**Praise for Christine**

"Heart-stopping action. Crazy sexy-time scenes. Tender emotions . . . [A] little bit of something for everyone who enjoys a solid paranormal romance." —Harlequin Junkie

"With a Feehan novel you know you will get well-developed characters and an engaging plot, so when you add a dose of sizzling sexuality, you have an unbeatable mix."
—*RT Book Reviews*

"Heady, passionate, seductive . . . Ms. Feehan does a fantastic job of building up to the climax for a smashing finale that leaves you breathless and satisfied." —Smexy Books

"Readers . . . will be seduced by this erotic adventure."
—*Publishers Weekly*

"Another wild ride . . . enter the lair of the shapeshifters."
—Romance Reviews Today

"A passionate, jam-packed adventure."
—Fallen Angel Reviews

"The passion runs high and the sex is hot!"
—The Romance Readers Connection

"Sizzling and exciting . . . surprises erupt at every turn."
—Fresh Fiction

"A phenomenal story . . . Christine Feehan knows how to weave a tale of action, suspense and paranormal passion that has earned her so many fans and keeps bringing new ones." —Romance Junkies

## *Titles by Christine Feehan*

# LEOPARD'S BLOOD

## CHRISTINE FEEHAN

JOVE
New York

A JOVE BOOK
Published by Berkley
An imprint of Penguin Random House LLC
375 Hudson Street, New York, New York 10014

Copyright © 2017 by Christine Feehan
Excerpt from *Judgment Road* copyright © 2017 by Christine Feehan
Penguin Random House supports copyright. Copyright fuels creativity, encourages
diverse voices, promotes free speech, and creates a vibrant culture. Thank you for buying
an authorized edition of this book and for complying with copyright laws by not
reproducing, scanning, or distributing any part of it in any form without permission.
You are supporting writers and allowing Penguin Random House to continue to
publish books for every reader.

A JOVE BOOK and BERKLEY are registered trademarks and the B colophon
is a trademark of Penguin Random House LLC.

ISBN: 9780399583971

First Edition: October 2017

Printed in the United States of America
1   3   5   7   9   10   8   6   4   2

Cover art © Danny O'Leary
Cover design by Judith Lagerman

*Kathi Firzlaff, you have to know why this one's for you!*

## For My Readers

Be sure to go to christinefeehan.com/members/ to sign up for my PRIVATE book announcement list and download the FREE Ebook of *Dark Desserts*. Join my community and get firsthand news, enter the book discussions, ask your questions and chat with me. Please feel free to e-mail me at Christine@christinefeehan.com. I would love to hear from you.

# Acknowledgments

This is always the time when I must really think about everyone who helped me in some way to finish this book. Thanks to Brian Feehan and Sheila English for power-houring with me on the daily. Thanks for the competition. We all know how truly competitive I am. Thanks to Lisa Benson and Captain Neil Benson of Pearl Echo Tours in Slidell, LA (catch it from New Orleans, they shuttle you). They gave me so much information. They took me on both day and night tours several times and answered every question until I'm fairly certain Neil wanted to toss me out of the boat, but of course he was too gentlemanly for that. Thank you SO much! Thanks to Domini Walker for helping me with research and editing. You're my right hand all the way. And thanks to Denise for keeping me sane!

# 1

NIGHTS in the swamp were often sultry. Heat and moisture drifted through the cypress groves and clung to the long shawls of lacy Spanish moss hanging from crooked branches. The long-fringed drapes swayed in the slight breeze, adding a macabre feel to the already eerie night. Frogs chorused loudly, hundreds of them, calling out joyously while raccoons slipped noiselessly down to the duckweed-filled water to wash their paws. Two bull alligators challenged for territory, their bellows reverberating through the air.

Sonia Lopez followed the narrow game trail, the one she'd widened over the last few weeks that led deeper into the swamp. Insects droned all around her, a loud cacophony of sound. None stopped when she stepped lightly along the ground, a tribute to the fact that she'd spent every night for the last two months learning every inch of the piece of swamp that belonged to her. She owned forty acres and wanted to become acquainted with all of it. For this. She'd known it was coming, and she was very, very glad she'd prepared.

"We're almost there," she whispered softly. "Hold on. I know it's hard."

Something moved beneath her skin, a wave that pushed outward and then slid away, leaving behind a horrible itch that made her want to scratch until she bled. Her joints ached. She burned in her most feminine core, a savage, brutal need driving her deeper and deeper into the swamp. She was on fire. Every part of her, her body so sensitive, clothing hurt. Every movement brushed streaks of fire from her breasts to her sex. She ached. She needed. The only safe place she had was the swamp.

The grunt of a wild boar had her quickening her step. She had to get to the very heart of the swamp where she'd constructed a small blind, just big enough so she could have a thin mattress, strip, leave her clothing in relative safety and shift. *Hurry. Hurry. Hurry.* The words thundered in her ears accompanied by the drumming of her heart.

Sonia had allowed her leopard to run free when there was opportunity, ever since that first, shocking, terrifying appearance when the cat had saved her life. It had never been like this. This . . . this . . . *necessity.* She breathed deep as her joints began to pop. Her knuckles were on fire, the ache becoming a terrible pain that wouldn't let up. "Wait. Just try for me, Gatita. Just try to hang on. We're close."

She didn't dare let her cat loose anywhere near civilization. Not now. Not ever, but now was the most important. Gatita was definitely in heat. That meant Sonia was in heat and couldn't be any place a man might be. She didn't trust herself. She had had no idea the heat would be so intense, such a terrible force driving her beyond all endurance.

Her leopard was in need, and if the way her body was burning was any indication, her cat was going up in flames. She tried running, but stumbled when her toes began to curl down. The blind was just ahead and she threw herself forward those last few feet, tugging her shirt over her head and pulling off her shoes. Her jeans were next. She was usually good about folding clothes and being neat, but there was no time. Her female was in trouble, and Sonia was driven to help her.

Nothing had prepared her for the brutal hunger, the need filling her mind and body until she wanted to scream. Nothing helped. She'd tried. Toys. Fingers. She'd given up, sobbing, standing under the cold of the shower until she realized that wouldn't help. Nothing would help. And it was far worse for Gatita.

She found herself on her hands and knees, breathing as deeply as possible to ease the pain of the shifting. Her skull hurt, feeling too tight. Her jaw, her toes and fingers. Every muscle and joint. Still, the pain helped her forget, for that one terrible moment, the relentless hunger swamping her.

Shifting only took seconds now that she'd practiced, but those seconds were excruciating. Then her leopard was there, sleek, agile and beautiful. She was on the smaller side, her fur thick with so many black rosettes that one appeared to touch another from her head to the top of her tail. Her coat looked black with traces of thin, gleaming golden rings appearing to streak around the black. All leopard patterns were unique, but Sonia was a little vain about her cat's fur. She thought Gatita was beautiful and her fur different and rare. Of course, that meant she had to be more protective than ever.

There had been no time to gather clothes and shove them into the pack to put around Gatita's neck, so she knew she would have to get the leopard to return to the blind where she'd set up the small mattress for the cat to rest on after her run. She urged the leopard back into the swamp, whispering encouragement.

"Run it off, *pequeño* Gatita, for both of us, run it off."

Gatita had never been in heat before. Sonia knew it could last a week or even a few days longer than that. It was going to be hell for both of them. She'd known she'd have to face the female's heat sometime, but she hadn't thought about the possibility that she would feel what her leopard felt.

Letting Gatita run free was a little on the dangerous side. As a rule, Sonia knew she had no trouble controlling her, but right now, she could barely control herself. Every cell in her body demanded she find a man. Any man would do at this point. She had taken time off work, avoided town and wished she'd thought to board up her home with steel plates on the windows and doors so neither of them could escape. Letting the leopard run in the swamp was better than both suffering and tearing up the house she was working so hard to restore.

Gatita ran through the swamp, leaping over rotting tree trunks covered with moss. The fog had begun to drift in, fingers of mist creeping through the trees, adding to the mystery and beauty of the land. An owl screeched as it missed its prey. The two alligators continued to bellow and posture.

Sonia, hidden deep in the leopard, cautioned her to stay away from the water's edge. The big bull alligator would defend his territory. He was nearly thirteen feet long and up to any challenge from an upstart coming into his world. The male had twelve females in his three-mile range, and he wasn't going to give even one of them up. Her leopard didn't need to be food for any of them, especially when the male was so aggressive.

The little female placed her paws delicately on the damp leaves and vegetation making up the swamp floor. Leaping effortlessly over the termites eating the rotting trunks, she landed in absolute silence. Sonia admired the way Gatita could be so utterly quiet as she moved through brush and trees so fast. She'd constructed the blind as close to the middle of the swamp that she called her own as possible, giving the leopard as much of a territory as she could.

Her property included a good forty acres of land, mostly

swamp no one wanted, and was ideal for her. She had the road to the front of her property, swamp to the back of her property, fanning out to meet the edges of two other properties, one just swamp land and one her neighbor, a huge piece of property that seemingly had endless acres of swamp. That gave her leopard a good-sized territory to roam.

Gatita rubbed her head and body everywhere, all over the trees and bushes. She scent-marked and called loudly for a mate. There was nothing Sonia could do about that. She knew the sound would travel for miles, but she couldn't force the heat-driven cat to stop vocalizing her need.

Abruptly, Gatita halted and then lifted her muzzle into the air. Every whisker reported back to her, a radar telling her everything about the neighborhood, who was in it and where. The whiskers could even extend over her mouth to give her the exact location and distance of her prey or enemy so she could deliver a killing bite.

Without warning, Gatita let out a distinctly different call, one that sent chills down Sonia's spine. It wasn't the fact that the noise was like a rusty saw going through a block of wood, it was the fact that the little female leopard was calling out to something . . . or someone.

*What are you doing?* Sonia hissed, but she knew. The female had come across the scent of a male in his prime. He had marked the territory for his own. What were the odds? Louisiana didn't have leopards, did it? Granted, she didn't know that much about the state, or the swamp she had just moved to, but she'd been certain there were no leopards. There might be a mountain lion or two, but certainly not a leopard.

She found herself tense, worried for her female. The last thing she wanted was a fight between her leopard and a male cougar. She should have checked the area much more carefully. She'd fallen in love with the house. She'd needed a place for her leopard. The house and land were perfect for them both, and, most importantly, the seller had wanted out.

She'd fallen into the best job possible for her. Everything had seemed so right, but her female couldn't fight a male and win.

*Let's go back,* she whispered. *Turn around.*

Gatita ignored her and rubbed and sprayed all along the trees, leaving her alluring scent for males to find her. Every six or so minutes she called out as she moved through the swamp. The third time Gatita called, a sawing roar filled the swamp in answer, nearly stopping Sonia's heart. There was no mistaking that sound. It was a leopard. The call was very distinctive. By the sound of it, the animal wasn't small.

Heart pounding, she tried to exert some control over the little female, but the cat was too far gone, too in need from her heat. In all her wildest imaginings, Sonia had never once considered this scenario. She'd been afraid the female might get loose around people, that a hunter might discover her. She'd feared that she might react to the cat's heat and attack some innocent man at a bar, which was the reason she'd holed up at her house. But the last thing she'd thought of was that a male leopard might be close by—close enough to hear Gatita calling out in need and readiness.

The little hussy continued her call as she rubbed her scent over every tree and bush in the vicinity. Sonia knew the moment the big male parted the brush to discover her little female. Gatita swung around to face him, hissing a warning, but then rubbing seductively along a tree trunk to entice him.

He was big. Roped muscles moved beneath the thick coat of fur. There were a few scars on him, declaring him a veteran fighter. Sonia took a breath as she studied him from behind the eyes of her female. He was definitely in his prime. Gatita was pleased, practically vibrating with excitement.

*A mate worthy of us.* Her purring was more felt than heard. Her words not words, but images and the feeling of intense satisfaction.

Sonia knew there was no point in protesting. Gatita deserved a mate. More, the heat was intense, burning the two of them until they both thought they might go insane. Sonia hadn't known a drive could be so powerful. She tried not to think about the problems that could arise from this pairing.

She knew it was too late to stop the two leopards from mating. The male had the scent of the ready female, and he wouldn't give her up. That was evident in the way he took charge, close, but not too close. He patiently followed her when she moved away from him. She played like a seductive kitten, and the large cat watched, moving closer to her, rubbing his fur along hers and shouldering her. Rather than rebuff him, Gatita nuzzled him back.

Her female moaned softly and rolled onto her back, legs in the air. She came to her feet, her rump raised, her long tail lashing as she presented her alluring body to the male. She brushed her head and body on everything she could, providing him with temptation. She approached him, signaling he was her choice. She rubbed her face along his, nuzzling him repeatedly. He responded, rubbing his scent all over her. They moved off together again, going deeper into the swamp, the male allowing the female to lead him.

He chuffed. She answered. She moved a few steps from him and crouched. The male was on her before Gatita could rebuff him, a common practice with females. As the male extended his back, leaning over the female, Sonia retreated to give them privacy. The male took the female without hesitation, moving in her over and over. Eventually he let out a long growl just before sinking his teeth into the female's shoulder, holding her in place.

The male held her still for several long moments, and then he released her from his teeth and simultaneously leapt away. She growled and swiped at him with her paw, ran a few feet and collapsed, her sides heaving. The male approached her cautiously. When she showed no signs of attacking him, he rubbed his face over hers and then, while she slept, paced around her, scent-marking the trees, making certain that any other male leopard knew this was his territory and his female.

The big male rubbed his face over Gatita's, nuzzling her several times. She rose, and the two of them started all over again. They found a small stream that trickled through the swamp and both drank and rested between their rough sex. As the night began to wane, the female led the male back toward the blind Sonia had set up so they could rest after the female's run.

Gatita collapsed on the mattress, shifting as she did so. Sonia found herself completely naked, the terrible burning hunger not in the least assuaged. Every cell in her body was on fire. She needed a man more than she needed air to breathe.

It was still dark. All around her the cacophony of insects was so loud it drowned out everything, until she heard the exhale. Her body stiffened. She felt the focused stare. Her heart nearly stopped beating and then began to pound. Her mouth went dry. Very slowly she turned her head and found herself staring into the eyes of the huge male.

Once they locked eyes, Sonia couldn't look away. The normal color of a leopard's eyes was amber, but this animal had blue eyes. She'd heard of a rare finding in India of several blue-eyed leopards, all suspected of being from the same family, but she'd never thought to see such a thing herself. The piercing stare was the same, blue or amber.

Up close, the cat was terrifying. He was huge, with roped muscles and savage teeth. Nothing, not even having her own leopard, could have prepared her for finding herself only a few feet from a wild leopard, one clearly dominant. His coat was beautiful, a deep ochre, more on the orange side beneath the scattering of large black rosettes. His eyes, had they been amber, would have been lost in the black and ochre of his face, but the startling blue stared straight into her eyes, taking her breath.

Sonia didn't have a weapon, nothing at all to protect

herself with. She couldn't imagine what the male thought, one moment with his newly found mate, and the next a human crouched next to him, staring straight into his eyes.

She couldn't help herself, even though she knew better. Cats hunted prey. The last thing she should do was run. In any case, a leopard could outrun her. Still, self-preservation demanded she do something, and she threw herself sideways, trying to get to the other side of the mattress.

Instantly he was on her, his heavy body pinning her down, his teeth sinking into her shoulder. She screamed at the flash of pain, closing her eyes, knowing what was coming. At the last moment, Gatita rose to defend her—except she didn't. The female didn't take over, didn't push to return to the male. She rose as if touching the male and then she subsided. The male purred as if recognizing her and slowly released Sonia.

His heavy weight still pressed her down, held her to the mattress. She no longer felt fur, but the roped muscles were there. The breathing. Warm. Soft. A tongue swept over the bite in her shoulder.

"Shh, you're all right now. He wouldn't hurt you." The tongue touched her ear. Lips brushed there. Teeth tugged on her earlobe. "Your leopard is his mate. He knows that." The lips traveled down the side of her neck, creating a trail of flames she felt traveling over her skin. "He claimed her, by putting his mark on you."

The voice was in her ear. Soft. Seductive. A low, but deep, very masculine voice washed through the pain and fear and brought her straight back to raging hormones. It didn't help that he was naked too, and that she felt his cock hard and thick and pressed against her buttocks.

She didn't speak. She couldn't find her voice. She didn't want him to move. If he did, she was afraid she would attack him. She needed what he had that much. The need was so strong, the burn so deep, she feared she would go insane if he didn't do something.

His hand stroked down her back. Just that touch sent streaks of fire straight to her sex. She heard herself moan and knew she was giving him consent when, any other time, she would have run for safety.

"Your skin is so soft," he whispered.

His voice was sheer temptation. He was leading her straight to hell, where they were both going to burn together for their sins. She knew that, but she didn't care. He was a shifter, just as she was, and he had to be on fire, his need and hunger every bit as strong as hers.

His hand slid over the left cheek of her buttocks, a caress that sent a wave of need so strong she heard a low, keening wail coming from her throat. Everywhere he touched sent those flames dancing, tripping over her skin, rushing through her veins to settle deep in her core like a firestorm.

One arm caught her hips and yanked her up to her knees, while the other held her head pressed to the mattress, his palm curled around her nape. She couldn't move, pinned as effectively as her female had been.

"Say yes."

It was a demand. She closed her eyes tightly. She needed him desperately, but he wasn't going to give her what she needed unless she gave him permission. There would be no pretense in the morning that she hadn't agreed to this. But if she didn't comply, he might go away, and she'd be left burning up.

Her breath came in ragged pants, so labored she barely recognized herself. She was squirming unashamedly, pushing back to try to entice him. She hadn't even seen his face. She didn't want to see it. She didn't want him to see hers.

Then his hand was there, his fingers. She heard that same low keening cry coming from her throat. The need shook her. His tongue moved up the inside of her thigh and then touched her center.

"Yes." She hissed it. "Yes." She found more strength and pushed assent into her voice so he couldn't fail to hear it.

He took her hard and fast. One moment his hand was at her entrance, testing her slick heat and then he filled her. He was thick and hard and long, stretching her ability to take him. The friction nearly set her on fire. The burn of him pressing against those tight inner muscles, stretching them beyond what she'd ever known, should have hurt. The only hurt was that he didn't move faster or harder.

"I need . . ." She gasped as his cock withdrew and then plunged deep again.

"I know what you need. Trust me. I need the same thing."

She was grateful that he admitted she wasn't alone in her wild needs. He couldn't be rough enough. Or hard enough. He couldn't be too deep. Or too anything. She needed his hands and his mouth and his teeth. She needed a wild mating without thought, only feeling that burning pleasure that bordered on pain. Maybe it was pain. She didn't know or care. Only that he had to take away the terrible burning inside.

Her fingers formed fists in the sheets as she pushed back hard, catching his rhythm and adding to the strength of his plunging cock. He was like a wild machine, out of control, and yet at the same time in complete control. He certainly was in control of her, when she wasn't. The orgasm took her by complete surprise. She felt the coiling tension gathering and gathering until she thought she might go insane.

"Let go," he hissed.

She had no idea how. She'd never actually had an orgasm, and she'd never felt like this. The hunger. The need. The intensity. She didn't know what to do, only that it had to stop before she lost her mind.

"Let go," he said again. This time that soft velvety voice growled with command. His finger was on her clit, stroking, then flicking. Hard. That shocking bite started a tsunami. It grew and grew, sending waves of that pleasure-pain swamping her, taking her on a wild ride she had never been on.

She felt the heat of his release, hot splashes of his seed deep inside her. He collapsed over top of her, his weight taking her to the mattress, pinning her there. All she wanted to do was sleep. She kept her eyes closed. The sound of his breathing was soothing to her. His body kept hers warm in the cool night air. All around them the sounds of the swamp created a familiar lullaby.

She woke to pure fire. Rolling onto her back to try to ease the way her skin felt so inflamed, she tried to piece together where she was. She couldn't think with the flames burning through her, scorching her. Her breasts ached, her nipples two pinpoints of pain. Her sex didn't just ache—the fire was so hot it was excruciating. She moaned and writhed, tears forming behind her eyes.

"It isn't going to stop," she whispered in despair. She'd humiliated herself and had sex with a perfect, nameless, faceless stranger, and yet it hadn't stopped.

"I'm here." His voice came out of the darkness. He loomed over her, tall for a shifter, broad-shouldered, the heavy roped muscles of their kind. His hair was shockingly blond, his eyes a rare, crystal blue-green.

He knelt between her legs, gripped her thighs, fingers digging into her soft skin. His eyes staring with the complete focus of a leopard into hers, he yanked her thighs apart. "You're mine," he hissed. Anger simmered beneath the velvet of his voice. His hand stroked her center, taking her breath. "Your female belongs to my male, and you belong to me."

She could barely hear him with the hunger roaring through her, crashing in her ears, burning through her center until she wanted to scream. His fingers weren't doing enough. Barely touching her. Circling her clit, never touching it. Her hips thrashed, and he gripped her harder.

"Say it," he snapped.

She would have promised him anything at that point. She didn't want to talk to him. She was using him. She knew that and it shamed her, but she was desperate. "I'm yours," she hissed between her teeth.

He rewarded her with a finger pushing into her. Just like before, she felt tight, as if her muscles had clenched down and now he was having to open her all over again. The thickness of his finger took her breath, robbed her of the ability to process anything, let alone have a conversation with him. She didn't understand why he was angry, unless he knew that she was using him and didn't like it.

She didn't care what it was, only that he get inside her and take away the terrible burn. The emptiness. The need and hunger that wouldn't go away. "Hurry," she pleaded. "Please." She even hated that, asking him, practically begging him.

She was free. She had a life. She didn't have to ask for anything, and yet here she was. *She* should be the one angry. All she could think about was the way her body demanded his. That need that wouldn't go away.

He pressed the head of his cock into her entrance and hissed, his eyes still holding hers captive. She couldn't look away, mesmerized by him, by that look of utter possession stamped deep in the lines of his face. He looked like sin incarnate—the devil taking her.

"You are scorching hot." He bit out the words between his perfect white teeth. "So fucking tight I might lose my mind."

She was already losing hers. He was pushing in slow, inch by inch now, not taking her all at once like he'd done before. She was tight, her body refusing to give him entrance and then slowly giving way to his invasion at his insistence. He didn't stop that slow entry, just kept a steady pressure, forcing his way through her reluctant sheath until he was fully in her, until she felt him up against her cervix.

His thickness pressed tightly against her inner muscles, stretching her again to the point of pain. It burned, that stretch, but it felt good, just what she needed. "Move," she commanded. He *had* to move before she imploded.

"My name is Joshua. Say it."

She shook her head. She didn't want to know his name. She didn't want him to know hers. She wanted him to take her hard and fast and then go away so she could be ashamed and humiliated alone. She lifted her hips, trying to move, but he wouldn't budge, and he wouldn't look away, or allow her to.

"Say my name," he ordered. He kept his voice low, but it was no less demanding.

"Why?" She practically wailed the question. She burned. Surely he did. Surely he could feel his leopard's need.

"You know why."

She didn't. She really didn't, but it didn't matter. If it would get him to move, she'd say it. "Joshua." She'd always liked that name. "Please, just move." She could play nice, but her fingers curled against the mattress, nails digging deep.

He still didn't move. "Give me your name."

Her eyelashes fluttered. She didn't want him to know her. Not at all. Not one thing. "After tonight you'll be gone. So will I."

"She'll be in heat for seven days. This doesn't go away. You think my male's going to allow another male anywhere near her?" There was a growl in his voice she couldn't mistake for anything but a male on the verge of rage.

"I'll lock her up."

"How will that help either of you?"

"I don't know," she wailed. "Please. Hurry."

"Your name."

He couldn't be feeling what she was feeling. Panic set in. She was moving, writhing beneath him, unable to stop. He leaned down and bit her shoulder. The bite of pain sent liquid heat surrounding him. Scorching him. She couldn't help it. Humiliation set in when he bit her other shoulder and then stroked his tongue over the sting, earning him more heat. More burning liquid. Her muscles spasmed around his cock, gripping him harder.

"Sonia." She gasped it. Nearly crying. Burning from the inside out.

He moved immediately, withdrawing and then surging forward. Then he was pounding into her, pulling her body into his when he moved into hers. Her breath rushed from her lungs, her breasts swayed with each hard jolt, her head thrashed on the mattress as he pistoned into her, over and over again. She never took her eyes from his, and he never once looked away.

She came immediately, the wave taking her hard, roaring through her with a terrible force and then instantly building again, coiling tighter than before. The need stronger. It built and built in her. He yanked her legs up and over his shoulders, changing his position, throwing her into another wild orgasm that raced through her body; every cell should have been sated, but it wasn't.

She cried out, terrified of losing herself in him. Never once did those eyes allow her to look away. She had to depend on him, and he was letting her know he knew that. He was the only one who could help her. The third time, he went with her, her body gripping and milking his, forcing his orgasm with the sheer strength of hers.

She whispered his name, the burn of tears in her eyes as she braced herself for the release. His cock was still heavy as he withdrew and there was that bite of pain she expected, the one that flashed through her and sent another heat wave. Before he could say anything, she rolled onto her side and let the swamp soothe her to sleep. He curled his body around hers, one arm sliding around her waist, his breath in her hair.

She woke close to the dawn. In the blind it was still dark, but light was beginning to creep through the trees, bringing those gray fingers of fog. Joshua rolled over top of her and took her mouth before she could protest.

He kissed like he fucked. Hard. Hot. Spectacular. Fireworks went off behind her eyes. His mouth traveled over her

chin, down her throat to her breasts. Finally. Her nipples,
always on fire, had the attention of his mouth. She realized
then she wasn't the only one feeling the burn of the leopard
mating. He was wild, his mouth hotter than hell. His teeth
were everywhere. He was rough, savagely so. He treated her
body like his own personal playground. She loved it, the
way he growled if she moved. The way his tongue lapped
at the sting of his bites.

This was what she'd needed. The heat. The fire. The rough
mixed with tender. His mouth was on her, claiming every
square inch of her body. His teeth marked her. His tongue
brushed caresses to soothe her. His hands were everywhere.
Then he was kissing her again, after the long exploration of
her body. Kissing her until she couldn't think, only feel. Only
need. Want. So much hunger spilling over until she could
hear herself pleading.

He caught one leg and pulled it around his waist. His
hand circled the girth of his cock, and he nudged at her
entrance. When she tried to impale herself, he shook his
head. "I want to feel your hands on me."

She hadn't wanted to go that far. She knew he'd been
committing her body to his memory, but she'd never had
anything like this before. It was too intense. Too passionate.
Too sinful. Too . . . everything. She knew she'd never forget
him as it was, let alone if she gave in to her desire to explore
his body.

Reluctantly, she complied. She didn't want him to stop,
so she did what he asked, putting her hand on his shoulder.
Then he was inside her, slamming deep, driving through
her tight folds, the breath hissing out of him. Once again his
blue-green eyes trapped hers so she felt she was caught in
crystal, exposed to him. Every vulnerability. Every flaw.
Every humiliating need and desire.

Her body wouldn't be sated without rough. Somehow he
read that in her, and it shamed her. Her nails dug into his back
when fire streaked through her. It was good. So good. The

way his cock drove deep, retreated and drove in again. Over and over.

She wrapped her other leg around his waist and used her hands down his back, over his buttocks, her nails driving deep, scoring a path in his skin, while he took her over. She knew he owned her body. There was no retreating from this. No getting away from it. Not when he could drag another three orgasms from her. Not when his kisses set fire to her soul. Not when his mouth on her breasts sent flames licking over her skin. He owned her body, and he always would.

He emptied himself in her while she floated somewhere she'd never been, his body collapsing over hers, pinning her to the mattress, her legs and arms still wrapping him up, both fighting for air.

He lifted his head first, his lips brushing her eyelids, the tip of her nose and then her mouth. Very gently. The difference between his rough and gentle was soul-destroying. It alarmed her. A woman could get used to a man like him, but she didn't dare. There was no man in her future. No rough. No gentle. No anything.

He brushed the hair from her face. "You're beautiful. This face. A man would fall forever for this face alone. Put it with your body and he's lost."

There was nothing lost about him. Nothing at all. He was still very much in charge. Still very much the dominant male. He didn't move off her, his body still locked in hers. She braced herself for that flash of pain when he withdrew, moving subtly to let him know it was time. He just smiled down at her, and that took her breath.

She'd tried not to look at him as a whole. He had a purely masculine body. There wasn't a soft spot anywhere. And then there were his eyes. So beautiful, all that blue-green in a sea of crystal. She had deliberately not focused on his face. She didn't want to see him as a man. A shifter, mate of her female, that was fine, but if she looked at his face, she'd have to see him.

He was beautiful in a masculine way. Okay, gorgeous. Hot. Everything women dreamt of in a man. That made her self-conscious of her too-wide hips, full breasts and wild, too-thick dark hair. She cleared her throat, trying to think what to say to make him leave.

"Don't," he ordered softly. "I see it on your face. This is normal for a shifter. You probably had no idea about your female. Most don't. But she's beautiful and healthy, just like you. She'll be this way for the next week. You can give me your number . . ."

She shook her head. Emphatically. "No." She said it for good measure. "I'll keep her in. I told you."

The gentle smile disappeared, replaced by a short shake of his head. His eyes went to that piercing, scary stare his leopard had. "My leopard will hunt yours. You have to allow them to be together."

She bit her lip hard enough to draw blood. Her teeth felt sharper than usual. The bite stung, but only because he'd already marked her there and she'd just aggravated the small injury.

He immediately bent his head and licked at the small red drop and then caught her lower lip between his teeth. He tugged and then let her loose, his tongue soothing the ache. "This is mine. I don't want you biting it."

"You did," she pointed out.

"I can. You can't. Now give me your number. The sun is coming up, and you're naked out here. I don't want any others to find you. There would be a fight, Sonia. The leopards would fight to the death over a female. My male will never give yours up."

She tried not to panic. She couldn't begin a relationship with a man. Then again, he wasn't claiming her. He wasn't saying *he* wouldn't give *her* up. He said his leopard. She touched her tongue nervously to the indentation, where she still felt his teeth. "I don't know much about shifters. I'm learning as I go along, so I'll have to accept your word on that. I'll meet you here tonight. I think I'll sleep most of the day, so I don't know what time, but I'll come."

"Give me your word."

"I just did." She pushed at his shoulders. "I have to go. Really. I have to get back."

"To what?" He shifted his weight and began to withdraw.

Her breath caught in her throat. The pain was exquisite. The pleasure almost intolerable. Streaks of fire raced up her spine. Why did it have to be so good with him? She knew his brand was stamped into her bones. He did own her body and she could—and would—deny it, but she knew better.

"Seriously, move." She pushed harder.

He laughed softly and took her mouth. To her horror, she kissed him back immediately. His tongue did a lazy exploration, sliding along hers, coaxing her response until her tongue tangled with his in a bizarre dance that told her more than words could have, that he knew he was in there deep.

When he lifted his head, he moved off her. She rolled away from him, coming to her knees. Her body protested. Ached everywhere. Every muscle. Every cell. But it was a good kind of ache, sated. Satisfied. She could breathe on her own again. She didn't need mouth-to-mouth from a stranger.

"Don't follow me." She yanked on her jeans, heedless of his seed spilling down her leg. "We didn't use a condom. Do you realize that?"

"Yep."

He didn't sound in the least upset, and she paused in the act of pulling on her shirt to glare at him over her shoulder. "Don't smirk. Think of the consequences." She jerked the shirt over her head and reached for her boots.

"I have. Condoms and other forms of birth control don't work on shifters. Either you'll get pregnant or you won't. Believe me, baby, you're pretty damn fertile."

She could hate him. She really could. But there was his

body. He hadn't even attempted to cover up and just looking at him made her body come alive. She felt the burn starting all over.

"I'm leaving now." There was no retort she could think of to wipe his male-superior-amused smirk from his face. In any case, she had to get out of there before she jumped him again.

"See you tonight."

She didn't deign to reply, but she knew he would see her. She'd be back, because now she was addicted to him. She kept her back to him as she began the long walk of shame home.

# 2

SONIA groaned and buried her face in the pillow. The nagging alarm wouldn't stop, and she couldn't reach it because she'd already thrown it across the room. The pillow did nothing to muffle the sound. Why couldn't she have gotten one of those soothing alarms? The kind that woke one up gently? The clock blasted its horn-blowing, nerve-jangling message again, and she rolled over and threw the pillow at it. The pillow hit the wall and fell—right beside the shrieking alarm.

She groaned again and forced her body into a sitting position. It wasn't easy. Every muscle hurt. *Every* muscle. She felt as if she'd been run over by a truck.

"You *so* deserve this, Sonia," she chastised aloud. She dropped her throbbing head into her hands and sat on the edge of the bed, legs dangling over the side, and rocked to try to ease the soreness, the aches and the embarrassment of her awful, no, *terrible* behavior.

She forced her body to move, mostly because the alarm was driving her crazy, making her head, already pounding, hurt more. With every step, deep inside, she felt the delicious soreness, her inner muscles protesting. It didn't matter how many hot baths she'd taken, her body still ached with every movement.

It hadn't mattered how many times she'd promised herself she wouldn't go back because it was humiliating that she couldn't stop herself, but she'd returned every night for seven nights. They hadn't talked, they just stayed up all night, just like their leopards, all over each other. The rougher, the better—it had assuaged the horrible need that just wouldn't let up. It had driven her night and day, so much so that she'd been tempted to get his number just so he'd meet her there during the day. She wasn't going to admit to him she was that far gone.

Fortunately, her female's heat had begun to subside and Sonia had managed to breathe. She didn't tell Joshua. She knew he would insist on her number. She knew he thought he would eventually wear her down, or she wouldn't be able to do without his sex. Instead, she'd walked away early in the morning, just as the sun rose, just as she always did, and left him, knowing she wouldn't go back.

It was day three without him. She'd slept nearly thirty straight hours and then slept on and off for the next day and night. She couldn't remember why she'd set her alarm, but it had been important.

"The walk of shame," she muttered aloud. It was funny when she'd thought about that phrase, or envisioned talking about it with girlfriends. Not so funny when one actually had to walk the walk—and she'd done it seven nights in a row. Was that a record? Could she get in the walk of shame hall of fame? Probably.

She didn't know his last name. She'd never seen him before that first night, so if she was lucky he wasn't from around her neighborhood or town. She hoped to hell she'd never see him again. She closed her eyes for a moment, wishing she could take back the week. Maybe if she had girlfriends she'd be able to find some humor in the situation. She'd own her walk of shame, but right now, all she could think about was the utter humiliation of what she'd done— and how spectacular it had been.

"Okay. There. I admitted it." She turned off the alarm, thankful the thing wasn't blaring at her so accusingly. She could judge herself—and she did—harshly. It wasn't Joshua's fault that she'd been in heat right along with her leopard— that she'd used him ruthlessly.

Her lip stung, and she touched it with the tip of her tongue. He'd been equally as ruthless. He'd ruled her their half of the night. She found it strange that the leopards had given them so much time together.

*Gatita? Why did you shift every night halfway through the night?*

*My mate insisted.*

Her heart thudded. She pressed her hand over it. If Gatita's mate had insisted, that meant Joshua had insisted. Joshua had absolute control over his leopard even when the female's heat was driving all of them. She touched her lip with her finger. It was slightly swollen. She didn't remember this time how that mark had gotten on her, but he liked to use his teeth, and he'd been wild and she'd been out of control.

The man knew how to kiss. Seriously. She'd thought she knew what kissing was until he'd kissed her. She'd gone up in flames. Both had. She'd been married, had had an experienced husband, but not once had she ever had an orgasm. She'd thought she couldn't—that she just wasn't that into sex.

She'd had so many orgasms with Joshua she'd lost count. Night after night, they'd burned together. Who knew? Joshua had taken her in so many ways. He'd demanded so much of her, and she'd given him everything he'd demanded. She'd wanted him to rule her body. She'd given herself to him. It had been the most amazing, beautiful, savagely wild experience of her life, and it had to stop. She couldn't let it go any further. She hissed a small reprimand to herself for even thinking about him and his spectacular ownership of her body as she made her way to the bathroom.

There were only three rooms properly renovated in the beautiful plantation home she'd bought. It was run-down, out of date and yet beautiful to her. Her bedroom, the master bath and the kitchen were the only rooms entirely finished, and she was grateful she'd started with her bathroom.

The water was hot and soothing. She had a huge bathtub, separate from the very large shower. She had a thing for water, and so did Gatita. She worried that Gatita would try to swim in the canals or the river. Alligators were everywhere around them, and she'd tried to warn her cat, but Gatita had sniffed at her, acting as if she needed no warnings.

*When do we go running with our mates again?*

The hot water was working its magic, clearing her head, but the cat's question brought her up short. Her female was no longer in heat, but Sonia couldn't say the same thing. The terrible burning drive was gone, but the need for him was still there. She had to work to keep from thinking about him or having silly girlish fantasies.

"What do you mean? I'm not mates with the man. Your heat is over. We aren't going to see them again."

There was a long silence. Sonia stopped massaging the conditioner into her hair and just stood there. Waiting.

*He said you were his man's mate.*

Her breath caught in her throat. Her heart clenched at the idea. "He was wrong. I don't even know him. We had sex. You know it was driven by your heat."

*Our heat,* Gatita corrected. *We both were in need. I know you're still in need. When you are lying on the bed thinking of him, you . . .*

"I know what I do," Sonia broke in, not that it worked. Not that *anything* she did worked. "I can't help it. You don't have the same drive as humans."

Again, there was silence while Sonia rinsed herself off. She slowed when she reached the junction between her legs. She was still feeling him. How could she not think about him and the things he'd done to her body?

*I think of my mate. I think of being with him that way and still want him.*

That was a revelation. "I read about leopards when you showed yourself. After you saved me. I was so scared, and I couldn't find anything on shifters that wasn't science fiction. Leopards go into heat, and after they don't stay with their mates. The males don't help raise the babies, so I thought it was the same. Isn't it?" She began toweling herself off.

*I don't know about the others like me, but I want to be with him. I want to stay close to him. I want you close to his man.*

"That isn't going to happen. I'm sorry, Gatita. I had no idea you would feel that way. I can't be with another man, you know that. It's too dangerous for us and for him. We came here because of the swamp. It's a lot like the Florida swamp, a place for you to run free . . . I can't just take you anywhere, you know that. This was the best place I could think of."

*I know it is dangerous. I didn't think you were protecting the man. He seemed strong. The man calls my mate Shadow. He likes his name and likes his man. He says his man is very strong and dangerous. Maybe we should try it. I am not like an animal leopard any more than you are like a regular human. We're both different, and he is too.*

Sonia had to agree with her leopard there. Joshua was different. He was much more dominant than a regular human male, and who wanted that for a boyfriend? He talked to her as if she belonged to him—that it was a forgone conclusion that she would come when he called her. She'd been smart enough never to bring her cell phone or give out her last name or her number.

A small shiver crept down her spine. In fantasies, relationships like that worked, but in reality, dominant men were a pain in the neck. She knew from experience. It didn't matter that her body craved him and she was fairly certain his name was carved deep inside her body; she wasn't making another mistake.

"I'm sorry, Gatita, I have to keep both of us safe. A man like that is not good for me. You know what happened . . ."

*The man you chose did not do that. It was the others. He wouldn't have given you up, but he was not your mate. You know he wasn't.* There was no reprimand in Gatita's voice. *You have been with your mate and it was . . . different.*

Her body flushed at Gatita's impressions. She was referring to sex. "Sex isn't everything," she whispered, trying to convince herself.

Sonia stared at her reflection in the mirror. She was covered in his marks. They were everywhere. She touched the signs of possession. His brand. Her breasts. The inside of her thighs. Her neck. He'd liked marking her. He'd liked telling her she was his. For seven nights, she'd been his. All his. He'd owned her body and she'd loved every single second of it. He'd made her nights pure paradise.

"Even if it were true," she said to her cat, "he didn't say a thing about permanent. Nor did he ask me out on a date. It was just sex to him. That's a good thing. It would be too dangerous for him to be in our lives."

*Do you want to spend the rest of your life alone?*

Of course she didn't. She wanted what everyone else had, but she knew better. "I don't have a choice. In any case, I'm not alone. I have you." She was more than grateful for Gatita. Being a shifter presented its own set of problems. She had to ensure her leopard was taken care of at all times, which meant having a place for Gatita to run free without being seen. She'd found this swamp. She loved it. She loved everything about it, even the heat and humidity. She had been lucky enough to find the old plantation house for sale. The real estate agent had advised tearing down the house.

She'd spent her time talking about the land and what pieces of property along the river were worth. Although the land was needed for her leopard, Sonia had fallen in love with the house.

Made of cypress, it was a house that wouldn't rot, despite the dampness. There were no hallways. The rooms ran one into the other in a long sprawling wide straight line on both stories. She was going to have to modernize everything, but she was determined to keep the original architecture as intact as possible. The first thing she'd done was rewire the entire house. That hadn't been easy, as electricity wasn't her forte, and it was extremely important to get it right. Her boss had helped by overseeing her work. Her boss and You-Tube. The videos had helped teach her things she'd had no idea about.

Sonia snapped her fingers. "I forgot, Gatita. I set the alarm because Jerry wanted me to call him first thing this morning."

*You took your vacation.* This time there was a reprimand in Gatita's voice. *You need to rest. What if you're pregnant?*

Sonia paused in the act of dragging on a pair of her favorite jeans. "Don't even think that. Don't say it. Don't think it. Talk about irresponsible. Sheesh. I'm the first person to think about that, although with him, I'll admit, I didn't. Fortunately, I'm using birth control. I didn't tell him because he was so smug. Let him worry."

*It could still happen.*

"It had better not. How would I take care of us? Can you see me up on a roof eight months pregnant? I have to work, Gatita. That's how I keep us with a roof over our head and food in our tummy."

Her head came up, her color flushing a dark red. "I didn't think about STDs either. Oh my God, Gatita. I have to go to a clinic and get checked. I'm not only going to the 'walk of shame' hall of fame, I'll be in the 'most irresponsible of all time' hall of fame as well."

Gatita subsided, curling up and closing her eyes, not bothering to answer. Sonia rolled her own eyes. The last three days without her mate, Gatita had been moody as all leopards could be. Sonia was a little moody herself.

She finished dressing and hurried down to the kitchen to fix breakfast. She opted for a smoothie and called her boss while she was drinking it out on the wide, inviting verandah. The verandah went on forever, wrapping around both stories, giving her the best views. That had been the first thing she'd fallen in love with about the house.

"Hey, Jerry," she greeted. "What's up?"

"Need you to come into town and talk as soon as possible."

There was something in his voice that tipped her off that this was a big deal. "Now? Today? You mean during my vacation?"

"You can have two more vacation days," he wheedled, confirming to her that whatever was up was very important to him.

She glanced at the clock. "Be there in twenty."

"Thanks, Sonia."

She loved Jerry Corporon. She'd do practically anything for him, but she didn't need him—or anyone else—to know that. Jerry was sweet, but he took advantage if he could. She wasn't one to say no too often, and he knew that. She wanted the world to think Jerry was just her boss, and she clocked in and clocked out without caring too much about him or the job, but in truth she adored him and loved her job.

He'd seen desperation, and he'd held out his hand to her. She'd seen a man needing help, and that had made it easy to accept his offer of a job. Over time, she'd grown to really love who Jerry was. Funny, intelligent, talented and a bit broken. He owned a successful contracting business, and then his car was hit by a drunk driver, killing his wife and children, leaving him in a wheelchair.

Sonia's pickup truck had been one of Jerry's older vehicles. It ran so well it practically purred, but Jerry had claimed it was on its last leg and sold it to her for a steal. She'd needed a work truck as well as something to haul supplies back to her house. Jerry had laughed each time he'd come out to oversee her putting in the wiring, telling her the house was going to fall down on her head, but he'd kept coming, and sometimes he'd tell her there was leftover dry-wall and to take it. That was her boss.

She parked just outside the double gates leading to the lumberyard and walked the rest of the way, counting it as her morning exercise. Jerry owned the local lumberyard and his office was at the southernmost end, tucked back where he hoped no one could find him. He parked his wheelchair behind his long, narrow desk and conducted business, on the phone more than he was off. He was a big man with a receding hairline, wide shoulders and biceps that bulged from lifting his large body in and out of the chair. He held up one finger when she walked in, indicated a chair and kept talking.

Sonia gave an exaggerated sigh, carrying out the ritual they were both familiar with. He was always talking. She was always waiting impatiently. After five minutes, she drummed her fingers loudly on his desk. At ten she paced. At fifteen she pointed to the door and started walking.

"Wait," Jerry called. "Gotta go," he added, and hung up abruptly on his client. "Sheesh, woman, you could have a little patience."

"That was me being patient," Sonia pointed out.

Jerry gave a snort of disbelief. "Regardless of your rude-ness, I have a job for you."

"Jerry, I have three already. Dickerson's porch, Molly Sheffield's garage and Donna Miller's outside kitchen that isn't really outside because she wants it enclosed with a wall."

"On three sides."

"Now four. It's a room, Jerry, and it's stupid."

To her shock he waved that ongoing argument away.

"This," he said, leaning over the desk, his eyes bright, "is a real job. The real deal. Rafe Cordeau owned one of the biggest pieces of land around here. One of the nicest plantation houses. Recently, it got shot up all to hell; at least, that's the rumor. Someone's moved in, and they apparently tried to repair it themselves, but it's a mess. He wants an estimate on repairing the outside damage, a kitchen remodel and possibly more work. He'll talk about that when you go out there and take a look."

"What do you mean, 'shot up all to hell'?" she asked, suspicion in her voice.

He waved that away. "Rafe Cordeau was a mobster. Bigtime. He left and hasn't returned. They say he's dead."

"They?" She was *not* getting mixed up with the mob. Been there, done that. Never again. "Who, exactly, are *they*?"

Jerry scowled at her, meaning to look intimidating, succeeding in making himself look cute. Jerry would hate being called cute, so she kept that for a different time when she really wanted to annoy him. "*They* are the people in the know. The point, Sonia, is that he's gone and we've got a new guy willing to pay money to fix up his house. That's what we do. We fix up houses. In fact, if I'm not mistaken, that's your particular love. You fix up old houses and restore them to their original beauty." He grinned at her. "He's got money. He can pay us."

Okay. That was good. "You sure?" Just checking because no one in town had much in the way of real cash. Molly bought three sheets of drywall at a time. Dickerson had Sonia building the porch in stages. The outdoor kitchen was in the planning phase, meaning Donna Miller changed her mind every other minute. She was the only one with actual money, although Sonia was beginning to doubt the truth of that.

"I'm sure. I had him checked out. He comes from an old family from the New Orleans area. The Tregre family has been around from nearly the beginning of the history of

New Orleans. The family is shrouded in secrecy, which means you have the opportunity to get to know them."

She rolled her eyes. "Am I restoring a house or becoming a spy, Jerry? Sometimes I think you live for gossip."

"Gossip is for women. I'm a businessman, Sonia. That means I need information. The more information I have on the people living in this town and the surrounding parishes, the better I can do at my business. You leave that side to me."

She knew he loved what he did. The wheeling and dealing. The mingling with the mayor and bankers. His men had deserted him when he'd been in the accident, a silly move on their part since there was nothing wrong with Jerry's brain. He brought in the jobs despite the slow time they were temporarily in. Winter had been harsh on everyone.

"Will do, boss. When do you want me out there?"

He handed her a Post-it note with *Tregre* and the address written on it. She recognized it immediately. The address was the only other home on her road. A chill slid down her spine. Her neighbor? "Um, Jerry? You said Rafe Cordeau was in the mob and bullets were flying around his house? How do you know that he was a gangster?"

"Everyone knows he had mob connections."

"Why the bullets?"

"When he disappeared, a bunch of his men tried a take-over, or something like that. I'm still getting details. Apparently no one managed the takeover."

"And this Tregre?"

Jerry shook his head. "Old family, not mob. I think there was some scandal attached to his grandfather, but not this man. He went off to some foreign country and did things like rescue kidnap victims. Hero shit. Not mafia."

She let her breath out. Okay, she could deal with bullet holes as long as any living, breathing mafia wasn't involved.

"He wants you out there as soon as possible. His people are making a mess out of his home. He loves the plantation house and wants it restored. Sonia, this is our chance. He's got the money, and you have the know-how. I can get a large work crew if you need one, and hopefully you will. We need this. We're surviving, but not by much."

She knew that. She sent him a cocky grin. "No problem. I'll charm the socks off Mr. Tregre." She was certain she had the perfect picture of him. Sixty-five or seventy. Gray hair and a neatly trimmed beard. Slightly pudgy, but not by much, still walked every morning, maybe with a cane just because it suited his gentlemanly looks.

"I have no doubt that you will."

She sauntered out, past the workmen in the lumberyard and made it to her truck, just outside the double gates. She was grateful she'd worn her newest old-favorite jeans, which meant threadbare in places but no holes. Her tee was tighter than she would have liked, dip-dyed from a royal blue all the way to a faded blue that matched her jeans. She had on boots—leather, girly, with rings of roped leather and gold around the ankle. She'd do. She was supposed to look like a carpenter, not a model.

She scented roses and turned her head to see Molly waving at her. Beckoning. A part of her wanted that—a friend. She genuinely liked Molly. The woman was only a year or two older than she was and every bit as alone. Sonia didn't know her story because she was afraid of getting close to anyone. Molly tempted her, though.

"You have time for a cup of coffee?" Molly called from across the parking lot.

With one hand on the door and the other clutching the Post-it note, Sonia had all the excuses in the world, but she hesitated. She was tired of not having a friend—at least one person to talk to.

"Come on. One coffee isn't going to kill you," Molly urged.

It might not kill her, but it could get Molly killed. Perhaps both of them. Her hand tightened on the door handle, but she couldn't make herself pull the door open. "I guess. But it has to be fast. I have to get to work."

Molly's smile got wider, but it didn't quite reach her eyes. "Finally. You actually have more than two minutes. The only time you slow down is when you're driving away and I see you singing in your truck."

"I'm not exactly slowing down. I've nearly gotten three speeding tickets," Sonia confessed. "I had to flirt like crazy with Bastien Foret."

"He's hot but knows it," Molly said, falling into step with her as they started down the street toward the local coffee shop. "I never speed, but once I had a flat tire. I was changing it, and he came along and insisted he would do it. He did more talking about himself than anyone I've ever met. I know about his camp out in the bayou, and his prowess at fishing and hunting. I know he was married once, but his wife left him and no one knows where she went off to. I know he does extra drive-bys around my street to keep the good citizens safe, especially single women who are at risk . . ."

"He didn't say that to you, did he?" Sonia asked, trying not to laugh. "Because he said the exact same thing to me."

"He apparently says it to all the single women he thinks may fall for him. He talks to Pete—you know, the man who delivers the gas to everyone around here—and Pete told me to be careful," Molly said. "Pete's a nice guy. His niece was taken by some of Rafe Cordeau's men and held out there for three months. Some men came in and rescued her."

Sonia glanced up at Molly as she held open the door to the coffee shop. Molly was really striking with her long blond hair and large blue eyes. She looked almost exotic with flawless pale skin and a generous mouth. She was tall and curvy, with legs that went on forever. Sonia could only dream about looking like her.

Jerry had said that Tregre, at one time in his life, had rescued victims of kidnappers. Was it possible he'd been in some way responsible for helping Pete's niece? She was beginning to like Old Man Tregre already, long before she ever met him.

They found a quiet booth in the corner, Sonia taking the side that had her facing the front door and bank of windows along the street. She liked to see anything coming at her. Suddenly, she felt awkward. It had been a long time since she'd had a girlfriend.

"I work so much I think I've forgotten how to talk to people," she admitted, deciding to tell as much of the truth as possible.

"Me too," Molly said. "I moved here about a year ago, and I don't really know anyone but the man bringing my gas, the grocery store clerk, and Bastien Foret, the biggest flirt in town."

Sonia laughed. "I've not met Pete, although I've seen him. Bastien and I have an unfortunate acquaintance because I can't keep my foot off the gas pedal, and Charity at the grocery store is an old favorite. I have to decide ahead of time which piece of gossip I can pay with or she'll hold me hostage until I spill my guts out on the floor to her."

Molly laughed, the sound like soft, well-tuned bells. Heads turned, and Sonia tried not to sink down in her seat. "That is so true. She loves gossip. She teaches line dancing with her husband at the community center. I've gone a couple of times, but it isn't fun without someone to go with."

"I thought line dancing was solo."

"It is. I meant a friend. Male or female. I just can't work up the enthusiasm," Molly admitted. "That and Charity is always trying to hook me up with someone."

Sonia groaned. "Jerry does that to me at the lumberyard. He doesn't think it's decent for a woman to be alone, especially considering where I live. He thinks it's the middle of nowhere. I fell in love with the house, and the location is part of that."

"I'd love to see it sometime," Molly said, her voice turning a little shy.

"It's a mess right now," Sonia warned. "I spent so much time on the wiring and plumbing and then insulation that actual work on the renovations has been slow. I don't have tons of money, so I have to choose a room and go from there. I was up on the roof the other day and discovered I'm not going to be able to wait another couple of years. Like everything, it needs work now."

"I wouldn't mind helping out," Molly volunteered. "As a friend. Not a paid one. I don't know the first thing about carpentry, but I'd love to learn."

Sonia heard the lonely note in Molly's voice. She heard it because she felt the same. "I've been meaning to ask you to come out to consult about the yards. I'm not working on them yet, but I know if I want them nice, I have to plant now. You're the best at landscaping. You know so much about plants native to the area and I was going to ask for help, so I'd love for you come out, see the place and give me advice. I'm a fairly decent cook. Maybe a dinner in return for your expertise?"

"I'd love that," Molly said. "My family was from around here, a long time ago. My grandmother still owned property that no one wanted. I paid the back taxes on the little house and got it. That's why the house is so run-down. No one had lived in it for years. I also got a piece of the swamp I haven't looked at yet because the boat that came with it had several holes in it and sank when I tried to take it out. Oh, and I used the last of my money to open the landscaping business. Mostly I sell plants, but several of my most recent jobs have come because Jerry or you recommended me."

That was true. They tried to keep Molly in business.

Molly wrapped her hands around the hot coffee mug the waitress had brought her. "I don't want to sound like I'm prying, but your lip is swollen, and you have bruises on your neck and arms. They look like fingermarks, or teeth marks. I just need to know you're all right."

Sonia felt the blush start somewhere in her toes and creep

up to her neck and face in a long, slow burn. "It looks bad, but it isn't. I'm perfectly fine, and no one hurt me."

Molly let out her breath, nodded and changed the subject. "Where are you from?"

Sonia's heart jumped. This was the reason she didn't mingle with other people. You had to lie when they asked questions. She shrugged. "I've moved around a lot. I like being out of town where it's peaceful. I think if I could live on an island in the middle of the swamp, I would. I go out at night and sit on the porch and just listen. It isn't quiet out there, so I can't say I'm looking for quiet, but it is peaceful. I love the way the frogs call to one another and the insects have this amazing symphony going on. It's loud and crazy, but it's soothing at the same time."

"I like looking up at the stars," Molly said. "That's soothing to me. When you're away from the town and all the lights, you can see all the way to heaven."

Sonia paused with her cup halfway to her mouth. "That's beautiful, Molly, and so true. I just never thought of it like that. I love to look up at the stars as well. Is there a house on your grandmother's land in the swamp? I love the little house in town that was hers, but often there's a cabin or maybe a camp?"

"She had a house on stilts, or at least it looked that way to me. It was really different, but pretty. When I was a child I loved to go there, but later, when she was ill, she moved into town. None of my relatives wanted to live here, so one by one they left, my parents being the first. My grandmother might have lived longer if she'd had someone to care for her."

"That's sad, Molly."

"It really was. I loved her. Where is your family?"

The dreaded questions again. This one she could answer truthfully. "I don't have any family left. My father died some years ago, and my mother died of cancer just under three years ago." It seemed longer. Much longer. So much had happened. "I don't have any other relatives alive. My family members are destined to die young."

"I'm so sorry about your mother. You have a faint accent. Where are you originally from?"

Sonia took a long sip of coffee, her mind working fast. She knew she could never quite get rid of that accent. She tried. She worked on it all the time. "We used to go to Spain often for my father's work and we stayed there for months at a time. My parents spoke excellent Spanish, and I learned as well. It was a huge influence on me, and I think I retain a little bit of that accent." It was thin, but it was the only explanation that was the least bit plausible and still safe. If she said they went to Cuba, or her parents were from Cuba, there would be more questions. Worse, having that small piece of information could put Molly in danger.

"So you're from Spain? I can see that. Your skin is beautiful. With that skin and those eyes, you're very lucky."

Sonia held out her arm. She was a shade lighter than her mother, but with nearly the same olive skin and dark, dark chocolate eyes. She thought her mother beautiful. They had the same mouth, but her mother hadn't carried extra on her hips and breasts. Sonia was curvy no matter how much running she did. "My mother gave me her skin," she said, wanting Molly to know how much her mother had meant to her. "I thought she was the most beautiful woman in the world. And courageous." Tears burned behind her eyes. "I miss her every single day."

Molly sent her a small, sad smile. "That's so amazing. I wish I could say the same. My mother doesn't like me very much."

Sonia frowned. "Why? That makes no sense at all."

Molly hesitated and then shrugged. "We didn't have a lot of money. Well, we had it, inherited it, but most of my family doesn't believe in working. They like to spend, not earn. I met a man, very wealthy, and my parents wanted me to marry him. It was their dream come true when he asked, but he wasn't always very nice." She touched her throat as if it hurt. "I told them, but they didn't care, so I left, got out of town. They told him where I was. He came and got me. I woke up in a little room, a closet really, with no windows. It was so hot I thought I would suffocate. I'm just going to say, it wasn't pleasant for a few weeks. In the end, I had to play nice to get out."

Sonia closed her eyes. Molly's own parents had delivered her to a monster in order to get money. "How did you get away?"

"I just acted like I didn't know why I'd left, that he was right in all things and our engagement could proceed. I knew better than to talk to my parents and tell them my plans. They didn't know I was the one who had bought grandma's property when I inherited my money on my eighteenth birthday. I didn't tell anyone, least of all them. So, I came here. I knew it was risky, but I didn't have anywhere else to go. So far, so good. No one has tracked me here."

"But they might figure it out," Sonia protested.

Molly nodded. "They might, but I know Bastien, and he puts extra patrols around my neighborhood." She laughed softly at her own joke and then sobered. "I've had a chance to put in a security system, and I'm careful."

Sonia didn't like it. "Have you told Bastien? He might be flirty, but he's a good cop. You can see it in his eyes. He watches everything and everyone. I think that flirty, arrogant crap is a façade he wants everyone to believe."

Molly shrugged. "Maybe. In any case, I've been here awhile now. I told you what I'm running from. Are you going to tell me *your* story?"

Sonia pushed the empty coffee mug away. "My story is I owe Jerry a lot, and he needs me to go get an estimate on a really big job. We need it, and I'm going to land it for us." She saw the hurt in Molly's eyes and had to do something. "But I meant it when I said I wanted you to come out and look at my yard. I could use the input."

"Name a good time."

"Come tonight around seven. I should be off work by then, and I'll have dinner made. Anything you don't like?"

"I'm a total foodie."

"You look like a model. I wasn't certain you actually ate food."

Molly pushed back her blond hair. "I can put away an entire large pizza when I'm having a pity party."

Sonia made a face. "Girlfriend, any woman worth her salt can do that."

"*And* a tub of ice cream."

Sonia grinned at her. "Now *that* impresses me." She left the money for her coffee and a tip for the waitress. Women had to stick together, especially those working their way through the world on their own.

"It should, I was making it up."

Sonia found herself laughing, and it was the first time in a very long time. "I should have known. You have such a perfect figure."

"Um, Sonia? This isn't called a figure. I'm thin. You have a figure. I try, but I've never been able to put on weight easily. This sounds so stupid, and I never say it as a rule, but I just can't eat calories fast enough without my body burning them up."

"You try to put on weight?"

"All the time."

Sonia laughed again. "That's crazy. I'm always trying to lose. I guess we're typical women, Molly. We want what we don't have."

# 3

SONIA drove up to the Tregre plantation house slowly. It was several miles up the road from hers, deeper into the swamp and bordering the river as well. There was a high wrought iron fence, very ornate, surrounding the front of the property. A booth sat between the side of the lane going in and the one leading out. It looked like a guard booth, but no one was in it.

She drove her truck through the open gates and nearly stopped dead in the middle of the road. Even from a distance, the house was one of beauty and elegance from an era gone by. She thought her home was gorgeous, but this one was even more so. Clearly both had been built by the same architect. He'd been brilliant, using cypress, which didn't rot or get bug infestations as easily as most other woods. She could see that both the upper and lower stories of the house had long, wraparound balconies just as her home did.

Her truck moved slowly up the winding drive. The grounds were being manicured. There was activity everywhere around the outside of the house that she could see. Gardeners weeded flower beds and trimmed unruly bushes. Emerald leaves fluttered in the wind. The trees were thick and sturdy, trunks wide and branches curved, deliberately shaped. She slipped from her truck and took the path leading to the side of the house so she could peer into the side yard at the trees, making a mental note to tell the new owner about Molly's expertise in the gardening and landscaping world.

This was a leopard's paradise. Had Rafe Cordeau been a shifter? No, more than likely, the family that had owned the plantation all those years ago, when the trees had been planted and the branches forced to grow a certain way to create a highway flowing from tree to tree, had been shifters. Gatita would love this. Sonia was in the middle of creating just such a play yard for her leopard.

Feeling eyes on her, she took a careful look around and slowly lifted her chin so she could sniff the air. Her long hair and the hair on her body acted like a leopard's whiskers, sending out sonar and receiving information back. Her hair allowed her to feel slight vibrations in the air currents as they changed. She also could detect, even in the dark, just how close she was to anything or anyone.

Her sense of smell was good and gave her the information that aside from the gardeners, there were three men close by. She couldn't see them, and her eyesight was beyond excellent. She didn't like that the men could hide their presence from her. It was unusual, and anything out of the ordinary bothered her. Still, she was moving around the house of a client—a man of wealth who had taken back kidnap victims from their assailants. He was a man who must have made enemies. If he had a few guards, who could blame him? There were so many different males around, it was difficult to sort out all the various scents. Several were familiar to her, but elusive as they all ran together.

Sonia moved back around to the front of the house, deliberately looking up at the structure, noting any signs of aging. The house had held up when so many others had rotted in the intensity of the humidity, heat, insect attacks and neglect. There were very few signs of insects or neglect. This house had been loved by those living in it. She liked that.

She went up the long, wide steps onto the porch. Like hers, this one was massive, covered and used by the occupants. She moved closer to one of the columns and touched the long rake mark made by a large cat. The mark was old. Even painting it would feel like taking away a piece of history. Most seeing that mark wouldn't realize it was made by a leopard. Most probably wouldn't notice it unless they were purchasing the house.

She used the old-fashioned doorbell. The sound was melodious, pealing through the house to get all the way to the back of it. At once a man opened the door for her. He was young, not more than thirty. He smiled at her. "Miss Lopez? I'm Evan. Mr. Tregre asked me to show you around. He's running a little late. I hope you don't mind."

She shook her head and moved into the huge spacious room that was the existing great room. The floors were nothing short of magnificent. All gleaming wood, spreading through the room like sunshine. Windows were abundant, almost from floor to ceiling, and the ceilings were high, just as they were in her home. The fireplace was stone, very, very unusual for that type of architecture. She thought her home had been unique in that feature.

"This is beautiful. I can see why he wants to keep it the way it was meant."

Evan nodded. "I'll take you to the kitchen first. There was a shootout there. A bomb went off just under the eaves outside in the back. It did a lot of damage. We thought we could repair it ourselves, but we had no idea the house was so old and required a gentler hand. I think we did more damage than repairs. We also discovered a problem with the plumbing. The electrical was brought up to date by the previous owner, but the plumbing is a problem."

She nodded. "That's not unexpected. A lot of these older homes are updated in some areas and not others."

Evan was pleasant, and he didn't flirt at all. She glanced at his left hand. No wedding ring. His gaze had moved over her from head to toe when he'd first opened the door, after that—nothing. None of the other men they came across flirted either. She'd never had that happen. Not ever. Two women were mopping the upstairs floors, and they smiled down at her. That was more notice than any of the men gave her. The rarity of that bothered her so much she was becoming uneasy. Evan didn't give off threat vibes. No one did. Still, the unusual was setting off alarms.

The house was larger than hers, and she followed Evan from room to room. He showed her every one other than the master bedroom, bath and office. Nothing else was off-limits. She noted all the damage she could see in each room. There were bullet holes in doors, and the master bedroom door had been replaced, but it wasn't authentic or even suitable to the period of the building.

The destruction outside where the blast had hit was considerable. In terms of repairing a beautiful historic antique such as the Tregre plantation home, the fact that a bomb had gone off and only the verandah on the top story and bottom, along with the side of the house and windows, had been damaged was a miracle.

She whistled softly and touched the wood in awe. "This is amazing. Whoever planted that bomb knew what they were doing and directed the blast away from the house."

Evan's eyebrows went up. "You can tell that?"

She nodded. "I've worked with dynamite. The placement of this charge was very precise. Whoever planted it didn't want to injure the house."

"I agree." The voice came from behind her.

Sonia stiffened. She stared straight ahead. It wasn't just

any voice. It was low, velvet smooth, carrying a hint of a command, and she would recognize it anywhere. It wouldn't matter how much time went by, she would always know that voice. His. Joshua's. She raised her gaze to meet Evan's eyes. That was the reason none of the men flirted with her. Joshua had told them not to. He was the ultimate alpha. Leopard. Shifter. Of course he owned this house.

They were standing on the terrace on the back side of the house, examining the damage. Evan faced her on the first stair just below her. She shook her head and deliberately stepped onto the step with him. "Thanks for showing me around," she said, taking the next step and then the last one. Her heart began to pound. She felt like the rabbit in the middle of a pack of predators. She didn't know about Evan, but Joshua was one. She didn't dare run, although every instinct told her to; she knew it would set off his prey drive.

"Stop right there, Sonia." It was a command, pure and simple.

She glanced over her shoulder and kept walking. In the daylight, he was something to see. The man was drop-dead gorgeous. It didn't matter that he was hotter than hell, that sex with him was off the charts or that she wore his mark all over her body and felt him inside her with every step she took. She was leaving. *Leaving.* If Jerry wanted the job, he could get someone else to do it. Not her.

She felt a disturbance in the air and then he was in front of her, blocking the way. She halted so she wouldn't run into him, but she refused to back up even one step. Leopards could leap long distances, and evidently so could their human counterparts.

"Get out of my way."

"You're angry."

"You used Jerry to get to me."

He shook his head slowly, his blue-green eyes every bit as piercing as his leopard's. "I am in need of a contractor. Everything I told Jerry was the absolute truth." He gestured toward the house. "It's beautiful and damaged. I want it restored, but with more modern conveniences. It was Jerry who said he had just the person to do it."

"You followed me home." Her voice vibrated with accusation.

"Of course I did. I wouldn't be much of a gentleman if I didn't make certain you arrived home safely. I followed you every morning."

Sonia didn't know whether it was the fact that she'd told him not to and he'd done it anyway or that she hadn't detected him that bothered her most. "That wasn't cool."

"Maybe not, but you were safe. I like your home. It's a smaller version of this one. I looked it up to see if another family member had that house, but I couldn't find much on the family that had both houses built. They were secretive." His eyes told her he thought the family were shifters, and she agreed with that assumption. It made sense. The tree branches that deliberately formed a highway in the grove the family had planted throughout the acreage leading from the large mansion to her smaller one suggested shifters.

"I need someone to work on the house, Sonia," he reiterated. "I knew you worked for Jerry, but if he hadn't been the one recommended for this type of restoration, I wouldn't have chosen his company."

She tapped the notebook she'd been documenting the damage in against her thigh. "I don't like surprises, and you've given me quite a few."

"You're wearing my mark and my leopard's mark. Your female accepted him. You accepted me."

She looked around quickly, but Evan was gone and no one else appeared to be close. "For seven nights. That was it. Through her heat. Okay," she admitted when he continued to look at her. "*Our* heat. I was as bad as she was. I don't know about you, but I don't especially want anyone to know about my leopard. Rockets went off, you're that good, but I'm not looking for a relationship. I told you that."

"You told me you were mine."

"I was. For *seven* days," she insisted.

"Not going without you, baby," he said, stepping closer.

He took her breath, just like that, leaving her lungs burning and her heart aching. The way his voice went even lower, that note that caressed her skin like fingers, the intensity of his eyes—all of it got to her. When he stepped closer, she was once again surrounded by his scent, enveloped in him until she breathed him deep with every breath she took in. She didn't know how he did it, but he made her feel safe when she knew she wasn't. Especially not with him.

She couldn't have him. She wasn't going there. Seven nights of bliss, in the swamp, hidden from the world had to be enough for her. He was safe. She was safe. Gatita was safe. Safety would be gone if they stayed together beyond those days. She'd always treasure them, think of them, maybe even fixate on them, because the kind of sex he'd given her was addicting.

She shook her head. "Look, Joshua, I really, really had the best time with you a woman can possibly have, I'm not going to lie, but it can't possibly go beyond what we had."

He reached out slowly, as if she might bolt if he made the wrong move—which was entirely possible. Everything in her told her she was in fight-or-flight mode. She stayed frozen to the spot, unable to run, unable to draw her leopard out to fight him. She just stood there, allowing him to take possession of her just the way he had in the swamp.

His palm slid around the nape of her neck, and her heart thundered in her ears. His fingers curled around her neck, right over her pounding pulse. She felt the whisper of his warm breath as he bent his head toward hers, and then his mouth brushed lightly over hers. Her sex clenched hard. Her breath caught in her throat in absolute anticipation. He didn't disappoint.

Joshua's lips rubbed against hers like a cat, back and forth. His tongue traced the seam of her lips and then his teeth were there, tugging at her lower lip, biting down slowly, sinking deeper and deeper until, shocked at the stinging pain, she gasped and he was there, sweeping in, taking her over.

Rockets went off. Colors burst behind her eyes. His hands were in her hair, bunching, fisting, holding her still while he kissed her over and over. Long, drugging kisses that took every sane thought she'd ever had. Kisses that reduced her to incoherence. To confusion.

His kisses alone made it clear her body belonged to him. She forgot where she was. That it was broad daylight and they were out in the open. She would have done anything with him right then because she couldn't think straight. Only feel. He hadn't touched her body. He hadn't done one thing but kiss her, and she was already slick with need. That exquisite tension was already coiling tighter and tighter. Desire built until she was kissing him back, making her own demands, stepping closer, pressing into him to feel that hot, hungry length of him tight against her stomach.

"Baby"—he breathed the endearment—"we have to stop or I won't be able to."

He didn't step away from her but kept his body pressed tightly against hers. She had the feeling he was shielding her from too many interested eyes.

"Who are you, Joshua?" she whispered, because her voice refused to do more than that.

"You know who I am." He caught her chin. "I'm your man. Your mate. Are we done with the protests, or do I carry you upstairs and convince you a different way?"

"Your arrogance is annoying."

A small smile played around the edges of his mouth, capturing her heart. "I have reason to feel arrogant now that I've got you."

She shook her head. "You don't understand. I'm not in a position to have a man. Don't you think I'd say yes, if I could?"

That small smile was gone instantly. Her heart slammed hard in her chest and then accelerated alarmingly. That hot, gorgeous arrogance was gone, replaced by cool blue-green eyes. The green, turbulent, like a sea—just as cold—the blue like the deep of an iceberg. His features were a mask she couldn't read, all masculine and scary. He'd gone from warm and sexy to cold and dangerous in the blink of an eye.

She'd been around dangerous men before, but they were out of their league next to Joshua. She tried to take a step back, her hand going protectively to her throat. He caught her arm in a firm grip, looked around him and then started down the path leading under the canopy of trees, away from the house and anyone who might overhear them. She wasn't certain she wanted to be alone with him.

"You're scaring me." Honesty was the best policy. In any case, her leopard could always hear lies, and she presumed his leopard did the same for him.

"You should be scared," he snapped. "This is bullshit. You have a problem with someone, you need to tell me and tell me now."

"I don't know you," she reiterated, forcing her body to stay still when it was determined to tremble. She had Gatita, and that meant she could protect herself from him, at least long enough to get away. "I can't just blurt out personal problems when I just met you—if I had any," she hastily tacked on.

"You didn't just meet me, and you just confirmed you're in trouble. You're mine, Sonia, and I take care of what is mine. I know this is new to you, but you're a shifter. We live by different rules than the rest of the world. You should know that. You had to have been born into a lair."

She shook her head. "I don't even know what that is."

His gaze narrowed, more focused than ever, if that were possible. His eyes were back to crystal blue, all green gone. She could see the leopard staring at her.

"I want to leave. Right. Now. I want to leave." She could barely breathe.

"He isn't going to hurt you. That would be impossible for either of us to do," Joshua said. "I might be impatient or even angry with you at times, but I would never hurt you."

The ring of sincerity in his voice calmed her. He couldn't fake that. She took a deep breath and pulled him down into her lungs. He smelled of the outdoors. All masculine. "I don't know the first thing about shifters. I didn't know I was one until my leopard showed herself in an extreme circumstance." She chose her words very carefully.

"Extreme circumstance?" he repeated.

She nodded. "She saved my life." She didn't elaborate. "I came here because she needed a place to run. I needed a place for peace."

"To hide. You're hiding."

"If I'm hiding, you can see that the last thing I would need is the complication of a boyfriend."

"Boyfriend?" Amusement tinged his voice.

She was mortified. Of course he hadn't said a word about being her official boyfriend. They were more like . . . "Okay, fuck buddies," she snapped. "I don't have room in my life for you."

All amusement was gone from his face, leaving his features stony and cold. His ever-changing eyes were back to green-blue. She didn't know which was worse, knowing that his leopard was there staring at her like so much prey, or the man, doing the same thing.

"We are *not* fuck buddies," he hissed, between clenched teeth. "You are permanent. Mine. My woman. My mate. I'm not your damn boyfriend. I'm no boy and I'm not yet your friend. We're working on that. I'm *your* man. *Your* mate. I belong to you in the same way you belong to me. I have your body and you have mine. I want your heart and your mind. I want to be your best friend. And I want to be all that for you."

He was nuts. Crazy. Totally insane. He was the most gorgeous man she'd ever seen—and the scariest, and she'd seen plenty of scary men. She touched her tongue to her lips, trying to think. Up close to the heat of his body, breathing him in with every breath, feeling his dangerous pull, it was impossible to think straight. She looked around her, needing a reprieve. "What do you do? Why are all these men working around your home?"

"Have you ever heard of Drake Donovan? He runs a security agency."

She'd heard of him. As far away as Miami, Drake Donovan's name was known. She nodded without speaking, because she couldn't say where she'd heard the name if he asked.

"He has teams all over the world. We go in and take back victims that have been kidnapped. Or we do the drop to pay the ransom. Sometimes we act as bodyguards. I run one of his branches, and most of the men take the jobs when needed. Right now, we're trying to put this place together. There are cabins everywhere, all of which need updating. Aside from the main house, I'll need each of those fixed up or torn down and rebuilt. The grounds need work. We have enemies, so I need a decent, up-to-date security system. And then there's you."

He wasn't lying about any of those things. Gatita heard the truth in his voice, yet . . . Sonia didn't altogether trust him.

*I do.*

*You do because you want to be with his leopard, you hussy.*

"Tell me the reason you're afraid to be with me."

"I just met you," she repeated. "I don't really know you. I'm not going to make some crazy commitment when I don't have a real clue who you are."

"Fine. Then agree to work here." He gestured back toward the house. "You can see the work is legitimate. And agree to see me outside of work."

The temptation was strong, even though she knew better. "It isn't a good idea," she said reluctantly, but he was already smiling.

"Maybe not, but we need to try." He caught her hand. "Let me show you the cabins. I didn't tell Jerry about them because I wanted to ask you if they just needed to be torn down. If so, my men can start that work, and you can bring in crews to rebuild. There's history there, but the feel of them when I go inside is . . ." He trailed off. "I'd rather you judge for yourself."

Sonia went with him, terrified of what she'd just done, what she'd committed to doing in the future. Seeing him. What was wrong with her? She might get him killed. But was she going to live her life completely alone? He was leopard. He obviously knew more about that world than she did. He could explain things. Teach her. Everyone thought she was dead. There was no reason anyone would be looking for her.

They moved together in silence, walking along a worn path deeper into the grove of trees. She could see that small cabins dotted the trail. They were very old and some were so dilapidated, no matter how historical they were, they were too far gone to be saved. The cabin he took her to had been updated with more modern conveniences.

He stepped back, staying on the porch, opened the door and waved her through. For some reason, that made Sonia reluctant to enter. She studied his face for a moment. It was an expressionless mask. His face looked as if it could have been chiseled from the hardest stone, and his leopard was back, those crystalline blue eyes staring at her. A muscle ticked in his jaw, drawing attention to the darker blond shadow there.

Touching her tongue to the bite mark on her lower lip, she stepped inside the cabin and knew instantly what Joshua had been talking about. Gatita went wild, throwing herself against the restraints put on her by Sonia's human form. Snarling. Clawing. Raking for freedom. She smelled blood and torture. She heard the walls screaming. Death was there. Sonia had to fight to keep the cat from shifting. It wasn't easy, but she kept a firm hold.

Sonia stumbled out of the cabin, and Joshua instantly caught her arm and pulled her into the shelter of his body. He wrapped his arms around her and put his chin on top of her head. She stayed there, unmoving, fighting back nausea, trying desperately to breathe through Gatita's raking claws. Joshua's hand stroked calming caresses down the back of her head, his fingers whispering through her hair.

*It's all right now, they will take care of it.*

Strangely, it wasn't Gatita's voice she heard. It was the male leopard calming his mate, pushing his message through Sonia, giving her the impression of Joshua and Sonia tearing apart the cabin. The big male believed in the man, and he wanted Gatita to believe in him as well.

No one had spoken to Gatita but her. No one else had known about her until Joshua had come to them that first night of the female's heat. Sonia had counted on her. The leopard had been her only companion these last few months. A part of her didn't like sharing. She pulled out of Joshua's arms.

"I see what you mean," she said, still shaken. To cover the fact that her stomach was still churning and her body trembling, she stepped off the porch to solid ground. "If I were you, I'd pull them all down. Most of them have rotted, from the outside looks of them. These were slave cabins. Get rid of them, and if you need smaller homes for your men to stay in while they're here, I'd choose the best locations and make slightly larger houses, ones with full kitchens, good bathrooms with showers so they're comfortable. You could have the one with the best view be your guesthouse and make that special."

"I thought it might just be my leopard that could feel that. Historical or not, they should come down. Like you said, most are falling down anyway, and they're unsafe. The few Cordeau renovated, he didn't keep the historical look at all." He fell into step beside her, reached out and took her hand so that they moved together, side by side, along the path, their hands linking them together.

She bit at her lip. Just walking with him made her feel exhilarated. The feeling added color to the already bursting colors in the swamp and groves. Everything about being with Joshua felt intense. That was more than scary to her. She needed someone to talk to.

*You have me.* Gatita sounded a little annoyed.

*Maybe I do, but you're biased. All you can think about is having more sex with that male.*

Gatita preened, purred and stretched languidly. *That's what you're thinking about with your male.*

It was true. *So* true, but Sonia wasn't giving her cat the satisfaction of agreeing. She kept walking, debating whether or not to pull her hand away. Glancing up at Joshua's set features, she decided against it. He was back to looking on the dangerous side.

"You don't have a poker face. I can read every thought in your whacked-out-way-of-thinking mind. You promised me you'd try. Now you're back to thinking about running."

She glared at him. "Don't read my mind if you don't like what I'm thinking."

"Baby"—he shook his head—"I'm reading your beautiful face, not your crazy mind."

She couldn't help wanting to smile, but she didn't. She had very real concerns, although she couldn't share what they were. "Has it occurred to you that I might be protecting you?"

He stared at her for a moment, his eyes back to that blue-green, all man. All dangerous. All hers. She blinked. She couldn't think that way.

"No, that never occurred to me," he admitted. "But given the fact that I'm beginning to realize just how fucked up your thinking is, I should have."

She gave him her blackest scowl. "My thinking is perfectly logical. Just because you don't have all the facts doesn't mean there aren't good reasons."

"So share."

She shook her head. "I don't know you well enough."

She was looking at him, so she saw the dangerous ice that crept into the lines carved deep into his face, but then he flashed a humorless smile. He looked more like a predator with prey in his sights than a man.

"All right, baby, you're going to get to know me rather fast. I'm known for my patience, but with you, I find I don't have that much. While you're renovating the rooms in my house, don't forget to include a nursery."

She yanked her hand from his. "You are the most annoying man I've ever met."

"I'm just getting started. I'll pick you up for dinner tonight at seven. Wear something nice."

"Can't. I've already got a date."

It was the wrong thing to say, and she knew it the moment the last word slipped out of her mouth. His fingers shackled her wrist and he pulled her in close. Before she could say anything, his mouth was on hers, one fist in her hair. His hand tightened there, pulling her head back, his kiss dark and demanding. Her scalp hurt, but in a good way, adding to the pleasure bursting through her.

Then he lifted her, one-armed, his mouth still on hers. She barely knew she was moving until he put her down again and his hand caught the hem of her tee, pulling it up as he lifted his mouth from hers. He yanked off her shirt and was kissing her again. The air hit her body and she shivered. She felt his hand brushing along her back and then her bra was gone and he cupped both breasts.

Sonia was breathing hard, opening her mouth to protest, to try to think beyond the scrambled brains in her head, but his mouth closed, hot and wet over her left breast, pulling the soft mound deep, his tongue stroking and flattening her nipple against the roof of his mouth. His fingers were on her right breast, massaging and kneading, tugging and rolling her nipple. There was nothing gentle about the way he claimed her, and she didn't want gentle. He seemed to know exactly what would send flames racing through her blood-stream.

His mouth worked her breast while his hand dropped to the front of her jeans. He opened the front and then his fingers were in her panties, pushing them down to her thighs right along with the denim.

"You're already so hot and slick for me," he murmured as he switched his attention to her right breast.

The air on her left breast, which was already wet and aching, added to the need building in her. His fingers filled her, plunging, curling to find that one spot that could send her into another orbit. He withdrew his fingers and held them up, his eyes suddenly hard and dangerous, so blue they were shocking. "This is mine. All for me. You fucking don't have dates with other men." He licked his fingers clean and then dropped to one knee, his mouth covering her slick center.

She heard the keening wail snaking through the trees, the one she couldn't stop as he ruthlessly lapped at her, used his teeth to rake at her clit, then his fingers to bring her close. His tongue was back, flicking and thrusting until she gripped his hair and held him there, needing. The intensity of her hunger was so strong the world around her blurred. Pleasure was so close. So close.

He pulled back abruptly.

"What are you doing?" She was practically sobbing. "Please. Joshua. I'm so close."

He stood up, yanking up her panties and jeans. "No. Absolutely not. Not like this."

Furious, she glared at him. "Do you think I need you to get off? Because I don't. You can't dictate that to me."

One eyebrow shot up. "Really? Because your hand or your vibrator is going to do to you what I can? How many times did you try these last three days and nights?"

She couldn't hold his gaze. She looked away, tears burning behind her eyes. "Maybe you can dictate to me," she admitted. "I hope that makes you feel great, because it makes me miserable. Truly miserable. That isn't giving you points, in case you wondered."

"Sonia." He waited.

She didn't want to look at him, but she couldn't stop herself. She knew he would see the tears swimming in her eyes. It was one more humiliation among so many. She hated that she had no control over her body, but that he did. He clearly didn't feel the same way about her that she did him.

He caught her chin. "I'm not going to excuse my temper by reminding you I'm leopard. That's no excuse, and in any case, I think the man is jealous all on his own without his leopard feeding him that. Just so you know, it was the most miserable three days and nights of my life. My hand didn't do any better than your toys." He tasted her tears with his lips. "Who is taking you out?"

She was silent for a moment, wondering why the abrupt change in him made her feel cared for. Safe even. He didn't have to tell her he'd suffered as well, but he gave that to her and it mattered.

"I'm hoping it isn't a friend of mine, because I'd have to let my leopard hunt." There was a small teasing note in is voice, but she was leopard and she heard the half-truth there.

"My friend Molly is coming over for dinner tonight at seven, not that it's any of your business."

"Woman, you are truly exasperating. We just agreed we were going to get to know each other so you're more comfortable with the mate idea, but you know you're mine. You agreed. You carry my mark. You carry my leopard's mark. Leopards don't take well to their mates being around other men, especially other male leopards."

"I don't know your rules."

"The rules are in place so no one gets killed. Have fun with your friend Molly, and I'll come over after she leaves. We'll go over the rules then."

She wasn't certain having him in her space was a particularly good idea. If things didn't work out, she might not be able to cleanse her home of his presence. She wasn't even certain she liked him, but she loved his body and she loved the things he could do to her body. She was in way over her head.

"Would you rather come to my home?"

She shook her head immediately. "I have to work here. I have to face those men every day. I don't want them to know . . ."

"They know." His voice said it all. It was a decree. "They were told you were my mate and to stay the hell away from you."

That was why the men had barely looked at her, let alone flirted. He'd given them an order, and they'd obeyed. He was definitely the boss. If any of the others were leopard, then he was their leader. She didn't know leopards had leaders, but the men had done as he'd told them.

"You scare me. What happens between us scares me."

"I'll take that into consideration when handling you and the crazy way you think. I would really like it if you could take into consideration everything you know of leopards and their temperaments."

"Leopards don't mate for life. Females raise the young alone. In fact, male leopards have been known to kill the cubs." She couldn't keep the accusation out of her voice. She was still trembling, still hot, hating that her bra was on the ground with her shirt and she was standing half naked in front of him. Glancing down, there were those marks again, the way he'd scraped his teeth over her skin, the way he'd sucked until there was a bright strawberry. She refused to reach down and get her clothes to cover up.

"Shifters mate for life. We raise our young, Sonia. *I* mate for life with my woman and I certainly intend to raise my children with her." He reached down and gathered up her bra and shirt. He put one finger in the air and spun it in a circle, indicating for her to turn around.

She hesitated, but he didn't offer her clothes to her, so she reluctantly turned her back on him. He reached around her with her lacy bra and fit it over her breasts. "I hate to cover something this beautiful up, but you're already going to drive the men crazy. I don't need them looking at your body." He fit the hooks together and then pulled her T-shirt over her head.

She took a couple of steps forward before turning to face him again. Her gaze swept his body. At least he had a hard-on. The front of his jeans was pushed out and she could see the outline of his package, thick and long, straining the denim. She was grateful she wasn't the only one having a difficult time with what had occurred. Her sex clenched, and hot liquid dampened her panties. She was slick with need. Aching. She stepped farther away from temptation, putting space between them, not wanting to pull his scent into her lungs.

He moved with blurring speed. She knew leopards were fast, but his speed was astonishing and disconcerting. He was on her before she had processed that he was coming at her. His hand cupped her chin. "Tonight, Sonia. I'll take care of you tonight and we'll talk this thing out. In the meantime, I would appreciate you texting me when your friend leaves."

"I don't have your cell number." His thumb was rubbing across her lips and she could barely think again. She *hated* that she was that susceptible to him when he could think so clearly.

His hand slid into her back pocket where she kept her cell phone, pulled it out and handed it to her. "Put in your code and give it to me. I'll program my number in. Then you send me yours."

Her head screamed "no" but she found herself doing exactly as he'd asked—no, not asked. He'd told her. Still, even knowing that, she sent him her number when he handed her phone back.

"When you come up with the estimates for the main house, and the cabins separately, have Jerry send them to me."

She nodded. At least she hadn't lost the job for Jerry.

They skirted around the house, taking a path that led to the front, where her truck was parked. He walked with her. Close. His hand brushing hers. Fingers tangling. Gripping. He pulled her hand to his thigh. She didn't pull away.

When they reached her truck, he opened the door and trapped her between his body and the seat. "Kiss me." It was an order.

"I don't dare." She told the truth. Her body was already in full meltdown.

"I need you to kiss me."

"Joshua." She knew it was a weak protest.

The hand holding her palm to his thigh moved, pressed it over the hard length of him. "You aren't understanding me, baby. I *need* you to kiss me. I always feel as if I'm on the verge of losing you. I did lose you for three fucking days. I counted the damn minutes. You kiss me so I know you're with me, suffering the way I am. Thinking about me the way I'm thinking about you. I haven't slept in three nights, and that's the truth. I needed your body curled up in my bed, my body wrapped around yours. Don't know when I'll get sleep, but it has to be soon. You get me? It has to be soon."

She tilted her chin to look up at him. His cock was hot through the material of his jeans. She swore she felt his heart beating into her palm. Her gaze drifted over his eyes. His mouth. For just that moment, she was going to let him be hers, just as she had those seven nights.

She tossed her notebook over her shoulder into the car and then wrapped her hand around his neck. He didn't wait. He leaned down and took her mouth. Under her palm, his cock jerked hard and then that heartbeat pounded like a drum, so strongly she felt movement in her hand. His tongue was wicked. Commanding. He tasted like dark, carnal sin. He tasted like heaven itself.

Sonia didn't know how long she spent with her back pressed to the seat of her pickup and his hard body pressed into hers, but by the time she was back behind the wheel, her lips were swollen, her body on fire and her brain entirely gone.

# 4

"YOU know that song by Taylor Swift, 'Wildest Dreams'?" Sonia asked. She bit off the end of her fried zucchini. "That's Joshua. Tall. Handsome as hell. Okay, gorgeous. But he has the bad-boy thing down. Maybe more like badass. Either way, it isn't going to end well for me."

Molly frowned as she continued to eat. "You don't know that."

"Of course I do. Men like him don't really ever stay. They only say they're going to. And even if he did, he'd be hell to live with. He's a dictator." Sonia waved the zucchini in the air for emphasis. "Everything coming out of his mouth sounds like an order."

"Do you mind?"

"In bed, no. Out of it, yes. And he wouldn't confine his dictatorship to the bedroom. Trust me, he hasn't already."

"Hmm." Molly pushed her plate away even though there was still food on it. "I'm so stuffed if I eat one more thing

I'm going to explode. I need to get this straight. You didn't know him, didn't even know his name at first, and you had wild, crazy, out-of-control sex all night the very first time you ran into him."

Sonia groaned. "Just hearing you say it out loud embarrasses me. I've never done anything like that in my life. I've only ever been with one other man. I didn't even know sex could be like that. He's dangerous to women, Molly."

Molly laughed. "Well, we know he's dangerous to you. You kept going back, and so did he. What did you think was going to happen?"

"A week of the best sex in the world. That's what I thought and then it would be over. My heart wouldn't be totally involved, and I would pine away every night for just his brand of super sex." She was honest. "I thought I had it under control. Unfortunately, I think he's the one in control and I'm a mess."

"It didn't sound that way when he said you had to kiss him good-bye," Molly pointed out. "It sounded like he was the mess, afraid you were going to pull another disappearing act. He sounded a little desperate to me."

"I hope he was desperate, because every time I think about going to bed frustrated and aching, I'm dying for him." She sent Molly a mischievous grin. "Maybe not him. Maybe just his cock. Can a girl fall in love with just a man's cock? If he kept his mouth shut . . . No . . . wait. The things he does with his mouth are a miracle. If he just didn't talk, he'd be perfect. I could look at his body all day and take advantage any time I wanted."

Molly groaned. "You can't say things like that to me when I'm not getting any. I'm alone in my bed, remember? Toys are poor substitutes for the real thing."

"Now it isn't even a substitute," Sonia said and jumped up to pace across the kitchen floor. "I can't . . ." Frustrated, she halted in the middle of the room and flung her hands into the air. "You know. Nothing works without him."

"Okay, that's bad. Really, really bad. A girl has to be able to get herself off if she doesn't have a man."

"He says I do have a man."

"What do you say?" Molly asked.

Sonia took a deep breath. "I say he scares the living daylights out of me. I have no hope in hell of keeping up with him. His brand of sex is very adventurous. I mean *very*. Sooner or later he's bound to get bored with me."

"Sonia, you know better than that. You're looking for excuses not to be with him. *And* you're avoiding the question. Do you want to be with him?"

Sonia raked both hands through her hair. "I don't know, and that's the truth. I hate being alone. I love the sex. He's amazing. His voice. His hair. His mouth. His cock. His body. But, he's scary. He is. He can be looking at me one moment all sweet and the next he's cold as ice. He would demand I do whatever he wants. He has a temper. He was angry, but I couldn't tell if it was at me or because his—" She stopped herself from revealing their leopards. "His sex drive forced him to be with me, and he resents that."

Molly frowned. "I never thought about what it might be like for him." She shrugged. "I guess I think men just want sex any way they can get it without their emotions being involved. He must be as driven as you if he came back every night and just had wild sex. Why not try with him, Sonia?"

"I'd have to have complete trust in him, and I don't trust so easily."

Molly nodded. "I understand that. Still, what is really keeping you from trying it with him? You could always walk away if it doesn't work out."

Sonia shook her head. "I couldn't. Not with my heart. I know if I was around him too much, he wouldn't just own my body, that wouldn't be enough for him. He's already as much as said he'd want my heart—and he'd get it. I know I'd fall for him. He's just my type. I have a type, and it isn't good, Molly, it really isn't good."

"You like bad boys."

Sonia gathered the dishes from the table and took them to her sink. "Unfortunately. I don't know how it happened, but that seems to be my lot in life. Looking at them is awesome. The sex is good, or in this case, fireworks and rockets. But living with them, that's scary, dangerous and bad, bad, bad. Did I mention bad? Because it goes from bad to worse."

Molly studiously avoided looking at her. Instead, she rinsed the plates and put them in the dishwasher. "I'm sorry, Sonia. It sounds like your bad is right up there with mine."

"Did yours try to kill you?"

Molly almost dropped the plate. She caught it and rinsed it off. "How did you know?"

"No, I meant—" Sonia broke off. "Wait. That asshole tried to kill you? The one that kept you in that closet?"

"I'm not certain that was his intention, although he said if I refused to stay with him, I wouldn't be staying with anyone else," Molly confessed in a shaky voice. "He broke my arm in two places and three ribs. Both eyes were swollen shut, and my jaw had a hairline fracture. He had a friend, a doctor, who came to the house. I don't remember much of those early days, other than I couldn't do anything but drink through a straw for a few weeks after. They bandaged my jaw and told me not to move it. Blake told me I should thank him, that being on a liquid diet would keep me from getting fat."

"He did *not*." Sonia wanted to find the man and let her leopard loose. "He wasn't even arrested? He got away with it? And your parents still champion him?"

Molly nodded. "He's connected to law enforcement. The local DA schmoozing with all the bigwigs. Just the sort of man my parents want in their lives. He comes from a prominent family, and he's got tons of money. He's everyone's darling. Who would believe me?"

"I believe you," Sonia declared.

"I have a type too," Molly said. "Law enforcement every

time. I can't even look at Bastien without turning red. I'm sure he knows it. He always wears that smirk when he sees me."

"His cocky grin?" Sonia gave a little sniff. "No, hon, that's permanent on him. He's hot and he knows it."

Molly sighed. "Unfortunately for me, he flirts with everything that wears skirts, no matter the age, and he's law enforcement, which means if Blake had his friends put a fake BOLO out on me, Bastien would get it and turn me in."

"Bastien might flirt, honey, but he's intelligent. He wouldn't just hand you over without asking your side of things."

"Yeah, well I'm just staying out of his way as much as possible. I'm afraid to be alone with a man," Molly confessed. "I'm going to be a cat lady."

"Didn't you mention once to Jerry that you were allergic to cats? He told me the lumberyard cat had kittens before he could get her to a vet, and you couldn't take one because you're allergic."

"Yep. Totally allergic, so I'll be the cat lady that has rashes and sneezes all the time. So attractive."

Both laughing, they moved through the kitchen into the dining room. Molly looked around at the paintings on the wall. "These are beautiful. Are they all the same artist?"

Sonia blushed. She loved painting, but she had to hide her work. She couldn't stop herself from sketching nature, all the plants and animals she saw in the swamp. "I'm working with oil because I want the colors vivid. The swamp is beautiful, and I want others to see it the way I do."

"Everyone should see these. Honestly, Sonia, these are very good. I'd love to buy one from you."

Before she could answer, she caught the flash of lights through the trees. Her breath caught in her throat, and she stepped back from the window. "Molly, it looks like I've got more company. Why don't you stay in the kitchen while I go to the door?" If she had to shift, she didn't want an audience. "Just in case, you know."

Molly paled. "Didn't you say Joshua was going to come by later?"

They could hear the car coming up the gravel driveway. Sonia shook her head. "I was going to text him after we were done talking and having a good time. I wanted your advice, not his company tonight." Which was kind of a lie, but she wasn't admitting that to Molly or herself. "Just stay in there for a couple of minutes, hon. I'll go see who it is."

She hurried through the formal dining room to the great room. Pulling open the door, she slipped outside and moved to the left of the door on the verandah. She didn't have lights on outside and didn't turn them on now. She just waited while the visitor parked his SUV and then got out. Instantly her body relaxed.

She waited until he was up the three steps before she let him know he wasn't alone. "Bastien. What brings you out here tonight?"

He was in uniform. He paused on the wide porch. "Sonia. I didn't see you there in the dark." He looked around. "You alone?"

"Why?" she countered.

"I saw Molly leave town and when I cruised by your house, I saw her car. She doesn't normally travel this far out, and she never stays out this late. I was worried."

She could hear deception in his voice. He wasn't telling her the entire truth. The lie was mixed with truth.

"We had dinner together. Girl talk. Forming a posse."

He leaned one hand against the large column. He did look good in his uniform, and the lazy pose only served to emphasize how handsome he was. "Why do the two of you need a posse?"

She stayed in the shadows. The more still she stayed, the more the night covered her. He knew where she was, his gaze was directly on her, but she knew she blended in at night. She wasn't certain what he wanted yet and she wasn't going to let him get to Molly if his intention was to arrest her and send her back to Blake.

"Women stick together when men are circling. We compare notes and keep each other strong."

"Molly trying to be strong?" He flashed a grin at her. "Or is it you?"

"Maybe both." She wasn't in the least fooled by that easy smile.

"Invite me in." It was said nicely, but there was a subtle order underlying that pleasant tone. He straightened, going from lazy to meaning business.

"Why?" She got the message, but she wasn't giving in without knowing what she had to do to protect her friend.

"I have to see for myself that Molly's okay."

His answer was so unexpected she made the mistake of moving, presenting a good target if he wanted to take out his gun and shoot her.

"Why?" she repeated.

He sighed. "She's careful. She looks over her shoulder. She's in trouble. I'm not about to let anything happen to her. I'm getting her story, and then, I warn you, I'm going to get yours."

She liked that he wanted to look after Molly. The sincerity in his voice told her that much was the strict truth. She also was happy that he didn't think she was running from someone. She was a woman alone and he wanted to know why, but he didn't think danger was as imminent with her as it was with Molly. She was doing something right.

"Fine, but behave yourself. I'm not afraid of kicking you out if you upset her."

"Why would you think I'd upset Molly?" There was genuine concern, but also speculation.

Sonia knew she could never forget he was a cop. He had the mind of an investigator and the way she answered him or even got sassy with him would give too much away. She pressed her lips together and stalked back to the door.

*Keep close,* she warned her cat. She didn't need Gatita going to sleep on her when she might need her.

*He is no threat to you,* Gatita said.

Sonia pushed the door open. *Stop sulking. You're going to see your male tonight. I'm not worried about me. I'm worried Bastien might want to arrest Molly. Stay alert.*

"Molly, Bastien's here. He just wants to check in and make sure we're both all right. Why don't you come here into the great room?" she called, mostly to warn Molly. After what Molly had disclosed about her attraction to the cop, she wanted to give the woman plenty of time to shore up her defenses. Not that time would help Sonia if Joshua were there.

Bastien caught Sonia's shoulders and moved her, with surprising strength, out of his way. He strode through her house. The layout made it easy for him as one room flowed straight into the next. He was in her dining room almost before she knew what happened.

"Molly." His gaze moved over her, taking in every inch of her. "You good?"

Molly's chin lifted. "Why wouldn't I be?" She sounded out of breath and a little shy when she obviously meant to sound belligerent. "I may have overeaten. Sonia's a good cook."

Bastien glanced over his shoulder at Sonia. She stood in the doorway of the dining room watching them, but the light spilled across her face. His gaze narrowed instantly and he strode straight back to her, catching her chin and turning her face toward the light. "What the hell?"

She pulled away from him and stepped back. "I bit my lip when I fell. It was actually a couple of days ago when I first bit it, but then, this morning . . ." She licked at the small injury. "I keep doing the same thing. I have a bad habit." She knew she was stumbling over her explanation, saying too much and making it sound like she was lying.

He swung away from her back to Molly. "This sudden meeting doesn't have anything to do with Sonia's lip, does it?"

"No, of course not. Bastien, if Sonia was in trouble, I'd tell you."

"Would you tell me if *you* were in trouble?" he demanded.

Molly ducked her head, faint color flushing her face. "I'm boring. I don't get into trouble," she hedged.

He stepped closer to her. Sonia's breath caught in her throat. Bastien's entire body language screamed protective toward Molly. The man might flirt with every woman alive, but she had never seen him look at anyone else the way he was looking at Molly.

"There's nothing boring about you, Molly. If you're in trouble, you need to clue me in."

Molly looked to her a bit helplessly. Sonia rescued her. "Funny you should say that, Bastien. We were just talking about how, when you've been burned, it takes a lot to trust again. That's the kind of things women talk about over a kick-ass, spicy dinner."

"Her cooking is kick-ass and very spicy," Molly stated. "And look at her paintings. Sonia not only can build a house, and cook a killer meal, she can decorate with her artwork."

He hesitated and Sonia held her breath, willing him to let Molly off the hook. She had to tell him when she was ready, and that would take trust. A *lot* of trust. Molly didn't want to be handed over to Blake. Sonia made a mental note to find out his last name and where he was. Until Molly could trust Bastien, she was going to have to be Molly's protection.

"You paint these, Sonia?" he asked.

She nodded. "I've been painting since I can remember."

"Were your parents artists? These are good. Really good. Even I can see that."

She couldn't help but bask a little. She loved painting, but there was no chance now of ever knowing how good she was. She had no idea if anyone would ever really show her work in a gallery or if someone would really want to purchase one.

"When I paint, I just lose myself in it," she said. "I don't paint portraits, although I've experimented with them. I especially love nature." She indicated the three paintings she had on the wall. "When I get to this room and it's elegant, I'll shift these paintings somewhere else, but the room was such a mess I needed to brighten it up."

"You ever show your work in a gallery?" Bastien asked, standing in front of one, studying it carefully. "I know the owner of the most successful gallery in New Orleans. It's very high-end. She'd kill for a chance at these."

Sonia flashed a fake smile and shook her head. "I just paint for myself. I'm a carpenter, Bastien, just trying to make a name for myself renovating old houses."

"Did you really just drop by to see if we were all right?" Molly asked. She stumbled a little over the words and there was an attractive flush on her face, but she managed to meet Bastien's gaze.

"Yes." He looked around the house. "Are you ready to go?"

Molly nodded. "It's late. I've always hated going into my house after it's dark."

He stepped back to allow her to precede him into the great room. "I'll follow you home and do a walk-through."

"I have a security system. It's supposed to be a really good one."

"I'll do a walk-through," he stated, his voice firming. "And I'll leave right away after. I'm a cop, Molly. I love what I do and would never risk my career by getting out of line with a woman, no matter how attracted to her I am. Just for your information, I have a high regard for women, instilled in me by a good mother. I would never hurt a woman, and I don't like seeing them afraid or with bruises, or swollen lips." His gaze found Sonia's face.

She rolled her eyes at him. "You've been a cop so long I

think you're looking for a case. It's probably very quiet around here."

"Rafe Cordeau, the man who owned the estate just up the road from here, was a mobster. I'm uncertain whether the man who bought the property after him has taken over his business, but I suspect he has. Half the police department was on Cordeau's payroll. Believe me, honey, I don't have to go looking for work. It's all around me."

Sonia stiffened. She hadn't seen evidence that Joshua Tregre was in the mob. "I just came from there, Bastien. Jerry sent me to do estimates for repairing the damage done to the house and property. He told me he works for Donovan Security. It's international, and he heads one of the teams."

"Donovan?"

She nodded. "Jerry said Tregre rescued kidnap victims in other countries. Why do you think Tregre is a criminal?" Because if he was, she wasn't having anything to do with him. She'd leave everything behind if she had to and run again.

Bastien frowned. "He's good friends with Elijah Lospostos and Alonzo Massi. Elijah's family is well-known mafia, and he took over the family business some years ago. He's married to Siena, Antonio Arnotto's granddaughter. She inherited Antonio's crime business and appointed Massi as her business manager. It's known Massi took over the crime side of the business. He has a massive territory, and already there's been a war started with other factions. Massi and Lospostos make a powerful combination."

"And my neighbor knows these people?" That was scary. Very, very scary. She wasn't about to get anywhere near the mob. She'd heard of Siena Arnotto. Her grandfather had had a very successful winery. The family was very wealthy and had been written up in tabloids for years. When Arnotto had been murdered, it had come out that he'd been the head of a crime family. The scandal had occupied the newspapers and gossip columns for months. She'd felt a little sorry for Siena Arnotto. Who wouldn't for someone under that scrutiny? But then the woman had married Elijah Lospostos. The man's family went back generations in the crime business.

"Yes, he does," Bastien said. "But to be fair, so do I. It doesn't make Tregre a criminal, but it does make him someone to keep my eye on. When you're there . . ."

"I'm not spying." She was adamant. If she saw anything suspicious, she was gone. She wasn't reporting it, she was just plain gone.

"I don't want you spying. In fact, just the opposite. Do your work. Concentrate on that. Don't go anywhere you're not supposed to. If you do see something suspicious, just walk away."

She liked that he was so protective, but this new development was frightening and she wanted both Molly and Bastien gone so she could think about it and decide what to do.

Bastien stalked to the door and held it open, waiting for Molly. Molly hugged her. "Thanks so much for a great evening. It's the most fun I've had in a year. The food was delicious and the company and conversation even better."

"Thanks for giving me so many pointers for my yard. I love the ideas you came up with. If we land this job, I should be able to plant most of the bushes and ornamental trees as well as the flowers in the next month. That will give them time to grow while I work on my house. The roof should come first. I can't have any leaks when the rains come again."

"I'll come back soon," Molly declared. "And don't forget we're having dinner next week at my house. I can't cook like you do, but I won't give you food poisoning."

Bastien took Molly's elbow. "I think the two of you could set a record for the longest good-byes."

"Well, I'm fairly certain I should be a candidate for a couple of halls of fame, so throw my name in the ring for that as well," Sonia said cheerfully. It felt good to know she had a friend. She really liked Molly. "Don't forget to do that walk-through," she added.

Molly widened her eyes in a shocked, what-are-you-doing stare. Bastien nodded. "I won't forget. She'll be safe. I'm following you home, Molly, so don't speed."

"I *never* speed. That's Sonia."

Sonia shrugged. "Seriously? No one is ever on these roads. I don't speed in town."

"It's still breaking the law, Sonia," he said.

She rolled her eyes at him. "It's a stupid law when no one is on the road but me."

"It's designed to keep you safe."

She didn't like safe. She liked dangerous. She wanted safe, it was more comfortable, and now that she was out of danger, she thought it was exactly what she wanted. Then she met Joshua Tregre, and safe wasn't nearly as important as she'd thought it was. She ran both hands through her hair. She was messed up. Seriously screwed up. After the things that had happened to her, why would she even consider a relationship with Joshua? After the information Bastien had imparted to her, she should be packing. Running again. Instead, she stood on her porch and waved to Molly and Bastien. Once their taillights had faded away, she still stood there, listening to the sounds of the swamp.

Those crooning insects made up a lullaby just for her. The frogs chimed in for the chorus and continued to belt out a frenzied call and answer, while the swamp cicadas provided the endless melody. She loved the night sounds in the swamp. *Loved* them. Sometimes she lay in her bed with the window open, and other times she couldn't resist sitting outside on her balcony falling asleep to the music.

She wrapped her arms around her middle and rocked for a moment, trying to stop her body from burning. If her brain would stop thinking about Joshua, she would have a chance to figure out the intelligent thing to do and then actually follow through. Unfortunately, Joshua had set up a terrible addiction in her. The moment her company had disappeared, her body began to coil tightly, pressure building, her desire becoming a need.

Sex was temporary. It would burn out, and then she'd be left with a bossy dictator who probably would run around on her. And that was if he stayed—which he wouldn't. Men like him didn't stay. She was in for serious heartbreak if she was stupid enough to try to have an actual relationship with him.

She sighed and went back into the house. As she walked, she pulled out her phone and stared down at it. She didn't text him. She had to believe she was disciplined enough to go another night without him. It had been bad enough that she'd met him every night in the swamp because she hadn't been able to stay away, but she could blame Gatita's heat. She didn't have that excuse now. If she texted him to come, it would be on her. She would know she was too weak to resist him, and if he was a criminal, if he in any way was mixed up in mobster-type behavior, she was as good as dead.

She took a long, cool shower and pulled on a pair of red stretch boy shorts. They were a favorite because they were so comfortable. The lace stretched over her hips and made her feel feminine, even when she was working with hammers or a nail gun. She especially liked to sleep in them on hot nights. The matching camisole clung to her full breasts, but surprisingly gave more support than she thought it would, making it a favorite to sleep in as well. She knew better than to go barefoot, so she slipped on thin ballet slippers and went out to the back verandah to add soft easy music to that of the swamp.

It sometimes took hours for her long, thick hair to dry if she washed it at night. She played her favorite songs and let the breeze play through the wet strands. The chair she liked best was an egg-shaped swing suspended from the ceiling by a chain. She curled up in it and rocked gently while her fingers idly turned her cell phone end over end. It was going to be a very long night.

*You're sad.*

She was. Very sad. Not like when her mother died and she'd been so lost. It had been the two of them for so long. Her beautiful mother, who had cleaned houses for a very wealthy Russian family after her husband had died. "Murdered, Gatita," she murmured aloud. She lied so much about her father dying in an accident that she needed to hear the word.

"*Papi* was murdered."

*I know. I am so sorry. We are safe here.*

"They made me believe they were our friends. *Mami* worked for them, and she knew. All that time, she knew they murdered her husband. Can you imagine how awful that must have been for her? That night, when I found out my own husband was going to murder me, I also found out his father, Nikita, that man I thought loved us, forced her to sleep with him. I overheard him talking to Sasha. He said it was stupid to fall in love with me. In the end, he would have to kill me and it just made it harder if he loved me. Sasha agreed with him." Sasha, her husband. The man she'd trusted. The only human being she'd had left in the world.

Gatita soothed her, purring gently, so that the insides of her body vibrated, almost to the comforting music of the swamp.

"Nikita always acted like we were important to him. Always. I would never have believed this about him if someone had told me, but I heard him myself. And Sasha agreed with him. I thought Sasha truly loved me, that he'd fight for me."

She hadn't realized tears were falling, but one slid off her chin and dripped onto the upper curve of her breast. She wiped at them. She'd done enough crying when she realized how the Bogomolov family had taken advantage of her. Nikita Bogomolov, head of family, had ordered her father Roberto's execution. He'd been tortured first because they'd believed he had stolen money from them. Maybe he had. He had a lot of pride and didn't like his wife or daughter working. Roberto had brought them from Cuba, and he'd had connections to the Bogomolov family, so he'd had work immediately.

"It wasn't right, Gatita," she whispered. "Even if he stole from them, they didn't have to kill him. What were they looking for? Why would they have *Mami* work for them, use her like that and then pay for all her cancer treatments? She had round-the-clock care until she died." She knew the answer. Sasha. He'd made certain her mother had been taken care of. He'd been Sonia's rock throughout it all.

"I thought he loved me," she repeated sadly. "Nikita said we were not the type of women to marry, only to fuck. Not to love. Not to have children with. We weren't women to take into society. I hate how that made me feel."

Sasha had agreed with him. Her world had been shattered. She'd been seventeen when her mother was diagnosed and two months into her eighteenth year when she'd died. Sasha had taken care of the nurses, the hospital, paying the bills, organizing the service and burial afterward. She had looked to him for everything.

*He said he loved you and he didn't lie. I would have heard it.*

"Did you know that Nikita killed *Papi*?"

*How could I? You were never around a conversation regarding your father's death.*

Sonia scrubbed a hand over her face, removing more silent tears. They'd made their try, planting a bomb in her car—the car Sasha had given to her when they'd married to encourage her to get her license. The car had been blown to bits, crashing with a fiery orange-red and black tower of smoke and flames into the ocean.

She would have been a burned corpse, dead at the bottom of the sea, had it not been for Gatita. She hadn't known Gatita existed. The leopard had risen, bursting through skin to take over, leaping from the vehicle just as the bomb went off. The blast had catapulted the cat to the edge of the road on the far side from the ocean. Even injured, the leopard had known to run fast and get under cover.

They'd made their way back to the huge Bogomolov estate, where Sonia picked up the keys to the safety deposit box her mother had opened and told her to use for stashing money just in case. It had become a habit. No one was to ever know about the box. A few times she'd been tempted to tell Sasha, but she'd heard her mother's voice warning her it was only for emergencies and *no one* should know. She had a "go" bag, something her mother and father had always insisted she keep ready. It had clothes, identification, papers she would need and cash. Lots of cash. That had been kept away from the house along with the key to the safety-deposit box.

"*Mami* knew I would need money," she whispered to the leopard. "There was so much cash I have to wonder if *Papi* did steal from the Bogomolov family."

*We are safe here.*

"We *were* safe here," Sonia corrected. The slight breeze slid across her body, touching her burning skin. "Now I'm not so certain. You heard Bastien. Joshua Tregre very well could be a member of a crime family. If he is, Gatita, they're all connected. Sooner or later, we'd slip up, and he'd tell Nikita and Sasha we're alive."

*He wouldn't turn us over to them.*

"Technically, I'm still married to Sasha, at least I think I am. It isn't like I could file for divorce. He'd know I was still alive." She rubbed her temples. It was all very confusing.

*He tried to have you killed.*

"I'm very aware of that, thanks, Gatita."

Absently she ran her finger over her breast, tracing the soft skin through the lace. She tapped her thigh with the phone in her other hand. Over and over. Keeping beat to the music playing through her head. Drumming to the sounds of the swamp and the love song she listened to. The finger on her breast found her nipple. It was hard and aching. Because

Joshua was back in her head. Nothing she did seemed to keep him out, not even when she thought of the past.

"One would think I would learn," she said. "What's wrong with me that I can't learn?"

*You need to sleep.*

"I can't sleep. I'll have to go running until I can't move like I did last night." And every night after refusing to give Joshua her phone number or last name.

*I like running.* Gatita stretched languidly.

That made Sonia smile. "You just hope we're going to meet up with your mate."

*So do you.*

Sonia groaned. "I hate it when you're so smug."

*You hate when I'm right.*

"That too." Sonia jumped up and paced across the long length of the verandah. The wraparound porch was very long, just like the house. That gave her a lot of room to pace and she took full advantage. "He's so bossy. Doesn't it bother you that they boss us around? Even Sasha didn't tell me what to do."

*No, but he did try to kill you.*

"Maybe it wasn't Sasha. Maybe it was Nikita."

*I smelled Sasha's scent.* Papi *made bombs. He let you plant dynamite charges when you were working with him, learning to build things. You learned to plant charges in the rock. You knew Sasha built the same kind of bombs. You smelled the chemicals on him when he came home.*

She hadn't asked him about it either. She'd told herself it was because she didn't want him to know she had such a keen sense of smell. She'd known she smelled things others couldn't, and the few she'd told had accused her of lying. Mostly she hadn't told him because she'd been afraid to know what he was doing. By that time, she'd learned the dynamics of the household. The secrets. She'd always been good with languages, and her parents had spoken some Russian. She'd picked up even more living with Sasha.

She had been young enough and shocked enough by her mother's death to enjoy the privileges of being his wife without question. Once the shock was over and the wild grieving lessened, she'd taken the time to look around her, to listen when no one thought she was.

She had to admit, she had begun to suspect the Bogomolov family was involved in crime and that Sasha was a big part of that. She'd made up her mind to ask him, but she never got that chance. Her class at the college, the one on historical architecture, had been canceled due to a professor's illness. She'd gone home early and overheard the conversation between her father-in-law and Sasha. Her world had once again crashed.

She'd snuck more money and clothes into her "go" bag every chance she got, planning her getaway down to the smallest detail. She hadn't known that while she was planning to run, her husband and his family were plotting her death. She couldn't go to the police because some might be on the Bogomolov payroll, but more, she didn't have anything of value to trade for her life. She'd never heard one single deal go down. Not one. In her presence, they'd talked business, but it had always been a legitimate one.

Sonia pressed her fingertips to the corners of her eyes to try to stop the tears from leaking out. She'd loved Sasha and she'd believed in him. Looked up to him. If he'd been able to deceive her like that, what would happen with a man who didn't have his smooth, polished edges? His gentlemanly ways? His charm? Sasha had expected her to agree with him over most things, but he hadn't minded an argument and had listened to her. Joshua appeared to be a first-class dictator. It occurred to her that was a leopard trait. So was temper and moodiness, if her leopard was anything to go by—and Gatita wasn't in the least bit alpha.

Oh God. She was back to Joshua. The road always seemed to loop back to him, and she couldn't have that.

# 5

SHE wasn't going to text him to come to her. Joshua Tregre paced back and forth along the upper balcony of the plantation house. In the past two hours, he'd looked over toward Sonia's home a hundred times. Evan had told him repeatedly he was going to wear a hole in wood that had withstood a hundred years or more of wear and tear.

"She's afraid, Joshua. Look at you. You're intimidating as hell and you scared her," Evan pointed out.

He knew that. He didn't want to hear it. He'd been crazy with her. He couldn't keep his hands off her. "Never thought I'd find her," he admitted to his best friend. "Never. Not in a million years, and certainly not now, not when I've got this mess on my hands. We've got a huge deal coming up and I can't afford to be thinking about my runaway mate." That was *all* he was thinking about.

Normally, Joshua was known for his cool. His utter calm. He wasn't a hothead like so many leopards, that was why he'd been chosen to take over Rafe Cordeau's territory. He didn't get ruffled no matter the circumstance. Until Sonia. She was beautiful, sexy, intelligent and scared to death.

Shadow, his leopard, gave him impressions of a fiery car dropping into the ocean, of Gatita and Sonia running for their lives. Gatita hadn't shown much else, only giving the big male the impression of the two females dead and that meant they were safe. From that, he'd gleaned that someone had tried to kill them and thought they'd succeeded. That was unacceptable to him.

"She's in trouble, Evan, big trouble, and she isn't going to tell me about it."

"Have your leopard get it out of his mate."

"He had the impression of a car blowing up and falling into the ocean. That's it. Nothing else. When he pushed her for more, she ignored him."

"Sonia knows bombs. She recognized that the blast that took out the porch was deliberately directional," Evan volunteered.

"Damn it, she has to talk to me. I'm her fucking mate. She should trust me."

The truth was, he was used to being taken at his word. He answered to Drake Donovan and Elijah Lospostos, but no one else. And no one questioned his word. He was also used to being popular with women. He liked sex. A. Lot. His body was often hard, making demands on him, and after a long day, there was nothing better than a night of sex. But then he went home. He didn't sleep with them. He didn't cuddle them. He didn't want to inhale them with every breath he took—until Sonia.

Sonia was like a drug he couldn't get out of his system. Not just any drug, one that gave him such an intense release, he swore he could reach the fucking stars. She did that. He wanted to devour her. Her taste was addictive. Her body was paradise. He knew she was his. She'd been made for him. He'd known that even without the leopards, Sonia would have belonged to him. He wanted her to feel the same way about him. Possessive. Urgent. Explosive. And then, in bed with her after, holding her close, sated, completely at peace.

"Joshua, I'm your friend. You're leader of the lair here. You're getting this lair under control, and it was seriously fucked up. Most of the men here are unknown. We aren't positive we can trust them yet. We've got this Miami deal we have to set up. Elijah made it clear that the pipeline had to be set up as fast as possible, and we need the Russians in Miami. That's on you and you know it. Now this woman comes along at the wrong moment and adds a huge complication. You have every reason to be edgy and moody, especially with her in a heat, but you know, if you scare her, she might get it in her head to take off."

Joshua stood on the edge of the upper gallery, one arm circling the massive support post while he stared out over the swamp toward Sonia's home. The branches of the trees touched one another, laying out a long, complex highway that stretched to Sonia's as well as in the other direction and also deeper into the swamp. He had the perfect setup for his leopard. For all the leopards in the lair. They had freedom to run their leopards undetected by the outside world. He had the freedom to get to Sonia without anyone seeing— including her.

*God*. He wanted her. He fucking wanted her with every breath he took. "I can't think straight, Evan. I didn't know it could be like this. I know she's mine. I *know* it. My leopard claimed hers. I thought when that happened she'd just go along with the program, especially after all those nights together."

"Did you talk to her about this? Maybe she doesn't know about shifters. I've known that can happen. Drake said as much."

"She told me she didn't know the rules. I told her I'd come to her tonight and we'd talk. We didn't do much talking while she was in her heat." The thought of those nights made his body hard all over again. "I should have been more careful with her. Gentle. She didn't seem to want or need gentle and neither did I. I knew leopard sex could get rough during a heat, but I had no idea it would be like that. I about lost my fucking mind. Rough is my preference every time, and she was all over that."

"You're going to her." Evan made it a statement.

"I can't keep away, and it sucks that she doesn't feel the same way. It pisses me off and hurts like a son of a bitch at the same time." He rubbed his chest over his heart. "You know me, I'm not like this."

"You're going to have to resolve it soon. We've got a week, no more, and then you have to have your head in the game. If you don't think you can do that, Joshua, we've got to tell Elijah. Maybe one of the others can take over."

He shook his head. "Elijah and Alonzo are counting on me. I've worked hard on this and I know every detail from start to finish. I'm going to see it through." But first, there was the biggest deal of his life waiting to be brokered. Sonia Lopez. He'd already called Drake Donovan and Jake Bannaconni, two friends who would be able to learn every secret the woman had. He didn't like setting them on her, but he had no choice. She wasn't going to talk, and he needed information fast.

He took a deep breath, breathing in the swamp, listening to the insects and frogs dominating the night's sounds. He heard the plop of snakes in the water. The jump of a fish. The rush of wings as an owl flew close. He loved the swamp. He'd been born in Louisiana. It was home and always would feel like home to him.

The swamp wasn't for everyone, but Sonia had been fearless yet respectful, making her home there. She'd been careful not to disturb the animals and plants any more than necessary. He could see that she was trying to restore her home to its once-elegant beauty while keeping the grounds covered in native plants.

"You're good with women, Joshua. They're all over you."

"Not good with the one who counts." He sighed. "I can't stay here knowing she's over there. I'm going to her. You might want to cross your fingers she doesn't shoot me."

"She have a gun?" Evan was mildly worried.

"I wouldn't put it past her," he said and bent to remove his boots. "Can you find me a pack? I'll just take a T-shirt and pair of jeans."

"I'll leave you a pair of boots and socks at the corner of her property. The old tree where we stash clothes." He pulled a small pack from under his chair and handed it to Joshua.

"Thanks, Evan." He rolled his shirt and put it in the pack. Jeans were more difficult, they had to be rolled tightly to fit the smaller packs. The packs were fitted around their necks so when they shifted, they carried their clothes with them. They also made it a practice to stash clothing and shoes at various sites around the property just to be safe.

Joshua was relatively new as leader to the lair, having taken leadership from the leopard who'd claimed it when Rafe Cordeau disappeared. Joshua's leopard fought and killed the leader, and the remaining leopards opted to stay and swear allegiance. The first thing he'd done was decree that his men would befriend their neighbors and the townspeople. No business paid protection money. No one was shaken down or made to feel afraid. He'd set the example of buying locally and using local talent to help put the property back together.

Drake had sent him several leopards from Borneo, men Drake had worked with and trusted. Joshua knew them, and had fought alongside of them. All had volunteered to help him when Drake had laid the problems in the lair out for them. They knew the danger and were willing, as usual, to assume the risks.

He didn't wait. The moment he'd secured the pack around his neck, he shifted with blurring speed. Drake Donovan had drilled it into all of them that speed counted, and they'd

practiced, knowing one second could be the difference between life and death. Most of the time their clothing and
footwear were easily gotten rid of so they weren't slowed
down by stripping.

His leopard was a big, fearless male. In a fight, he was
fast and deadly. It was Joshua who held him back, tempering
dominance with compassion and mercy. That wasn't always
the best thing, not in a fight to the death, but it made for a
good balance as a leader of a lair.

Shadow ran along the branches, above ground, leaping
easily from tree to tree on the twisted, outstretched limbs.
Each branch was solid and thick, making them perfect
perches for the leopard to move fast through the swamp.
Joshua had run the swamp night after night, familiarizing
himself with every inch of the territory. He had explored
above ground, in the trees, and ground level. He'd seen
Sonia's home many times, never once imagining that his
own mate resided there.

The big leopard caught Sonia's scent and moved faster,
knowing he was close to his mate. He leapt to the tree that
would take him around to the back of her house looking out
over the swamp. Music filled the night. Not just the cacophony of insects, frogs and alligators, but actual musical
notes.

The leopard paused in the tree that had one branch extended toward the top balcony and another bowing down
toward the ground, leading straight to the lower verandah.
Joshua took over, pushing to shift again. The leopard instantly retreated to the background, leaving Joshua in the
crook of the tree, naked with a pack around his neck.

Sonia danced to the music, her body undulating like a
temptress's. Hands above her head, eyes closed, she moved
across the verandah, her hips and breasts swaying with every
beat. She wore red lace, and beneath it, nothing else. He
could see the marks of his possession on her soft skin and it
made something primitive and savage in him rejoice.

His breath hitched in his lungs when she turned around and he was looking at her smooth back and her butt. He was partial to her bottom, and the marks there proclaimed he'd spent time worshiping her. Just watching her made his mouth water and his cock throb with heat. She was the most naturally sensual creature he'd ever encountered. Everything about her appealed to him. Her hair was down and wild. It fell in waves around down her back, thick and glossy in the moonlight, making her appear an exotic dancer enticing her lover.

He was more than willing to oblige. Stark naked, pack in hand, he walked along the dipping branch leading straight to her porch, his gaze fixed on her. Predator hunting prey. Focused. Determined. Certain of his destiny. He knew with everything in him, his destiny was to love her. To keep her safe. To make sure that every day of her life with him was happy.

Sonia's head turned and she froze, her eyes on him. Her gaze drifted over his body, taking in the hard cock pressed tight to his stomach, his heavy balls, and then jumped back up to his face.

He stepped onto the gallery right in front of her. Close. She smelled like heaven. He tossed the pack onto one of the chairs and stepped into her again when she retreated. One finger drifted down her face to her lips, absorbing the softness of her skin. He had to touch her. The need was so strong it shook him.

Touching her wasn't enough. He recognized that immediately. He hooked one hand around the nape of her neck and took her mouth. That mouth he was obsessed with. The one he thought about when he should be working, should be thinking about staying alive and keeping his men alive.

She tasted every bit as good as he remembered. More so. Her mouth was paradise. Sweet. Hot. She gave herself fully to him, no hesitation, her tongue sliding along his, following his when he retreated, so that when she was in his mouth, his body shuddered with such need, such pleasure, he couldn't remember any woman who had come before her.

He kissed her over and over, a man starving, a man falling, but he ignored that and just let himself feel. Let himself drown. Little sparks jumped from her skin to his, flames licking over his cock like a scorching-hot tongue. His groin burned, an inferno threatening to consume him. Even his thighs were on fire. He lifted his mouth from hers and it took effort. Concentration. Discipline.

"You didn't text me."

Her eyelashes fluttered, betraying her nerves. "I know."

"I waited as long as I could." He took her hand and brought it to his cock. "Just thinking about you makes me hard as a fucking rock, Sonia." He pressed her palm to him. Tight. He needed that. Needed her not to pull away—and she didn't. "Sometimes I think I'm going to go insane with wanting you."

She touched her tongue to her lip, sliding it along that small mark. His cock jerked under her hand. She curled her fingers around the hard length, her thumb sliding over the drops leaking there, smearing them all over the sensitive head.

Fire streaked through him. He hadn't realized just how far gone he was. He hadn't intended to have sex with her, not without talking first. She used sex to keep him at bay. She might not know that was what she was doing, but he couldn't resist her. He couldn't now. Not with his body raging at him, making demands he couldn't control or ignore. He'd never been like that. He was always the one in control.

"Sometimes I think I'm going insane with wanting you too," she whispered.

He groaned. She looked sexy in her red lace. Her lips were full. Red to go with the lace stretching over her full breasts and hips. He loved what she was wearing. Her nipples were hard little knots begging for attention, and each time she moved, the lace strained to keep them in.

His cock jerked and his balls felt so tight and full he was afraid they'd burst. He put his hand on her shoulder and applied pressure. She didn't hesitate. She went to her knees, and the sight of her like that in all that lace nearly undid him.

"Look at me." He fisted her hair and pulled her head back so she was forced to look up. "I want to watch you. I want you watching me."

Excitement flared in her dark eyes. He loved that. He loved that whatever he asked of her turned her on. He knew she liked his brand of sex. Right now, he could scent her answering need, that liquid heat that tasted like an aphrodisiac.

"Open your mouth." He wanted to see her red lips stretched around his cock the way the red lace stretched around her curves. It was sexy as hell. She'd swallowed him more than once, but he'd never seen her, not like this. Not with the light on her, not with her body adorned by red lace and his marks. Not with her full, pouty lips so red. He loved her mouth, he lay awake at night thinking about it and how she tasted. How she smiled or frowned. That adorable lower lip he couldn't resist biting every time he got close to her.

Sonia obeyed him, licking her lips, her eyes on his, and then she slowly opened her mouth for him. Just that alone nearly made him erupt all over her face. He didn't know how he was going to keep it together.

"You're so fuckin' sexy." He hissed the words between clenched teeth as he guided his cock in, giving her the broad head, watching it disappear between her lips, feeling that burn that shook his entire body, that made his thighs harden and his blood run so hot he feared he might burn from the inside out.

Her mouth was on fire, scorching him the way her sheath did. Her tongue slid over the sensitive crown in a lazy curl and then stroked underneath in that sweet spot that nearly took his head off. He pushed deeper into that scalding-hot cauldron. She hollowed her cheeks and sucked. He didn't

know if it was the feeling alone of her mouth on him, lush
red lips stretched around his girth, or her eyes staring up at
him, but whatever it was, it set off an inferno inside of him.

His hips moved of their own volition, pushing deeper.
He tried to be gentle. He liked rough, but she deserved
gentle and he was determined to be careful of her. She
sucked harder and lashed him with her tongue. A low purr
emanated from her throat. The vibration tore up his shaft
like a wildfire out of control. His balls drew tight and hard.
He pushed deeper, not meaning to, but unable to hold back.

She didn't pull off him, not even when he felt those tight
muscles gripping his sensitive head and her eyes watered. It
was too much, the massage, the heat, the way she looked. He
couldn't hold back. The force started somewhere deep and
climbed, spreading like hot lava through his gut, up his
thighs, centering that violent flame, burning, stroking, so hot
he thought for a moment he would go insane with the brutal
pressure. Then he was erupting, hot jets of seed splashing
down her throat. He couldn't look away. He needed to throw
his head back and howl, but he was riveted on her, the way
her mouth worked him, the way her throat swallowed, massaging him more. The way her eyes had gone liquid and her
red lips stretched to accommodate his size. Her breasts
heaved in the red lace as her body fought for air, but she
refused to stop until she had all of him.

She took a long, deep, shuddering breath, and then gently swallowed him again, gliding a couple of times and then
lapping at him. Every touch of her tongue sent lightning
streaking through him, a white-hot pleasure that con-
sumed him.

His hands tightened in her hair as she licked her lips and
then sat back on her heels, still looking up at him. "You're
so fucking beautiful." It was all that he could get out of his
mouth. She was. Beautiful. Sensual. Sexy. *His.*

She just stared up at him, looking as vulnerable as hell.
It occurred to him she didn't have the first clue what to say

or do. She hadn't wanted him there and the moment they were together, they were at it. He could see her nipples, peaked, hard, desperate for his mouth. She squirmed, pushing her thighs together, every bit in need as he'd been.

He reached down and took her hand, tugging until she was on her feet. Without a word he lifted her, two hands at her waist, and set her on the table between the two chairs. He bent his head and sucked her left breast into his mouth. That soft mound had been driving him crazy as she swallowed him, swaying in temptation, straining against the thin, delicate lace. He sucked hard, used his teeth to rake at her.

She shivered, jolted, gasped and then moaned, her arms coming up to cradle his head. His hand went to her right nipple and he wasn't gentle, tugging hard, rolling, setting her on fire. By the time he switched his mouth to her right breast, her left was covered with . . . *him.* He left strawberries and rake marks decorating her soft skin. It looked beautiful, his signature, his name written on her. He claimed her right breast in the same way. *His.* All that beauty. He wanted her to do the same to him. Brand her name into his bones.

When her breathing was ragged and moans had turned to pleas, he kissed his way down the lace to her belly button. He dipped his tongue there, left his signature all around that sweet little enticing circle and kept going.

He wrapped one hand around her throat, feeling her pulse hammering into his palm. He exerted gentle pressure, giving her no choice but to lie back. He kept kissing his way down to that sexy little mound. He loved the way she had tiny tight curls that hid rosettes. Using both hands, he dragged the lace from her body and then pulled her thighs wide apart and lifted her to his mouth.

She screamed when his tongue swiped across her swollen bud. Her body jerked. Liquid heat met his mouth, and he devoured her. He wasn't gentle there either, driving her up ruthlessly, demanding her orgasm, and then doing it again.

He used his teeth on her thighs, leaving a string of his marks on both inner thighs, up close to her entrance.

"Again. I want it again," he demanded and lapped at her before using tongue, teeth and fingers to get what he wanted. He loved watching her face when she came apart. That beauty ripping through her, taking her someplace only he could give her. He loved the sounds she made. She wasn't quiet. Those hitches in her breathing. Her moans. Pleas. He loved that especially. Taking her up, keeping her right on the edge for as long as he thought she could take it. The way she said his name. Shocked. He loved her shock. The demand that crept into her voice. He could watch her come apart all night every night.

"I can't." Her head thrashed back and forth, fingers curled into tight fists.

He'd waited for that ragged denial. He knew she could. He fucking loved showing her she could. "You will, for me, you'll give that to me again, because I need it. You didn't text me." She hadn't, and he had to make certain she couldn't live without him any more than he could live without her.

He clamped his hands around her thighs, holding her open for his assault. He took her up again. So high. Watched her carefully as he pushed her limits. "That's it, baby," he whispered softly, breathing warm air into all that heat. "Now. Give it to me now." He needed to see and hear the music of her ragged breathing. He used his teeth and her body came apart for him, clamping down, shuddering, her muscles rippling from her stomach to her thighs with the force.

Joshua wiped his face on her thighs, dropped into a nearby chair and then laid his head on her abdomen. He felt her heat. Her body still reacting, the waves still strong enough for him to feel. Her breasts heaved as she tried to drag in air. He turned his head and kissed her mound. Her hand dropped to his hair, fingers sifting through it.

She'd done that once or twice in the swamp and he'd loved it. The caresses felt different, not sexual exactly, but more sensual, a gentle, peaceful connection between them. He wrapped his arms around her middle and stayed still, letting the swamp's symphony and her fingers in his hair soothe the heat out of his body. He wanted to lie with her at night. He would put a bed on his balcony and sleep under the stars with her just to get this closeness he felt with her.

He didn't know how long he held her, but it couldn't last forever and he knew it. Her hand lifted and she shifted subtly to tell him she had to move. Reluctantly he stood, tugging her body into a sitting position. He handed her the red lace panties.

"This is always going to be my favorite outfit." His marks stood out everywhere, and there was satisfaction in that. "I'm sorry I'm not as gentle as I should be with you. I try, and then the next thing I know, I'm completely out of control."

She pulled the stretch lace over her hips. Just that little movement, along with the sway of her breasts, sent a jolt of heat through him.

"It isn't just you," she admitted. There was an unexpected shyness, as if she didn't quite know how to talk to him. "I like what you do to me. *Everything* you do. If I didn't, I'd say so."

He nodded, relief rushing through him. "Good. I want you to tell me when I do something you don't like." He admired the fact that she gave him the truth when she was still uncertain of him.

"I would."

"You weren't going to text me." He hoped the hurt, mixed with anger, didn't show in his voice. "Sonia, you feel the same way I do. I know you do. You wouldn't react to me like this if you didn't. It can't all be sex."

"Why not? Why can't we just leave it at that? Sex. It's good. Better than good." She shivered and rubbed her hands down her arms.

Joshua realized the night had turned a little cold with the breeze rising to a wind. He slung his arm around her and walked her toward the door. Weather could change quickly, raining one minute and the sun breaking out the next. The moment he stepped into her house, his leopard went wild. *Wild.* He could barely contain the snarling beast. Every muscle contracted, his skin rippling as the cat tried to force his way out.

He thrust her away from him, pushing back at the animal fighting for supremacy.

"What is it?"

"He smells another man." He could barely get the words out. His skull didn't fit in his skin, the pressure causing blinding pain. His teeth filled his mouth, pushing to be more.

"It was Bastien Foret. He came here to check on my friend Molly."

The absence of any indication of hesitation or lie saved them. Joshua had never once experienced his leopard fighting for takeover. Not like that. That battle had been swift and brutal. He was angry with his cat. Furious. *What the fuck did you think you were going to do? Hurt her? Hurt my woman?* It was the first time he'd ever been truly incensed at his leopard.

The cat backed down immediately. *Never. I would hunt down and kill this man.*

*He is innocent. You reacted before she had the chance to tell us. You would have killed an innocent man. What the hell is wrong with you?*

The leopard was silent as if trying to regain his formidable temper. *She will not commit to us. She wants to take Gatita and run.*

Joshua's heart thudded, and he looked at Sonia. She stood waiting, knowing he was struggling with his leopard, but instead of fear, she was unmoving.

"You act scared of me half the time, the times you shouldn't be, and then now, when my leopard is losing his fucking mind, you just stand there. He might have killed you." He was angry with his leopard, himself and the situation.

She shook her head. "Gatita wouldn't let that happen."

"Leopards have vicious tempers. You know that. They can be very dangerous when they're angry."

"So can their counterpart," she replied, looking him right in the eye.

He didn't know whether she referred to him or to herself. "Tell me why Bastien felt he needed to check on Molly. She's the landscaper, right? I haven't been to her nursery, the gardeners have. We're trying to use all local people, and she's very knowledgeable according to everyone around these parts. Is something wrong?"

"That's Molly's story to tell."

"So, something *is* wrong." He moved deeper into her house, looking around her modernized kitchen. It was beautiful, with gleaming countertops and a tiled floor. "She's obviously confided in you. If she's in trouble, I need to know two things. You don't have to be specific, just tell me if there's something I can do to help. You know I have certain specialties. And if any of her problems leak over to you."

She ran her fingertips along the countertop. "I think she's talked herself into believing she's safe when she's not."

His head came up, his gaze focusing on her. She was talking about Molly, but she was also talking about herself. He heard it in her voice. He wanted to grab her, take her back to his home and surround her with guards night and day. A thought shimmered into his mind. One he didn't want to think about, but had to consider. *Husband.* Could she be married? His gaze strayed to her left hand before he could stop it. It was bare. He needed her to trust him enough to confide in him.

"Are you thinking of running? My cat thinks you are. It makes him uneasy and temperamental. That makes me the same way."

Her lashes fluttered again, drawing his attention to them. Long. Thick. Dark like her hair, framing her exotic dark chocolate eyes. She was looking down at the countertop as if it would somehow come to life and save her from answering. He refrained from speaking, letting the silence stretch out until she finally sighed.

"I don't know what I'm going to do. I can't be in a relationship with you."

His heart did an odd clenching that told him he was in deep trouble. She fought a relationship with him when she had to know they were meant to be together. She wanted to protect him even more than herself. The thought kept growing, and he didn't like it at all.

He took her hand, pulled her beneath his shoulder and kept walking through the kitchen. One room led straight into the next, just as it did in his home. "Why not?" They were in her formal dining room. She hadn't yet restored this room, but she had several oil paintings hung on the wall. They were all of the swamp. They were beautiful, and he stopped to admire them.

Her fingers tightened around his, and his heart clenched hard in his chest. He turned his head to look down at her. "You really are afraid of me." He caught her chin and tipped her head up, forcing her to look into his eyes. "I would never hurt you. Shifters mate for life. For *life*. I recognized you the moment I saw you. I knew we belonged. I knew I was born to protect you. To make you happy. To love you, Sonia, like no one in this world has ever been loved. Your leopard can hear the truth, so can you. Am I telling you the truth?"

She didn't have a poker face. Every thought moving through her mind was there on her face and in her eyes for him to see. Fear was uppermost. She wanted to believe him because she heard honesty, but she couldn't quite make herself get there.

"Give me a chance." He switched tactics. "Get to know me. Take the time."

"If it's just sex, I won't get my heart broken."

He knew that admission cost her with all it gave away. "Words don't matter as much as actions. Give me the chance to show you I mean what I say when I tell you, for me, there isn't going to be another woman." He led her through to the great room. It was spacious and beautiful, again, not fully renovated.

"How?"

His heart steadied. She wasn't going to fight him. He needed that reassurance as much as his leopard did.

"We'll go out. Meet together after work. I'll tell you my crazy life and you can tell yours . . ." He broke off when she shook her head.

"I can't tell you mine."

"Or won't?"

"I can't."

He was silent as they went up the stairs. She had scraped the years of neglect from the stairs, but hadn't finished them. As in his home, they were on the narrow side, but they were functional, large enough for a man to step without worrying his foot wasn't going to fit.

"That implies you think it would be too dangerous for me to know. Look into Drake Donovan's security team. He's considered the best in the world. We're called on to go into places others wouldn't even consider. You know I'm leopard. Unless . . ." He pulled open a door and peered into an empty room. "Unless the trouble is with other leopards." He kept his voice casual, not wanting to spook her.

He moved from that room straight into the next. This one had long windows just like the first, with glass doors that led to the balcony. She'd replaced the old windows with new ones, floor to ceiling, and the doors were French doors, the windowpanes big squares. The middle room was her studio. It made sense, it got the most light and overlooked the largest part of the swamp. From her vantage point she could see the river and the canopy of trees in the distance.

He flicked on the light, knowing this room was a big part of her world. Of who she was. If he wanted to get to know her, he had to see her through her choices of what she painted. He would be able to see the world through her eyes. How she saw things, what she chose to paint.

He wandered around the room, looking at the canvases. She had one she'd set aside, off from the others, and that was the one he chose to study. Most were of the swamp, but this one was different. The colors were different. Subdued. Not the vibrant colors of the trees and bushes she'd painted from her balcony, looking out over the land she obviously loved.

This was of a cemetery. Looking at it, one got the feeling of loneliness, sorrow, even a hint of anger. There were beautiful tombstones all around the plot she'd chosen to focus on. Light streaked through the grays of the morning sun. He stepped closer to see the markings on the graves. There were two crosses, but no name.

He glanced over at Sonia. She held herself very still, fingers twisting together until her hands were white. He reached out and covered them with his own, stilling the motion. "Your parents? This one is very personal, yet the graves aren't marked."

"Both were cremated. I scattered their ashes. I painted that for me." Her voice was strained.

He found the concept interesting. She'd cremated her parents, which was good considering one or both had to be leopard, but she depicted them together in a cemetery. The cemetery she'd chosen was obviously real and had been painted from memory. "Will you let me buy one of your paintings?"

He tugged on her hand until she went with him to stand in front of the one he most admired. It was brilliant. He knew the exact spot. He'd visited it a hundred times. There was his swamp in the dripping Spanish moss, fringed lace draped through the cypress forest. Knobby knees of the cypress trees rose from the water where duckweed floated and cranes walked in elegance and grace.

"I'd like to have this one to hang above the fireplace in the great room. The colors match perfectly with the room, and this happens to be one of my favorite places to go. Let me have it, Sonia. Name your price."

"I'll give it to you."

"I can't let you do that." He looked around the room. Paint and paper were peeling from the walls. "You're fixing up your home. Think of it like sheets of drywall, or roofing material. I'll pay you what I paid for the picture in the dining room."

She'd seen that picture. It was the real deal, no copy. And it was painted by an artist long dead whose work commanded hundreds of thousands of dollars. Which hers did not. She shook her head. "I don't have a name. I don't sell my work. If you want the painting I'll gift it to you."

He could see she was going to be stubborn about it. He could "gift" her whatever she needed in the way of material to renovate her home—not that he wanted her living there much longer. He wanted her with him.

"Thank you," he murmured, seeing she was braced for an argument. "I would love to have it. Is it signed?" He stepped closer to look.

She touched the right-hand corner of the canvas. An intricately intertwined *S* and *L* were very small right at the bottom inside the tangled roots of a tree. "That's it. That's my signature. I always use that."

"Not your name?" He had to admit, the small signature fit into the painting, making it look part of the root system.

She shook her head. "When I was a child painting, I thought it was cool and mysterious. I practiced painting that *S* and *L* together for months before I put it on my canvases. Now it suits me. I like just adding that into the foliage somewhere. It fits most of the work I do. I can hide it in vines draping down, or flowers, even the water. It just works."

"I'll send for the painting tomorrow. Or you can bring it with you when you come back."

"I'd rather do that. I prefer strangers not come around too often."

He resisted asking questions. He had to take it slow with her, and this next, nonnegotiable demand was not going to be taken lightly. "That's fine. Bring it when you come to work. I'll be staying nights with you, Sonia, so I can always drive over tomorrow, but I prefer no one knows I'm here so if they think they're getting away with an attack on you, I'll be a surprise."

# 6

SONIA'S breath caught in her lungs and she gave a quick shake of her head. Joshua couldn't stay. Not in her house. Not in her bed. Panic set in. His scent would be all over her sheets and pillows. She would lose her mind when he left her. For all his promises, men like him didn't stay. If they stayed, they strayed—that was if they didn't kill you first.

He ignored her head shake and continued walking through her studio right to the master bedroom. He flicked off the light as he went by the switch, taking her with him. She didn't know why she just followed, why she couldn't tell him no verbally. Maybe because he was the kind of man who would listen to her if she meant it. Did she mean it?

Her gaze strayed down his broad back to his narrow waist and hips. His backside. Her breath hitched in her throat and she nearly stumbled. Who wouldn't want *that* in her bed? She stroked a hand down her throat and followed him. He was already at the double French doors, opening them wide and walking out onto the gallery. She loved the upper-story balcony even more than the lower one.

Branches extended toward the gallery so a leopard might easily make the short jump to the house. She knew she had an escape route. Now he had another entrance.

"Do you really think it's a good idea for you to stay?" She wanted to go up behind him and slide her arms around his waist to feel his warmth against her body, but she made herself stay right where she was. She was falling for a man she knew nothing about.

He turned his back on the moonlight and swamp to study her face. His eyes gleamed that crystal blue as his gaze moved over her face, dropped lower to slowly, lazily drift over her body and then just as slowly come back up, first to her mouth, making her lips burn, and then her eyes. He focused there, holding her captive, refusing to allow her to look away.

"Staying here with you is as necessary as breathing."

"We could have sex, and then you could leave," she offered. She knew she sounded panicked, and it annoyed her, but who wouldn't panic? Once Joshua shared her bed she'd always want him there. She was getting in over her head.

"We're going to have sex," he agreed. "I want all night to worship your body. Hell, baby, I have to know every inch of you. I want to wake up with my cock in your mouth or in your body. I want to hold you all night. Every fucking night. Can't sleep without you now."

"I'm pretty certain you already know every inch of me," she said a little desperately. "Why am I the only one trying to be sane here? Sex this intense can't possibly last. It will burn itself out in a day or two and then what?"

He threw back his head and laughed. "Come here."

That low, velvet note of command sent a shiver down her spine. Instantly her sex clenched and her thighs danced with fingers of desire. She went to him because there was no resisting that voice or those eyes. He wrapped his arms around her, bringing her tightly against his body. His cock hit her stomach, and there it was, his heartbeat, under her ear, and in the palm of her hand. Just like that, her head was reeling. She was lost.

She tightened her arms around him, pressing her breasts into those rock-hard muscles and her mound against his thigh. She knew he could feel the tremors, but it didn't matter. His arms were around her, and for those few moments, she allowed herself to feel safe. He could do that even when he scared her. She didn't know how. She didn't understand how she could be so confused, but it felt as if she'd been there before, surrounded by him. Held by him. *Loved* by him. There was nothing like it. If she had his love . . . *What* was she thinking? Sex wasn't love. It never would be.

Still, she clung to him, a little ashamed of herself for doing so. She'd been lonely, and he'd changed that. She was a little shocked that he didn't press her sexually. He was naked, she might as well have been, but he just held her, his head over hers, protectively. She felt that. She knew the trait was strong in him.

"Are you married, Sonia? Is it your husband threatening you? Is that why you're afraid to commit to me?"

The questions were so soft, a beautiful low tone that mesmerized her. At first the words barely penetrated the fog in her brain. She stiffened when she realized what he'd asked. Stiffened, and tried to pull out of his arms. He tightened his hold on her, his chin nuzzling the top of her head.

"Shh. I knew it was something like that. I don't like that he's tied you to him, but you aren't his. You were never meant to be his."

She shook her head, trying to deny it.

"Don't." He pressed her close to him, so her mouth was against his bare skin. "I don't want you to lie to me. I'd rather you didn't answer."

That made her ashamed. He was being honest and she wasn't. "Yes. No. I'm married, but . . ." That's why the attack didn't make sense. None of it made sense. Him marrying her. Declaring undying love. Treating her like he did, which was good, and then telling his father . . . She pressed her knuckles to her mouth. How did one explain something she didn't understand? And then add the little part about them being notorious gangsters.

"You had to run from him."

She nodded, her heart beating out of control. His voice was so low, so hypnotic, she had to answer him even when she didn't want to. They were getting into things she tried not to think about—they hurt too much.

"The fiery crash into the ocean Gatita showed Shadow?" he pressed.

She took a breath. Nodded again. Her heart hurt. Her lungs burned. She was terrified she might have a panic attack.

"Why are you uncertain whether you're married or not?"

He wasn't going to drop it, but then they'd had more than a week of crazy, spectacular, fireworks-and-rockets-going-off sex. He obviously didn't want to be with a married woman. That was wrong. She knew it. He knew it. But she wasn't married in her heart. Even if her husband had lied to his father, they'd tried to kill her. Did that mean she had to be loyal? Bitterness had her pulling free of him, stepping away.

"I overheard them talking. My father-in-law, who'd always acted so loving to me, told my husband that one didn't marry women like me, they fucked them and got rid of them. They certainly didn't fall in love. My husband laughed and said the marriage wasn't legal and when he was tired of the fucking he would end it. My father-in-law then said, 'You know you have to kill her,' and my husband said, 'Of course.'" She looked at him. "So there you have my sad little story. Since you and I are brilliant at fucking, I . . ."

He didn't let her finish. He moved so fast he was a blur, on her in a quarter of a second, his hands on her upper arms, giving her a little shake, and he wasn't gentle. "We were mating, Sonia. *Mating*. There's a difference. I've never fucked you. I never will. My leopard marked you. I marked you. You're mine. My mate. We are tied for life. You don't see other men, and I don't see other women. I don't get tired of you, and you aren't going to get tired of me. This man who so carelessly was ready to throw you away is an idiot, and I'm fucking glad he is. I wouldn't have you otherwise. I'd go through my life alone because someone who has no right to you claimed you."

He pulled her up tighter against him, right up on her toes. "Look at me, Sonia."

He waited until her gaze lifted to his. It was an effort. Every word he said gave her hope, gave her the burn of tears, so that little voice in the back of her head reminding her that men lied to get their way was pushed back further. When her lashes came up she found herself looking into that crystalline blue. Dark green swirled through the blue, a turbulent sea. He was angry, and that scared her a little.

"I'm not leaving you. I'm not going to put a bomb in your car. You're mine to protect and treasure. I didn't think I had a chance in hell of finding you, and believe me, I searched the world for you. For Shadow to find Gatita right next door was a miracle. I don't throw away my miracles."

"You could be killed for being close to me, Joshua. I know you work for Drake Donovan and you think you're invincible, but not from him. I am not going to say anything else, because I won't be responsible for getting you killed." She *had* to give him every out. She was certain everyone believed her dead, but if they didn't, if they were looking, she had to warn him what could happen. The men she was dealing with were first-class killers.

"Fair enough. But I do need to know if he's leopard."

"I don't know if he is. I didn't know I was until Gatita saved my life. Believe me, I was shocked when she emerged. I had several shocks that day." She had nightmares. Not every night, but quite a few. She was traumatized by what had happened. She'd believed in Sasha Bogomolov. He'd been her rock when her world had gone to pieces. He'd taken such good care of her. She'd been barely eighteen and had no idea what to do. He'd sorted her life out for her and she'd believed in him.

"I've taken control of my life," she said, wanting him to understand. "I didn't know how to live before. I was barely eighteen when my mother died. He took over, paid the hospital bills, arranged her funeral and cremation. He helped me scatter her ashes in the sea. He did everything for me. When I ran, I didn't know how to take care of myself. Now I do."

He kissed the top of her head. "And you do it very well. When I made inquiries about the renovations, every single person I talked to said to go to Jerry, that he had a brilliant carpenter, an artist with restoration, and they named you."

"My father was a carpenter. He liked to work with wood. I don't know how he got mixed up—" She broke off abruptly. She was becoming far too comfortable with Joshua.

"My male needs to see your female for a little while. Are you comfortable with that? With letting them out to run together. If you're not too tired?"

That was so perfect. She wouldn't have to think and Gatita would be happy. She wanted her little female to be happy. Sonia nodded.

He caught the hem of the stretch lace camisole. "Let me. This thing is so damned sexy I can barely think when I look at you."

Sasha had rarely had sex with her. Only when she'd initiated it. He had always been gentle, almost reverent, the opposite of Joshua's wild, out-of-control, rough sex. She responded to Joshua's way of touching her. The way he talked to her. He'd given her an orgasm—well, the first of many. Why she felt guilty over that, she didn't know. Sasha had tried to kill her. She had no reason to feel guilty because she liked the way Joshua touched her.

She watched as he carefully folded the little top and put it on the table. He hooked his thumbs in the boy shorts and started to slide them down her hips. As he did, his head lowered and he caught her left breast in his mouth. Sucked hard. Fire streaked straight to her sex. He caught her nipple between his teeth and tugged.

She cried out as white lightning ripped through her body, shocking her. The things he did should have hurt, but the bite was a sweet ache that fueled the darker desires of her body. His tongue licked gently, a velvet rasp that sent more lightning arcing through her. She fisted one hand in his hair and with the other cupped her breast, guiding his head to that side for equal attention.

He obliged, his mouth closing over the soft mound. Her knees went weak. The brush of shaggy hair against her breasts and midriff sensitized her skin more. The bristles on his jaw rubbed the swelling curves, marking her the way his mouth did. Her boy shorts were around her thighs, forgotten as his hand slid down her mound, fingers curling to find her entrance.

She threw her head back and keened, a long, low wail of pure pleasure escaping her throat. His mouth left her breast, and he turned her toward the railing, one hand curling at her nape, pressing until she obediently leaned over it. She found herself looking down from the upper story while his fingers moved in her, sliding in and out of her.

"You're so tight, baby. So fucking tight I can barely get my fingers in you. How the hell you manage to take my cock, I don't know."

She didn't know either, but she did know she needed him in her right that moment. "Stop messing around and get inside me."

She should have known the way he would respond, slowly drawing down her lace panties so she could step out of them. She knew him now, the way he was with sex. He liked to do everything his way. She didn't mind because she reaped the benefits, but sometimes he took forever to get where she knew he needed to be. She caught the railing and held tight while he began his slow torture. Soft touches. A fiery lick of his tongue. The edge of his teeth raking her clit. Over and over, small tortures designed to drive her out of her mind—and he was succeeding.

Her breasts were mashed against the wrought iron railing, swinging with every movement, pressed tightly against the twisted metalwork the next. She heard herself sob, plead, her hips squirming and earning his hand. That felt good, spreading even more heat, more need. He did it again and again and then his mouth was there, right where she needed it. She pushed back, and he was gone. She cried out in protest.

"You want me?"

"Yes." She hissed her answer. "Hurry."

She felt the head of his cock, so broad, so velvet soft and hard at the same time, stretching her, giving her that burn she craved. She held herself still, knowing if she moved he would stop, maybe start all over from the beginning. He liked to play. Liked to make her body hum and vibrate. He loved her pleas, or the cries she couldn't suppress. She knew that, because he told her he did. Sprawled on top of her, he had confessed he loved her need of him. The "music" she made for him. He liked the way her lungs struggled for air when she was desperate to come or when he gave her his weight, holding her down with his body, gliding gently in her.

He pushed deeper. So slowly. The burn scorched her. Took every bit of air. With him moving so slowly, her muscles were forced to give way for his invasion and then stretch to accommodate him, burning more than they ever had. It was brutal. It was perfection. It was them. He seemed to know exactly what she needed, or better yet, he was right all along and she'd been born for him. Created just for him.

The wind ruffled the Spanish moss in the trees and her hair as it hung down over the wrought iron.

"Do you feel your beauty right now? The moon is shining on your body, spotlighting you. That glorious skin." He stroked his hand down her back. "I love your skin." His hand slid over her right cheek. "Your sweet ass is red with my marks. Do you like them as much as I do? You can't see them, but can you feel them?" He rubbed at the marks, and when she didn't answer, he added another one.

She cried out, and he felt the hot liquid surround him, enticing him into her farther. She pushed back subtly, trying to get him to fill her.

He laughed softly. "Yes. The answer is yes, my little cat. Say it. Say you know how beautiful you are with my marks on you."

"I love them," she admitted. "Every one of them, and I especially love how you put them there. It's sexy. Hot. And it feels good. Now please, please, please, stop teasing me."

"I'm making love to you, baby. Don't you feel that?" He smacked her left cheek this time, leaned forward and licked down her spine with that velvet rasp.

Her inner muscles tightened impossibly, and he groaned. "So fuckin' hot, Sonia. You give this to me every time." He slipped in another slow inch.

He was killing her with pleasure, if that were possible, and she was beginning to be afraid it might be. She lifted her head to look out over the swamp. Leaves rustled and branches swayed gently. For a moment she thought she caught the sheen of eyes.

"There might be something out there," she reported, her breath in her lungs. Her body was on fire, her muscles grasping at him, slick and hot.

He rubbed down her thigh, and back up her inner thigh. "I have guards watching the territory. They'll take care of anything straying our way."

"Would you stop if there was something?" she asked,

because nothing in the world would stop her. She wanted him that badly. She needed to hear that he did too.

His fingers crept up to her clit and flicked, sending shock waves through her. "Nothing. Not even if someone put a gun to my head. This is paradise. My paradise. When you're wrapped around me like this, I know I'm home." His voice dropped, became low and intimate. "This is me with you. Our world, Sonia. The two of us. No one can take it from us. The things I do to you are for you alone. No one else. I've never been able to be me. You're the lover I've waited for, the one I can give who I am to. The one I can give everything to. You take what I need to give."

She loved the ring of truth in his voice. "I love what you have to give. It's the same for me. I never knew what was missing. Why I couldn't feel what I was supposed to feel. I needed you." God help her, that was the truth.

He surged into her hard, filling her completely, driving through her tight muscles, the angle of her body allowing him to go deep. He set the pace, a hard, steady rhythm that sent her tumbling off a precipice into a place she'd never been. Everything seemed to go to bursting color behind her eyes, but there was no floating free.

He was moving hard in her, setting a brutal pace, his fingers digging into her hips to yank her back onto him as he surged forward. The streaks of fire threatened to consume her. The man had stamina, and he sent her over the edge again and again until she was crying for mercy, but not wanting him to stop. She needed him to keep going. To fuse them together.

One hand slid up her back to curl around her throat so that her pulse beat right into the center of his palm. She loved when he did that. Her breasts pressed against the bars, her nipples twin peaks of fire. Each time the breeze hit them, it sent fire shooting like an arrow to her clenching sex. Her lungs felt raw and burning, but that added to the churning fireball inside of her, coiling tighter and growing hotter.

She felt his shaft swell, pushing hard against the restriction of her muscles. The friction was superb. Perfect. Bordering on pain, tipping so close to it, she was light-headed with need.

"Now, baby. Come with me now." He whispered it to her in that hypnotic voice of his, and she couldn't do anything else.

Her body clamped down hard on his and milked him. He threw back his head and roared both triumph and challenge, his cock jerking hard, jetting hot splashes of his seed against her scorching walls, triggering a much stronger orgasm than she'd ever had. It came in waves, rushing through her entire body, sweeping every nerve ending with it. It went on and on, powerful and beautiful, a glorious tsunami that roared with intensity.

He collapsed over top her, his arm around her waist, his body tightly in hers, his mouth at her shoulder. He turned his head, burying his face in her neck, and then she felt the nip of his teeth and the pull of his mouth as he sucked the bite mark into his mouth, his tongue stroking and caressing.

She tried to turn her head but couldn't find the energy. "You are very oral."

His tongue touched her ear. "Yes, I am. Thank God you like it."

She did. She liked everything he did. "I hope Gatita can still run."

He laughed. "I'm sure she won't have any trouble. She isn't in heat right now. There isn't any danger with the other leopards around. Shadow will tolerate them."

"Other leopards?" she echoed. "There are other males out there?"

"When I go running, yes, of course." He kissed her neck, still gliding slowly and easily. Each glide triggered a weaker ripple through her body.

"You mean, shifters? Men? Actual men?"

"Don't act like you're interested in whether or not there

are other men in near proximity to you," he growled, and bit her earlobe.

She yelped and turned her head to glare at him. "Let me up. This isn't the most comfortable position."

He did so immediately, slipping out of her and helping her to stand. She gripped the railing to keep from sliding to the ground. He made her that weak. She could feel the mixture of the two of them slowly slipping out of her to drip along her inner thighs.

"I'm more interested in having the reassurance that they weren't watching us."

He frowned and looked out into the night. "I don't employ perverts."

"We were making a lot of noise."

His frown turned to a slow grin. "We were, weren't we? Screw 'em, baby. If they watched, they know how hot you are and how lucky I am. They also know if I ever got wind that they were watching you, I'd put them in the fucking ground."

He said it so mildly, she almost didn't catch the threat, but there was a ring of truth in his voice that was disconcerting.

"Um, honey, I don't think if someone watched us the right punishment would be to kill them. That's kind of taking it a little too far," she felt compelled to point out.

"I'm leopard, Sonia. I don't give a fuck if someone sees my body. In other circumstances, they might see yours. When I make love to you, it's for you. What I give you is yours alone. The way I touch you, the things I say to you, the things you say to me. That's mine. The sounds you make, those little hitches in your breath. That's what you give to me."

She nodded and slipped her arms around his neck, leaning into his body. "You're . . . unexpected. I don't know what to think about you half the time."

He tipped her face up to his and took her mouth. It wasn't

his usual rough, and that surprised her. Melted her. He tasted of something that made her heart pound and adrenaline rush through her veins. She pulled away, closed her eyes and clung to him.

"What is it, Sonia?"

The caring in his voice was her undoing. That note of reality. His kiss hadn't been about sex at all. It wasn't about claiming—leopard or man. It was something altogether different, and she couldn't face that.

"You're a good man, aren't you?" A part of her was pleading with him to be.

"I try to be."

How did one know? How could a woman tell if a man was a good man? He was so rough and dominant, even moody like his leopard. Sasha had been sweet and charming, always gentle with her when he touched her.

"Gatita wants to run, Joshua."

He tipped her face up, making it so she couldn't avoid looking at him while he searched her eyes. "All right, baby. I'm going to give this one to you. But when we're in bed, I'm telling you about me, about my life. You're going to get to know me."

"I'd like that." It was the best she could do, and she knew it came out hesitant. She wasn't certain it was a good idea to get to know him.

To avoid any further conversation, and mostly so he couldn't challenge the truth of her answer, she shifted. She was getting better at it. She still wasn't nearly as fast as she wanted to be, and it still hurt like hell, but she was used to it and not afraid.

Joshua stroked his hand through the female leopard's fur, looking into her eyes and seeing Sonia's dark chocolate eyes staring back at him. "She's beautiful, baby, just like you. Her fur's very rare." He traced a thin golden band that ringed a rosette. "You must love this little cat."

Sonia loved that he thought Gatita was beautiful. She

watched as he shifted. That alone was something worth seeing. He was fast, so fast she didn't see the actual transformation because she'd blinked. His cat was bigger than Gatita by quite a bit. The first thing he did was nuzzle her neck and rub along her body before licking her face. Gatita responded by doing the same to the male. As if they were talking to each other, they whirled around and leapt for the tree branch.

Shadow took the lead, with the female trailing him. They ran along the twisted limbs above the ground until they were close to the center of Sonia's land. Shadow led her to the ground and they played for a while in the leaves, rolling in them, leaping over downed trunks of trees, hunting for insects and fish along the bank.

He took her a little closer to the property line bordering Joshua's property, and Gatita scented other males. She grimaced and started to retreat. Shadow stopped her, nudging her forward with his shoulder.

Sonia moved closer to the surface the moment Gatita was uncomfortable. The female and her male had played and rested for well over an hour. She had crouched in front of him a few times and he'd been on her fast. They rested after copulating four times in less than two hours and then they ran again.

Sonia tried to soothe, to tell her to trust in the male, but she remained close, willing to put her life on the line if anything threatened her leopard. Out of the trees came three other big males. Gatita whirled to face them, and then backed up until she ran into Shadow. He nudged her and rubbed along her body with his.

One by one the leopards came up to the female and touched noses. Sonia realized Shadow was introducing the other shifters. She got the impression the three were bodyguards for Shadow. Not Shadow—Joshua. Why would the head of a security team need bodyguards? She needed to look into him. She could contact Drake Donovan's agency and ask if Joshua really worked for him.

114     Christine Feehan

Immediately she was ashamed of herself for thinking about checking up on him. She'd be furious if he started doing the same to her. She'd been deliberately vague about who she'd been married to. That was a good thing. He couldn't investigate her without tipping off her husband and his father. They had ears and eyes everywhere.

Gatita ran with the four males, exploring Joshua's territory. Shadow turned her after another hour, which meant Joshua wanted to take back his form. Sonia would have been happy to allow Gatita to have her form until dawn in the hopes that Joshua wouldn't have to spend too much time in her bed.

It wasn't sex she was afraid of. It was the way he held her. So close. His body tightly against hers. He held her like she was cherished by him. Like she was the most precious thing in his life. He whispered to her. He stroked her hair. Those things were what wore her down, not his creative brand of mating.

Shadow pushed Gatita to the verandah, where Shadow shifted. Joshua dropped his hand to Gatita's fur and the leopard walked with him to the French doors of the bedroom. He opened them and the two walked into her bedroom. She loved her room. It was enormous for her. Wide open spaces. She loved the high ceiling and all the glass facing the swamp. She loved the floor with its cool rings of various shades in the wood, a pattern of medium circles throughout. It had taken her a long time to do the floor right. She knew wood wasn't the best with a leopard, but she wanted to duplicate the original floor to the best of her ability, and it had been hardwood.

She shifted as Joshua turned back to get her red lace from the table and then closed the French doors. "They had fun."

"Yes, they did, but you're tired, sore and your muscles are achy." He moved past her to the bathroom, where her extremely large claw-foot tub was waiting. He turned on the gold taps and steaming water poured into the porcelain bathtub. "Do you have any bath salts? Something that might soothe away soreness?"

That made her blush, but she nodded and walked past him, trying not to be hyperaware of the differences in their bodies. She was certain he didn't have an ounce of fat on him. He had defined muscles in his chest, his abs and more muscles forming a vee as his waist narrowed into his hips. His thighs were twin columns of muscle.

Then there was her body. She had muscle, but she was fairly certain no one could see it, except maybe those in her arms. She was tempted to pump her bicep to see, but she crouched in front of the sink where she kept boxes of salts. She handed him one of the more neutral scents. He took it from her, smelled it and grinned, one eyebrow shooting up.

"Grapefruit."

"I have oranges and spice."

"Grapefruit it is." He poured it into the steaming water.

He was really built. She had ample curves, with the stress on the *ample* part. Her breasts were full, her hips full, and because her rib cage was narrow and so was her waist, it only served to emphasize the generous endowments given to her. Then there were her thighs. She ran all the time, why weren't her thighs bone skinny? She was *not* model material.

"You keep it up, and I'm going to bite you somewhere that will make you unable to sit down for a week or two."

Startled, her gaze jumped to his face. He didn't look as if he was joking, nor did he sound it. He looked intimidating. "You already did that."

"I'll do it again much harder."

She decided to ignore the threat, mostly because it sounded intriguing to her. "You can't possibly read my thoughts."

"I told you, you don't have a poker face. More, you were staring at me and rubbing your hand along your thigh with a scowl on your face. You don't like the way you look. It doesn't matter that I tell you you're the most beautiful woman in the world to me, that I love every inch of you, you don't believe me."

"I wasn't thinking that at all," she lied. She tried a mock glare, hoping to make him laugh, but it didn't work.

He stepped even closer to her, his hands framing her face, his thumb sliding over her lips. The caress burned. That burn spread through her body, turning her veins to hot molasses. "Look at me."

Her heart beat hard. She knew if she looked into his eyes she'd be lost there. She always was. There was something so beautiful and deadly about the turbulent sea there in the depths of all that crystalline blue. He waited. She took a breath and lifted her lashes. His gaze burned into hers. Burned right through her until she felt him taking a piece of her heart. She'd known it would happen sooner or later, but how could it right there? Right then? It was the way he looked at her, that mixture of affection and exasperation, that sent her heartbeat skipping.

"I don't know who made you feel as if you aren't perfect, but whoever he was, he doesn't have a fuckin' brain in his head. You understand me, Sonia? You take my breath away. Our leopards may have found each other first, but had I laid eyes on you in the street before that night, I would have been coming after you. Nothing, no one, would have stopped me from pursuing you. That's the truth."

Just like that he had a second piece of her heart. He was stealing it away, and there didn't seem to be much she could do about it.

"You get me, baby? You get what I'm saying to you? I know every man in my employ thinks you're beautiful. They talk, and I listen. You walked into that house and they were pissed you weren't theirs. They're out there now, watching over us. Making sure we're safe. They're good men and they deserve the best. But I have you and I'm keeping you."

She didn't know what to say. He meant every word. She knew he did. It was there in his tone, in his set features and most of all, in his eyes. She nodded, because what else could she do? He made her feel beautiful and worth something. Not a woman one fucked and threw away. Not one to blow up in a car because you were through with her.

"You don't know me, Joshua." She whispered it, trying desperately to keep their relationship to sex.

"I know that you're trying to protect me from some danger you have chasing you, Sonia. I know you help out Jerry when you don't need to. Everyone knows you've got talent, and you've got that reputation. I know you're kind and caring and talented beyond anything I've seen both with your work and your art. I love the way you laugh. The way you put your hand in my hair just to let me know you're with me. I could go on and on but . . ." He took her hand and led her to the tub. "You need to get into the water, baby. Turn around."

She did, wondering what he was up to.

Immediately his hands were in her hair, dividing it into three sections and braiding it swiftly, so quickly she knew he was skilled.

"Where did you learn to do that?" She kept all expression from her voice, and it was easier to ask him with her back to him. "You're good at it."

"I can do fancy braids as well," he bragged, amusement and something that was suspiciously like sorrow in his voice. "My mom, Elaina, had long hair. She loved it, and even when she got sick, she didn't want to cut it. So I learned how to take care of it for her."

He could break hearts. That was all there was to it. She didn't turn around, but went to the drawers where she kept her hair ties and secured the end of her braid. Pinning it on top of her head, she turned back to him. "How old were you?"

"I had her until I was sixteen. We were living in Borneo, in the rain forest. Drake was already running a crew to get back kidnap victims. It was becoming a way of life for some to kidnap tourists and extort money. I joined him then."

Sonia sank down into the hot, steaming water and scooted to the end of the tub to make room for him. He fascinated her. She watched him climb into the deep tub with ease, as if he'd been sharing the bath with her for years. He stretched out and then took her ankles and pulled until her feet were in his lap. His hands began a slow massage under the water.

"I've seen pictures of Drake Donovan. He doesn't look much older than you."

"He isn't. How old were you when you lost your mother?"

"I'd just turned eighteen. I didn't have a clue what to do."

"That's when he swooped in and married you, taking care of everything, right?"

She nodded, reluctant to talk about her past with him. She had to protect him somehow. The less he knew, the better.

"So, you were with him a year? Two? You don't look very old."

She shrugged. "Almost two years. I feel old. It isn't every woman who can say her husband set a bomb in a car to kill her. If we weren't legally married, why bother? Why take the chance?"

"That's the million-dollar question, isn't it? Did he carry an insurance policy on you?"

She hadn't thought of that. She knew there was one on both of them and the payout was enormous, far more than one million dollars. She leaned her head back, tired of thinking about how stupid she was for falling for Sasha. How stupid she was being for falling for Joshua. At least he was a good man. Anyone who worked for Drake Donovan was a good man. She had to hold on to that, because she was falling.

"You're so tired, you can't keep your eyes open," he said, amusement in his voice. "Go ahead and fall asleep, Sonia, I'll get you to bed."

"Tell me more about your mother."

"She was the best. My father risked his life to get us out

of a bad situation. In the end, he was killed, but we got away. She raised me alone. She was young, but she never even looked at another man. She told me my father was the only one and when I found the right woman, I would know and she'd be my only one. I was lucky, baby. I found you."

She drifted off, his declaration running around in her mind, taking one more piece of her heart.

# 7

"WHAT'S he like?" Molly asked, taking a bite of the club sandwich she'd ordered. "It's been a week now. You've been with him every night."

Sonia nodded. "I go to work, so does he, and then he comes over at night." She didn't say they talked nearly all night when they weren't all over each other and every morning she made breakfast for him. They talked then too, laughing so much they could barely eat. He was winding himself around her heart far too fast.

"He doesn't ever take you out?"

"Out where?" she asked, although she knew what Molly was implying—that Joshua wasn't seen with her in public.

"To dinner. At least take you to dinner."

Sonia shook her head. "That's on me, not him. I'm the one who doesn't want anyone to know we're seeing each other." She didn't like being in public too much, and Joshua drew attention. She liked to cook and it was nice to have someone to cook for.

"Why?" Molly frowned at her. "I've heard a few rumors, but most of the gossip says he works for Donovan Security."

"Most?" Sonia pounced on that. "What do the others say?" She hoped her name wasn't linked with Joshua's in any way. She was working out at his place, drawing and coming up with ideas for the renovations. She'd studied the time period for her own home, so she knew what was needed, but she wanted his home to be special. Modern, but with that old-world feel to it. The house had once represented elegance and class. She wanted that same feel and was determined to get it.

Molly leaned toward her and lowered her voice to a whisper. "Some say he took over Rafe Cordeau's territory with the mob."

"Why would they say that?" She knew what it was like being around mobsters, and Joshua's crew didn't fit that at all. They were friendly. Hardworking. Nice to delivery people. No one stood around looking mean. "I thought they put those rumors to rest."

"They carry guns. *All* of them carry guns."

Sonia's breath exploded out of her lungs and she realized she'd been holding her breath. "Of course they carry guns. Is that why they're being judged? They work for an international security company, and they make enemies taking back hostages."

Molly nodded. "That's what Bastien said."

Sonia's eyebrow went up. "*Bastien* said that? You and Bastien are talking about Joshua?"

"Well, I knew you liked him, so I casually asked Bastien about the rumors. He said he'd looked into him and couldn't find a single thing that linked him positively to the mafia, other than that he knows Elijah Lospostos and Alonzo Massi. He also knows Jake Bannaconni and Eli Perez. Eli was DEA, and Jake is a businessman." She leaned closer again so her whisper would carry. "He's a *billionaire*. Joshua knows a billionaire, Sonia."

Sonia couldn't help but smile. "You had quite the conversation with Bastien. Was this over dinner and drinks?"

Molly blushed. "It isn't anything like that. We just ran into each other here at the café, and it seemed silly to eat alone so we sat together."

"He just happened to come in at the same time as you?" she teased.

Molly shrugged, trying her best to look casual and failing as she took another bite of her club. Sonia kept quiet and just watched her until Molly burst out laughing, wadded up her napkin and threw it across the table at her. "Stop."

"You're turning red."

"I know. You're making me. He just happened to come in at the same time as me. Twice. Okay, maybe three times." She covered her eyes with one hand. "Stop looking at me like that."

"*Three* times. That's not coincidence, my friend. That man is after you. Has he asked you out?"

Molly shook her head. "I wouldn't go out with him. That would mean he would pick me up at my house and then drop me off after and then we'd be all alone together. Meeting here in public is safe."

"You like him."

Molly nodded slowly. "I do. I really like him. He's smart and funny. He's in law enforcement, which is my thing, for whatever reason, and you know he's smokin' hot."

Sonia laughed. She loved the fact that she could laugh. She hadn't done that in so long, but Joshua had given that back to her. He often made her laugh, in between their wild, out-of-control sex, which she couldn't even think about without going damp and needing him. He stayed out of her way while she worked, which she was grateful for. Just seeing him sent her body into meltdown. She was afraid he was programming her that way.

"Why wouldn't you go out with him if he asked?" she persisted. "You could insist on meeting him wherever he wants to go. If he doesn't agree, then don't go."

"Or we could double-date," Molly said. "You and Joshua with Bastien and me. I'd feel safe if you were there."

Sonia pressed her lips together. She wanted to help Molly out. Molly deserved to be happy, and Bastien was definitely interested, Sonia had seen that when he'd come to check on them. It had been all about Molly. "I would. You know I would do anything to help you out," she said reluctantly. "But I can't. I'm hiding, just like you are. The man after me is incredibly dangerous, and he'd kill Joshua first. I know he would. Probably in front of me. I shouldn't even be seeing him. I told myself when I moved here it would be enough without friends or a partner, but then I met you and Jerry and Joshua and it isn't that easy. I still have to protect all of you, though. So, you see, just being my friend could put you in danger."

Molly stared at her a long time in silence. She heaved a sigh and put the last of her club down. "I knew it. Damn it, why should we have to be the ones hiding and living in fear for our friends? For ourselves? Afraid to have any kind of a relationship. It isn't right, Sonia."

"You're telling me."

"I told you about Blake. His family is a big deal, and his pockets are deep. If he's looking for me, he'll eventually find me. I don't want you or Bastien caught up in my drama. Still, I told you, I took that chance, but you didn't say a word about your problems."

There was a small note of hurt in her voice that Sonia couldn't fail to hear. "I'm sorry," she whispered, glancing around the café. They had the table she preferred, her back to the wall and looking out onto the street. Molly always got that table. "He's more than deep pockets, Molly, and he's ruthless. Completely ruthless."

Molly pushed her mostly empty plate away. "Did he hurt you? The way Blake hurt me?"

Sonia shook her head. "No broken bones. No locked in a closet. He just tried to kill me by planting a bomb in my car."

Molly gasped, one hand flying defensively to her throat. "He really did?"

"Yep. I was lucky and the car blew into the ocean. I went the other way. I'm not certain what tipped me off, but at the last second, I dove out of the car." She hated lying, but there was nothing else to say. She couldn't very well admit her leopard had saved her.

She would never forget the pain of that first shifting. The terrible sound of joints cracking, the feeling of teeth filling her mouth. She had kicked off her shoes because her toes had curled alarmingly, the ends stinging and burning, just like her fingers. She'd ripped off her tee and shoved down her jeans because she hadn't been able to stand the feel of anything against her skin.

She'd itched. That was one of the worst things—a full-body itch. When she'd looked down, she'd seen something moving beneath her skin, like a parasite, alive and seeking a way out. It had pushed against her, her skin rising and lowering as it moved around her. Every muscle had screamed in pain.

She remembered the feeling of doom. The need to exit the car. It had been so strong she'd managed to clumsily push the door handle. The driver had glanced back over his shoulder, a look of horror on his face at what he'd seen. Then she'd been flying out of the vehicle as it sped into one of the tight turns overlooking the sea. She'd been in another body, the cat leaping a good thirty feet and clearing the road to land in the grass on the other side. She'd turned briefly, crouching as the car blew apart, pieces of the vehicle raining down into the ocean below.

She'd been so scared as the leopard ran, going into the grass, instinctively heading for home. *He has betrayed you.* Sonia would never forget that either. Those were Gatita's first words to her. That quiet, very calm statement. Making it a fact, one she hadn't been able to dispute with the car in the ocean.

Gatita had taken her to the small guesthouse where Sonia had stashed the bag she kept with clothes and money, just as her mother had instructed her to have prepared. She had two ready now, one in her house and the other buried down the road. She'd gotten them to the Everglades and Gatita had taken over, telling her what to do and how to do it. Later, she'd caught a ride from a trucker, heading to Louisiana. That had sounded good to her. She'd ridden in silence, crying silent tears, but he hadn't asked questions. When they'd stopped for gas, or a food break, she'd used the restroom, checking carefully first to make certain no cameras could catch a glimpse of her. She'd never gone inside to eat, just told the driver she wasn't hungry. He'd brought her food without a word.

When she'd told him to let her off near the swamp, he'd objected, but finally pulled the truck to the side of the road. He'd offered her money, which she'd turned down, and then he was gone. He'd been nice, leaving her to absorb all that had happened.

"I heard them. My husband and father-in-law. My husband said the marriage wasn't legal and then they talked about killing me." The moment she'd overheard the conversation between Sasha and his father, she'd really stashed money, as much as she'd been able to get her hands on in preparation. She'd wiped out the accounts that morning and had hoped to get away from her driver at the mall where she was going shopping, return unseen, get the "go" bag and disappear for good. "I took my time planning how to leave, getting as much money together as I could. I wanted to do it before I left, so they didn't have a starting point to track me."

"That is so horrible. Couldn't you go to the police?"

Sonia shook her head. "Like you, that's not an option for me. He owns a few cops, and I don't know which ones. He could get to me. It's better that he thinks I'm dead. It's safer."

"Are you certain they think that?"

"I read all the papers, everything I could get my hands on. It was sad, my poor husband, a widower so early in his life. He was thirty-three and his young bride had died. They found pieces of her burned clothing, but not her body. My father-in-law loved me like a daughter, poor man. They really played to the press."

Molly took a deep breath and let it out. "I really hate that men did this to us and we can't make them pay. I have to live in fear for the rest of my life, and so do you. Why?"

Sonia forced a small grin. "Bad judgment? I think we're in the same boat there. We went for the wrong men and now we're in a mess."

"I love that little accent, the way you twist your words. Has Joshua noticed it?"

Her heart reacted with a small thud. "He has mentioned it. Just last night." What else had he found out about her? Her age. He'd been clever going about it. How long she'd been married. When her mother had died. He worked with Donovan in security. They had to investigate the people they were going to go after. That meant he had the resources to have her investigated. Were the things she'd told him enough to ferret out who she'd been married to?

"I bet he loves it."

Sonia nodded a little absently. "That's what he said, but he's always saying things like that. He compliments me quite a bit."

"I wouldn't mind a few compliments," Molly said with a soft, almost dreamy sigh.

"Bastien doesn't compliment you?"

At the mention of the detective's name, Molly blushed again. "He does, but he flirts so much with other women, I think it's just what he does naturally to anything female."

"He's seeking you out. How many other women has he dated around here? Surely you got the gossip on him."

She shook her head. "I've never asked."

"Well, I did," Sonia said. She crooked her fingers until

Molly was leaning across the table very close. "I asked Jerry, and he gets all the good gossip on everyone. He said Bastien flirts with anything in skirts, but he's never taken a woman out that he can remember. Not in four years. If he's seeing anyone, she isn't from around here. He got it from Charity at the grocery store that he's smitten with you. That's the word she used. *Smitten*."

Molly's wild blush turned to a deep rose. "He's not smitten. He just sat with me because neither of us had anyone else to sit with and it gets lonely always eating alone."

"He has sat in here dozens of time alone and never once ate with anyone else that was alone. He's into you. Seriously into you."

"You think?"

"I know. Call him up and ask him out. Women can do that."

"Not this woman. If he wants me to go out with him, he has to ask, and he'd have to be okay with meeting me at our destination. I'm not going to be the trusting soul who gets in trouble again. Once was enough for me."

Sonia glanced at her watch. "I've got to go, honey. I'm going to be late if I don't get a move on. I told the work crew I'd be out there this afternoon."

Molly caught her wrist as she tossed bills onto the table. "Just be careful, Sonia. Just in case. Sometimes rumors are grounded in fact. Maybe ask Joshua about how he knows Elijah Lospostos, just to be safe. Where did they meet—that sort of thing. I don't want you getting hurt again."

Sonia knew her heart was already at risk. If Joshua wasn't who he said he was, she was afraid the consequence was going to be worse than what it had been when she'd discovered her husband of almost two years didn't really love her—that he never had. She'd been too young and too desperate and shocked to know what love was. She'd been grateful to Sasha and she'd needed him. She'd loved him, she knew that, but not the way a wife should love her husband.

Maybe over time she would have come to love him the way she was supposed to.

Joshua talked to her more than Sasha ever had. They spent hours on her bed, the plans she was drawing spread out for him to look at. He had a few good suggestions, but mostly he liked what she envisioned and gave her the go-ahead each time. Sasha would never have even glanced at her drawings. He would have told her they needed someone far more experienced than she was. Joshua complimented her all the time. Sasha rarely had. Joshua loved her paintings. Sasha had told her she needed more work before they could ever be shown in public.

"You've got that goofy look on your face again," Molly said. "I'm getting envious. I want that look on my face."

"Then ask Bastien out. Go to bed with him. I recommend sex highly."

Molly laughed. "I have a toy."

"Not the same, I can testify to that." Sonia jumped up, waved and rushed out, hurrying to her truck. She hadn't been late once. She wanted Joshua to take her seriously. She loved what she did, and she was good at it.

As she pulled onto the highway, she glanced back and noticed the dark SUV that had been parked just down from her truck. She recognized it immediately. Joshua's men favored the four-wheel-drive, tinted-windows kind of vehicle. This was one she'd seen two of them use. One was named Kai and the other Gray. They were close friends of Joshua and came from the rain forest in Borneo. She'd noticed them more than once when she was in town. Now she had a sneaking suspicion they were following her.

She turned into the main gates of Joshua's estate. The guard post was there, still unmanned. That always made her feel good. The surrounding fence blocked off all roads other than the one from the swamp to the back of the house. Joshua hadn't built the fence, someone else had. That someone else had also put in the guard shack. The gates were open and no one was there, no grim-looking men walking around looking all kinds of scary. Still, the SUV followed her up the drive to the main house. She waited for the two men to exit their vehicle before she got out of hers. Smiling, she walked right up to them.

"Are you following me?"

They exchanged a glance over her head, and then Kai nodded. "Yep."

"Why? You do know I'm perfectly capable of finding my way from point A to point B without help. I also, just to make you feel better, have GPS. If I break down, or get a flat, I'm fairly well-versed in knowing how to fix things. I keep the tank filled. It's very sweet of you to worry, but I can handle things all by myself."

"Gotta talk to the boss, Sonia," Gray said. "He gives the orders, we just follow them."

She nodded. She didn't like bodyguards. She'd had that. Those guards hadn't been there for her protection, they'd been there to make certain she didn't get away. She should have been suspicious when Sasha and Nikita had sent her off to the mall with just a driver. Not once had that ever happened before.

*I was suspicious.* Gatita was smug.

*You smelled conspiracy.*

*That too.* Now there was the impression of amusement.

*Why did Joshua send them after me?*

*To make certain no one hurts you.*

*Is that what his leopard told you?* Gatita was such a little hussy. Every night she wanted to go running with her mate, and if Sonia was too tired from work, she sulked, so Sonia made certain she was never that tired.

Gatita settled down again. *Yes. But I talked to their leopards as well. I don't leave your protection to chance. Not anymore.*

That shocked Sonia. She had no idea the other leopards communicated with one another. She also hadn't realized that Gatita blamed herself for what had happened.

*That wasn't your fault. None of it was your fault.* She waved at the two men and went into the house. *You know that, don't you? You hadn't even emerged. What made you come to the surface when you hadn't had a heat?*

*I sensed a conspiracy. I sensed you were in danger. I began to listen whenever you were around those people. They aren't nice.*

*No, they aren't,* Sonia conceded. *I got us into that, not you. You saved us.*

*I will always save you, even from my mate.*

Unexpectedly, there was burning behind her eyes. She loved her leopard.

*I love you too. Now go fight with your man the way you always do. You won't win, but he likes the argument.*

*He does not.*

*He thinks you're very sexy when you argue with him.*

*Oh my God. How could you possibly know that? Wait, don't tell me. Shadow told you.*

Sonia stomped up the stairs to the first small bedroom, which would be the nursery. Joshua was adamant that they restore the nursery. He said they would need it. She always ignored those statements. She had no way to respond. She wasn't going to fantasize any more than she already did.

She walked through the master bedroom and looked around. She'd never gone in Joshua's room before. It was huge, almost as large as her entire second story. The front and back windows were glass. She looked closely and thought maybe it was bulletproof glass. If so, Rafe Cordeau had spent a fortune on it. The French doors were similar to the ones in her home, but again, these were custom-made. The upper verandah stretched wide and long, giving Joshua a good view of the swamp and river. Tree branches led straight to the wrought iron railing, making it easy for a leopard to make the jump from the tree to the house.

Joshua's bed was made and his clothes put away neatly. The room looked lived-in, but clean. Very clean. She hadn't seen a maid go in other than once. That time, the woman had come out with sheets, presumably to wash them. Sonia ran her hand over the duvet spread across his bed. It was masculine, a black and red Asian theme. She liked it.

His scent was all over the room, making it difficult not to breathe him in. She didn't want to be surrounded by him, but it was impossible not to be. She forced herself to keep walking right on through to his office. She knocked on the doorjamb, although the door was open.

"Joshua?" She poked her head in, half expecting him to be angry with her for disturbing him at work. Sasha would have been angry. Now she knew why. He wouldn't have wanted her to know his businesses weren't legitimate.

Joshua was frowning at his computer, his shaggy blond hair falling across his forehead, making him look more like a surfer than a businessman. His head came up; the frown was gone and his smile spread light across his face. "Sonia." He jumped up. "Come in, baby. What a surprise. You've never come near my private lair."

Her heart jumped at his words. Just looking at him sent that liquid heat dampening her lacy little boy shorts, the ones she wore comfortably under her jeans. Her nipples burned and ached, pushing against the lacy bra. She wore a simple T-shirt, but it was tight and she knew not only would he see her arousal, but since he was leopard, he would smell it.

His smile widened until his look bordered on arrogance. He had every right to be arrogant where she was concerned, she conceded. He didn't have to do much, just smile at her and she was ready, but that wasn't the point. She refused to smile back. "You're having me followed."

"Of course." He didn't deny it. He leaned his butt on the desk, arms folded across his chest, faint male amusement evident in his eyes.

"That's your answer? 'Of course'? Be serious, Joshua. Why in the world would you have two men follow me around? Don't you have jobs for them to do? Are you getting desperate because Donovan Security has no work for anyone right now?"

"Their sole job is to follow you. Their sole purpose is to keep you safe at all times."

She shook her head. "No, their sole purpose is to keep *you* safe. You, Joshua. For whatever reason you've acquired enemies, and I get that, someone would be after you, not me."

"Someone tried to kill you, not me."

"I've seen the scars on your body. You have more than slashes from a leopard fight. You have knife scars and bullet scars. I don't have any of those things. In fact, I doubt you'd find too many scars on my body."

"You have one just above your left knee. A small indentation."

She made a face and waved that away. "I fell off my bike when my father was trying to teach me to ride."

"And the larger one on your left forearm?"

She was silent for a moment, and then she sighed. "Really, Joshua, don't change the subject. We're talking about why you have Kai and Gray following me."

"No, *you're* talking about it. I'm looking at you. My God, you're beautiful. I'm a very lucky man. Come over here and kiss me."

"I'm not going to kiss you. We're going to talk about Kai and Gray and you're going to call them off."

"Come here and kiss me. You wouldn't want me to be so distracted that I'm ruined for the rest of the day."

"I'm working. I'm not your girlfriend when I'm working. Those were the rules we set down. We talked about this."

His smile widened. The lines of strain instantly disappeared. He looked young and almost carefree. He also looked so hot she thought about stripping for him, seducing and claiming him right there, draped over his desk. Instead, she gave him her deadliest glare.

"Baby, I listened very carefully to the nonsense you laid out, but if you remember, I didn't agree. I just listened."

"Silence is agreeing."

"Silence means I think what you're saying is bullshit, I won't agree to it in a million years, but you're cute as hell and I want my cock buried in your body with every breath I take."

"*Bullshit?* You think my rules are bullshit?" She wanted to pull her hair out; at the same time, she thought having his cock in her mouth and driving him insane might be another alternative.

"Yep, total bullshit. Come and kiss me."

She put her hand on her hip, deliberately scowling, trying to appear as if his demand didn't slice through her, as if her blood wasn't already hot and her body aware of him. "Not. Going. To. Happen. Well"—she held up her hand when he shifted his weight on his feet and set her heart pounding—"it might . . . *might* . . . if you agree to call off your men. Otherwise, kisses are going to be out until you do." She could never go without kissing him, and that was a fact.

He moved then, fast like he did, blurring speed, catching her around the waist as he sprinted, tossing her over his shoulder, his momentum taking him halfway across the bedroom before she even realized she was over his shoulder, upside-down. He had a very nice butt and she swatted it hard, trying not to laugh. She loved the way he played. Sasha had not been playful, but she'd put it down to his being older than she was. She guessed that Joshua was at least ten years older than her, but he took the time to play and laugh.

He tossed her on his bed and came down over her, pinning her there with his superior weight. She pressed her lips together and turned her face to the side. "Not kissing you, Joshua Tregre. Not now. Not ever. Unless you call those men off."

"They stay, and you're kissing me." His warm breath

stirred the tendrils of hair escaping her fishbone braid. He'd shown off his skills in the morning after they'd showered.

"It's against the carpenter code. There is one, you know. The third rule is no kissing on the job." She did her best to sound superior and snippy.

He blew warm air in her ear and then caught her earlobe between his teeth, biting down gently. "I call bullshit on that one as well." His lips moved against her ear as he whispered to her.

She almost turned her head but realized at the last minute that was what he wanted. She clamped her lips together and pressed into the pillow, trying not to laugh. It took a minute to get herself under firm control. "You can't call bullshit on everything. We need rules if I'm going to be working in your home every day."

"Fine. You want rules, the number-one rule is when you get your gorgeous ass to work, you come find me and kiss me." He bit the spot between her neck and shoulder. Hard.

She yelped and turned slightly so he could see her glare. "Stop that. And that can't be a rule."

His tongue touched the spot. "It's the *only* rule." His kissed the sting and then began a slow journey up her throat. Tiny kisses that drove her crazy.

Laughter bubbled up, laughter and desire all wrapped in one. "I do like your kisses," she conceded. "Some days you get it right."

He caught her jaw and turned her face to him. His blue-green eyes smoldered with sex. Every line in his face was sensual, the devil tempting her to sin. The smile faded as his lips came down on hers. She expected wild. Rough. It was stamped there in every line of his face. She got sweet. Tender. One hand spanned her throat, holding her in place while he explored her mouth, coaxing her tongue to follow his. He deepened the kiss, but was so gentle it brought tears to her eyes. He was saying more than she wanted to hear, but she loved what she was hearing.

She kissed him back, giving herself to him in the way she did. She never held back when she was in his arms. When he lifted his mouth from hers and rested his forehead on hers, she realized he might have been teasing her, even playing around, but there was something else in him, something upsetting him.

"Honey, talk to me," she said softly. She rarely invited him to share his world with her, and he lifted his head to look into her eyes. She ran her fingers through his thick, shaggy hair. He needed a good haircut, but on him, the longish hair looked good. "I can tell something is bothering you. Is it me? Something to do with me?"

Joshua shrugged and rolled off her. "I've got an important meeting tomorrow and I've got to have everything worked out. I've been getting threats and need to increase security around here, and I'll have to do that before my meeting."

"Kai and Gray can help you," she said, meaning it. "If you want them to follow me around all day after you don't need them anymore, I'll put up with it for a little while just to make you feel better, but you can use them. It isn't like you have a huge resource pool around here."

He rolled over and stared at the ceiling fan, his fingers linked behind his head, his legs over the side. "I put them on you because you mean more to me than anything else, and they're that good. I'm not pulling them off. I don't like you being upset over it, though."

She rolled to her side and propped up her head with one hand. The other slid over his chest, her fingers idly writing her name. "I won't be upset, although I prefer them guarding you, if you're getting threats. The threat to me is over. I'm dead, remember? I know they think that. I'm far away and nothing I do will ever impact them."

He kept looking at the ceiling fan. "*Them?* You often use that instead of 'him.' Do you mean his family?"

"Yes." She wasn't going to lie to him. "His father was the one who told him he had to kill me and he agreed. Very casually, I might add. No argument. So yes, I say 'they' because I think his father would want me dead even now."

"Why, Sonia? I turn that over and over in my mind, trying to put the threat to you into a logical conclusion, but there is none. Were they in some shady business and you overheard something you shouldn't?"

It helped that he kept his eyes on the fan and not her. "I didn't, though. I think it had something to do with my father." She touched the faint scar on her forearm. It was long and thin, white against the olive of her skin. Still, it was so faint, no one had ever noticed it, not even Sasha, whom she'd lived with for nearly two years.

"Your father," he prompted when she fell silent.

She pulled his white, button-down shirt from his jeans. He did that a lot—paired a dress shirt or a shirt and jacket with jeans. She thought of it as his signature look, one she appreciated. He looked good in jackets and collared shirts. His skin beneath the shirt was very warm. She drew circles over his hard muscles. "He was murdered. I was there. He was a good carpenter, and I loved wood. Really loved it. The smell, the different textures and looks. He taught me so much, but I suspected he was doing something else, something not legal. Men came and did things to him. Horrible things. They made me watch. I get nightmares sometimes. I fought them, and one had a knife. It sliced my arm open. The laceration was fairly shallow but it hurt like hell and needed stitches to close."

"So maybe not so shallow."

She shrugged. "Maybe. In any case, I now have this scar. By the way, I saw you hung the picture in the great room. I saw it when I was walking to the stairs." Her hand dropped to his jeans, fingers fiddling with the snap there. She opened it. "You're right, it looks good. I didn't think it would go so well over the fireplace, but the colors are perfect. I like knowing something of mine is in your house."

"I do too." His hand slipped into her hair. "I like you in this house."

"I am here." Very, very slowly she slid down the zipper. He was already hard and ready for her. "I kind of like this afternoon break thing. Now, that might be a decent rule to add." She slipped off the bed to her knees, nudging his legs apart so she could fit. She took off his shoes and socks first. Grasping the waistband, she pulled his jeans down his legs until she could get them off.

She loved looking at him sprawled just like that, draped over the bed, hands back behind his head, his eyes on her face.

"Do me a favor and lose the clothes."

"*My* clothes? I don't think it's necessary when I plan to have your cock in my mouth, devour you and then go to work."

"Your clothes. I want my cock in your mouth and then I want you riding me. Hard. Face-to-face. And I want to look at your body while you do that."

She cupped his balls, her thumbs sliding over the velvet sacs while she contemplated what he wanted. "I have to admit, I like the idea of riding you hard, but I'm giving up a lot here, so I should have some concessions."

She pulled off her shirt and flung it to one side. Her bra followed. She removed both boots and then shimmied out of her jeans. She liked the way his eyes were on her every second. He didn't blink, giving her the full focus a leopard would its prey. That familiar shiver slid down her spine.

"What concessions?"

"Tonight, I get to take you all the way before we let the cats run. I have something special I want to try."

"I have to let you blow me again? Twice in one day. That's tough, baby. A really tough sell. I don't know."

"Let me try to persuade you." She knelt between his legs and licked up his shaft. His cock jumped and he groaned.

"That's cheating. Cheaters get in trouble. Their asses get marked."

"I am cheating, but I want my way." Before he could reply, she took him deep, sucked hard, her tongue lashing and curling around him. She'd had plenty of practice, and she loved watching his face, watching the pleasure spread, the lines of carnal sin deepen, the dark passion turn his eyes more blue than green. It was *such* a turn-on.

"All right, baby. But don't expect to sit comfortably for a day or two."

She purred softly around his shaft, watching the vibrations take him up another notch. She loved that. Loved it almost as much as she loved what he did to her. Everything he did to her. "I'll look forward to that, honey, but in the meantime, you're going to have to stay strong," she murmured around his shaft, and then went to work.

She loved making it difficult for him to leave her mouth. If he came in her mouth, it was paradise, but then he missed her sheath grasping him with scorching-hot, tight muscles. Milking him. Pulling his seed right out of him.

He groaned, and his hips began that helpless thrusting she knew meant she was giving him exactly what he needed. She increased her suction, took him deeper, held him there, muscles squeezing, took a deep breath and started all over.

Then he caught her braid in his fist, forcing her head up. "Sit on me. Do it now, you little cheater. Right now."

He was leaking all that salty goodness she had tried so hard to get. Laughing, she licked at him, took him deep while he held his cock at the base and then, with a show of reluctance, let him go. She straddled his thighs, and lowered herself onto him, all the while watching his face. She loved that. She loved the way his gaze dropped to her breasts, his hands came up and then his mouth was on hers, kissing her fiercely. She felt as if she was home.

# 8

"DAMN it, Drake, I've given you everything I have on her. I need to find out who the hell tried to kill her and why. We have an entire team of investigators. Are you telling me they can't find one single thing on her? She's been here a year. Surely somewhere in the United States, a car blowing up was reported a year ago. That can't be that fuckin' hard to find."

"I've never heard you rattled, Joshua. You really have found your mate."

As always, Drake's voice was calm. It didn't matter that Joshua had been growling at him for the last three minutes solid, probably blowing out his eardrum. Joshua could picture the man, pacing with the phone to his ear, just waiting for his friend to get over his tantrum. Joshua made an effort to calm down.

"Sorry, man. I just have this feeling. Gut deep. I don't like that she's hanging out there when I don't even know what or who is threatening her."

"It's possible she's safe. It's been a year. They aren't looking for her, or our team would have caught wind of it when they were putting careful feelers out."

He took a deep breath and let it out. "The thing is, Drake, I've never been wrong. I know trouble's coming. I can't get a handle on where it's coming from, but it's coming. I can't lose her. She's already skittish. Sometimes she feels like water in my palms just slipping away." He hadn't meant to whine, but, hell, every night they were magic together, and every day she smiled that sweet smile and looked at him as if she expected him to turn into a monster. He knew sadists. His grandfather had been one. He wasn't that. He had faults, but he wasn't that.

"This meeting with the Russians is important, Joshua. You have to be certain you're all in. One slipup and you're dead. It's too late for me to get there. I'm in San Antonio at the moment."

"I can handle the meeting. You and the others put me in this position, but I took it willingly. I didn't think I'd find my mate and it seemed like a good thing at the time."

"Rafe had a big territory. You've gotten most of it under control in a short amount of time. You worked hard to get us that pipeline. The Russians are the last step."

"You certain reaching out to them was a good idea, considering Alonzo's past? We're in bed with several Russians some are looking to kill."

"We have to know if they're hunting Alonzo. *I* have to know. He's a friend, Joshua, and he'd lay down his life for any of us. We have to know how much trouble he's in."

"You think Nikita will casually tell us they're looking for him, don't you?"

"I'm betting on it. This is the first time we've really reached out to the Russians and they know it's significant. They're always looking to take over more territory. We're solid here and they can't move in, so they want peace with us. They want allies. They want a look inside. They'll drop it that they're looking for Alonzo, his brother and cousins. They'll use us to try to find these men and at the same time, give us the opportunity to cement relationships by helping them out. That's what we want. We need an 'in' with them. We know Nikita Bogomolov is one of the worst."

"I'll handle it," Joshua assured. He liked Alonzo. Not Alonzo, Fyodor. Fyodor Amurov. He wasn't about to let anything happen to the man, especially since he was mated to Joshua's cousin.

"We'll push the investigation into your woman, Joshua, but try to get a little more on her. A starting point would be good. Telling me she has a Spanish accent doesn't help me much."

"I'll try. She keeps things to herself. What about Molly Sheffield? Did you get anything on her?"

"She's an open book. The Sheffields are originally from that area. They left fifteen years ago, leaving the grandmother behind. As far as we can tell, Molly was the only one to consistently visit her. She purchased the swampland and house when she inherited money, but didn't live there until recently. She got hooked up with a man by the name of Blake Garritson. Big-shot district attorney. Comes from big money. Has an ego the size of Texas. I can tell you with certainty, the man is dirty as hell, and he's looking for Molly."

"Is he close to finding her?"

"It took *me* all of three minutes," Drake said. "I'd have to say yes. He's got to be on her trail, or already has someone there watching her."

Joshua swore under his breath. He didn't need that added complication. Sonia had her own troubles, she didn't need to take on Molly's. But she would. She was going to be right in the middle of it. It infuriated him—call that terror—but it was one of the reasons he was falling so hard.

"Molly is seeing the local law. I sent you his name as well." Joshua glanced at the clock. The Russians would be showing up any minute.

"Bastien Foret. I checked with my brother-in-law, Remy. He's a detective in New Orleans. His brother is a sheriff here. They both say Bastien is as straight as an arrow. He's a better-than-average detective. Intelligent. He's not the type to try to blackmail or bribe."

"Good to know. Sonia's been feeling me out, trying to set up a barbecue with Molly and Bastien. I've managed to put it off, but sooner or later, I'll have to say yes."

It was Drake's turn to swear. He did it so rarely that it shocked Joshua. "I can handle this," he assured again.

"I put you there," Drake said.

"I could have said no," Joshua pointed out. "I've got Evan and the others. They're good men. It's going to be fine." He wished he believed that, but his gut was saying something else.

"Boss." Evan stuck his head in the door.

Joshua flipped him off for calling him "boss." They'd been friends for years. They'd watched each other's backs when the bullets were flying.

Evan flashed a grin. "They're coming up the drive."

"Gotta go," Joshua told Drake and hung up.

Under any other circumstances, he would have been elated to run a meeting with the Russians. He welcomed the cat-and-mouse games. He was good at them. He found most men underestimated him because he looked young, and for being in their business, he *was* young.

"You certain no work crews will show?" he asked Evan. He meant Sonia. The last thing he wanted was for Sonia to show up when every one of his crew was walking around armed, looking tough and deliberately intimidating. He didn't want the Russians to know about her. She would be a liability, making him vulnerable.

"I'm certain. Sonia's in town. Kai's on her. Gray's here. Kai just reported in, and Molly and Sonia are eating lunch together in the café."

That was a relief. He walked down the stairs into the

great room, waiting for the Russians to get to the door. Evan opened it and escorted the small group of four men into the room. Instantly Joshua's leopard went wild, confirming his belief that all four men were leopard. He'd have to be careful, make certain every statement was truthful.

"Nikita Bogomolov," the oldest of the four men said, his hand outstretched.

He knew. Joshua could read it in his eyes. He knew Joshua and his men were shifters as well. That instantly evened the playing field, taking away the advantage Nikita thought he'd had. His smile didn't falter as he shook Joshua's hand and acknowledged his introduction.

The two men sized each other up. Nikita Bogomolov was fifty-seven years old. His face was lined, although he looked younger than his age. He wore a suit worth several thousand dollars, custom-made, and it fit like a glove. His shoes cost almost as much as his suit. His handshake was firm and his faded blue eyes sharp.

The three men with Nikita were clearly bodyguards. They didn't make any bones about it, fanning out around their boss in a semicircle. They wore the same expression, eyes moving restlessly, their leopards close to keep them on high alert.

Joshua waved the four men toward the comfortable leather chairs. "Hot coffee or something cool?"

"Coffee would be welcome," Nikita said. He looked around the room. "Beautiful place."

"I'm in the middle of renovating it." He sent the Russian a brief smile. All teeth. Showing his leopard. "The previous owner must have had a gun battle here. Lots of bullet holes."

Nikita had stopped listening. He jumped up, his face a mask of fury for a moment, and then it settled into more amicable lines as he slowed his pace, wandering across the room to the fireplace. "This painting is quite unique. Where did you get it?" His voice was falsely casual, when clearly, he wasn't feeling in the least casual.

Joshua was grateful that he'd learned from an early age never to show emotion. Fear ripped through him, leaving him feeling raw and exposed. He had the desire to take out his gun and shoot Nikita right in the head. His painting, the one he'd talked Sonia out of, hung in its place of honor, the colors of the swamp vibrant in his home.

"It was given to me by a friend." That was true. He had to stick strictly to the truth. Later, the crime lord would go over every word and nuance. He had to hear the truth or he would come back and torture everyone until he got what he wanted. Joshua had to handle this just right.

He walked over to stand beside Nikita, staring up at the painting. "I saw it and wanted it. It reminded me of good times years ago." He smiled at Nikita. "And it goes perfectly in this room."

"I'd like to buy it from you," Nikita said. "Name your price."

Joshua turned away. "Nikita, we're here to discuss business, not paintings. That painting is special to me for a lot of reasons, and I don't want to part with it." That was all true. Every word.

"My son, Sasha, was widowed a year ago. She was a beautiful, vibrant woman. She painted. This style reminds me of her. I would like to buy the painting for him."

"I can't sell it, Nikita, as much as I would like to oblige you." Joshua gestured toward the chairs and the coffee Evan brought in. "I know you don't have much time and I'd like to make this count."

Nikita's features portrayed a flash of anger, and then he was smiling, turning his back on the painting. Joshua's leopard clawed at him in warning. That amicable mask hid a deadly anger. The Russian didn't like to be thwarted in the smallest thing. He was used to getting his way, or taking it. Joshua, standing in his way, was an unexpected show of strength.

Nikita picked up his coffee mug without sitting down. "At least tell me the name of the artist so I can contact them to purchase a painting of my own."

Joshua shrugged. "I didn't buy the painting from the artist." He was careful to keep his statement strictly the truth. Sonia had refused to take money. He was arranging to send a truckload of building supplies to her home in exchange, although she wasn't aware of his intention. He deliberately hadn't told her, because she'd argued the first time he'd tried, right after she'd delivered the painting.

Nikita frowned, but he dropped the subject. Throughout the next two hours while they brokered a deal for their pipeline, Nikita's gaze continually strayed toward Sonia's artwork. It made sense to Joshua now. Sonia had somehow gotten involved with the Russian mob. The fact that her father had been murdered made him believe it was him who had first gotten mixed up with them. He'd pulled his family in, perhaps through a gambling debt.

If the Bogomolov family was anything like the Amurov leopards, they wanted sons, not wives. Their lairs didn't tolerate loyalty to anyone but the *bratya*. The women providing children, more often than not, ended up dead. Sonia had probably been scheduled for termination because she hadn't gotten pregnant. Alonzo had explained how the males in his family murdered the women to prove their loyalty. That meant the Bogomolov family might somehow be connected to Alonzo's family.

He understood why Sonia didn't want to involve him. The Russians were ruthless, very, very dangerous. He'd known, sooner or later, they'd be dealing with them because of Alonzo and the others, but he hadn't expected it would become personal.

They talked, Nikita trying to get every advantage, but Joshua held firm. In the end, they shook hands and the Russians stood to go. Nikita wandered over to the painting, looked at it closely until he stiffened, lifting one finger to trace the *S* and *L* woven into the foliage. "You are certain you cannot tell me who the artist is?"

"I can't," Joshua said with the utmost sincerity.

Nikita took out his cell and snapped a few pictures of the painting. "I may be able to find the artist by asking around the art world."

Joshua walked the Russian toward the door. "Thanks for coming all this way. I hope you take the time to enjoy yourself. New Orleans is a beautiful city. There's so much to see and do."

"I must get back immediately," Nikita said.

"Oh? I'm sorry. I thought you were staying a few days. I must have misunderstood."

Nikita flashed a fake smile. "Something of great importance has come up," he explained.

"Anything I can help with?"

Nikita turned back as if just remembering something. "There is one small thing."

"Yes, of course," Joshua said swiftly.

"We are hunting a very dangerous man. His name is Fyodor Amurov. Along with his brother, Timur, and his cousins Gorya and Mitya, he murdered a dozen or more people. We are looking for this man and his brother and cousins."

"Of course we'll help. I'll put out the word to our friends and see if we can locate them for you."

"We would be very appreciative." Nikita's gaze once more strayed over Joshua's shoulder to the painting. He quickly looked away and headed down the stairs to his vehicle, the others falling into step around him.

Joshua stood in the doorway, cursing as the car pulled back down the drive toward the road. Sonia hadn't been marked. There were no bite marks on her shoulders, no rake marks. Nothing indicated Sasha's leopard had known about her leopard. Gatita hadn't risen because of her first heat— she'd risen to save Sonia's life. Sasha's leopard didn't know about her. He never would have allowed her to go, not without giving him a child. Then he would have killed her.

Alonzo had explained that the males in the lair purposely mated with a woman not their own mate so there was no chance of falling in love. They wanted males to make the lair stronger, but to prove loyalty, they murdered their wives after sons were provided.

Joshua ran his hands through his hair in exasperation. He couldn't bring up the Russians to Sonia and confirm everything. She'd ask questions he couldn't answer, and she was already skittish. If she thought he had any connection to the mob, she'd leave everything behind and run from him just as she'd run from Sasha Bogomolov.

Evan stood in front of the painting. "He recognized this work as being hers. Sonia's. Didn't he?"

Joshua nodded. "No question about it. He was more interested in the painting than he was the pipeline, so much so that he didn't force me to make more concessions for him. He knows Sonia. They had to be the ones who tried to kill her. If I confront her about it, she'll want to know how I know Nikita."

"She's hiding a pretty big secret. You think she was married to Sasha Bogomolov?"

"That's the only answer, as much as I'd like another one. All the pieces fit." Joshua pressed his fingers to his throbbing temple. He was getting a massive headache. "I'll call Drake and update him. Do we have eyes on them?"

Evan nodded.

"Warn Kai the Russians are on the move. They may stop in town. I don't want them to run into Sonia accidentally. Have Kai get her out of there if possible. Tell him he needs to drop it that he was at the lumberyard, and he overheard me giving a huge order of roofing material to Jerry over the phone. Tell him to say he hadn't thought we needed a new roof. Sonia will go ballistic and head straight to Jerry to tell him to cancel the order."

Evan nodded and took out his cell, texting with one hand. Joshua paced across the floor like a caged leopard. If Sonia were with him, she'd be safe. She'd just refused. She hadn't once spent the night at his house, preferring her own. She wouldn't go out in public with him. Essentially, she called all the shots in their relationship. He might be the dominant in bed, but that seemed the only place. Because he had been giving her space, she was in danger.

He cursed himself again, nails digging into his palms. Flecks of blood proved the leopard's claws were very much in evidence. The pain helped clear his mind. He had to trust Kai into maneuvering Sonia out of harm's way. Tonight, he'd have to talk to her, even if it meant she would have to be told the truth about who and what he was—what he'd become.

If she'd been involved with the Russian mob—and they'd tried to kill her—he couldn't imagine her reaction when she learned he'd taken over Rafe Cordeau's territory. Joshua Tregre was the new crime lord. He looked like the friendly neighbor. He acted the friendly neighbor. He ruled his territory with an iron fist and made deals with murderous Russians.

He'd managed to fool everyone. The rumors of his taking over for Cordeau had mostly died down. He'd worked hard to gain the trust of the locals. His men had been given strict instructions never to push anyone around. Most of his crew were men he'd worked with in Borneo, but a few were leftovers from Rafe's crew. Those were the ones he watched the most. He wanted his reputation around his town spotless. He wanted his reputation with others in his world ruthless. It was the only way to keep everyone safe.

"Is Bastien Foret going to be a problem, Evan?" he asked.

"It's a possibility. Good men can be a pain in the ass. Smart men even more so. Foret is both." Evan tapped his fingers on his phone. "Let's see what these bastards do. You got the best of him in the deal. He didn't expect that and he didn't like it, but he wanted an 'in' with us bad enough to take what he could get. I liked that you pointed out he wasn't the only game in town, but you'd come to him out of respect. I wanted to laugh at his expression."

"He knew it was bullshit but he couldn't call me on it, not without losing the deal. Mostly he was upset over the painting and what it meant."

"He lost that deal," Evan said. "You look like a kid. You came out of nowhere and took hold of Rafe's territory and made everyone aware right out of the gate that you weren't playing games. Even with that, there wasn't a trail of dead bodies. He has to respect that. Few could have pulled that off."

"I had a little help from my friends." Joshua couldn't stop the restless pacing. His phone sounded off, letting him know he had a text. Glancing down, he grinned. "Kai must have made his move." He held up the phone for Evan to see. **You didn't.** Two words. "Man, I love that woman." The grin faded when he realized what he'd said. He couldn't afford to love her. Not yet. Not when he hadn't told her the truth.

"Gray just reported in. The Russians are headed out of town. They didn't stop; in fact, they're going to get a speeding ticket if they don't slow down. Nikita's been on the phone the entire time and he doesn't look happy."

"He just found out his daughter-in-law is still alive." Joshua wanted to punch the wall. "I have to tell her. She has to know."

His phone pinged again and he glanced down. **Thanks, man. Sonia's in here ripping me a new one. She wants me to cancel the order.**

He texted back. He was fast and he sent the order immediately. **Do not cancel the order. Tell her you need the money. Give her a sob story and she'll relent.** He knew his woman. The sadder the story, the more likely she would back down. **I have faith in you. She needs those materials.** He knew how Jerry felt about Sonia. The man would do anything for her.

"She's going to give you trouble," Evan prophesied.

"Don't sound so fuckin' happy about it," Joshua said. He walked across the room to stand in front of the painting. "Why would he want to buy this? Why make a big deal out of it and just go home without tipping us off that something isn't right?"

"Good question."

"He wanted proof, Evan. He wanted the painting and when he couldn't get it, he took photographs to give someone the evidence. He wanted his son to know—and believe him—that Sonia was alive. The painting depicts the swamp here in New Orleans. He had to know that. I couldn't very well lie and say I bought it in a city. His leopard would have heard that immediately."

"You were careful. It was a good thing that we sprayed the house with the scent-canceling formula we got from Remy. It worked when Sonia first came to the house. If we hadn't, Bogomolov's leopard would have scented her. She's been all over the house. I think he bought it that you didn't know the artist."

"He bought it for the moment. He'll have time to think about it and convince himself that I know more than I was telling him, and they'll come back."

"You have to talk to her. Get Drake down here. Bring Eli Perez, someone she might trust."

"As opposed to me." Joshua wanted to pound the wall. It was a very unusual reaction for him. He was always the calm one. His woman could make him crazy.

"Come on, Joshua. She's scared with good reason. How can she trust her own judgment? The Russian told her he loved her, married her, promised to take care of her and instead, tried to kill her. Along comes you. You're all over her. Your leopard is all over her. She really doesn't have much choice because you didn't let up for a moment and give her breathing room."

"She would have run from me."

"She lives next door," Evan pointed out.

"Fuck you, Evan," he snapped, but was ashamed the moment the words came out of his mouth. Evan was right and he knew it. He hadn't been able to be away from her. Not for five minutes. The more Sonia ran, the more he chased. He shook his head. "Sorry, man. You're right. I know you are." He ran both hands through his hair. "How did they do this? Tell their women? Alonzo? Evangeline is my cousin. She's about as sweet and as innocent as one can get. I think she knew from the beginning what Alonzo was. Sonia is running from the mob. The last thing she's going to want to do is even discuss this with me."

"You have to tell her, Joshua."

He nodded. "She's safe right now. I'm going to go over everything we have on the Bogomolov family. Drake gathered a lot of information on them."

He climbed the stairs slowly, his chest hurting. His head was throbbing. Sonia was the most important person in his world and he was going to have to ask her to stay with him knowing what he was, what he'd gotten himself into. Once in, there was no getting out, not without a hefty price on the head and running for the rest of one's life.

*Damn it, Shadow. I got us into a mess.*

The big cat yawned. *You'll work it out. You always do.*

The confidence the leopard had in him settled him. He was always the one to figure out how to keep the peace. How to get things done. He was given the job of forming a new pipeline through several territories in order to have access to each of those territories. The goal was to find the worst of the mobsters and take over their territories. It would have to be done slowly and systematically, hitting shipments and their books, siphoning money from them, shutting down the businesses that laundered their money and making them weak before the big strike. Once the boss was killed, it left the territory wide open, so they could place one of their allies in the position. It was his job and he excelled at planning it.

Sitting in front of his computer, he opened the file on the Bogomolov family. They were known for being ruthless. They killed entire families in retaliation for the slightest misdeed. Now that he knew what he was looking for, he went back, trying to find a reference to Sonia's father. It took him a while to find it.

They'd had the information on Sonia all along. It was in the enormous file the investigators had collected on the family. If he'd thought to do a name search for Sonia Lopez in that file, he would have found it. It had been impossible to read the entire thing before his meeting, so he and Drake had chosen to concentrate on Nikita Bogomolov as head of the family and the crimes they'd committed in Miami.

Roberto Lopez, originally from Cuba, had been a low-level runner for the Bogomolov family. His wife, Valeria, had had one child, Sonia. Roberto had been found dead when Sonia was twelve, obviously tortured and partially burned. He'd died hard and he'd been put on display for all to see, a common practice to show others what happened if they were disloyal or stole from the Bogomolov family. Strangely, his wife and child had been spared.

Valeria had worked in the Bogomolov home as a housekeeper. She'd worked for them for five years before being diagnosed with cancer. She'd lived in the guesthouse on the Bogomolov property with her daughter, and once she was ill, it had been the Russian family who took care of all her bills and brought in nurses to attend her around the clock until she died.

Little was known about the daughter, Sonia. *His* Sonia. There were pictures of her at her mother's funeral, with Sasha Bogomolov, his arm around her. He studied every picture carefully. The man's body language screamed protective. Two photographs caught him looking down at her. Both showed what appeared to be genuine emotion. If Joshua had seen them together, he would have sworn he was looking at a man in love.

Still, there was no marriage certificate to be found. He sent out a quick message to the investigative team to search every public record for that certificate. There was little on Sonia after that. Sasha Bogomolov had been seen at night-clubs, but without Sonia. Sonia had been home, thinking she was married to the man while he was out wining and dining with his friends and business acquaintances.

Joshua sank back in his chair and stared at the evidence. Sonia had never gone out with him because she hadn't known about going out. She didn't dress up and go to dinner. She didn't go dancing out in public. She danced on her ve-randah. She'd been in the Bogomolov home from the time she was twelve. She'd grown up there. She'd trusted them. They'd been family to her. She'd eaten at their table, swam in their pool, laughed and cried with them—but she hadn't gone out in public with them. Why?

She'd been barely eighteen when her mother died. Sasha had been thirty-three. He'd supposedly married her. She'd lived with him in the home after that. She'd been a prisoner in a gilded cage, she just hadn't realized it. He couldn't imagine the betrayal, overhearing the man she believed in telling his father she wasn't married to him, it had all been a sham. The man who was supposed to love her agreeing to murder her. The pain of that. How had she survived?

She had to have figured out from the conversation that Nikita had ordered her father's murder. He'd slept with her mother and then dismissed both women as trash one got rid of. Sasha had agreed. Joshua groaned, thinking how that had to have made Sonia feel. She'd been so young and had already suffered too many losses.

Joshua went back to studying the photographs of Sonia's supposed husband. What if he had loved her? What if he'd tried to keep her safe, even from his father? There was a reason Valeria and Sonia hadn't been killed when Roberto had died. There was a reason Sonia had been kept out of the public eye. Even the lack of a marriage certificate might have been a protection. Had Sasha known his father wanted to kill the women and he'd found a way to save them?

Joshua rubbed his eyes. He sometimes got headaches. Migraines. He detested them and tried never to give in to them. He believed a man should be able to overcome all physical ailments and get the job done no matter what. He hated that sometimes it was impossible. He could take a bullet—and he'd taken more than one—but a headache? No, that got to him.

He had blocked out most of the early years of his life deliberately. He hadn't wanted to remember his grandfather, but he could hear his voice calling his father a sniveling baby for lying in bed in the dark because of a headache. Real men didn't acknowledge headaches.

He forced his eyes to focus on the screen. Sonia looked so young and grief-stricken in the photographs taken at her mother's service. She had been young. She still was. She'd never had the chance for a real courtship. She'd never had a chance at all. He understood better why she didn't trust him with her story.

"You loved her, didn't you?" he murmured aloud. "You bastard. You loved her, and you didn't have the balls to kill the son of a bitch who wanted her dead." Nikita Bogomolov had known his son loved Sonia and hadn't wanted his son's loyalty divided. One didn't fall in love with their woman. They got a son, or sons, and then they murdered her, preferably in a gruesome way to show their boys the *bratya* was their first loyalty.

The Bogomolovs were leopards, and they were every bit as cruel and ruthless as the lair Alonzo had come from. He had to find the connection between the two families. If this was a lair out of Russia, chances were, they were in some way related to Alonzo. He texted Alonzo, rubbing at his temples. His stomach was beginning to react to the pain. He was seeing spots. He'd have to darken the room and lie down for a few minutes.

Cursing, he waited for Alonzo's answer. It came a few minutes later. Maira Amurov had been given to Nikita Bogomolov. Maira had one son, Sasha, and then she'd been killed when she gave birth to a second child. Murdered by her own husband. That wasn't known, of course. To the outside world, she'd died in childbirth. The little girl hadn't survived either. Alonzo said Nikita had beaten Maira to death when the child wasn't another boy.

Joshua stood abruptly, his desk chair rolling back as he paced across the room. How had Alonzo, his brother and cousins managed to stay sane in such an environment? Husbands murdering their wives, often right in front of their children? A man killing his newborn daughter?

Joshua pulled the heavy drapes to block out the sunlight. The darkness was a bit of a relief, but he needed medication. His grandfather had been like those men. Depraved. Vile. He would have been the type of man to kill his woman without a thought. Joshua hated the idea of Sonia growing up in a house with a man like that. Joshua had always thought his grandfather was the worst of the leopards, had every bad trait there was, but Nikita was just as vile. Not just Nikita, but Alonzo's uncles and father.

He took the medication the doctor had prescribed. Drake's doctor. The man was leopard and a highly skilled surgeon, yet he'd taken the time to figure out medication that would help a migraine. How did some men turn out like the Doc and Drake and others like Nikita and his own grandfather? That ran in his genes. It ran in Alonzo's genes, and Joshua had worried for his cousin, Evangeline. He'd been so certain he wouldn't find a mate of his own that he hadn't worried as much about his own genetic code. Now he had to worry that another woman he cared for, Sonia, was once again mixed up in a lair where the leader was insane.

Cursing, he stretched out on the bed, wishing she was there with him. Her fingers in his hair. He loved when she did that—and she did it often. Little caresses that massaged his scalp and made him feel loved. Her touch was always gentle after they made love. Sex with her was wild and rough, but afterward, he was always tender, and she was so gentle and caring that sometimes he almost couldn't bear it.

She had been hurt so deeply by the Bogomolov family, just the way his mother had been hurt by the Tregre family. How did she recover from that? How did she trust again? Especially when he had to tell her that he'd taken over Rafe Cordeau's territory and he was involved with the Bogomolov family. More, he had to tell her that Nikita knew she was alive.

He took out his phone and stared down at it for a long time before he texted her. **Where are you?**

It took a moment before she replied. He knew she didn't like him tracking her. **Hasn't Kai reported in?**

**Baby.** He sent her a one-word reprimand.

**Still at Jerry's going over this enormous list of supplies, trying to trim it down.**

**I need to see you tonight.**

Again, there was a brief pause. **Is there something wrong? Are you all right?**

She had a sixth sense, he knew she did, at least when it came to him.

**Nothing big. Stupid headache.** That was hard to admit to her, but if they were going to live together she had to know he wasn't always going to be manly. **Nothing a dark room and a little bit of meds won't cure.** And Sonia's fingers massaging his scalp.

**Joshua, do you need me? Migraines are the worst. My dad used to get them. My mother showed me how to massage his temples for him. It helped. I can come over after I'm done here.**

I told Molly I'd drop by her house before I left town because she wanted me to look at some odd wormhole or something like that she thinks is in her bedroom. She's afraid her entire house is being eaten by woodworms. I can put that off.

He studied the text for a long time, happiness bursting through him. Right away. She'd change her plans to get to him right away. He hadn't thought she would ever do that. Sonia seemed so elusive, except when they had sex. Every other time she was just out of reach.

I want to take you dancing. And out to dinner. I want to have a barbecue with you and your friends. I want to show you off, let everyone know you're mine.

Again, he got that long pause, as if she was trying to figure out why he said those things to her. She didn't know he had a file on the Bogomolovs or that she was in it. She didn't know his investigators were digging up everything they could find on Sonia Lopez and her family.

Joshua, I'm coming over.

He needed a little time for his headache to ease before he saw her and told her everything. He would need all his wits about him to convince her to stay with him. He texted Gray to meet Kai in town and help watch over her. Then he turned his attention to Sonia.

No, babe, go to Molly's and ease her mind. She doesn't have it easy. She wouldn't have asked if she didn't need you. I just have a headache. I took meds and it will go away soon. We'll have dinner tonight, my house. I'll have a chef in. Or we can go to a restaurant if you prefer. Whatever you'd like.

You'll have a chef in? Just like that?

And candles. You like candles. They're all over your house. You never come here.

You know why. I'm working there.

Today you've been off work. I want the world to know you're mine. We can start with Evan and the others.

Ha. Ha. Ha. I'm pretty sure they already know.

He liked that she didn't object to him calling her his.

Go look at Molly's wormhole and tell her it isn't a wood-eating worm, even if it is. She'll never stay home and she'll want to come over to your house and if you won't come here, I have to be there. I want you with me tonight. Got that?

Got it. You rest. I'll see you tonight and you can tell me all about your meeting.

His meeting. With Nikita Bogomolov, the man who had tried to kill her. He closed his eyes, wondering how that was going to go over.

# 9

MOLLY'S house was on a quiet street, tucked back into a cul-de-sac edging the outskirts of town. The river and swamplands were just a scant half mile away in the distance, across a field from her backyard. The house was small, but the yards surrounding it were extensive and beautifully land-scaped. She worked in them all the time.

Her front porch was large, like many of the verandahs in the neighborhood. She had a two-person covered swing and one egg-shaped basket chair that dangled on a chain from the ceiling. It was a woman's home. First her grandmother and then Molly lived in it and the stamps of the two women were clear. The house was painted a soft, barely there green with lacy white trim around the windows. The cushions in the swing and egg basket chair were green-and-white striped.

"I sit here every single night," Molly confided as she turned the key in the lock. "It's my favorite thing to do."

"I almost always sit on my back porch," Sonia said. "It

faces the swamp, and I love to listen to the frogs and swamp cicadas. It's just so beautiful."

"All I could think about if I owned your property was a big alligator sneaking up on me. Or biting insects." Molly gave a delicate shudder. "Mosquitoes."

"They don't bother me," Sonia admitted. "I think I give off some kind of chemical that repels them. I guess that's why I don't mind going out day or night in the swamp. I don't have the bug problem a lot of other people do."

"I wish I had that repellent." Molly pushed open the door, hurried inside and punched in the code to disarm the alarm.

"It's because you're so sweet, Molly," Sonia said. "Even insects know it."

Molly burst out laughing. "That sounds like such a line. I would expect Bastien to say something like that."

"He might, but like me, he'd mean it. You really are sweet. I don't understand how your parents could throw you under the bus for money."

"They both have addiction problems. They'd do just about anything for money. They grew up with it, were given everything and never held accountable, and the two of them were toxic for each other. It started in high school. They were in and out of trouble then, and their parents bailed them out and paid people off every single time. My grandmother really regretted how she raised my mother."

"How were you raised? You said you had a lot of money at one time." Sonia followed her into the kitchen.

The house was cozy. One story. The great room was larger than the other rooms, but far smaller than Sonia's living room. It was painted in pastels, and somewhere, Molly had found a rug of the softest wool, patterned with soft blues, golds and creams. It took up most of the floor, giving a room that might have been cool a rich warmth.

Molly shrugged. "My mother started taking drugs after she had me in order to get thin again. She really blamed me for her weight problems. By the time I was four, they both were into drugs so heavily, I don't remember any other way of life. They liked going out and were gone more than they were home."

"That's awful," Sonia said, thinking about how wonderful her mother had been to her.

The formal dining room, right off the kitchen, was very small, holding a four-person gleaming oak table and chairs. A single chandelier hung over the center of the table. Dark wood made up the sideboards and cabinets.

"Maybe, but I didn't realize it because I didn't know anything else," Molly said, her voice matter-of-fact. "I think there are a lot of kids growing up the way I did."

Sonia had to agree with her, but it didn't make it right. Her father had been murdered and her mother forced to do unthinkable things by the very man who had ordered her husband's murder. Through it all, her mother had made her life wonderful.

Molly's kitchen was small, but very efficiently built. There was a breakfast nook in the corner by the windows, so one could look out as they drank their morning coffee. Molly opened the fridge and pulled out a large pitcher of strawberry lemonade. "I made this before I left the house. It should be ice-cold."

Strawberry lemonade was a weakness. Sonia nodded. "Love some. We'll have to sit for a while before I tackle the woodworm thing."

"Ha. Ha. Ha. There are holes, like some horrible creatures bored through my walls. I've been on an extensive wall search and I marked every hole I found," Molly said, filling two tall glasses with ice and then pouring the lemonade. "I counted seven of them." She handed one glass to Sonia. "Two in my bedroom. Two in the great room. One in my dining room and two in the kitchen."

"The worms have managed to bore a hole through the kitchen wall too?" Sonia tried not to laugh. "*All* the way through?"

Molly nodded solemnly. "I noticed the holes because there were tiny bits of sawdust on the floor. That's how I found all of them."

"Sawdust?" Sonia couldn't help the frown. Joshua had told her she didn't have a poker face. She put down the glass. "Show me. I want to see the wood shavings."

"I threw them away. It just looked like sawdust to me. Why? What's wrong?"

"Nothing. I thought you were a little paranoid, but if you saw sawdust at every site, that means whatever is boring a hole through the wood is on the outside to begin with. It's weird that there would only be one or two holes in each of the rooms. No holes in the bathroom wall? Show me the two in here."

Sonia had a bad feeling. The house was made of cedar. It wasn't very likely that there would be an infestation of bugs. More, they would be grouped in one or two rooms, not spread through the house like that. She went through the list of bugs in her head. There were a couple of types of beetles, termites, carpenter ants, certainly old home borers . . . She frowned. She hadn't seen any evidence outside on the porch of any destruction by insects. She'd been there to give an estimate on redoing the garage and had looked at the wood. It was something she couldn't help.

One or two holes in different rooms? Sawdust on the floor, on the inside? She didn't like that. She followed Molly to the side of the kitchen away from the street, facing the backyard. Molly pointed to a place about two feet from the floor. Sonia crouched down to inspect it. Sure enough, there was a very small hole, perfectly round. She stared at it for a few minutes, trying to puzzle it out in her head. It looked like a hole a 5/8ths of an inch drill bit might make. Maybe a little larger, but definitely a hole that was drilled by a tool, not a bug.

"Show me the other one in here." She looked around the kitchen, trying to see the line of sight one would have from the outside, if they could see anything through such a small hole. It might afford them a view of the breakfast nook, depending on what was outside.

The second hole was in the front of the house. It was a little higher, maybe three feet up, and this one also looked drilled, not chewed. It was in line with the sink and cutting boards where Molly worked.

"I'd like to look in your bedroom," Sonia said.

"What is it?" Molly asked. "Do you think the walls are riddled with bugs? I've heard of bees making their nests inside walls and people having to move." She led the way down the narrow hall to her bedroom.

"It's definitely not bees, Molly."

The bedroom was about the same size as the kitchen. The bed was a four-poster, in antique seafoam. The duvet was white lace as were the curtains. The dresser and vanity were scrolled wood in antique seafoam. A woman's room. Sonia thought it was beautiful and classy, just like Molly. The wall separating the interior from the outside was the only wall that might have the "wormhole" on it. The other three were all interior walls.

"I checked that wall yesterday," Molly said. "If I'd found anything, I wouldn't have slept in my bed."

Sonia saw the telltale pile of sawdust. The hole faced the bed. She touched the hole with the tip of her finger. It felt like a hole one might drill through wood. She crouched low to examine it, shining the light from the small flashlight she carried on her keychain.

"Do you get dressed in here? In your bedroom?"

Molly sank down onto her bed. "It isn't worms, is it?"

"There's something inside the wood. I'm going outside to look."

"What do you think it is, Sonia? Has Blake found me? Is that what you think?"

"I don't know yet. I'll be right back." She hurried outside and sprinted around to the side of the house, her heart beating wildly in her throat.

On the outside, she found the entry point. Using her flash-light, she located the thin tab and pulled. A tiny, wireless camera fell into her waiting hand. She smelled Kai and Gray before they got to her and whirled around to face them, the camera in her palm.

"What the hell?" Kai said. "Where does that lead?"

"Molly's bedroom."

"How many?" Gray spat the question at her, already striding around the house, using his leopard's ability to smell and his visual acuity to find the other cameras.

She followed him. "At least seven more. She undresses in that room, Gray."

Kai had circled around the house in the other direction. In the end, they found nine cameras. Molly came out onto her porch and watched them, her knuckles jammed in her mouth and tears running down her face.

"It's him, Sonia. Blake. He's found me. I should have known not to come here. It isn't like I had tons of money, and I don't have much now to be able to pick up and leave. What am I going to do?"

Sonia put her arm around Molly's waist. "You can stay at my place while we figure out what to do."

"I don't sleep with clothes on," Molly whispered. "They have recordings of me without clothes and—" She broke off, looking horrified. "Sonia." She began to sob.

Sonia knew exactly what she meant. She was alone a lot and needed sex. To have someone violate one's home and record every private moment, that wasn't right. "Pack a bag and let's get out of here. We can talk at my house."

A dark-colored SUV pulled up to the curb and Bastien Foret slid out. He walked toward them; his sharp gaze took in the group on the porch, touched Molly's tears and then dropped to the two men. Both slid the cameras into their pockets as he approached.

"Molly? Are you all right?" It was a demand, spoken in a low tone of complete authority.

Molly dropped her face into her hands and cried louder.

Bastien moved right past Kai and Gray to pull her away from Sonia and into his arms. "Someone better tell me what's going on here. And I mean right now." There was steel in his voice.

Kai and Gray separated. It was a subtle movement, but it put them to either side of the detective.

Bastien narrowed his gaze on Sonia, not in the least intimidated. "Tell me."

"Molly?" she asked. She wasn't going to tell Molly's story, not without permission. She had no idea if Molly had confided anything at all to the sheriff.

Molly nodded, her fists curling in Bastien's shirt, her face pressed tightly against his chest.

"I hope that means it's okay to fill him in," Sonia said, giving her a second chance to protest.

Molly just nodded her head again. Bastien tightened his hold on her. Sonia noticed he did that with one arm—the other was close to his weapon.

"Molly was held prisoner by a man for weeks. He beat her, raped her, broke bones and threatened to kill her. Unfortunately, the man has money, and he's connected to law enforcement. Her family wants money to feed their addictions, so the first time she got away from him, they sold her out. When she got away again, she came here to hide. We think he's found her."

Bastien's face was a mask of fury, and Sonia stepped closer to Kai without thinking. "You didn't think to tell me this sooner?"

"I couldn't break her confidence. She was terrified you'd believe him because he has that connection to law enforcement. He's a district attorney. Apparently, he knows everyone in his hometown. The cops are on his side. Molly was terrified of being sent back there. She thought he might put out a BOLO on her and you'd arrest her."

Bastien ran his hand down Molly's hair. "Honey, how

could you think I'd do that without talking to you? You have to know I would have believed you."

"We found these," Gray said, pulling the tiny cameras out of his pocket. "Someone drilled holes in her house and stuffed these into the walls so they could record her every movement. Foret, they recorded her in her bedroom."

Their eyes met over Molly's head, Bastien's betraying his fury for one moment.

"There has to be a remote around here somewhere to collect the data." Gray glanced around the neighborhood.

"Open field, up to five hundred feet, but that's pushing it," Kai said, looking toward the field behind Molly's house.

"Or one of the houses across the street. A neighbor's house, or the field," Gray suggested. "I'll take a look around."

"I can take her to my house to be safe while you all look," Sonia offered. "I don't want her here for all this."

"That's a good idea," Bastien said. He peeled Molly from his chest, one hand catching her chin so he could look into her tear-drenched face.

Sonia wasn't at all surprised to see that Molly looked beautiful even after crying her heart out. If Sonia had done that, she would have had a red, splotchy face, swollen eyes and nose and even her mouth would have been puffy, because when she cried, the biggest puffer fish in the world had nothing on her. She swelled up like a balloon and turned red like a boiled lobster.

"You can't go alone, Sonia," Kai said. "I'll have to go with you."

She shook her head. "You can come the moment you find what you're looking for."

"I have to go with you," he repeated.

Bastien frowned at her. "Damn it, Sonia. I had a bad feeling about you too. You can tell me your story later. Go, and take Molly with you."

Sonia ignored Kai. She wasn't going to argue in front of a cop and get him any more curious than he already was.

She caught Molly by the hand. "Come on, honey, let's go pack you a bag."

Molly shook her head. "I don't want to go in there."

Sonia understood. She hadn't wanted to enter the Bogomolov home once she knew her husband had planned to murder her. "I'll get you a few things. You need any meds? Something along those lines?"

Molly shook her head again and then sank onto the porch swing. Kai hesitated and then walked out toward the left side of the house, toward the nearest neighbors. Gray had gone around to the back to cover the field. Sonia knew both men were utilizing their leopards' abilities to help them. Bastien went straight toward an abandoned house two houses down and across the street.

"There's a bag under my bed. I'm sorry for being such a baby," Molly said.

"No worries. I'll get everything you need." She hurried inside, dragged the bag from under the bed, managed to find underwear, jeans and shirts, raced into the bathroom, collected makeup, toothbrush, hair tools and found birth control pills. She added them, although it looked as if Molly hadn't started them yet.

She found a pretty dress hanging in the closet, rolled it and added it and then raced back outside. "Let's go." She held out her hand. "We can get you settled, and I'll put on coffee and something for the boys to have. It will be done by the time Kai gets there."

"Are you certain he didn't mean he had to ride in the car with us?" Molly asked. She looked around her, fear on her face.

"They always come right behind me," Sonia said. She whistled and when Kai turned his head, she pointed to her truck.

He nodded and had started back when Gray came up to him. The two conferred. Sonia and Molly hurried to her truck and got in.

"Thank you for finding the cameras," Molly said in a low voice. "I haven't had a friend like you ever."

"You found them," Sonia pointed out. She glanced at Molly. "I've never had a friend like you either. I think we've both gone through similar situations. My husband tried to kill me, your boyfriend tried to kill you. We're both really, really bad at picking men. You're involved in a relationship with law enforcement again. I'm involved with a man who looks like he should carry a neon sign that flashes *danger, danger, danger.*"

Molly's smile was a little wobbly, but it managed to make her face look like the sun had just come out to shine. "I'm not in a relationship with Bastien Foret."

"I think you are. I think *he* thinks you are. I think the town might think you are."

Molly's soft laughter filled the cab of the truck. "You're so crazy." She twisted her fingers together in her lap, her smile fading away. "I'm so sorry you got dragged into this."

Sonia shook her head. "Don't say that. You haven't dragged me anywhere I haven't been. Actually, I've been in worse. My father worked for the Russian mob. He wasn't Russian, so he was very low level. He was a carpenter with a gambling addiction. To cover the gambling, he took jobs for the mob. *Papi* taught me most of what I know about carpentry. He even allowed me to set dynamite charges when he moved rocks and land from plots to build."

She glanced at Molly to see how she was taking the truth. She hadn't allowed herself to think about what her father had set in motion all those years earlier. He'd created a debt that had had to be paid. They were lucky Nikita Bogomolov chose to keep them alive rather than kill them along with her father.

"Keep going," Molly said quietly.

Sonia sighed. The pressure in her chest was painful. She felt Gatita rising to comfort her. "He stole from the mob. That's never a good thing. It was a lot of money and they made an example of him. Then they went to *Mami* and demanded that the two of us work off the debt. I thought, at first, they were good to us. Much later, after my mother died, I found out that my father-in-law forced *mi madre* to sleep with him. She cleaned his house and apparently had sex with him. We lived in the guesthouse on their property. I helped her take care of the house, but she was careful not to let me see what was really going on."

"I'm so sorry," Molly whispered. "That must have been terrible for you."

"Sasha, his son, was fifteen years older than me. He was always looking out for me. Always taking care of me. The entire time we worked for his father, he treated me like a younger sister. I loved him. I really loved him. Then my mother got sick and everything changed. I was so scared. For her. For me. For us. Sasha took care of every detail. The nurses she needed around the clock. The bills. He got her the best care. I loved him for that. When I think about those times, I still do. That man. The one who was so good to my mother."

"Of course you loved him," Molly said. "I love that he did that for you."

"I was so lost and he was so strong. He married me to protect me, he said. I knew I loved him, maybe not the way a woman loves a man, but he was so good, I knew in time I'd feel that for him as well. For almost two years we were together. He didn't like me going anywhere because he said he had enemies. When I did go, I had bodyguards with me." Which was why she resented Kai and Gray looking after her every minute. "I didn't have friends. I didn't even realize just how isolated I was until I overheard that conversation and I knew they were planning on killing me."

"The bastards. They were your family." Molly glared out the windshield. "That is one sick, twisted man. Or men. Both were twisted. Did you know they were mafia?"

"No. Everyone kept that from me. When my father was

murdered, I had no idea it had anything to do with them. When *mi madre* took me to live with them, I still didn't know. There were men with guns, but I thought they were there because we'd been threatened. Later, Sasha told me that their family was threatened all the time because they were wealthy Russians. I believed him. I believed everything he ever told me. His father hired a tutor for me and I was homeschooled. Again, I was told it was for my safety."

She parked the truck in her driveway and both women slid out of the cab. She caught up Molly's bag from the bed. "You can see why I'm reluctant to start another relationship. It's kind of hard to believe what he says."

Molly nodded. "It's very understandable. Have you told Joshua?"

Sonia unlocked the door and pushed it open, stepping back to allow Molly to precede her inside. "No. I was afraid if I told either of you, something bad could happen to you if they found me. I think I'm safe, but I don't know for certain. Still, I know I have to tell him. It isn't something you just walk up to a man and say."

Molly's soft laughter somehow made that terrible pressure in Sonia's chest disappear. "Hey, babe," she said. "I forgot to tell you. I may or may not be married to a Russian mobster. He's out to kill me and he favors bombs and torture. Still, I'm really cute so I'm the girl for you." She made a face. "He's going to run for the hills, and that's the best-case scenario."

Molly's laughter, which had swelled in volume, ended abruptly. "What's the worst?"

Sonia sobered instantly, her heart accelerating. "He'll sell the information of my whereabouts to my father-in-law. They'd pay a lot of money to find me." She glanced at Molly and then at the floor, a little ashamed that she'd been afraid to tell her for the same reason.

"Sonia," Molly said softly. "I was afraid to tell you or

anyone else anything. I'm still freaked out that Bastien knows. And those two men. Your bodyguards."

Sonia winced. "Don't call them that. They're not mine anyway. They're part of a security team Joshua runs. I don't know why he insists on having them follow me around, but in this case, it was a good thing. They know what they're doing when it comes to this kind of problem. They've been all over the world taking back kidnap victims. I've overheard Kai and Gray talking and they definitely aren't lying. They've done it. They also talk about Joshua and how he's so good at slipping into camps unseen and gathering the information needed to get hostages out. If they can do this, surely they can handle Blake Garritson."

"Maybe Joshua suspects you're in danger, just the way Bastien suspected with me. I tried not to look at him because he's a cop and he's all wrong for me, but he kept coming around. Now I realize, it was all about his gut, his detective instincts that made him look interested."

"Yeah, that was it," Sonia said, smirking at Molly as she closed the door and locked it, just to be safe. Kai would be there soon, and she had Gatita to warn her, but she didn't want to take any chances with Molly's life. "Bastien Foret was willing to take on both Kai and Gray just because you were crying."

Molly put her hand to her face. "Is my mascara running? Why do I always look awful when that man comes around?"

"As if you could ever look awful. I was thinking of doing you in myself when I saw you looking hot while you were crying. You're like one of those women on a soap opera, looking even prettier with tears in your eyes."

Molly laughed, the sound surprising both of them. Some of the fear faded from her face. "Bastien is really a good guy, don't you think? He didn't sound like he'd turn me over to Blake without first investigating and finding out what really happened."

"Is there evidence of your broken ribs and arm?"

"X-rays were taken at his doctor friend's clinic. We went there after hours. After that the doctor would come to the house."

"Were you ever alone with the doctor? Did you try to talk to him?"

"Blake was always in the room. He insisted on being with us. I know he was paying his friend, but the doctor was angry with him. He might testify, although it would mean his license. I think there was more than money between the two of them."

"Do you know if Blake was seeing someone before you? You couldn't have been his first girlfriend." She carried Molly's bag into the guest room. "Sorry about the mess. I haven't had time or the money to fix these rooms. There's heat, though, and the bed is nice. Just keep your eyes closed and don't look at the walls." Sonia scowled, looking down at the floor. "This room really needs work."

"So does your roof. This is fine. I feel safe here with you, especially if Joshua has a couple of his hotshot security team members watching over you."

Sonia rolled her eyes. "I think he assigns them jobs to keep them from being bored. Watching me go to work and come home must be super-exciting after rescuing kidnap victims and hostages in exotic places. I think if they don't get a legitimate job soon, there's going to be a rebellion."

"Does that mean if they do get a job, Joshua leaves the country?" Molly asked uneasily.

Sonia hadn't thought about that. She didn't like the idea of Joshua leaving, especially if his job put him in danger, but on the other hand, it might be the perfect solution. If he left, she wouldn't have to tell him about the Bogomolov crime family and how she might just be married to one of them.

"I hadn't thought of that," she said, pushing open the door to the guest bathroom. "Plumbing works, so toilet and shower are fine, but again, it isn't very nice." It wasn't. The tile was cracked and broken. The walls were peeling, faded paper and paint.

"It will work."

"I guess it's better than camping," Sonia conceded. "Come on, let's get something to drink. I don't have your strawberry lemonade—which, by the way, kicked ass—but I've got plain lemonade."

"Sounds perfect," Molly said. "We can sit out on your upstairs balcony so the alligators can't eat us and listen to the sounds of the swamp. I could use a little relaxation." She followed her to the kitchen.

Sonia loved her kitchen. She didn't have to be embarrassed by it. Everything was perfect. "I'm in charge of remodeling Joshua's kitchen. Well, his entire house and the houses on the property," she said. She pulled open her refrigerator, unable to keep the smile from her face. "It's my dream job. Seriously, Molly, the perfect job someone like me dreams of for a lifetime and never gets because I don't have the right credentials. That old plantation home is so beautiful and unique. The builder did things no one else building in this area during that time period did. All the tiny little details, the exquisite moldings and carvings, the floors, I could go on and on."

She poured them both a tall glass of lemonade, with plenty of ice. "I love what I do, and I never thought I'd get such a chance."

"The bonus is, the owner just happens to be gorgeous."

"That isn't a bonus." Sonia led the way up the stairs. "I haven't made up my mind what to do with him."

"You seem to do just fine with him," Molly teased.

Sonia forced the blush back down. "That part is easy. It's all the rest of it that's difficult. Remember the may-or-may-not-be-married thing? The Russian mob would come in force if they knew I was still alive. Joshua isn't the type of man to back down, and no one takes on the Russian mob. They're violent. They kill entire families. If you look at what they normally do, my mother and I were very lucky."

Molly gave a little sniff of disdain. "Lucky? Those men were assholes. The worst kind of human being, pretending to love you, to be family and then turning on you. Even if you were married to one of them, he doesn't deserve you, and I'm pretty certain the fact that he tried to kill you cancels out the marriage."

She stopped in the middle of the studio and looked around her at the paintings. "These are beautiful, Sonia." She moved closer to study the canvas Sonia hadn't quite finished. "You make everything come to life. I could fall in love with the swamp just looking at this painting."

"Thank you, Molly, that's an amazing compliment."

"It's true, though. I can't believe you've got such a talent. Bastien is right, these paintings belong in a gallery."

"Russian mob looking for me, remember?" Sonia repeated and opened the French doors to the outside verandah. "Come sit down. I at least have decent chairs out here." She waved Molly toward the most comfortable seating she had.

This was her favorite spot. The studio had a beautiful view of the swamp and river. Cranes waded through the thick duckweed floating in the water. The knobby knees of the cypress trees rose around the larger trees just at the shoreline or in the shallower waters. The colors were vivid, shades of green, explosions of pink, purple and yellow where flowers fought for space in the heavier bushes and brush. Leaves took on a silvery glint or yellow and gold so that colors seemed to vie for space.

Birds circled overhead and flitted from branch to branch. Squirrels ran along the twisted limbs and chattered to one another. Alligators bellowed. Boars grunted. Always the vibrations of the cicada filled the air. Frogs called back and forth. Fish jumped from the water and landed with a splash. The occasional snake plopped from a tree branch into the river. Sonia couldn't imagine a more beautiful place. She knew it wasn't for everyone, and she was grateful it wasn't, otherwise it would be gone, overrun by people.

"Have you noticed the way the tree branches lead straight to your balconies? That big thick one twists down to your lower verandah and this huge, gnarly one nearly touches this balcony. The branches are so big that anyone or anything could walk right on them," Molly observed.

Sonia leaned on the railing, peering down at the trees as if studying the branches. It would be difficult not to see that, and Molly wasn't stupid. Sonia was an artist. She would have noticed the branches. She nodded, but kept her back to Molly. "I've been thinking about how best to paint them," she said. "There are quite a few really large trees in this swamp. Thick ones, with massive branches that reach from tree to tree. If I was going to build a treehouse, this would be the perfect place."

She turned to face Molly, her hips resting against the railing. "Have you ever looked at books with treehouses in them? There are beautiful homes. Actual homes."

"You're thinking of building a treehouse? Aren't there, um . . ." Molly frowned and took a sip of lemonade. "I think I've become so paranoid I can't enjoy anything, not even beautiful trees. Why are you able to carry on with your life and I'm such a terrible baby? I *cried* in front of Bastien. That's so awful. I can't imagine what he thinks."

"He thinks you're a beautiful, desirable woman with a madman chasing after you. He thinks you're human, Molly." Sonia turned back to stare out over the swamp. She needed that swamp to keep Gatita safe and happy. She *wasn't* human. She had no idea why or how she ended up a shifter, a woman with a leopard living inside her. She didn't know if her mother or father was a leopard, but she did know she wasn't human. There wouldn't be a human man in her future.

*You have a mate,* Gatita weighed in.

*I don't know how to tell him about Sasha. He would try to protect us and no one can take on the Russian mob and live—not even Donovan Security.* She sighed and pushed at the hair falling out of her haphazard ponytail.

"I'm really scared, Sonia," Molly confessed. "I don't think I'd survive if Blake found me again. I can't take pain very well. It hurt so much."

Sonia whirled back around, forgetting for a moment to keep Gatita's speed under control. "No one is going to get to you, Molly. *No one.* I'll protect you, I swear it."

"He could hurt you," Molly pointed out.

Sonia shook her head. "Since Sasha turned on me, I've made it my business to learn a few things in this last year." She was getting faster at shifting, although she hadn't figured out how to get out of her clothes as quickly as she would like. She was still working on that. "He's not going to get to you. Kai will be here any minute and then Gray and probably Bastien. Once Joshua knows you're in danger, which he probably already does because Kai and Gray tattle every chance they get, he'll come too. Most likely, because his security team is bored as hell, he'll bring them along and then . . ."

Molly burst out laughing. "We'd better start making food. Lots of food. If we have an army to feed, we can't be slackers in the cooking department."

"Wait. Are you saying I should have been offering Kai and Gray dinners this entire time?" Sonia asked, half serious.

"I would have. You did, at least, offer them coffee."

She hadn't. Not once. She'd been annoyed they were even around. "You're so much nicer than me."

"No, I'm not," Molly said. "It isn't like you've had a chance to figure out who you are and what you want to do, not when you were married at what? Eighteen?"

Sonia nodded. "I married him a month after my mother died. He wanted me to continue staying at his house. I just let him carry me while I was grieving. I didn't think about anything but how awful it was without her. I stayed within the grounds that first year. Sasha encouraged me to take the time, to let myself grieve. He was so good about it."

"He was keeping you prisoner."

"I didn't know that, though," Sonia pointed out. "I thought he was looking out for me. He even brought in a personal shopper when I needed new clothes."

"What happened when you wanted to leave the house?" Molly asked.

She shrugged. "Bodyguards. That's why I haven't been so thrilled with Kai and Gray. I don't like anyone watching me. It feels too much like him. Sasha. I thought, at the time, it was to protect me, but it was much more sinister than that."

*Sonia. They are here.*

For a moment Sonia thought Gatita meant Kai and Gray, but the feeling hit her hard. It didn't drift into her mind the way warnings could, this one flashed in bright red neon signs in her mind. *They* weren't Kai and Gray. *They* didn't mean Bastien. *They* meant Blake and his men.

# 10

SONIA put down her glass of lemonade and reached for Molly's hand to tug her up. When Molly flashed a smile and looked as if she were about to speak, Sonia shook her head. Instantly the smile faded, replaced by fear. No, not fear, terror. Sonia hated putting that look on her face. She indicated the French doors and put a finger to her lips. Molly nodded and went inside.

Sonia closed the doors as quietly as possible. "Someone's here," she whispered. "I don't think it's Kai. Whatever you do, stay in this room. You're on the upper floor and protected here. I'm going to take a look around." She pulled out her cell phone. "I programmed Bastien's number into my cell when he left his card the other day. I'm texting him to step on it, that there's possible trouble."

"How do you know? I didn't hear anything."

"I have excellent hearing, and I'm used to living here in

the swamp. I know every noise possible. Just hang in here. I'll be right back."

Molly caught her arm. "Blake is sick. He'll look charming and sweet, but if it's him, he's really mean."

She was willing to face mean for her friend. She also knew Kai would be there any minute and she had Joshua. She texted him as well. Possible trouble. Can you come? Might have weapons. She would never have done that if it had been Sasha or his father. In that moment, she made up her mind, Joshua wasn't getting anywhere near the mob. She could see the stark terror on Molly's face and guilt in her eyes that Sonia might be facing Blake instead of her. She wasn't going to feel the same way. She was never going to put Joshua in harm's way. His bodyguards had to go after this. If Sasha or his father killed either man, she wouldn't be able to live with herself.

"I have to go check the house. It's locked, but that doesn't mean someone can't get in. I'm just going to check. You stay here and wait for me."

"Do you have a gun?"

"Yes." She said it firmly. "I'm giving you my Glock. Have you used one?" She'd practiced until she was a very good shot.

"You might need it." Molly sank down onto the bed, the gun in her lap.

Sonia also could use a knife, and she pushed her favorite down into her boot. Without looking at Molly, she hurried out of the room, using her lightest step, knowing the house creaked. Certain floorboards would give her away if she stepped on them, so she was careful to avoid them.

She crept down the stairs, wishing it was dark out. The lighting in the house was dim, but she could see everything easily, which meant so could an intruder. When she moved to the archway leading to the great room, she saw a man seated in her best armchair. High back, wide seat and low, padded arms, the chair had been on sale. Even with the sale, it had been pricey, but she'd fallen in love.

She stepped into the room. "That's my chair you're sitting in."

The man turned his head to look at her, but he didn't get up. He wore a suit like he was born in it. He could easily have stepped off the cover of *GQ* magazine. His hair was short without one strand out of place. His shoes gleamed, Italian leather if she wasn't mistaken. He looked her up and down, his face a mask of utter contempt.

She wasn't tall and beautiful like Molly. That was his preference. He wanted his woman to be fashionably thin. She wasn't and never would be. She knew he wanted her to feel small and ugly and ashamed. He was handsome and knew it.

"I'd like you to leave my house. I've called the police."

"That won't do you any good," Blake Garritson said. "It's best if you call Molly down before there's trouble."

"There's already trouble." Sonia stepped out of the archway and moved to her left, putting her back to the wall. She doubted if anyone could sneak up behind her, but she didn't want to give them the opportunity.

*Gatita, make certain to listen for anyone on the stairs. Tell me when you know Joshua or Kai is here.*

*There are five more of them. They are outside the house. One is trying to climb the tree outside in the back.*

Her heart jumped. Of course a human could climb those trees. The trees were big and sturdy, the branches wide to accommodate a leopard.

*I could kill this one.*

*Then humans would hunt you forever. If necessary that's what we'll do, but only if we have no other choice.*

She waited, locking eyes with the intruder. He sat in her chair as if he owned the place. She knew he thought it shabby. He would have razed the house, torn it to the ground. He would never see the beauty of the old architecture.

"I don't understand Molly's choice of friends. She has

such poor taste," he said, shaking his head slowly as if he really were puzzled. "Fat, ugly women living in falling-down old mansions, pretending to be women of means. She's sunken to new lows."

She didn't even wince. She might not be beautiful, but she wasn't fat or ugly. She knew that. She was attractive enough that everywhere she went, men sat up and took notice. His opinion wasn't going to make her sit down and cry. She did, however, need to stall him.

"I take exception to you calling this house a falling-down old mansion."

"It's deplorable. It should have been condemned. Go get Molly. I don't have patience to deal with women of little intelligence, which, clearly, you are."

"And if I don't?"

He stood up and walked toward her. "Then you are going to be very, very sorry."

"Not just sorry. Very, *very* sorry? What's the difference?"

He swung at her face with his fist. He was fast, but Gatita was faster. Sonia managed to block the first blow, but the second connected with her face. It felt as if her cheek exploded. White-hot pain flashed through her body, making her feel nauseous. Gatita roared her anger, leaping toward the surface so fast and so ferociously that Sonia could barely contain her. It was nearly impossible to fight two battles on two different fronts, one external and the other internal.

She managed to block the next two punches. Blake was swinging fast at her, a flurry of punches low then high then low again. The second punch to get her clipped her chin, but just barely. Blake's eyes widened, and he was flung backward away from her. He hit the floor hard and roared, furious to find himself facing a blond giant of man.

Joshua was shirtless and barefoot. He wore only a pair of jeans, and she knew his leopard had come fast through the swamp. She didn't want to see the carnage outside, especially since Bastien would be arriving soon.

Joshua ignored Blake and tipped Sonia's face up. The sight of her red, swelling cheek sent a rage snaking through him. He slid the pad of his thumb gently over her cheek and then turned to face the man who had hit her. Was this the same man who had tried to kill her? He wasn't leopard, that was for certain. He wasn't Russian. Then who was he?

Blake was on his feet, stepping back to give himself room. He smoothed down the jacket of his expensive suit, his gaze jumping to the door as if he expected his men to come through it any minute.

"They're dead," Joshua said softly.

"Excuse me?"

"All of them. They're dead. The ones left behind at Molly's house were killed in a shootout between my men, a sheriff and your men. The ones you brought to my woman's house were caught trying to break in. Sadly, there are all kinds of animals in the swamp and your men ran right into them. They're dead."

Blake held up his hand when Joshua took a step toward him. "Wait a minute. You've got this all wrong. I'm just here for Molly. We thought she was held prisoner . . ."

"I can hear lies. I've been able to hear lies since I was a child." Joshua stepped in and hit the man, using the strength of his leopard. Bones crunched with a satisfying sound. He hit him three more times, just as hard. Cheek had been first. Chin second. Ribs on the right. Ribs on the left. He let the poor excuse for a human step back and pull a gun.

Blake's breath was coming in short, labored pants of distress. His eyes were wild as he fired off a round at Joshua. Joshua was already in motion, springing off the balls of his feet, using his leopard's ability to leap with blurring speed and force. The burn of the bullet caught him along his bicep, but didn't slow him down. He crashed into Blake, knocking the other man back several feet and to the floor. The gun went off again as Blake dropped it. Even as he was on the intruder, Joshua heard Sonia's breath hitch and his heart nearly stopped. He caught Blake's head in his hands and, staring down into his eyes, wrenched. He waited a heartbeat to be certain the man was dead, and then he slowly turned his head to look at Sonia.

She was sitting on the floor, back to the wall. Her eyes were wide with shock as her gaze met his. "That son of a bitch shot me."

Evan burst into the room just ahead of Bastien. Joshua ignored them and crouched beside Sonia. "Show me."

"It isn't bad." She lifted her hand and showed him the blood seeping across the denim along her thigh. "This is my favorite pair of jeans."

"Where's Molly?" Bastien demanded.

She pointed upstairs. "Thanks for coming, Joshua."

"You gave me a heart attack. Why didn't you annihilate him?"

"I was afraid if I used Gatita then Bastien or Molly would see or, even if they didn't, I couldn't explain the kill marks of a leopard. I don't want hunters coming here looking for cats."

She closed her eyes as Joshua ripped the material off her thigh to see that the bullet had skimmed along her skin. "I told you I was lucky." She touched his shoulder. "Evidently you were too." Blood ran down his arm.

"First aid kit, Sonia?" Evan asked.

She pointed vaguely toward the bathroom. She kept a kit in every bathroom. It was something her mother had always done and she followed that tradition.

"Are you feeling faint?" Joshua asked, his thumb once more skimming her cheek.

"No. Just tired. Really, Joshua, thanks for coming. I didn't know what to do. I would have had to use Gatita and I didn't want her to have to kill a human being."

"When Kai texted saying they were in a firefight, I was relieved to hear you'd gone ahead of him. Then your text came in and I came close to panicking. I didn't wait for the others, I just threw jeans in a pack and came. Evan and the others used a truck."

"The others?" Sonia looked around the room for the first time.

There were seven men in her home. She recognized the faces from seeing them when she was working at Joshua's estate, but she hadn't been formally introduced to all of them.

"Sonia?" Bastien was there. "You okay?" He dropped to his knee beside her, surveying the damage.

"He hit me a couple of times and then tried shooting us both. Joshua charged him." She brushed her fingers over Joshua's bloodstained sleeve. "I think he's dead, Bastien. That's a good thing for Molly, isn't it?"

"Yeah, honey, it is, but I don't want you saying anything more right now. I'm going to call an ambulance." He did so, his face grim.

"I don't need . . ."

"I have to call them to check both of you out. That doesn't mean you have to be transported. Let me do my job. You don't talk to anyone without a lawyer, do you understand?"

"Am I in trouble? Is Joshua? He broke into my house and tried to kill us."

"No, of course not. This is clearly self-defense. Still . . ." He broke off. "Tregre?"

"I've texted my lawyer. He'll be here any minute," Joshua assured.

Bastien stalked over to the body and crouched down, observing the damage done by Joshua's fists. He glanced over his shoulder and when Joshua started to speak, gave a slight shake of his head as other officers hurried in.

Joshua stayed close to Sonia, his back to the wall, his shoulder wedged close so she could lean on him. She closed her eyes and that scared him a little. He needed to be alone with her. He wanted their own doctor to look her over, not some paramedic, although that was just paranoia. Mostly he wanted her surrounded by a dozen guards armed with the latest in weapons.

He wasn't able to speak with Evan until the paramedics had stitched his shoulder and taken care of Sonia's thigh. They answered questions until his lawyer declared they were finished. Only then did he carry Sonia up the stairs. Molly sat in the rocking chair and when he carried Sonia into the room, she jumped up. Tears tracked down her face.

"I'm so sorry. I'm so very sorry, Sonia," she said. "Bastien said you'd been shot but it wasn't bad. How could it not be bad if you were shot?"

"They put a Band-Aid on it, that's how much it can't be bad," Sonia said.

Joshua set her in the rocking chair Molly had just vacated. "She's all right," he assured.

"You're shot too," Molly said, grabbing his bloody sleeve.

"That was also treated with a Band-Aid." Joshua tried grinning at her, but it was too late. A fresh flood of tears started.

"Need to talk to Evan, baby," Joshua said. "I'll be back in a few."

Sonia nodded, and he hurried back down the stairs to find Evan waiting. They went outside and the others followed in tight formation, enclosing the two so it was impossible to see them, let alone hear what they said.

"The bodies?"

"Took them deep in the swamp. Tonight, they'll go out to the ocean," Evan said. "No one's going to find them and if they do, they won't find a way to connect them to us. They were killed by a leopard."

"Is everything cleaned up outside?"

"Very little blood. You suffocated them or severed the spinal cord. You didn't rip the shit out of them. We're in the clear."

"The less said about those men to Sonia, the better."

"Number-one question they kept asking is, was he alone?"

Evan pointed out. "Foret has some suspicion that Garritson didn't travel without a big crew."

"Sonia never saw anyone other than Blake. Molly didn't see anybody. As far as they know, Blake came here alone. Sonia speculated to Bastien that Blake must have followed Molly and her home while his men fought with Bastien, Kai and Gray. It makes sense."

"That's what Bastien said to the other officers," Evan agreed.

"We're safe enough. Just double-check. I plan on taking Sonia back to the house with me. She won't like it and she'll probably throw a fit, but she's still coming home with me."

Evan grinned at him. "She'll use her friend as an excuse."

"I happen to know Foret is planning on taking Molly to his house. He told the other detective Molly was his girlfriend so he'd give his statement and turn over the case to someone else. He's well liked and has the reputation of a straight shooter. They believe his every word. He made it clear that Garritson had already terrorized Molly, that he'd stalked, kidnapped, raped and beaten her. I think it's fairly open and shut."

"Even when Garritson's family comes down here and refutes that charge?" Evan played devil's advocate.

"They may try, but more likely, they won't want the story to get out. They'll want to do damage control more than try clearing his name."

"If they're anything like him, they could send someone after Molly," Evan said.

Joshua nodded. "Bastien's making it clear that she's his. I think that's in his head, but if it isn't, we'll make certain he understands that's a possibility. People like Blake use contract killers to get back at the people who offend them. Blake was after Molly. He obsessed over her. I know what that's like. Can't eat. Can't sleep. Think about her night and day. Now I know the worst. Fuckin' Russian mob."

"You think it's really a good idea to bring her to the

house? The way that Russian was fixating on the painting, I'd be afraid he'd come back with an army to take it."

"He took pictures of it. He wanted to show his son. They'll be back. Both of them. Nikita and his son, Sasha. They're both coming back and they'll bring that army when they do."

"You'll need to inform Drake and come up with an alternate for the pipeline. We still need to have a route for distribution," Evan said. "More, how does this impact Alonzo, his brother and cousins and Evangeline?"

"I've already been thinking about that," he admitted. "I sent word we needed a meet immediately. They're setting it up."

"Right. At your house." Evan pointed out the obvious.

Joshua swore under his breath and glanced up toward the upper balcony. "She's still coming to my home, where we can watch over her. I'll just have to talk to her about everything."

"I don't think you have much of a choice," Evan agreed. "But when you do, give her some space to be upset. She has every right. She isn't going to like what you are, given who she was involved with."

Joshua hoped she didn't try to leave. He'd give her all the time and space she needed, as long as she didn't try to leave, not when the Russians knew she was alive.

MOLLY tucked a thin blanket over Sonia after helping her to the bed. "You're shivering."

"I think it's shock more than anything else. Blake was so full of himself. I wish I could say I'm not happy that he's dead, but he nearly killed Joshua and I think he would have tried to kill me if Joshua hadn't come." The intent had been there on his face. He had *wanted* to kill her to punish Molly. There were consequences to Molly for leaving, and that was her friends paying the ultimate price.

"I'm happy he's dead," Molly confessed. "Does that make me a bad person?"

"If it does, then we're both bad," Sonia said. "Kai was supposed to be right behind us, Molly. I wouldn't ever have exposed you to danger. I wasn't trying to get away from him. Right as we were leaving, Gray told him he'd found something. When they both started back toward the house where Gray thought the recorder was, Blake's men opened fire on them."

"Are you blaming yourself for what happened?" Molly's face paled. "You *saved* me. If you hadn't stopped by to see those wormholes for me, Blake would have taken me back with him. That was his intention. I would never have gotten away."

"Yes, you would have," Sonia said. "I would have gone looking for you. I would have known it was Garritson who took you and I would have found a way to get you back. Joshua would have helped." She smirked deliberately. "That is his forte. This time, instead of a bad boy, I chose someone like Bastien. We both maybe got good ones." She wasn't going to think about how he might be crazy enough to go after a Russian mobster for her. She was going to just let that go for the night and get through this one without any more drama.

"You're such a good friend." Molly had tears in her eyes. "Bastien wanted me to go home with him, but I'm going to stay here and take care of you instead."

"That's not necessary, Molly. I'm going to just go to sleep for a little while. I want you to go home with Bastien. I know you'll be safe with him. The fact that he declared in front of his partners that you were his girlfriend means something big."

"It means he's crazy," Molly said, but her face flushed and her eyes went bright. "He had to say something. He felt bad about not stopping Blake from recording me in my bedroom. The recordings were uploaded to a site for Blake to see. Bastien was very upset about that on my behalf. I think he just felt really bad and wanted to do something nice for me."

Sonia rolled her eyes. "Seriously? That doesn't even make sense. Bastien had no way to stop something he didn't know was going on and you know it. Stop being a chicken. You were the one telling me to take a chance on Joshua."

"Wow. And again, I have to say it: Joshua is hotter than hell, Sonia. Of course you have to take a chance on him. No shirt? Barefoot? He runs across the swamp or whatever he did to come to your aid because you texted him? How cool is that?"

"And there you go, changing the subject. Although I wouldn't mind talking about the no-shirt part for hours, because I have *lots* to say on the subject, we were discussing Bastien. I have a lot to say about him as well."

"You do?" Molly's voice had a little squeak in it.

"He ran right past a dead body to get to you, Molly. He didn't look at me with my bleeding thigh, or Joshua with his bleeding arm. He just demanded to know where you were and ran for the stairs to see for himself you were alive and well. I think, given the fact that he's considered a really good detective, that is saying a lot."

A small smile lit Molly's face. "He did, didn't he? That's sort of sweet."

"*Sort of?* The man has a career he loves and he just forgot all about it in order to make sure you were safe. That deserves something more than 'sweet,'" Sonia said decisively.

Molly's smile widened. "I agree, but going home with him? I wouldn't know what to do. It's been a long time and I get afraid very easily. What if I freak out on him because the wind rattles the window?"

"I guess he'll have to hold you even tighter than I expect he already will be doing." She reached for the pills Joshua had left on the end table. The aspirin would help, hopefully, with the pain. She sent a wry smile to Molly. "I'm not really all that stoic about being shot. It hurts like hell and it isn't more than a flesh wound."

"I overheard Bastien telling someone that you were lucky and that the bullet took off a chunk of skin. He said you might have a scar there."

Sonia frowned, giving her friend her best stern look. "You are not responsible in any way. Blake's responsible. He was an obsessed stalker." Her frown deepened. "I wonder if I can be considered a stalker. I think I'm a little obsessed with Joshua. At least with his cock." She peeked at Molly from beneath her lashes to see if she was beginning to laugh. "His abs too. I think about all that muscle a lot. And I like his hair. His eyes are way cool, and his mouth. Wow, his mouth. I'm *really* obsessed with his mouth. He does this thing with his tongue . . ."

"*Sonia, stop.*" Molly's laughter was genuine. She sank onto the end of the bed. "You are so wrong."

"His tongue is *so* right. That's what you need, girlfriend, a little tongue action."

"I can see myself asking for that. Oh, Bastien, by the way, I'm terrified of being alone with you, but do you think you could get busy with the tongue?" She erupted with more laughter.

Sonia was grateful for the silliness. Molly had been feeling needless guilt. "It would be rather awkward if you weren't alone with him and you asked him to get busy. If you're going in that direction, make certain it isn't in front of me. At least, not if Joshua isn't around. I'd be all jealous, and who wants to be jealous of their bestie getting a little action?"

Molly tossed one of the decorative pillows at her. "Stop."

"Not until you agree to go home with Bastien. You already have a bag packed, it isn't as if you'd have to go home."

"Fine. I'll do it. I'll be brave, but if I freak out and you hear me screaming all the way from his house, which I have no idea where it is, you have to come rescue me."

"That's a promise. I won't let you go until I have his address. His number is already programmed into my phone. He gave me his card that day he came to check on you."

"*Us.* He came to check on both of us."

"Girl, you spend your life in denial, but since you agreed to go with him, I'm skipping the lecture." Sonia leaned her head against the pillow. "Is this over? Will your family or his family do anything else to you?"

"I don't know," Molly admitted. "I'll be careful. I'm used to being careful."

"You've got me to watch out for you."

"Thanks, Sonia. By the way, I put your gun under the pillow when I heard Bastien coming up the stairs. I thought you probably didn't have a license for it."

"You'd be right. Thanks, honey. Are you going to go tell your man you're going home with him, because I think he plans to sleep downstairs if you stay."

Before Molly could answer, Evan's voice called up the stairs. "Your boss is here, Sonia. Can you come down?"

"He'd better not be referring to Joshua," Sonia whispered.

"I heard that," Joshua called. "And I *am* your boss. In this case, he's referring to Jerry. If you want to come down, I'll come up there and get you."

"How could he possibly hear that?" Molly asked. "You were whispering."

"Big ears," Sonia said in a loud voice. "I don't need you to help me walk," she added. She wasn't about to be carried like some little child in front of everyone. She threw back the blanket and swung her legs over to one side. Her thigh hurt, but it wasn't that bad. Her face hurt more. She could hear Jerry muttering something about "damned kids." There was genuine worry in his voice. She saw the same anxiety on Molly's face. She had friends. Good friends. She'd done that on her own.

Joshua padded in on bare feet, so silent she scented him but never heard him. His shaggy blond hair fell over his

forehead, drawing attention to his eyes. She could see his
leopard was staying close, watchful, the crystalline blue
giving the cat away. Fresh blood was seeping through the
sleeve.

She drew back before he could lift her. "You're bleeding
again."

"I popped out the stitches."

"What were you doing?" There was a wealth of suspicion
in her voice.

"Things, baby. Taking care of business." He slipped his
arms under her knees and lifted her against his chest. He
was gentle, taking care to bring her in close against him
where she was safe. "Put your arms around my neck."

She did, burying her face against his shoulder and inhaling to draw his scent deep. "How can you smell so good
after a long run, a fight with a madman and getting shot?
That's not fair."

"Not fair is a gun going off and hearing your woman's
breath catch, knowing she just took a bullet. Scared the
ever-living fuck right out of me."

She smiled against his shoulder. "I hope not."

"It isn't funny, Sonia." There was no answering laughter
in his voice. "That second took a few years off my life. I
never want it to happen again."

She pulled back to meet his eyes. "Uh-oh. That sounds
like you telling me you're doubling security around me or
something."

"Or something," he agreed as they reached the bottom
of the stairs.

"What are you planning? Whatever it is, just forget it.
This was Molly's drama, not mine. I'm perfectly fine. No
one's even thought about me for over a year. I'm dead to
them, remember?"

Before he could answer, Jerry rolled his wheelchair right
to them. Fast. Nearly knocking Joshua over. He was wild-
eyed, his hair disheveled. If Jerry could look pale under his

permanent tan from all the years working outdoors, he did. "How bad is she hurt? Why isn't she in a hospital? If it's the money, Sonia, we can handle that."

"If she needed to go to the hospital, Jerry, she'd be there," Joshua said.

He set her in a dining room chair. Forensics had taken photographs and there was an outline of a body on the great room floor. Tape roped off the large room, denying any of them access. Jerry kept looking from the mess in the great room to Sonia's face.

She glared up at Joshua. "I'm *perfectly* fine, Jerry. They put a Band-Aid on my thigh. Thanks for coming to check on me, though. I really appreciate it, although I didn't expect it."

Jerry rubbed his chin. The stubble was present. The appearance came around the five o'clock mark just as if Jerry's shadow was the one talked about most. Instead of being attractive, as she found Joshua's, Jerry's was mostly salt and pepper, giving him a patchy look.

"I can't afford for you to be off work," he said gruffly. "You run my crews, remember?"

"I will be at work tomorrow," she affirmed, knowing he said it to deflect what he was feeling. He had driven all the way out to her house in his special van just to make certain she was alive and safe.

"She won't be," Joshua contradicted. "She's taking tomorrow off."

"She isn't." She gave him a look that should have withered him on the spot, or had him dropping dead. "She will be at work as usual, Jerry."

Joshua shook his head. "She's taking a day. Medical advice."

Jerry nodded enthusiastically. "Yes. Yes, of course, she needs a day at least, maybe the rest of the week to recoup. I want you to take the rest of the week off, Sonia. You were shot. You need it. I'm going home, but I want you to call me every day. Let me know how you're doing."

She gasped. "I can't take a week off. It's a freakin' Band-Aid. We need to keep the crew working."

"I'm capable of running a crew," Jerry said. His tone warned her against arguing.

She glared at Joshua as Jerry swung his chair around and started toward the kitchen door. "This is your fault," she hissed at him. "I *like* working. Jerry doesn't. He likes to sit in his office and play with his paperwork and the telephone."

Jerry paused in the doorway. "I heard that. I'm working when I'm in the office."

"Working is actually doing something besides playing those video games you don't think I know you play," she said.

Jerry looked over his shoulder. "I have no idea what you're talking about. I'm too old to play video games. I wouldn't even know how."

Her mouth dropped open. "Lightning is going to strike you, Jerry Corporon."

In answer, he let the door slam behind him. She turned her attention to Joshua. "Do you see what you just did there? He as much as told me I couldn't go back to work for a week."

"How is that my fault?" Joshua asked. "I said a day."

She narrowed her eyes at him in suspicion. He *had* said a day, so why did it feel as if she'd walked right into a trap he'd orchestrated?

"I'll go pack you a bag." He moved fast, heading for the stairs.

"Wait!" she called after him. "What do you mean, pack me a bag? I'm not going anywhere. Joshua, stay out of my drawers." She jumped to her feet. Her cheek throbbed. If she was admitting it, so did her thigh. He had a head start, but desperate times called for desperate measures.

*Gatita, move it.* She called on her little female. Utilizing the leopard's speed and agility, she leapt across the room, landed with a jolt on the stairs and then was up them in two bounds.

For the first time ever, the door to her bedroom was closed. She caught the door handle, twisted and pushed. Her body ran into the thick wood. The door didn't budge. "You locked me out," she accused, rattling the door handle.

"I did? It must have locked when it swung shut. You've got yourself a faulty lock there, baby," he called.

"I'll just bet I do," she sniffed. "Open this door. Right. *Now.*"

"Busy, darlin', give me a minute."

"I'll *darlin'* you. Don't you dare touch my things. And stay out of my drawers."

"Too late. Already found your vibrator. Nice one. You'll have to show me. I'll enjoy watching you."

She closed her eyes and slid down the wall. Heaven help her. She was never going to live it down. Not ever. She knocked the back of her head against the wall three times. Gently. Her cheek still felt a little like it had exploded and jarring it wasn't smart, so she was careful, but still, there was no getting around the fact that Joshua made her crazy.

"Sonia?"

His voice bubbled with laughter. That was so much better than the worry. The fear. That growl he made in his throat when he was going all badass protective on her. She kind of liked the growl. Just thinking about that sound sent a little shiver of desire sliding down her spine. "What?"

"I like this sexy dress you have hanging up. It's red. I have a thing for red."

She'd found that dress in a boutique in New Orleans and hadn't been able to resist it, although she'd had nowhere to wear it. She didn't want to talk about that dress, or think about why she'd bought it. The purchase had been pure impulse, to try to lift depression. She'd been alone night after night convincing herself she was the worst-looking woman on the face of the Earth. The dress had been an attempt to feel sexy and daring. She'd told herself she'd get it lined and then she'd go to a club. She hadn't. Instead, she'd packed the dress away and only took it out to look at it when she was seriously depressed.

"It belongs to my sister."

"You don't have a sister."

"You don't know. I could have one stashed away somewhere."

He laughed and flung the door open. "What are you doing?"

"Sulking." It was the truth. She was going to go home with him. She shouldn't. It was only going to get her deeper into trouble, but there was no resisting him when he was being sweet and funny.

"Come here, baby. You just need a little TLC."

"I need you to be real, Joshua." She looked up at him, feeling fragile. Vulnerable. Terrified. He made her feel things she had no business feeling. She didn't even know if she was free to fall in love with him, and she didn't have a safe way to find out.

He sobered instantly, crouching in front of her. His thumb slid over her swollen cheek and drifted lower to her lips. He rubbed her bottom lip. "I'm real, Sonia. One hundred percent real. You're safe with me."

She hoped so. She couldn't take another betrayal. She'd survived because there was a small part of her that had been asleep, too grief-stricken to know what the Bogomolov family was, but as she'd begun to waken, she'd absorbed their deceit and treachery through her skin. It hadn't come as a complete surprise that they were criminals. The shock had been the casual way they'd been willing to kill her after deceiving her into believing they loved her.

She looked into Joshua's blue-green eyes. That field of crystal blue with those intriguing swirls of green. She had to trust someone. She wanted that someone to be him.

# 11

SONIA was in his house. In his bed. Joshua glanced up to the ceiling. Flames from the fireplace sent light flickering across the crystal chandelier, making it sparkle like diamonds. He noted the beauty absently. She was up there, and he would have to tell her everything. Tonight. He couldn't climb into bed with her again without telling her the truth.

She had to know that Nikita and Sasha Bogomolov would be coming for her. He had the feeling she wouldn't take that very well. At least not the part of his confession about Nikita having been an invited guest in his home. He had cleared out the scent of the Russians in preparation of her coming, but that wasn't to deceive her so much as to buy him time to find a way to tell her the truth.

He'd put it off, letting her sleep last night, and then spent the day waiting on her, staying up in his room with her, just talking about everything but what they should have been talking about. He'd stalled. Now he had no more time. He had to tell her. He'd planned it all out and hoped everything went the way he needed it to go, but . . .

"Damn it, Evan. Why the hell does life throw these kinds of curves?"

Evan shrugged. "Don't know."

"I can't put it off. You saw him. Nikita is coming back, and he'll do it soon. I've been expecting a call from him any minute. He's going to give me a bullshit story about how he needs a sit-down with me to iron out expected problems with our deal. His son will come with him, and he'll bring a lot more of his men on the pretense someone has threatened his son."

Joshua hated that he was right most of the time. It was very rare for someone to outthink him. Drake had put him in this trusted position because he was a problem solver. He figured out what the enemy was going to do long before they thought of it and he was prepared. Nikita would call, tonight or tomorrow.

"I'll tell her tonight. After dinner. I want a few more hours to persuade her to give me a chance. I need to lock her in tight before she knows the worst."

Evan nodded. "I'll agree with that, Joshua. She needs to know who you are. Give her that. As much of yourself as you can."

"I've had the cook preparing a special dinner. The table's set. I'm going up to take a shower. You and the others can disappear for the night."

Evan stood. "It's going to be okay."

He replayed Evan's assurances over and over in his head as he showered in the guest bathroom and dressed in the guest room for dinner. He'd told Sonia to wear the red dress. He wanted to see it on her. It wasn't the kind of dress a woman could wear with underwear. It fit like a glove. The front was simply two strips of material veeing up from the narrow waistband. It left the sides and back bare. The skirt fit like a glove with one long slit up to the top of her thigh.

He couldn't wait to see it on her, although he wasn't certain he'd want anyone else to see her in it.

She hadn't even protested when he'd told her to wear it. She'd disappeared into the master bathroom and locked him out. He supposed he deserved it. He'd locked her out of her bedroom. He straightened his tie and went to the master bedroom door. Knocked. Like a gentleman. He supposed once in a while he could put on the charm for her. She deserved a gentleman, even though that wasn't him.

She opened the door. Her scent enveloped him. Orange citrus and vanilla. It was a heady combination, but it was the dress on her that drove out every sane thought he had. The thin material clung to her body like a second skin. The darker shadow of her nipples barely showed beneath the spun crimson threads. The swell of her breasts pushed at the stretchy fabric so that it showcased her figure. Every movement sent those soft mounds swaying temptingly.

She tilted her head at him, smiled and when he spun his finger she turned slowly. His breath caught in his throat. The back was bare to the indentations just above her shapely butt. He loved her ass. The red stretchy fabric showcased that favorite part of her to its advantage. The material was just thin enough that he felt he could catch a glimpse of her skin beneath it, just the hint was there, that seam between her cheeks, the twin dents he loved to lick.

"You look beautiful."

"It's almost sheer," she said, her voice shy. "I planned to have it lined, but I didn't have anywhere to wear it so I never spent the money."

He took her hand and pulled her from the room. She'd left her hair down, which she rarely did, and clouds of it surrounded her face and fell down her back in thick, dark waves. The dress sparkled under the lights. He had the mad desire to lean down and put his mouth right over her breast, to suckle right through the material. Before the night was over, he would do just that. He wanted to see one side wet and dark, a forbidden pleasure, maybe while she sat across from him at dinner.

He led her into the dining room to the small intimate table that had been set up for them. "You don't need a slip under the dress. Not here. Not with me." He bent to brush her mouth with his as he pulled out her chair. He stepped closer, preventing her from sliding into it. "You look provocative, Sonia. Sexy as hell."

She smiled at him and lifted both hands to her hair, pushing it over her shoulders. The action lifted her breasts. "I was going for sexy."

"You more than succeeded." He stopped trying to resist and fastened his mouth around her left breast, both hands on her hips as he suckled strongly. He drew material and nipple into his mouth, soaking the fabric, teased with his teeth and tongue until she was squirming and giving him that little mew she sometimes did—the one that made his cock as hard as a rock. She didn't try to pull away or tell him the dress was expensive. She cradled his head, one hand in his hair, fingers stroking little caresses through his scalp.

He lifted his head and surveyed his handiwork. "That should do." He drew his finger down from her shoulder, over the curve of her breast to her nipple. "Mmm. Not quite."

She raised an eyebrow and looked down at the wet spot that made the fabric totally sheer. "Not quite?"

"Hold still. I have one more thing to do before we eat." He turned her slightly and put his mouth on the side of her breast. It was open from her waist to under her arm. He took his time, decorating the strip of bare skin with his mark, a string of strawberries that danced up her side right over the swell of her breast.

When he lifted his head a second time, she smiled at him. "Are you happy now?"

"I was happy the moment I laid eyes on you. I'm satisfied for the moment." He stepped aside to allow her to sit.

Sonia slid into the chair's seat, and he lit the candles,

wanting the light to play over her. The ice had done wonders. He'd kept her in bed all night, and all the next day, icing her cheek, spoiling her, letting her rest. They'd lain in bed together, talking about the things he loved to listen to, things she was excited about, like her painting—not the men who wanted her dead. Her dark eyes were bright with happiness and he was glad he'd gone to the trouble of seeing to every detail, because he wanted to keep that look in her eyes. The food had been prepared and plated in the kitchen and he retrieved their entrées.

"Do you want wine? My leopard isn't as thrilled when I drink."

She shook her head. "Sparkling water is fine."

Seated, he looked across at her. He'd never seen a woman so beautiful. More, one that suited him perfectly. She seemed to be made just for him. She loved everything he did in the bedroom. Everything he tried. She never protested. If she hesitated, he was careful to slow down and be as gentle as he could until she was less apprehensive. He found he loved sitting across from her, looking at her gorgeous body, knowing whatever he asked for, she would give him. Knowing he would do the same for her.

"Tell me about your mother," he invited. He knew she loved her mother. It was in the softness of her face, her voice, whenever she spoke of her.

Instantly he got that smile. The way she smiled sent a slow molasses heat moving through his veins, setting him on fire, inch by inch.

"She laughed all the time with me. She loved frozen yogurt. Not just loved it, that's too mild. She was *obsessed* with it. Sometimes she only wanted frozen yogurt for dinner and nothing else. We'd giggle like a couple of schoolgirls when we'd go into the ice cream parlor to order it. The clerks knew her, and she knew everything about them. She asked after their parents, siblings, children and spouses. She always knew them by name."

He watched as she put a fork with a small bite of chicken on it into her mouth and closed her lips around it. His cock jerked. He eased his legs wider. Who knew that just sitting across from her, knowing she wasn't wearing underwear, would have him aching? Another minute and he'd have to ease down his zipper to give himself a little respite.

He barely comprehended what she said, he was too busy watching her every move. The flutter of her lashes. The close of her red lips around her fork, the way she parted them just before she took a drink of sparkling water. He kept the talk light, making her laugh, watching the way her lips curved. Her laughter was like music he'd never heard before, but needed to hear for the rest of his life.

They talked about Molly and Bastien. They talked about their leopards and how the cats enhanced their lives. He wanted to give her time to know him better before he brought up the Russians and how Nikita Bogomolov had come to be in his home. Maybe a lifetime of getting to know him would be enough time.

He sat across from her feeling genuinely happy, something he couldn't remember feeling since his mother died. He liked his life and he was good at it, but happiness was family to him. Joy was having a woman of his own. Having Sonia. He knew she was the one. He'd known it the moment he'd kissed her. Almost before that, when he'd still been in his leopard and she'd turned her head and looked at him with her dark eyes, so vulnerable.

He waited until the meal was almost finished before putting a small rectangular case on the table and pushing it across to her.

Her gaze jumped to his. The box was a jeweler's box, but too big to be a ring or earrings. "What's this?"

"Something I've been wanting to try with you for a while."

She licked her lips, her gaze jumping from his face to the box. He read anticipation in her eyes. She knew him now.

She knew the way his mind worked. He was very sexual, and the sexual tension in the room had spiraled almost out of control despite the light conversation. She opened the case slowly, her gaze widening as she took in the jewelry. There was a small golden egg gleaming at her. She glanced up at him. "This is for . . ."

He nodded. "It goes up inside you, fits right over that sweet little spot you love for me to scratch for you. I thought tonight we could try this out."

"Now? At dinner?"

"Yes." He watched her for any signs of discomfort. She looked intrigued, not upset. He liked to play, but only if the things he chose to do brought her pleasure. She liked to play too, and her eyes had darkened with desire.

She licked her lips again and he groaned, his hand dropping to his swollen cock. "You can't do that, baby, or my cock goes crazy hard."

She smirked a little. "Are you having problems with control, Joshua? There are things that help that, you know. Maybe a cock ring?" Her face flushed a dark rose, and her eyes went hot.

He knew his face was carved with carnal lines of pure sin. "You don't have the first idea what a cock ring is, do you?"

Her laughter teased his cock like fingers. Or tongue. He felt the strokes brushing over his hard flesh. "Nope, but it sounded good."

He lowered his voice until it was pure velvet. Pure sin. "Put it in now."

She took the egg from where it was nestled in the box with the other items. She started to rise, but he shook his head. "Right here. Pull your chair back so I can see. Just spread your legs and put it in. Get it wet first."

It was a dare more than anything else, although he thought he might go up in flames just watching her. She looked so damned innocent. Sexy as hell, but innocent. She didn't always act that way. She didn't now. She licked up the side of the egg, her eyes on him. Then she sucked it slowly into her mouth. His cock hurt so badly he opened his zipper to let it spring free.

Trying to be nonchalant when his hands were shaking, he took a sip of the sparkling water, never taking his eyes from her. Very slowly she pushed back with her chair until it was away from the table and he had a good view of her body. Her legs stretched out in front of her and then she began to pull up the skirt of her dress. Once she had it up all the way, she spread her legs wide. "Like this?" Her question came out breathless, as if she couldn't find air. Her nipples were hard little pebbles pushing against the fabric of the dress.

"Just like that. Slide the egg inside."

She licked her lips and then the egg one more time. Very slowly, she pressed it into her, her chest rising and falling rapidly, her eyes dilated with excitement. Never once did she look away, connecting him, making him part of the intimacy. His hand closed around his shaft tightly, his thumb smearing the droplets over the crown. Fire raced up his spine.

"You like this, honey?" she asked.

"Very much." He watched the egg disappear. "Now tidy your dress and slide your chair back to the table. "We'll see if it works."

She did as he said and then sat demurely across from him, once more looking the innocent. He couldn't believe she'd just been sprawled out as wanton as hell right in front of him. He pressed the remote, turning the vibration to low. She jumped. Bit her lip. Smiled at him, her eyes darkening even more.

"Oh, yeah. That's good. Really good." Her breath came in a little rush.

He indicated her plate. She glanced at the open jewelry box. "There's more."

"For later. Right now, you need to finish up. We have dessert."

She pouted. "I thought you were going to be dessert."

"You're so greedy."

"I am. You taste good. Besides, I love to watch your face when you're coming." She picked up her fork and pushed the last of the chicken around her plate.

He pushed the button to medium, his gaze on her face. She gasped, her eyelashes fluttered, her skin flushing more. "You look so beautiful. I love watching you."

He took another sip of the sparkling water and pretended interest in his meal. "Tell me how you became interested in renovating old houses. I know your father was a carpenter and taught you how to work with wood, but renovating houses is much different."

She took a breath, pushed her plate away and took the fluted glass in her hand. "I've always been interested in older homes, the various styles and designs of earlier time periods. Other girls played with dolls." She squirmed, her breath hitching.

He waited in silence, never taking his gaze from her. Sonia touched her tongue to her lip, and he did a lazy slide with his hand. His cock felt like a steel spike. There was nothing more decadent than sitting at a table, dressed up, his woman across from him, desire devouring her, desire devouring them both.

"I always stopped to look at the houses in the neighborhood. When we went to the library, I'd get my mother to find books on architecture. I'd look at the pictures and have her read to me about the various designs and why they were built that way." She gasped and threw her head back with a small, sexy moan.

He thumbed the remote, turning the vibrating egg back to low. She hissed her displeasure at him. He smirked. "Tell me more."

"I can't talk."

"You can talk."

"I can't breathe."

"You can breathe."

She took a deep breath. "I studied the really beautiful older plantations, like the Destrehan Plantation and the Oak Alley Plantation."

He kicked the egg up to high. She gasped and gripped the table, her gaze flying to his.

"Keep going. I'm learning about plantations."

She shook her head. She was close. So very close. He read her easily now. He'd watched her fly apart dozens of times. He smiled and reduced the setting again, denying her. She moaned and pushed at her long hair. A few tendrils were damp. He loved that she was so close, but waiting for him.

"Come here, baby," he ordered softly and pushed the dishes to the far side of the table. Right here." He pointed to the spot in front of him.

She swallowed hard. "I'm not certain I can walk."

"Come here and I'll take care of you."

She stood up gingerly, her grip on the table nearly turning her knuckles white. Very carefully she moved around the table until she standing in front of him. He enjoyed every step. The way she pressed her thighs together. The hiss of her breath. Her soft moan.

"Pull your dress up around your hips." He started the egg again, his gaze never leaving her face. That red flush, the haze in her eyes, all of it made his cock jerk and throb. He kept a slow, controlled slide with his fist. She was nearly desperate. He felt that way just watching her.

She began to bunch the thin, stretchy material in her fists, dragging it slowly up her thighs until it slid over her hips, her eyes on his. He could tell that her skin was so sensitive that just dragging the dress up caused ripples of heat to rush through her veins. He watched how it slid over the little Band-Aid on her leg, making certain she didn't wince as the shimmering red pulled over it. She didn't.

She bit her bottom lip. He shook his head. "Baby, stop that. I claimed that lip, remember? You keep doing that and I won't be able to concentrate. You want my full attention, don't you?"

Sonia nodded, allowing her full lower lip to slide from between her teeth. He groaned as the red skirt bunched around her waist and her thighs gleamed with liquid honey. He caught her around the waist with both hands and lifted her onto the table.

She gasped and caught at him, as if she might fall. As if he would ever let that happen. "What are you doing?"

"Having you for dessert. Spread your legs for me."

"Joshua . . ." There was hesitation in her voice.

He smiled at her and bent his head to the feast. Her entire body shuddered when his tongue slid along her inner thigh, collecting that honey that was all for him. She tasted like heaven. He knew he was addicted and always would be. He'd been craving her sweet spice.

One hand guided her back so she was propped up by her elbows only, sprawled out decadently on his table, his dessert. He thumbed the remote, turning up the egg so that it vibrated right over that little spot that made her unravel. At the same time, he put his mouth over her clit and sucked hard.

She screamed as she came apart for him. The orgasm ripped through her, wild and unyielding. Her hips came off the table into his hands and he caught her, pressing her tighter to his wicked tongue, sealing his mouth over her, stroking and suckling. He used his teeth, his fingers and that wonderful golden egg, driving her higher and higher, devouring her while she fragmented, soared and floated. Fuck, he loved that. He loved it almost more than he loved what she was going to do to him.

His cock was so hard, jerking and throbbing in time to her cries and pleas. When she caught his hair in her fist, shaking her head, so dazed with pleasure she couldn't speak, he turned off the egg and laid his head over her mound, breathing her in. She smelled like arousal. Like sex and sin. Like paradise waiting for him.

He let her float down gently, his hand massaging her rib cage and stomach, feeling the little aftershocks that rippled through her. When her breathing settled and her fingers were back to caressing his scalp instead of trying to pull his hair out, he lifted his head.

"Better?"

"Mmm." She nodded to emphasize the dreamy sound. "I wasn't certain I was going to survive that." There was a smile in her voice.

"We're a long way from finished." Again, he watched her closely. If she had to stop for a while and rest, he might have to take care of himself, although he knew that would never satisfy him. Still, her comfort was paramount.

"We aren't?" Her smile widened. "I hoped we weren't."

"Glad to hear that, darlin'. You have no idea how happy that makes me." His hand fisted his cock once more. He was dripping now, he needed her so much. "Tell me how your face feels. Are you hurting at all?"

She shook her head, her gaze riveted to his cock. He liked the way her tongue touched her lower lip in anticipation. "God, you're beautiful," she whispered. "Joshua, you really are."

His heart clenched hard in his chest. She really did appreciate his cock. He knew that wasn't the case with all women, but Sonia matched him sexually. She was adventurous and more than willing to do anything he asked. She played. She loved playing. When her mouth was on him, she feasted and let him know she loved what she was doing.

"Thank you, Sonia. I appreciate that you think so."

"Mmm." Her tongue licked along her lip again. "I know so."

"I'm going to sit you up, baby. You ready for that?"

"I think. I'm still floating somewhere in space. You may have to come looking for me." There was soft laughter in her voice, but honesty as well. She let him wrap his arm around her waist and pull her into a sitting position. He kept her close, just in case.

"I'm going to kiss you. You taste so fuckin' good, Sonia. I wouldn't share the honey you give me with anyone but you."

He tipped her chin up and took her mouth, sharing her taste. He wanted to be gentle, he tried. He started out that way, but his cock drove him hard. His kisses went from gentle to rough fairly fast, but she didn't seem to mind, her tongue dueling with his until he knew he was going to explode if he didn't stop.

Joshua helped her to stand again, right in front of his chair. He pushed the shimmery red strips of material to the side of her breasts, so the fabric pushed the firm mounds closer together. He cupped the soft weight in his hands and took her right breast into his mouth. She cried out, both hands going to his head to hold him there. He laved with his tongue, stroked, bit down gently, drew her nipple to a hard peak. Just what he needed. Picking up the golden chain from the velvet box, he gently clamped her nipple. Her breath hissed out. He smiled at her and blew on her nipple. When she moved, little bells jingled. Tiny golden bells hung from the chain, and two just a little larger hung off the nipple clamps.

"How does that feel?"

"It startled me, but it feels like you're pinching gently with your fingers."

"Good." He kissed her again. Hard. He loved kissing her and he continued to stroke her left breast, tugging and rolling her nipple. He kissed his way down her throat to the curve of her breast, sucked until there was a gorgeous red strawberry and then suckled strongly at her breast, tugging on the chain gently to hear her breath hiss out. He bit down gently and then pulled back to fasten the clip.

He sat back, stroking the inside of her thigh. "You look beautiful, baby. So fuckin' beautiful. I knew that chain would be perfect on you." He tugged on it, watching her face.

She moved experimentally, her breasts swinging. She gasped and the tiny bells sounded, calling to him. He kissed her again and then kissed his way down to her breasts, all the while stroking with his hands between her inner thighs. Every now and then his knuckles rubbed along her sex and she shivered. He couldn't help but smile. "You were born for me, Sonia. So perfect for me. I fuckin' love this." He gently tightened the nipple clamp, wanting the tension the way she liked his hands on her. He knew when he hit the maximum she could handle and he stopped, but tugged on the chain until she was forced to come forward. He kept tugging until she had to slide off the table to stand in front of him.

"Love this so much, baby," he whispered and put a hand to her hip, forcing her to her knees between his legs. His cock was hard and aching. He tugged on the chain very gently, lifting her breasts, loving the way she looked kneeling there in that red dress, his chain on her. "Can't wait much longer. Get busy. I need that mouth right now and I don't plan on being gentle. You don't like something, you let me know and we change it up."

She nodded and let him tug her forward by the chain. He guided his cock to her mouth. He didn't wait for her to lick up his shaft, he just pushed deep, stretching her lips around his girth because he fucking loved how that looked too. He dreamt about her mouth sucking him dry. He began to move, keeping each thrust gentle, letting her get used to the feel of him filling her. He switched the golden egg back on, turning it to shuffle, so the vibrator went from one setting to another every couple of minutes.

Her eyes widened. He tugged on the chain, pulling on her breasts so they jutted straight out and the bells jingled over and over. She swallowed hard, taking him deeper. He held himself still, her tight mouth working him until he wanted to roar with pleasure. The sight of her alone had his balls so tight he thought he'd explode.

"You look so fuckin' sexy, Sonia," he growled. His voice was so low and husky he knew he was already close. He didn't want it to end. The fire in his groin spread through his body, hot and wild. "I love when your lips are stretched around me and your eyes water as you try to take all of me. You do that for me. Never had anyone lovin' on me the way you do. You love my cock, don't you?"

She nodded. The bells went wild. His cock slid farther into her. She was taking more than she ever had. Her tongue stroked and danced and then she swallowed him again, and he heard the roar start in his belly. He let loose, a long stream of curses, his fist on the chain, pulling up again so her breasts nearly pointed at him, forcing her head back farther.

Her hips squirmed, reminding him the little egg was pushing her toward another orgasm. She was ultrasensitive, the evidence of her need on her thighs. Her tight mouth was scorching hot. Her muscles worked him as he pushed deeper. Her eyes widened, but she didn't pull off him. He allowed his cock to be squeezed hard and then he pulled out enough to give her breath.

"You all right?" He whispered it, praying she would nod. Would say yes. He'd stop if she couldn't take it, but . . . "You're taking me someplace I've never been," he added. Admitting it. Not just his body, but his head. His heart. She was taking him straight into new territory.

"I love doing this to you," she whispered, her eyes on his, so he could see she meant it. So he could hear she meant it. Her tongue swirled over the broad sensitive crown and then, deliberately looking into his eyes, she engulfed him, taking him deep, urging him to move his hips with one hand clamped to his thigh, fingers digging in. Her other glided down her smooth belly to her mound, fingers curling, circling.

Joshua watched, mesmerized. He moved because he couldn't stop himself. Her admission that she loved what she was doing seared through him. The sight of her fingers working on her clit and her lips stretched over his cock was the sexiest thing he'd seen. He felt the volcano start somewhere low and build and build. His balls hurt they were so tight, boiling hot. The blast was scorching hot, an explosive detonation, jet after jet, his shaft so hard and thick he didn't think it was possible to sate him.

He pulled back slowly, watching her throat work. Watching her lick her lips, follow his cock to lap at him gently. He closed his eyes, knowing he could lose her if he didn't handle things just right, and he couldn't afford to lose her. His heart was already involved. She had it, and there was no getting it back. He stopped the egg's vibration, giving her a respite.

Her mouth was so gentle as she finished him and then sat back on her heels, looking up at him. Every breath she took made the little bells jingle. He would never hear that sound without thinking of this moment. The fiery explosion, the overwhelming purely carnal pleasure, so perfect he knew it was sinful.

"Come here, baby," he said softly, tugging on the chain to remind her to get to her feet. He helped with one hand, keeping possession of the chain with the other.

Sonia stumbled a little, still light-headed, but he wrapped his arm around her, bringing her close. "I want you to take a deep breath and let it out," he instructed.

Her gaze clung to his. He saw the trust there. The moment she exhaled, he hit the remote on the egg so that it vibrated again, and he removed the clamp on her right breast. Her eyes went wide and she gasped, but his mouth was there, soothing the pain as the blood flowed back into her nipple. His tongue worked her, stroking gently as she came down from the combination.

"You good?" he asked again. He kissed her nipple and then left a trail of kisses to her throat. "I need to hear you say it."

"I am. This is so sexy, Joshua." She pressed her bare

mound against his thigh. He was still fully dressed. He'd simply opened his trousers to get to his cock, but she was rubbing along the material, leaving a wet trail.

"Do you see what you're doing, naughty girl?" he asked.

She laughed softly. "I know exactly what I'm doing."

"Take a breath, baby," he cautioned. The moment she did, he jumped the egg to high and removed the second clamp. He drew her breast into the heat of his mouth, tongue stroking away the pain while the egg distracted her.

She moved against him, her hips rocking urgently. "Joshua." She wailed his name. "I'm going to lose my mind."

His cock had already returned to his usual state around her. Hard and aching. He turned her, tossed the clamps on the table and shoved her head down so that her breasts were on the table. She spread her arms wide so she could grip the table's edge. His hand stroked her ass. So perfect. He turned off the remote and reached for the small wire. Yanking, the egg fell into his hand.

"Hotter than hell, baby," he said, and put the egg right next to her face. "You're hotter than hell, and I swear I'm going there with you. Fuckin' hell."

He entered her from behind, in one forceful surge. She cried out, her knuckles turning white as she hung on.

"Hard, Joshua. Don't hold back."

"Don't want you sore, Sonia."

She pushed back. "*Hard*. I need you *now*." There was a little sob in her voice.

He couldn't stop himself, not with her pleading. He had plans for the evening and her getting sore wasn't one of them, but damn him, he couldn't resist her. He began moving, holding her hips, his cock hard and aching, slamming into her over and over. Each stroke sent flames burning over his cock and fire roaring in his balls and belly.

How the hell she did that to him, he didn't know. It had never been like this with any other woman. He had control. Always. Control was important to him. He'd seen too many leopards out of control, yet with Sonia, he could barely see straight, let alone think.

Her sobs sounded like music, playing along his belly, tapping a rhythm in his thighs. Her heart beat right through the tight muscles of her sheath, surrounding him. The friction was unbelievable. He held off as long as possible, thankful he'd come once already and could spend time moving in and out of her.

"You close, baby?" he asked. He knew she was. He knew her body. He knew the sounds she made when she was going to get off and get off big. It was building in her, coiling around him so tightly she was practically strangling his cock.

"Yes." She nearly spat the word through gritted teeth.

"Let go with me." He ordered it, clenching his own teeth as the fire roiled and leapt, threatening to consume them both. *"Now."*

He knew she would do as he said, because she was Sonia. She was with him, connected to him. He felt her body tighten even more, gripping his shaft, squeezing down like a vise, stealing his breath. Stealing his heart. Stealing his damned soul. She took him with her, forcing the seed out of him, milking him with her scorching-hot inner muscles, draining him of every single drop.

Her cries penetrated the air, mixed with his hoarse shout. He wrapped his arms around her middle, holding her shuddering body to give her support and to keep himself up when his legs threatened to give out on him. That was another first. He'd never had such a hard orgasm that he could barely keep on his feet.

He hadn't planned to take her this way. He wanted her in his bed. He had planned to make love to her slowly. To worship her body. Show her with every touch and stroke of his fingers how much he wanted her. How much he needed her.

The egg and clamps were for appealing to her sense of fun and adventure. He wanted her to know she had it all with him. He would spoil her. Protect her. He wanted to know everything about her. He would spend his life making her happy, giving her every reason to stay. He'd planned on wining and dining her, playing a sexy, exciting game and then carrying her upstairs and making love to her. Now he was lying over top of her, afraid of moving, afraid he might shatter into a million pieces.

He listened to the sound of her ragged, labored breathing, all the while his hand slid up and down the back of her thigh. The muscles jumped there. Her heart beat wildly into his hand where he slid it up from her waist to her breast. He cradled the soft mound in his palm, afraid his weight might smash her nipples into the wood of the table and hurt them.

"Your nipples sore?" He rubbed his face along her spine. "We didn't go much over ten minutes. It's not a good idea to keep them on for much longer than that."

"Good kind of sore," she acknowledged. "I'm a good kind of sore all over my body and a little tired, which is so wrong after spending the day just lounging in bed. Who knew sex could be so exhausting?"

"Too tired to let the leopards have their run together? Shadow always goes on a nightly run. He complains if Gatita isn't with him now."

She laughed softly and the movement pressed her breast deeper into his palm. He liked that. He liked holding her. "Gatita is so smitten with your male she whines all night if I don't let her out to run with him."

"So, you're good with it?" He didn't move.

"Yes, but I'm not moving for a while. She'll just have to wait while I rest here on the dining room table."

"A pretty ornament." He rubbed her bottom. "I love your skin."

"That feels good."

"When they come back, I'll give you a massage," Joshua stated. "It will help you relax."

"Honey, if I was any more relaxed, I'd be a puddle on the floor. That being said, I'm not turning down a massage."

He kissed the nape of her neck and allowed his body to slide from hers. "Good thing. Let's get that dress off. When you shift, your face might burn. I looked at your thigh and it's just a scratch. It should be all right."

"I burn all over. I think I went up in flames and all you're seeing right now is pure ash." She didn't move.

"Baby."

"Ashes don't move."

He swatted her ass, admiring his handprint. She yelped and turned her head to glare at him over her shoulder. "You're kind of mean."

"You don't want my male to be pacing up and down the dining room. He's close, Sonia, pushing for freedom."

She gave an exaggerated sigh and straightened gingerly. Her hands went to the two wide strips of material at her shoulders and pushed them off.

# 12

THE two leopards ran together through the swamp, heading in the opposite direction of the houses. The river dissected the land masses, and without hesitation, the male jumped into the water and swam for the other side. Gatita followed him. Sonia was going to have a thing or two to say to Joshua about his male's daring behavior, but it was clear the leopard wanted to take Gatita exploring.

Her little female hadn't had nearly enough time discovering creatures in the swamp and she stopped for every lizard and insect she ran across. Shadow became impatient and ran back to her after calling repeatedly. She looked amused and swiped at him with a paw, warning him she wouldn't be hurried, when he nudged her rather hard with his shoulder.

The island was new to Gatita though Sonia had been there before, and she cast back and forth for scents, took the time to rub along every tree and bush, just to let all the males in the neighborhood know she was around. *Hussy,* Sonia accused. *You're going to get in trouble. Shadow has a nasty temper and he's jealous.*

*I like it. Besides, it never hurts to let him think he's not going to get everything his way,* Gatita answered, smug and sage at the same time.

The land was solid, and from what Sonia could tell, big enough for several camps. She spotted three cabins on stilts a good distance from one another. Gatita approached one of them and lifted her muzzle to the wind, showing her teeth in a wide grimace. She laid her ears back and called out softly to her mate.

*What is it?* The scent was elusive, not one she recognized, but Gatita might.

*Man. Not good man.*

Sonia didn't like the sound of that. What did Gatita mean? Sometimes things got lost in translation.

Shadow returned and moved around the cabin, circling the entire structure before climbing up the stairs to the porch. Gatita followed at a slower pace, letting the big male take the lead. Sonia strained to see, hear or smell anything that would bother the female leopard. She caught the scent of a dog and stiffened.

*He's a hunter. He brought dogs with him. We have to get out of here. We shouldn't have come here, Gatita.* Sonia held her breath, willing the dogs to remain quiet, not to catch a whiff of the cat's scent.

Gatita listened, backing slowing away from the front door, heading toward the stairs. Shadow stayed close, but kept his larger body between his mate and the cabin. He pushed at Gatita's shoulder and she crouched, slinking along the floor of the porch as she made her way toward the stairs.

To Sonia's horror, Gatita was enjoying herself. More, she liked the adrenaline rush that came with the potential for danger. *This is no time to get crazy. This is dangerous. If those dogs wake, they'll chase you into the swamp and a man with a gun will shoot at you.*

*You like the danger too. You would want them to chase you and you'd circle back and go after the man with the gun.*

Sonia was shocked at the response, but then she knew she shouldn't be. Gatita was right. She was exactly the same way. It was why she loved the sexy play Joshua enjoyed. She never knew what he was going to do next. She liked the unexpected. She loved the rush she got from being with him. She loved running Gatita in the swamp because that was always a bit of risk. She drove her truck too fast. She liked taking chances.

*You're always the voice of reason, Gatita. This is no time to switch roles.*

Gatita marked a bush, ran a few feet forward and then rubbed her fur along a tree. She rolled in the damp vegetation.

*Oh. My. God. You little hussy, stop that this minute. On top of everything else you're a little exhibitionist. You are not going to have raunchy cat sex with a hunter a few feet away. I'm not letting you put Joshua in danger. Get moving right now.*

The little cat ran toward the river just as a dog let out a howl from inside the cabin. Shadow was on Gatita immediately, shouldering her so that she turned toward the bank with the long sandbar. He plunged into the river just as two other dogs took up the cry. Gatita followed him. They swam in the darkness back to the mainland. Both leopards ran toward the back of Joshua's property.

*Ask Shadow if he's ever seen that cabin occupied before. Ask him if the dogs have been there.* Sonia was suddenly uneasy. She'd certainly explored that strip of land, but the cabins had always been emptied and seemed abandoned. She knew a lot of the locals had camps out in the swamps and bayous, but as long as she'd been there—admittedly it hadn't been that long—she'd never seen a single sign that those cabins were used.

*He says no. They've always been empty. He was cutting*

*across that part of the swamp to get to the land Molly's grandmother's family owned. The swampland she bought with her inheritance. He said there is a cabin on it and wanted us to see it.*

Sonia would love to see that. Molly had wanted to go out to her grandmother's camp but had never made it. Sonia didn't want to see it badly enough that Gatita and Shadow would be hunted or killed. That nagging feeling in her gut refused to go away.

*Joshua says you are safe.*

She wanted to believe that she was—that both Joshua and she were safe. There were camps strewn all through the swamp. Many of the locals relied on hunting and fishing to survive lean months or years. She shouldn't have been so uneasy, but she couldn't quite make the feeling go away.

She was happy. She hadn't been happy in a very long time. She loved being with Joshua. She loved the way he was so sweet, and so adventurous, but careful of her. She knew any time she said no, or hesitated, he would stop. He made certain she was comfortable. He made her feel beautiful, and he listened to her. He pored over the plans with her, clearly respectful of her work. He'd loved her painting enough to hang it over his fireplace.

She hadn't had those things in a long while and she wanted them. She wanted them with Joshua. She had a good friend in Molly. Maybe she could even count Bastien as a friend. Certainly Jerry, who detested driving his special van, but had done so just to check on her. She had a job she loved. She had Gatita and now Shadow. Her life was good, and she was terrified someone was going to come along and take it away from her.

She stayed quiet, listening to the distant baying of the dogs. A light shone on the shore of the strip of land, beaming out over the water, then was directed to the ground as if the hunter was looking for tracks. She hoped the cat tracks were lost in the sea of dog tracks.

*Did you catch the scent of the man?*

*Yes.* Gatita wrinkled her nose and her ears went flat again, indicating she didn't want to think about the man in the cabin.

*Was it familiar? Sasha? Nikita? One of the men working for them?*

That was her worst fear. Once she'd realized Sasha and his father were part of the Russian mob, she'd read everything she could get her hands on about them. They were spreading across the United States. They had a strong presence in Miami. She understood why. The city was a natural gateway to both the United States and Latin America. She knew they were firmly entrenched in San Francesco, Los Angeles, Chicago and New York and were becoming so in Sacramento. She knew because she'd overheard Nikita talking. He'd spoken in Russian.

She had an ear for languages, and over time, with her mother working for the Bogomolov family and living on the estate, she'd begun to learn fast. She hadn't trusted herself to get the accent right or choose the proper word, so she hadn't spoken in their language—but she'd understood. She'd also known they were making major deals with the Italians and others.

Had they tracked her here? The only reference to the mafia she'd heard was when anyone brought up Rafe Cordeau. She had looked up that name and read what she could about the man. No one really wanted to talk about him, and if they did, they spoke in hushed tones, as if he might overhear them.

She hadn't heard that particular name spoken in the Bogomolov home. She knew a few names—they were repeated often. She knew Nikita was especially anxious to find a man by the name of Fyodor Amurov and his brother, Timur. Also, Mitya and Gorya Amurov. She thought they might be cousins of the much sought-after Fyodor. She felt a little sorry for those men. She knew Nikita planned on killing them. He had offered a hefty reward for anyone telling them their whereabouts, but he wanted to look them in the eye when he gave them what they deserved. She knew that meant torture.

Just the fact that Nikita wanted them dead made her feel as if she had a connection with them, even if they were criminals. *What are we going to do, Gatita? It isn't fair to Joshua and Shadow not to tell them, but if I do, they'll hunt Sasha and Nikita. The Russians won't stop coming at us if they find out we're alive.*

*Then don't tell them.*

Life was simple for Gatita. She loved Sonia and kept her safe. Nights running in the swamp was her favorite activity, especially now that she had the big male with her. Some nights, other leopards joined them. Living where they did was part of the world she approved of. It didn't matter if Joshua knew about the Russians. As long as she had Sonia and Shadow, Gatita was happy.

*You aren't much help,* Sonia groused.

She kept quiet, worried now about the hunter and what to say to Joshua about the threat hanging over her head. The leopards played in the swamp for another hour and then started back. Sonia remained quiet, considering what to do. If she went out into the swamp by herself in the light of day and the hunter wasn't really a local, but had been sent by Nikita or Sasha, then she was dead. If she didn't go . . . Either way, she was screwed.

"You're very quiet," Joshua observed as he led Sonia into the large master bathroom. "You've been quiet since we shifted. What's wrong? You're not still worried about the hunter, are you?"

She shrugged. Joshua was casual about nudity. He didn't seem to notice, but she was still very aware of her body and the differences between them. Not just the obvious ones, him being all male and her female, but the fact that he had the hardest body she'd ever seen. He was totally fit. She had muscles, but she looked soft and she knew it.

"Baby, a shrug doesn't tell me jack. If you're worried, don't be. I'll go with the boys in the morning and we'll pay him a visit."

Her breath caught in her throat. What if he was a hit man for the Bogomolov family? She wanted to cry. This wasn't fair to Joshua. She either had to end their relationship or tell him the truth. There was no middle ground. She told herself she didn't know what to do—but she did. If she told him the truth, he would get all chivalrous and white knight on her and go after them. He'd get killed. She had to end their relationship. Just not now. Not tonight. She deserved one more night with him.

She stepped into the shower with him. She couldn't help being nervous. She'd never showered with Sasha. It felt very intimate, but also something committed couples might do together. The shower was enormous, with two heads spraying overhead and four coming from the sides.

"Are you going to talk to me, Sonia?" Joshua asked.

His voice turned her heart over. So gentle. Almost tender. He made tears burn behind her eyes and a million butterflies take wing in her stomach as he took the gel from her and lightly rubbed it over her body.

She couldn't look at him. She didn't dare. He was too good at reading her expressions. She placed both hands on the wall and leaned there, letting him soap her skin. He was thorough, exquisitely gentle, careful of the small laceration on her thigh. The hot water felt good and she closed her eyes, giving herself up to the sensation.

There were a million arguments running around in her brain—things she needed to say to him. She should tell him the truth, that if the Russians knew she was alive, she'd never stop running. She wasn't good for him, he could get killed getting involved with her. The problem with telling him was simple. He'd try to get rid of the threat to her and get himself killed. It didn't matter that he worked for Drake Donovan, Nikita would find a way to kill her. Sasha, out of pride, would kill Joshua. He'd probably make her watch. The arguments ran over and over in her mind, a terrible loop she couldn't seem to stop.

"Tell me what's wrong." He ran his hand down her hair. When he got to the ends, he tugged hard enough to pull her head back.

Her eyes met his. She realized it wasn't the water from the shower that was causing blurry vision. She shook her head and attempted a smile. "I'm good. Just maybe a little tired. The leopards covered a lot of territory tonight."

"You're crying, Sonia." He began rinsing her body. Again, he was very thorough, making certain that every inch of her was gel-free, using the handheld to pour hot water over and onto her. She was grateful for the luxury of hot water on sore muscles.

"Damn it, baby, you have to start talking to me. I can't fix something if I don't know what's wrong."

"You are." She blurted it out, pressing her forehead hard into the shower wall, closing her eyes tight. "You are, Joshua." Now her voice was a whisper, squeezing through the lump in her throat, coming out strangled. "You're so good to me. You're so right. I never thought I'd meet someone like you. I didn't even know men like you existed."

He was silent for a long time, just using his hands in her hair, massaging her scalp until she wanted to melt into a little puddle at his feet. He was the one to turn off the shower and wrap her in a large, oversized towel. "I'm not, you know, what you think. You know I'm not. A woman like you deserves to be put on a pedestal, not have a man who gets hot thinking about watching her blow him. I'm fuckin' going to hell for the things I want to do to you."

Her gaze jumped to his face. There was far too much speculation and condemnation in his voice. No remorse, she noticed. She didn't want him to feel either of those things.

"If I didn't love the things you do to me, you wouldn't be doing them," she said decisively. "I can't imagine a man more perfect than you."

"Finish it, Sonia. For you. I'm perfect for you. You keep leaving that part out. I'm not a perfect man. I'm not 'right.' I'm right for you and I'm perfect for you. No one else."

Did he know? Did he suspect she was going to end their relationship? She turned away from him, wanting to hide, but there was nowhere for her to go. Light bathed the room. She didn't have clothes nearby. She felt vulnerable and exposed. Not just her body, but raw feelings that shouldn't ever see the light of day.

"Get on the bed."

His voice had turned gruff. He wasn't asking. Sometimes when he did that, ordered her around, she wanted to defy him, to tell him she wasn't about to follow an order. Other times, like now, she was grateful she didn't have to think. She just had to do what he said. She hurried into the master bedroom, uncaring if he thought she was running from him. She was.

The bed was positioned across from the long bank of windows so, if the lights were off, she could see into the swamp. She shivered and rubbed her arms, staring out into the night. With the light on, the room, and everything in it, was illuminated, but that didn't matter because she heard the music that always lulled her into peace. She slowly unwound the towel from her head as she sat on the very end of the bed, her feet firmly on the floor, facing the windows, needing to know the swamp was close and she could run if she had to.

"There's no drying my hair tonight. It would take forever. I'm going to have to braid it and dry it in the morning. The pillow's going to get wet."

"I'll dry it," Joshua said. "I had Alice, one of the women working here, get me a blow-dryer." She'd gotten a few other things he thought his woman might need as well. "I fell in love with your hair and imagined . . . things."

He stood in front of her, naked, all muscle, his cock still semi-hard after the wild sex they'd had, armed with a blow-dryer. She burst out laughing because Joshua managed to make everything fun. "You're crazy, you know that, don't you? Absolutely crazy. What can you possibly do with a blow-dryer besides dry hair?"

He thumbed the switch, turning it on and off, brandishing it like a weapon, a little smirk on his face. "I've got a vivid imagination, darlin'."

She rolled her eyes, but held still as he climbed onto the bed behind her. He slid his legs on either side of her hips, surrounding her with him. His scent was fresh, clean and wildly masculine. She tried not to breathe. Tried not to inhale him, but she had no choice and then he was inside her—deep. In her lungs, moving through her bloodstream, everywhere, until she knew she would never get him out of her. She'd never be free.

She sat quietly while he brushed out her hair. The tug of the brush, the bristles sliding through her hair felt good. She swallowed hard and kept her eyes glued to the windows. She couldn't see out, not with the light, but the swamp was her lifeline and it was there, just behind the glass.

"I was sixteen when my mother got sick," Joshua said. "It started with a small wound on her leg that just wouldn't heal. I didn't think anything about it, but within days she was tired, black circles under her eyes. She couldn't eat anything. Drake Donovan came with the doctor, but I could see it on their faces the moment they saw that wound. It had grown so big, eating away at her."

"A bite of some kind?" Sonia guessed, her heart hurting for that sixteen-year-old boy. She'd been sixteen when her mother was diagnosed with cancer. She remembered the terror of realizing she could lose her. Her mother had been the most important person in her world.

"I didn't have anyone else. My mother was . . . extraordinary," he said, his voice soft with love. "You would have liked her, and I know she would have liked you."

Sonia felt a fraud. She was certain his mother wouldn't have been very happy with her for exposing her son to the very real danger of the Russian mob.

"I remember her laugh. I think that's one of the things I miss most about her." He brushed a kiss on her bare shoulder. "Hold still."

Triggering the blow-dryer, he began to dry her hair. Ordinarily, Sonia would never have used the dryer. Her hair would have been frizz, but he was careful, using a lower setting and drying small sections at a time. She couldn't believe his patience.

"My grandfather raped women. That was his thing."

He rubbed his chin along her shoulder, right over the spot where he'd kissed her. The shadowy stubble on his face scratched across her bare skin, sending fingers of awareness walking down her spine.

"No one was spared. Not his daughters, or granddaughters. Not his daughters-in-law. He took it as his due that he could have any woman he wanted, no matter who they belonged to. I think he lived in a fantasy that he was a feudal lord. He liked hurting both men and women. The more others suffered, the happier he was."

"Joshua." She whispered his name. Her childhood had been relatively happy, at least until her father was tortured and murdered in front of her.

"When my grandfather turned his sights on my mother, my father took us out of there—or he tried to. Later, my mother speculated that one of the other women tipped him off that we were running. Old Man Tregre murdered his own son, shot him and then beat him to death. While that was happening, my mother took me and ran. We made our way to the rain forest in Borneo. She was originally from there, although her parents were no longer alive."

The blow-dryer felt good moving through her hair like a warm wind. Sonia found herself leaning into it, turning her head in the direction he indicated. She loved the sound of his voice, and learning about his past. He had always talked to her, but not about things that mattered. She knew his past had shaped him—made him into the man he was now just as her past had shaped her.

"What was it like, the rain forest?"

"So truly beautiful, Sonia. I'll take you there one day. Every leopard should go sometime, to see it and experience it as a leopard. It can be a violent way of life, but here can be just as violent."

She knew that to be true. He shut off the blow-dryer and divided her hair into sections. She loved that he could braid hair. She pictured him with his daughters, three little girls, all waiting for him to braid their hair before going off to school. The fantasy was very vivid in her mind, and again, she had to blink back tears. After tonight, she wouldn't have him.

She was going to do one thing right, even if it meant giving up her beloved home, her friends and the world she'd built. He deserved better. She knew he'd feel as if he had to protect her—or save her. She couldn't let that happen.

"The rain forest has so much color. The trees, the canopy, all the birds, the exotic flowers winding around the tree trunks, all of it. It's amazing." His voice was low, soft. Reverent even as he talked about the place he obviously loved.

"It sounds like it."

"Lie down. I want to give you a massage."

"Joshua, maybe we shouldn't . . ." She trailed off when he caught her braid and forced her head back so she was looking at him.

"*Tell* me what the fuck is wrong, Sonia. You're already leaving. In your head, you're leaving me. You think I can't feel that? You retreating from me?"

She should have known he would feel her withdrawal.

They were that connected. It had happened that first night. She'd looked into his leopard's eyes and there he'd been, looking back. She'd seen him and she'd known right then he was the one. She shivered at the look in his eyes. Turbulent. Crystalline. His leopard close. Both watching her. Wary. Alert.

"I'm not retreating from you," she denied.

"Lying to a leopard is never a good idea." He moved away from her, giving her room. "Lie down. And if you think I won't find you anywhere in this world, you're dead wrong. I could and I would. It's what I do best. You run, Sonia, and you don't have a damned good reason such as I beat the holy shit out of you, then know I'm coming after you."

"Beat the holy shit out of me?"

"Yeah. I do something like that, something like my vile monster of a grandfather did, then you go straight to Drake Donovan. I wouldn't deserve you, and I'd want you safe. Drake's the best man I know. He'd protect you from me."

Her breath caught in her lungs. Stretched out, facedown on the bed, she turned her head to study his hard features. "Joshua, you aren't anything like your grandfather. You're a good man. You have compassion for people. Look what you did in Borneo. You risked your life to take back hostages, to return kidnap victims to their homes."

He poured oil into his hands and rubbed them together to ensure warmth. "It's easy to put your life at risk when you don't have a fuckin' thing to protect. To love. I didn't go home to someone at night, Sonia. I didn't have someone to talk to or laugh with. I had no one. Putting my life on the line didn't seem like such a big deal."

His hands went to her shoulders, and she closed her eyes. The feeling was indescribable. She hadn't known just how sore and stiff she was, but his hands should have been insured. He was strong, his fingers digging deep into aching, inflamed muscles Gatita's antics had caused, working magic. She moaned.

He brushed a kiss along her spine, his hands never stopping. "That's the same sound you make when I've got my mouth between your legs, devouring all that sweet, sweet nectar you give me."

She found herself smiling. "I can't help it, it feels that good."

He looked down at her naked body. The woman was his. He knew it with every breath he took, yet she still was elusive, ready to slip away no matter what he did. He felt it. She had one foot out the door, ready to flee at the first indication they were in trouble. He knew they were. Huge trouble. The worst.

He was stalling. He had to talk to her. Tell her the truth. It wasn't fair to her. More, it was dangerous. Nikita would come after her, and she had to know the threat to her was very real. He wanted to curse, to hit the wall, to break someone's neck, preferably that of her coward of a husband.

He worked his way down her back. She was beautiful. Soft, glowing skin. He hadn't thought skin felt like hers did. "You going to tell me what's wrong?" He massaged her butt. Those beautiful ass cheeks, firm, round. He was certain she could model thong underwear.

His hand slipped between her thighs and pressed, silently commanding her to spread her legs for him. She did without hesitation. "Do you have any understanding of why I know you're the one for me, Sonia? I'm sexual. I probably always will be. I like sex, but I don't like sharing my body with someone I'm not emotionally connected with. That said, I need a lot of sex, especially with you. I think about it all the time. Every place I go, every piece of furniture. When you're standing there, all anxious while I'm going over the blueprints, shifting your weight from one foot to the other, all I can think about is peeling your ridiculous overalls off you, or stripping you of those jeans that fit your ass like a fucking glove and making you come apart for me."

"You like my body," she said, her voice muffled by the mattress.

"No, baby, I fuckin' *love* your body. I've never wanted another woman the way I want you. I'm adventurous in the bedroom. I like to play. You do as well."

"Joshua, that's sex. It's just sex."

She sounded so weary it broke his heart. She'd once said to him that Nikita had told his son women like her were to be fucked, not married.

He took a breath and let it out slowly, feeling as if he was in the fight of his life, but not knowing how to proceed. She wasn't understanding what he was trying to say. "The things I do with you are yours alone. No one else's. Ever. When I wanted sex before, it was the sex, not the woman. With you, it's all about the woman."

He kept his hands on her body, working the sore muscles in her legs, all the way down to her feet. "I love touching you. Going to sleep with you curled next to me. Waking up with you in my arms. I like to lie in bed all night and watch you sleep. Watch you breathe. I know every inch of your body. Your laughter is like music, and something inside me comes alive. I was fuckin' dead, walkin' through life, Sonia. I didn't care if I lived or died. I had nothing. No one. I *know* it's you."

He could see the side of her face and tears leaked out, caught on her long lashes and sparkled under the light. "Turn over."

She shook her head. "I can't. Not yet."

"I wasn't askin', baby." He waited to see what she would do. She was his. He knew it right down to his soul and when she slowly turned so she was faceup, he understood she recognized it too. She'd fought the desire to please him, to turn over for him, wanting to hide, but in the end, she'd done it—for him.

He stretched out over top of her, a human blanket, his hips cradled in hers, his thighs keeping her legs spread wide for him. He reached down and caught each ankle, drawing it up until both knees were bent and she was open to him.

He kissed her throat and then took her mouth. Gently. Just the way he'd wanted to from the first.

He felt love welling up. It was so strong, so intense, it was disturbing to him. He deepened the kiss, taking her mouth, keeping it as gentle as he was capable of. She needed to feel him. He wanted to tell her with his body because he didn't have any other way.

"Some men have fancy words, Sonia. They can be poets. Was he a poet? The man who took such advantage of you when your mother died? Did he give you pretty words?" His teeth closed on her lower lip and tugged. He licked at the marks and whispered into her throat. "Tell me if he did. I want to know."

"Yes." She nearly choked out the answer.

"I don't have those words to give you. I don't know how to say them. I can only show you. I will love you better than any other man ever would. I can give you that and mean it. I will support you in anything you want to do. Your painting. Your renovations. School, if that's what matters to you. Every fuckin' dream you have, baby. I'll stand with you. Good or bad, I'll stand with you."

He kissed the tears running freely down her face. That was killing him. Desperation rose. She was crying because she was thinking of running. "It's him, isn't it, Sonia? You don't want to stay with me because of him."

That hurt. Just the thought of her loving another man hurt.

She shook her head and opened her eyes to stare into his. "Absolutely not. Whatever you're thinking, Joshua, it isn't that. How could I think about him after being with you? You've given me so much. I can be me. You listen when I talk to you. You make me feel important and even beautiful. Your brand of sex gave me my first orgasm and another million after that."

"Can you love me?" He knew he was pressing. He shouldn't. She needed a little time, but they didn't have it. "I'm crazy in love with you. I want that back. I want that same intense, insane emotion from you. It might not be right for everyone else, but it's right for us. Do you feel it at all?"

Her hands were on his back, stroking caresses up and down. Her breasts pressed into his chest, those twin nipples rubbing along his muscles every time she moved. He loved them the way he did her lower lip. He took more of his weight so he could draw first one soft mound then the other into the heat of his mouth. Gently. He had to be gentle, he reminded himself. She needed to know. To feel.

"Of course I feel it for you, Joshua." She whispered the admission in a low, shaken voice. "You don't understand."

"I'm asking if you can love me. It's a simple enough question." He wasn't going to let her get away with bullshit. "I need this now, baby. Give it to me."

He felt her breath. Knew it was for him. His gaze jumped to her face even as his hand slid down between her legs to test her readiness for him. She was damp. Slick. Elation burst through him. She was his. All the way, she was his. "Say it, Sonia. Don't be a fuckin' coward. Give me that much."

"You already know. I don't understand why you're insisting I say the words out loud. I'm here. I'm in your house. I'm in your bed. Do you think I would have allowed another man to put nipple clamps on me? Or an egg inside me? Do half the things to me you do? I wouldn't. I would never trust them that much."

He caught his cock in his fist and guided it to her entrance. So hot. Right away. The broad crown barely managed to fit and instantly he felt those tight muscles surround and grip him. He couldn't decide, heaven or hell, but either worked as long as he was in her. Surrounded by her. Her fingernails dug into his ass, and the sting had his cock sinking another inch or two into that scorching vise, robbing him of breath. He forced himself to stay still. It was difficult when he wanted to bury himself deep in her scalding hot sheath.

Gently, he reminded himself. He was making love to her

the way she thought making love was. She didn't understand
that every single time he touched her, kissed her, clamped
her, devoured her, he was making love to her.

"Would you have trusted him?"

She blinked up at him. He could see she thought about
it before she answered. She shook her head slowly. "No. I
don't know why, when he was so good to me."

"Because your leopard and you scented deceit. He was
deceiving you. You know I'm not. I love you. I told you, I'm
not the best with words, but I show you in everything I do.
Say it. Tell me you love me. Feel it, Sonia. In your heart. In
your fuckin' soul, feel it the way I do."

He sank into her because there was no holding back, no
real control, not when it was his woman. Fire gripped him.
He threw his head back and roared. It was the only way to
stand the flames. She was burning the life out of him. Giving him the kind of pleasure that could take a man's head
off when he blew, the kind he dreamt of, but knew he'd
never get.

Her whisper was soft—so soft he barely caught it with
the roar coming from his burning belly. *I love you.* Three
little words. They gutted him. *She* gutted him. Who knew
a man could love so deeply? Fall so fast? Who knew a
woman could mean so much?

"Mean it, Sonia. Please fucking mean it." He began to
move in her, long, deep strokes, keeping it gentle when his
entire body was in flames. He found that slow could be good.
The burn was scorching hot, the friction as he pushed
through those tight folds was incredible.

"I mean it. It's just . . ." She broke off again, but her eyes
were on his and he saw the truth there. She gave that to him,
and his heart actually hurt in his chest. Thunder crashed in
his ears. She meant every word. She loved him. That would
get them through the next few hours with the things he
would have to say to her.

He kept the pace slow, but caught her ankle again and

wrapped her leg around his waist. She hooked her other ankle behind his back with the first, changing the angle, allowing deeper penetration. Her breath hissed out of her lungs. She moaned—that sound he loved.

"Look at me, baby. Keep looking at me. I want to see it this time."

Her hands gripped his hips, fingers digging in. "Everything you say is always so sexy."

Every hard jolt sent her breasts swaying, her nipples sliding over his chest. "You are sexy. Keep looking at me. You're close, but wait. I want you to wait, I'm right behind you."

She lifted her hips, matching his heat and rhythm the way she always did, taking him deep, letting the fire get close. "Hurry, honey," she whispered, her voice an ache.

He loved that too, the urgency, the plea. He loved the look of near desperation. He kept moving in her. Watching her. Her breath hitched. "Joshua." His name came out a wail. "You have to hurry. I can't . . ." She broke off.

"Close, baby." He was right there, riding the edge. The way she struggled to keep control, the way her inner muscles gripped him, nearly dragging his orgasm out of him, threatened to tip him right over the edge, but he needed this. Needed to see it on her face. That look she gave him. The one that would be there any moment . . . and there it was.

*"Joshua."*

She hung on for him and now she was giving herself to him, trusting that he'd bring her home in a spectacular way. He didn't want to disappoint. He let go of his last remnant of control and surged right through that tight sheath, feeling his cock swell, push against the grip of her muscles creating a fiery friction that was his undoing.

"Now, baby. Let go now."

"It's so big." Her head thrashed but her eyes remained glued to him. Her anchor in the midst of the wild storm.

"I'm here. I'm not going anywhere." He meant every fucking word.

Her eyes widened and her body took over, a quake that rippled through her with the force of a hurricane, sweeping every nerve ending along with it. Her mouth opened and that long keening cry escaped, the one he loved. His body reacted to the fresh liquid fire surrounding him. The hot grip, squeezing down, clamping around his shaft, pumping, draining him dry. He felt the rush in every part of his body, fire consuming him.

He collapsed over her, letting her take his weight, knowing from experience that her hand would be in his hair, stroking and caressing. Giving him love without words. He recognized what it was now. Her way of talking without saying it aloud.

# 13

JOSHUA wanted to keep Sonia pinned under him. It was safer that way, but her breathing was impaired by his weight. She didn't complain, she never did, no matter how long he stayed holding her. He kissed her. Hard this time. Rough even. More him and less the man she deserved but would rarely have.

He drew his hand down her body, from her throat to her mound, as he rolled to the side. Claiming her. He'd been afraid when he knew his mother was dying. He hadn't felt like this. Terrified. His leopard rose, pushing close to the surface, feeling his wild emotions and wanting to emerge to spare him.

"You're always on the verge of flight. I can feel it, so can my leopard. You have to commit, Sonia. Normally, I'm the man others look to in a crisis because I stay calm. Drake has always said I have nerves of steel."

He bent his head to brush his mouth over hers, needing

the reassurance again. She kissed him, no holding back, but then she never did. When he lifted his head, that same urgency was there, the need to hold her to him. It was exasperating to feel that no matter what he did, she was close to slipping away from him.

"Got a lot to tell you," he said. "Don't go to sleep." He forced himself to open the dialogue. He couldn't put it off, not when he knew Nikita Bogomolov was probably on his way back to Louisiana and he'd bring his torpedoes with him. Sonia would have to understand that he was putting her in protective custody. Before that happened, he had to confess to her that she was in bed with the very thing she'd run from.

He groaned and rolled onto his back to stare at the ceiling. She immediately shifted to her side, turning toward him, drawing her knees up. She was close to him, and he noticed the little shiver running through her body. He pulled up the sheet to cover her.

"You need a blanket, baby?"

She shook her head. "I'm good. What do you need to tell me?"

He knew it was going to be rough. He hated this. Hated what it was going to do to her. His revelations had the ability to destroy her. It certainly had every potential to destroy them—their relationship. It was already fragile. For a moment, he considered stalling another day, but every minute meant the danger to her increased.

"I need you to listen to me. All of it. Everything I have to say before you jump to conclusions or react. I want you to promise me."

She frowned, propping her head up on one hand, elbow to the bed. "Now you have me worried. How can I give you a promise when I don't know what you're going to say?"

"Baby, I know trust is difficult to give. I understand why. I do. You're safe with me. I'm that man for you, the one that would do anything for you. You keep that in mind and we're going to be fine."

She sat up slowly, pulling the sheets over her breasts. It was the first time she'd covered up deliberately and he knew the sheet was armor for her. She put her back to the headboard and drew up her knees, her gaze steady on his face.

He sat up as well. He needed mobility. She was feeling vulnerable, he could see that on her expressive face. Her leopard was capable of huge leaps. He didn't want her getting out of the bedroom before he could finish his explanation.

"Joshua?" Her eyes told him she was beginning to panic. "Just tell me."

"I have to go way back, baby. Remember I told you about my mother taking me to Borneo and growing up there? I met Drake Donovan. He was a huge influence in my life. When my mother died, he befriended me and gave me a purpose. It was Drake teaching me how to be faster and stronger, how to fight as both a leopard and a man. He gave me the edge to stay alive when I was working."

Some of the panic faded from her eyes and she took a deep breath and let it out, nodding her head for him to continue.

"After she died, I worked a lot for Drake. I can't tell you how many missions I went out on, but there were a lot of them. Most were relatively simple. I collected information, or made a drop. Most of the kidnappings of tourists or wealthy families living there were fairly straightforward. It was a business, and Donovan Security delivered the ransom and retrieved the victims."

He rubbed the bridge of his nose, watching her carefully. The tension had drained out of her while he talked, and she rested her chin on her knees, her gaze on his face.

"I like hearing about your life."

"It isn't all pretty, baby," he warned. "I haven't always made the best choices."

"No one always makes the best choices. Look at me. My life has been a disaster, thanks to my choices."

He didn't want to touch that one, not with having to tell her why Nikita Bogomolov had been in his home. He sighed and ran both hands through his hair. "Some of the jobs weren't quite that easy. Certain cells kidnapped victims but had no real intention of returning them. We had to go in and take them back. It could get dicey."

She frowned at him. "Joshua, are you worried about telling me the things you had to do to get these people back home safe?"

"They didn't always get back home safe. Sometimes they were killed before we could reach them. There were firefights. I'm not going to lie to you, baby. I did what I was trained for. I kill people. I go in and execute them when I'm ordered to do so." He pressed his fingers to his eyes, fighting back the sounds of gunfire, the smell of blood and death.

Her tongue touched her lip and she swallowed. Nodded. "You said 'kill' as in present tense. I thought, because you're here, that you head up a team, you don't actually participate anymore."

His gaze shifted from hers. He shook his head. It was much harder than he'd thought it was going to be. His life was a tangled web of deception. Sorting it out for her was difficult enough without having to tell her the entire mess he was in—the mess of his own choosing.

"I've gone on three out-of-the-country missions since I've been in the United States," he admitted. "I worked security for Jake Bannaconni before I came here. During my stint with him, I volunteered to go. None of the three were easy, meaning we had to kill the kidnappers to take back the victims."

"I see." She drew her legs in tighter against her body. "I don't like that you're in danger, Joshua."

His heart clenched hard in his chest. She wasn't upset about *what* he had to do. She was worried about his safety. There wasn't going to be a bullshit argument about how wrong it was, which he was happy about. The things he'd seen were enough to convince him that some monsters didn't belong in the world. But then, she'd seen her father tortured and killed; maybe she already understood that concept.

"I thought I'd spend my life in Borneo." His chest hurt. He had to push rage down, rage he could never quite get rid of, no matter how far he traveled or how much he learned about meditation. It was a part of him that he kept separate, compartmentalized, until he had to face it. It was rare for him to allow it to be seen, but he was going to ask a lot of Sonia, the least he could do was show her who and what he truly was and how he got to be where he was.

"I traveled to other rain forests and wherever work took me, I looked for my mate, but I always thought I'd settle permanently where my mother had taken me." He shifted his weight, turned, so that he was sitting close to her. Very close. Thighs touching. He caught her hand and pressed her palm against his thigh, needing her touch.

As if she could read him, she shifted closer until she could brush her fingers through his hair with her free hand, her fingers working magic as they massaged his scalp. He loved when she did that—and she did it often.

"We got word that a new group was working in our area. They were a small band of men, very elusive and able to navigate through the rain forest where others couldn't. Drake sent me to track them. I'd been on their trail for three days. There were five of them, all younger men. I could tell by the way they moved. Fast. Efficient. They knew the forest, and I began to suspect that they were leopard. I knew all the leopards there and I should have been able to identify them, but I didn't have a clue who they were."

He fell silent, his gut churning. "I was slow. A day or so behind them." He shook his head, cursing, trying to find calm when the raging storm was on him once again. He rubbed his jaw, feeling the day-old growth. Back then, the stubble had been growing into a full-fledged beard. He let himself concentrate on her fingers, the way they moved almost hypnotically through his hair. She remained silent, but her gaze never once left his face.

"They raided a small village and took three girls, the daughters of a wealthy family. They were really young. Six, seven and nine." He shook his head and let go of her hand. He needed to move, but he didn't want to pull away from the fingers massaging his scalp so gently. She was his lifeline. His anchor. So delicate, those fingers, conveying her love. He felt it surrounding him.

"They'd set fire to several houses, and the village was in chaos when I arrived. They hadn't asked for ransom and that alarmed me. Why destroy the village when all you were after was money? They weren't staying true to the form of extortionists. Even if they planned on killing the girls later, they would still ask for money."

He took a breath, inhaling the scent of smoke. That terrible smell that never quite left him. Bile rose. "I found them two days later, two fucking days. Those girls were so traumatized they were catatonic by the time I got there. It hadn't mattered to the five of those bastards. They kept using them in every way possible. Sick, vile pieces of shit." He turned his face away from her, feeling tears burning behind his eyes. He couldn't face seeing that again, what those men had done. What leopards and humans were capable of. What *he* was capable of.

"I killed them all. The five of them. They died hard, and I fucking burned them and then buried their ashes so deep no one will ever find them. The girls were . . . damaged. If I'd found them sooner . . ." He trailed off, shaking his head. He would never forgive himself for not catching up with those men. Not ever. He would remember the first glimpse of the camp and what the men were doing to those little girls for the rest of his life. He still had nightmares.

"Once, a good friend of mine told me I didn't have a killer's instinct and I'd always have the disadvantage in a fight. I wish that was the truth, but I learned that night just what's inside me. A monster came out. I had no idea I was capable of anything like that. I didn't want to kill them clean. I wanted them to suffer the way those girls had suffered."

"It's all right, honey," she crooned softly. "It's done and over." Her fingers brushed at his face and then her lips were there.

He realized there were tears on his face. He didn't know if he was crying for the children or for himself, for knowing a monster lived inside of him, fully capable of taking revenge in a way that was so unacceptable to him that he could barely stand looking at himself in the mirror.

"I came back to the States. Drake was working security for Jake Bannaconni, and I joined him. Told him everything. Drake isn't the kind of man you hold back with. He knows what I did, every fucking detail." Joshua pressed his fingertips to the corners of his eyes and willed the migraine hovering so close to stay away. "Drake has been the constant in my life, and he got me through a bad time."

"From everything I've ever heard about him, he's a good man," she murmured.

"He is, Sonia. He's a very good man. I owe him." He wanted her to remember that. He took her hand again and locked it against his bare thigh. "He asked me to take a position for him, one that once I did, I could never get out of. It would be dangerous and I'd be stuck there for life. I said yes. I didn't hesitate or think about it. I was single. I'd looked all over the world for you and didn't think I'd find you, so I said yes." He turned his head to look at her.

Her eyes were dark chocolate. Melted chocolate. She looked at him as the white knight. He hadn't given her the graphic details of what he'd done to those five men, but she had an imagination and yet she still looked at him with love. With that look. That gave him hope. If she could accept the worst in him, the monster, maybe she could accept what he was now. What he would be for the rest of his life.

"I took the job, Sonia, and there's no going back." He had to make that plain. "I don't know where to start when I tell you this. I have to tell you. You need to know for two reasons. The first is that I want you with me, which means you'll be accepting my way of life and all the ugliness that comes with it. Friends turning away, people whispering behind your back."

She frowned, her gaze glued to his. She gave a little shake of her head but remained silent. She clearly had no idea where he was going. He usually had the right words to say, but now, in the most important conversation of his life, his mind was all over the place.

"The second reason is that you're in danger. They know where you are."

Her eyes widened. Her tongue touched her lip. The lower one. The one he loved. God, he hated this.

"Nikita Bogomolov saw the painting hanging over my fireplace and he recognized it as yours. He didn't say so. He tried to buy the painting from me, and when I wouldn't sell, he went up to it and found your signature, the *S* and *L* you loop together. He took pictures with his cell and left abruptly. He was supposed to go to New Orleans for a few days, but said he had an emergency and needed to return immediately."

As he gave her the information, the color drained from her face. Slowly terror crept onto her expressive features. "Nikita was *here*? He found me? Oh my God, Joshua, you can't stay here. You have to leave. He's going to come back and he'll torture you to try to find my whereabouts. I have to leave. I have to run. When was he here? How much time do I have?"

There was terror in her voice, not just for herself, but for him. She still thought he was the good man, the white knight, and the last thing he wanted to do was change her opinion of him, but she had to know.

"Remember I told you I had an important meeting the other day? We canceled all the work because we were meeting here at my house."

"Of course."

"The meeting was with Nikita Bogomolov." He dropped the bomb quietly, watching her carefully. Sonia was smart, but she wanted to believe in him.

"With Nikita? Why would you have a meeting with him?" She shook her head. "If he's kidnapped someone and Drake Donovan wants you to pay the ransom, whoever it is is probably dead. You can't deal with him and win. I know him. They kill entire families."

"It had nothing to do with a kidnap victim," he said, as gently as possible.

"What, then? Why would you meet with him?" The comprehension was there, she just hadn't allowed herself to believe it.

Her heartbeat suddenly accelerated, sounded like a drum to him. Hard. Fast. The rhythm of a prey animal knowing the predator was focused on her. Her tongue touched her lips again, her mouth suddenly dry. He knew all the signs. Her eyes showed shock. Knowledge. The dark chocolate deepened. Swirled with amber. With gold. Her leopard was close.

"Rafe Cordeau. The rumors about him were true. He was a crime boss, wasn't he?" Her voice quivered and she slowly, inch by inch, started to slide her hand from under his. The one in his hair was gone. She made herself very small, curling into her body, but her gaze never left his, as if mesmerized by a viper—or a leopard.

Joshua nodded. "His territory was very large." He had to let her hand go, although every instinct told him to hold on to her. When it slipped through his fingers, he felt as if she were slipping away from him.

"There were rumors that you took his territory over, but because you work for Drake Donovan, no one, not even Bastien, believes them." She paused. Swallowed hard. "But they're true, aren't they?" She whispered the last. Her voice shook. A tremor went through her.

"Baby, you're safe. Know that you're safe. I can take care of Nikita Bogomolov." He needed to reassure her. The last thing he wanted was for her to think he'd struck a bargain with Nikita to turn her over to him, or even that he'd sent word to him. But of course she'd think that. He would have thought that in her place. Her eyes had changed color. They were dilated with the pain of betrayal. Not just any betrayal, but a visceral, soul-shredding betrayal.

He tried to take her hand back, but she shrank back against the headboard, looking at him as if he were a monster. Which he fucking was. But not to her. Never to her.

"Sonia, I didn't know Bogomolov was your father-in-law. You never told me who they were. There's no way I would ever call that son of a bitch and tell him you were here. I didn't know who you were involved with, remember?"

He tried to keep his voice low and even. Soothing. Calm. He willed her to be calm and listen. "You have to know I wouldn't call Bogomolov and let him know you were here. The meeting was already set in advance of Shadow ever finding Gatita—and me discovering you."

She was shaking almost uncontrollably, and she'd made herself so small, he doubted if she'd be able to untangle herself if she didn't relax soon. Her limbs would be locked in that position for eternity. Her skin had grown cold to the touch, something rare in a leopard.

"What other business could you possibly have to be meeting with a man like Nikita Bogomolov?" She whispered the question, but she didn't need an answer. "Unless you're one of them. Unless you're like him. You really did take over Cordeau's territory, and you've got some deal in the works with Nikita." Her mind was allowing her to take in what he was saying and what it meant a little at a time.

He nodded. "I'm not like him, but yes, I have a deal in the works with him. Technically, yes, I did take over Cordeau's territory but . . ."

SONIA couldn't breathe. There was no breath. None. All the air in her lungs had been used and there was no more in the room. That dinner. That sensual dinner and the hot, wild sex after, that had been Joshua, *her* Joshua leading up to this moment of absolute triumph. He had tricked her. *Used* her. Just as Sasha had. It was one thing to have sex and keep it that way, but he'd deliberately tied her to him. Deliberately made her fall in love with him.

She knew she loved Joshua. She'd felt gratitude and affection for Sasha, but she *loved* Joshua and he'd deceived her. There wasn't a doubt in her mind that he had sold her out to Nikita. The two men were in the same business. They were criminals, and they cared nothing for the people they hurt.

*Gatita. What's wrong with me that I attract horrible men? I can't breathe.* She couldn't think, only curl into a ball and wish the earth would open and swallow her. *How do I get away from him? From Nikita. Now they know I'm alive and they'll hunt us to the ends of the earth.*

Her entire body shuddered with pain. She couldn't hear anything Joshua said over the screaming in her ears. She wanted to scream. To shred her vocal cords. Her heart was shredded. He had eviscerated her. No sound emerged. Everything she felt was locked inside. Deep. Where no one could see or hear. She was locked there, unable to cope with another betrayal.

Sasha had been her savior. She'd looked up to him for years before she'd ever agreed to be his wife. Nikita had treated her like a daughter long before she'd learned he'd been behind the murder of her father. She'd been horrified and shocked to hear him tell Sasha that the price for Sonia's life was her mother in his bed. That was how one did things.

Now Joshua. Joshua forcing her declaration that she loved him. Would they compare notes? Tell each other how best to control and amuse themselves with a human being? Her life? Her emotions? She held herself tighter. She was looking at him, but she couldn't see him. She didn't want to see him, not with the tears blurring her vision and the ones inside of her, so many, threatening to create a flood. *Gatita, help me. Tell me what to do.* She had no one else. There was her leopard. She'd let her cat down. *Gatita . . .*

JOSHUA swallowed what he was trying to say. He was no longer looking into Sonia's dark chocolate eyes. Gold swirled through them, driving the brown out, taking over until he was staring into the fierce, angry eyes of her leopard. He held up his hand. "Sonia, stay in control." He made it a command.

It was too late, far too late. Joints cracked. Sonia was naked, just as he was. She didn't need to take the time to rip off her clothes. Her body unfolded, contorted, and then she was on her hands and knees, muscles sliding beneath the skin, fur pushing through until the black leopard with the gold outlining of every black rosette stood on his bed, no more than a foot from him.

He threw his arms up to ward off the sleek leopard. It was in a fury, the rage palatable, the cat protecting its human from the betrayer. Gatita hit him hard, knocking him off the bed and slashing his chest. It hurt like hell, a hot fire burning through his skin straight to his cat. Shadow clawed and raked, just as furious, not understanding what happened but desperate to protect him—even from his mate.

Joshua pushed to his knees, his eyes on Gatita, fighting

his own leopard back. They didn't need a full-on war between two leopards; neither would win. She whirled and slashed at him, raking across his thigh as she spun back and leapt for the door. One paw contorted again and she was out, easily jumping for the nearest branch and running along it toward the second branch.

"Evan!" He roared it, leaping up, bloody, his body raging with fire. His cat fighting him every step. He rushed to the balcony, gripped the rail and sent out his call. It was a low-high snarl, the sound unmistakable to his men. He let his cat growl this time, letting Gatita know the males would be coming and her best bet was to return.

Only when he heard the other males call, taking up the hunting roar, did he allow Shadow to the forefront. The male was in a fury, his human hurt and bloody, his mate escaping and the adrenaline rush of the hunt on him.

THEY were coming for her. Gatita heard the male leopards and she paused for a moment on the branch leading to home. *They are coming.*

Sonia tried to clear the chaos from her mind. She'd heard them too. At least six. Maybe more. She identified Joshua's leopard from his voice when he roared out his challenge. They were hunting Gatita. Once again, she had failed to protect her leopard and the cat was in more peril than ever.

*Get us home.* The leopards couldn't attack her in the truck. She had weapons. She had been careful to keep that fact from anyone other than Molly. She was good with guns; her parents had insisted she practice daily. Her father had taken her out to the firing range every single day. Her mother had insisted she continue practicing. She had a shotgun as well. Point and shoot. That would stop a leopard. But . . . Oh, God. She was really thinking about killing Joshua.

Anguish welled up, sharp and terrible, her mind allowing more of the betrayal to slip in. She couldn't face it all at once. The idea that Joshua would deliberately get her to fall in love with him, even going so far as to force an admission out of her . . . Tears leaked out of her eyes, and out of Gatita's eyes.

*Fast, Gatita, get us home fast.*

Maybe she could get a head start, get in the truck and drive. They'd come after her, but she could find sanctuary somewhere. Bastien and Molly? Could she endanger them? Bastien was a cop. He had cop friends. She could go into protective custody. But for how long?

She'd never hurt so much in her life. Not even when she'd discovered Nikita had been the one to order her father's death. Not when she'd found out he'd forced her mother to sleep with him. It hadn't hurt this much when Sasha had discussed killing her so casually with his father. That had been brutal, but this was even more so. This shattered her soul, and she wasn't altogether certain she would make it through.

*You will. I'm here with you.*

Gatita. She could always count on her leopard, but she'd put her in such danger. The big male would come for her and he was very experienced in fighting.

*He will hesitate and I won't,* Gatita assured. *He is my true mate; his human is treacherous. Shadow had to know what Joshua was and what his plan was, but he chose not to tell me. He deserves whatever he gets.*

Gatita made the jump onto the upper balcony leading to her bedroom. She shifted, and Sonia ran into the room, yanked her "go" bag out from under the bed and raced for her closet. She kept her weapons behind a wall where she'd made a secret compartment. Thrusting the smallest handgun into her pack, she added two clips and then pulled out her shotgun.

*They are coming. We have a better chance in the swamp. I'm smaller and lighter. They can't go into the places I can.*

Sonia swung her head toward the swamp. She hadn't turned on lights. It was dark inside the house and no one could see in. It hurt to move. Every muscle and joint ached, along with her heart. She was still having trouble finding enough air. She needed to be able to breathe, when she felt as if she were choking, strangling, hands around her neck slowly snuffing the life out of her. He'd done that. Joshua.

*Are you certain? Gatita, if they catch you, they might kill you.*

*I've spent time looking for places I can go. Like you, I was afraid and wanted to make certain we had a way out. I can do this.* Gatita was unafraid and very calm in the midst of the storm. She was hurt, but the anguish and agony Sonia was feeling simply made her every protective instinct come forward.

Sonia had to make the decision fast. She tossed the shotgun on the bed, slung her bag around her neck and ran to the balcony. Shifting was getting easier. Gatita jumped to the ground, making for the swamp fast. Leopards weren't known for sustained speed and Sonia tried to keep hers from using up her energy with too much speed. They were in this for the long haul.

*He made love to me, Gatita. There's a difference and I could feel the difference. How could he do that? How could he be so deceptive? How could Sasha? What's wrong with me that I choose men like that? I don't understand it. They have to enjoy seducing and then betraying me or they wouldn't go to such lengths.*

*I would kill them both for hurting you if I could.* Her little female seemed fearless.

She could feel the rage smoldering in the cat as she moved through the swamp. She was sure-footed and light on her feet. Sonia knew the males would scent her, although the female was being careful not to rub her body along the trunks or brush. Their advantage was that Gatita had gone out nightly to run and play. Sonia knew her scent was everywhere.

They angled away from both the road and Joshua's estate,

keeping away from the river, although Gatita stayed parallel to it. Once they were past the area where the hunter was staying in his cabin, Gatita wanted to use the water to conceal the direction she was taking.

*There are a number of alligators,* Sonia cautioned.

*I am aware,* Gatita returned. *We will get away from the bull's territory and I can keep from being attacked by the females.*

*It's all the bull's territory. Those females are his. We need to get farther upriver before we go in.*

*The males will know. To get to the escape route I planned, we need the river.*

Sonia felt it was too big of a risk. Those alligators were larger than most in the area, and she didn't want Gatita tangling with them despite the leopard's assurance.

*Let me take this part. I can run through the swamp and get us to the place you're looking for. Maybe I'll leave less scent for them to find. They won't be expecting that.*

She would be naked and barefoot. Not at all practical in the swamp. She didn't care. Joshua had stripped her of all armor and then he'd ripped her apart. Shattered her until she knew she would never be the same. He'd taught her a lesson she would never forget—if she survived.

*No, I will get us there. You could get hurt.*

*Do you think anything will ever hurt me more than I'm already hurting? He gutted me, Gatita. Gutted me. There's nothing left. He didn't even leave me the ability to protect you, and that's the worst hurt.*

Gatita kept moving. *We protect each other. This is my time to step up when you need me. I know you're hurt, I can feel you curled up in a little ball, in the fetal position, because he took your heart. It's my time to protect you, Sonia. Let me.*

*I love you so much.* Sonia hadn't thought herself capable of loving anyone ever again. She was so certain she couldn't feel. That she would eventually go completely numb. Frozen was what she wanted—no, needed. So far, that hadn't happened.

Gatita picked her way through downed trunks and vegetation, moving through the brush with care. Behind them, they heard an ominous crack, a tree limb breaking. Were the male leopards pursuing them already that close?

*If they find us, Sonia, will they kill us?*

*I hope so.* That was the simple truth. *I don't want to be tortured by Nikita. I think he's angry enough to use us to teach everyone a lesson about what happens when someone runs from him.*

*When Joshua turns us over to Nikita, show him me. He will keep us prisoners, but he won't kill us.* Gatita sounded certain of that. *Together we will find a way to escape.*

*He'd put us in a cage. He might even skin you and use your fur for a rug. I wouldn't put it past him.* She would never be able to stop Nikita from harming the leopard once he knew about her.

*We would have to take that chance if he decided to kill you outright.*

Gatita had taken them far from the house into a part of the swamp Sonia hadn't yet explored in her human form. She was present when Gatita went running, but she didn't always pay attention. Now she wished she had. Gatita crouched low and entered a tunnel made by a smaller animal. Perhaps a fox? It smelled like fox. The labyrinth was narrow and very low. Gatita dragged herself through it, following the twisting trail that took them very close to the river. Before Sonia could stop her, the valiant little leopard jumped into the water.

Sonia's breath hissed out. She had to stay alert, as did Gatita. The bag around the leopard's neck was waterproof and everything inside had been double protected against water except for her weapon. She'd thrown that in carelessly, a stupid, stupid mistake. It would have taken seconds to secure it, but she'd been panicked.

The leopard swam through the river, staying close to the shore. Sonia expected her to swim toward the island, but the cat avoided the other side altogether.

*They will expect that.*

Of course they would. *You're so smart, Gatita. Thank you for helping me.* The panic and shock she experienced at the betrayal were beginning to recede enough that her brain was starting to work. The problem with that was now she had to cope with the intensity of her pain. It was brutal and she wanted to retreat into a catatonic state, but she didn't have that luxury, not with Joshua and the others on her trail.

Gatita moved a little faster, but still stayed at a safe, steady speed. Running would get her out of breath and she couldn't sustain it for long. Swimming was equally as difficult. Already, she was beginning to breathe hard, her sides heaving with every breath she drew.

*Almost there,* Sonia encouraged her.

It was a good thing that Gatita had been running every night in the swamp. Not only had she explored extensively, but she was in good shape. She had to be. The males were larger, and if anything Joshua had told her was true, they were kept in fighting shape. She didn't want Gatita to have to fight them. She wasn't about to let that happen. Better her getting torn apart than her leopard.

It wasn't Gatita who had fallen in love. Sonia felt another rush of pain, of bile. She'd sat across from Joshua, doing everything he asked. She'd *wanted* to have that egg inside her. Not just because of the pleasure it had brought her, but to see his face. She'd liked watching him watch her. The sensual lines had deepened, his eyes had darkened and become heavy-lidded with passion. She knew what she did to him and it felt powerful and wonderful. Sexy as all get-out. She'd done that to herself.

Joshua had made certain every step she'd cooperated with him had been her choice. She'd loved him all the more for that. He'd made it clear he would stop if she didn't like something he did. He'd made her feel safe and loved. All along he'd been playing her. A sob escaped and bubbled in her mind. Hurting. It was more than hurting. It was agony.

She had to stop, not think about it. Not think about him. Nothing had been real. It was all a ruse, including after dinner, when he'd made slow love to her. When he'd touched every inch of her skin so reverently. She should have known.

Nikita had said it. She just had refused to believe it. Girls like her were for fucking, not marrying. She was trash. That's what Nikita had meant. Evidently, Joshua had read that in her as well. Bastien was a good man. He'd looked right past her to Molly. Molly wasn't like her, the type of woman one fucked and then threw away.

She tried to jam her fist figuratively into her mouth to prevent any more sobs from making it into her mind. It hurt too much. Still, they were there along with the silent screaming.

*We're close. We're coming out of the water to the place near the road where I think you can get us a ride.* Gatita sounded elated.

They'd made it. Triumph surged through Sonia. Even with the leopards on them, they had outsmarted the males. Well, Gatita had outsmarted them. She had planned an escape route just in case.

*I learned from you, Sonia. You always have a plan for us. You're always prepared.*

She hadn't been prepared this time. Joshua had taken her off guard. *Thank you, my beautiful and intelligent Gatita. I don't know what I'd do without you.*

Gatita swam for shore and when the river was shallow enough, walked out of the water. Every step was slow, and she padded a distance from the canal to ensure an alligator didn't spot them and come looking out of curiosity.

*Need to rest for a moment,* Gatita explained as she powered forward the few more steps that took her back into heavier swamp. She flopped down beneath the shade of a black gum tree. Sonia remained alert, scanning the area, her heart beating hard.

*I can take us to the road.*

*No.* Gatita was adamant. *It will take me less time and be easier.*

She got to her feet just as they heard a twig snap. Then another. And another. Seven twigs snapped. Each sound came from somewhere around them, as if they were surrounded.

Heart pounding, despair hitting hard . . . Sonia thought each move out. She would have to shift fast, hands first, reach for the bag, unzip it, pull out her gun and be ready to fire before the males could do so. If the men didn't shift as well and their leopards attacked, it would all be over fast.

# 14

GATITA took all decisions from Sonia's hands. As the males came out of the swamp, ringing them, making it impossible to escape, the little female charged. She didn't snarl or slap at the leaves with her paw to show displeasure. There was no ritual to give her away, she simply rushed her mate before Sonia could stop her, slapping at his face and slashing at his neck as she went past, intending to break through the circle.

Instantly two heavier males closed on her from either side, slamming her to the ground. One had her throat in his mouth while the other held her. Her heart beat wildly. Air sawed in and out of her heaving lungs. Her tail swished. Hot breath blasted in her face, making her narrow her eyes to slits.

*Kai and Gray,* Sonia identified, another sob bursting through her brain like a heated missile. *I liked them. I really thought they liked me.* Could she shift just one paw and get to her gun before either stopped her? She doubted it, but was she going to just lie there and hope they didn't kill her? She could get off one shot. Maybe two. It had to be Kai and Gray, the two men she was closest with. She wanted it to be Joshua, but she wasn't certain she could pull the trigger. She loved him, and that didn't just go away because he was a liar.

"Don't hurt her."

She couldn't see him because at the angle Kai had taken her down, he was blocking her view of Joshua. But that voice, filled with command, made her body jerk in protest. That was Joshua—the boss.

No, she couldn't kill Joshua for herself. Not for self-preservation. But she could kill him to save Gatita. She used the leopard's radars, taking in all the information coming from whiskers and hair to find Joshua's exact location. While Gatita appeared to be refusing to submit, she practiced what she would do in smooth order, over and over again until she felt she could do it in her sleep.

*Now, Gatita, submit. Relax.*

Every ounce of fight went out of the female leopard at once, the tension draining from her, leaving her limp, staring up at Kai's big male while he had his teeth around her throat. His big head had pushed the pack up, which meant Sonia would have to reach farther than she'd hoped, but the gun was loose and would be easy to grab.

She waited a heartbeat. All the leopards turned their attention—and their heads—toward Joshua for further instructions. Sonia took a breath and exploded into action, one leg and paw shifting. Her arm wrapped around the head of Kai's male and zipped open the bag. She dropped her hand inside, and for one heart-stopping moment thought she'd lost the gun. Then it was in her fist. She thumbed the safety off as she drew it from the bag and shoved it into the side of Kai's neck.

Triumph and despair mixed again. She didn't want to kill anyone. That wasn't in her nature, even though she'd learned sometimes it was the only thing to do that stopped monsters.

She had to shoot him while she had the chance, and the next target would be Joshua, not Gray.

Movement caught her eye, and Joshua stood in front of them. He was naked. Totally naked, every muscle on display. His genitals were heavy and impressive. Blood streaked his thigh, chest and face. Blood dripped but he did nothing to stop it.

"Sonia, baby, you didn't give me a chance to explain everything. I asked you to hear me out. You don't want to shoot Kai. He had nothing to do with what's true between the two of us. Point the gun at me if that makes you feel safe, and we'll talk."

If she did, she'd lose all advantage and she knew it. Still, his voice was so powerful that before she could think it through, she'd started to turn the weapon away from the huge male. Something hit her arm from behind, dragging it at an odd angle, wrenching it. The gun was yanked from her hand, leaving her defenseless. There was no way out and these leopards weren't killing Gatita; she was going to force them to kill her.

She tried to take control and her leopard fought her for supremacy. She detested Joshua in that moment. He'd deliberately distracted her, coming close while naked. Exposing himself in his most vulnerable form in order to give his men a chance at stripping the gun from her.

*Gatita, let me shift.*

*No, I won't let them kill you.* The cat had her most stubborn tone, the one that told Sonia all the best commanding and pitiful whining wouldn't budge her. She shifted her arm and hand back, leaving the playing field to the little cat.

Kai and Gray slowly let Gatita up, but stayed close, boxing her in to keep her from having room to attack. She snarled at Joshua as she came to her feet, but made no move toward him. What would be the point? She had to conserve energy.

"Sonia, you can't win. There are seven of us and one of you. You don't want your cat torn to shreds. Head back to the house with us and don't do anything crazy. I know you're scared, but there's no need to be. I'd protect you with my life. We can't stay here and talk. There's a hunter just across the river and he isn't local. I'm asking you to think about what that could mean and do the right thing, just come with us quietly."

So many scenarios ran through her head. She didn't have a gun, but she could make him kill her right there. If they took her back to his house she would have a very small chance that she could escape again, but if she couldn't escape he'd turn her over to Nikita, and she didn't want to be tortured. Nikita wasn't going to just kill her outright. Still, going to his house might be better than getting torn to shreds.

Gatita snarled, showing her teeth. She slapped her paw at the ground, sending a long trail of leaves into the air to show her displeasure.

"Boss, back away. They aren't going to let her move until you get to safety," Evan said.

Sonia shifted her gaze to him. The man had partially shifted so he could speak. She had thought him a friend as well. She'd worked around these men. They'd meant something to her. She waited while Joshua studied her little female.

"I would never hurt you, Sonia. Not. Ever. I can understand why you think I might have sold you out. I can understand why you think I've betrayed you. Think about this rationally. Right now, you're in fight-or-flight mode. You aren't thinking. You have to know what we have between us is real. All the same, even knowing how fucked up your thinking is, it's still fucking insulting." He turned his back on her and shifted as he walked away.

She felt small. He made her feel that way. In front of his men, he'd reduced her to the aggressor with him as the victim. He'd even looked and sounded hurt. She didn't want to think about the honesty she heard in his voice. He'd sounded honest when he'd told her he loved her—but then so had Sasha. What explanation was there for that?

*Is it possible you can't tell a lie from the truth, Gatita?* She relied heavily on her leopard's senses.

*I am very confused. Shadow says I am his mate and cannot leave him. His male thinks the same of you. He seems sincere, although he is very, very angry with me for hurting Joshua.*

Gatita was slow in starting. She stood without moving, just staring at Joshua's big male as if he might have all the answers. That made Sonia uneasy. If Joshua could get his male to convince her female he intended them no harm, he'd be able to do almost anything.

Shadow approached. The moment he did, every male went on high alert. The big male shouldered her to get her moving; she snarled, turned her head and raked him with her teeth. Shadow leapt away so the teeth barely scraped his shoulder, but he whirled around and slammed his body hard against Gatita's, sending her to the ground.

Fury raged through Sonia. She took control immediately, taking advantage of Gatita being stunned at her mate's actions. She burst to the surface, driving Gatita back to take her own form. She didn't care how naked she was or how many men saw her that way. She was a shifter and shifters didn't care. How many times had Joshua said that?

She kicked the large leopard hard with the ball of her foot, a perfect front kick, snapped out hard and fast to his side, followed by a heel hook. She drove her heel into his side in the exact same spot, hoping to break his ribs.

"Fuck you, Joshua. You want me dead, you kill me, not my leopard!" She shouted it, so angry she kept driving toward the furious leopard with her feet.

The leopard sprang back, but already he was shifting, and Joshua was coming at her, his face a mask of anger. Those crystalline eyes glittered at her, every bit as turbulent as the most violent storm. Her breath caught in her lungs as he blocked her kick and stepped inside, one hand catching her fist and twisting hard so her body slammed up against his.

"What part of 'we don't know who that hunter is or what he wants' didn't you understand? He isn't local. He could be Nikita's man. Is that what you want? To go back to Sasha Bogomolov? To a man who agreed to kill you?"

He held her too tightly, and she knew she'd have bruises. The bruises on her skin didn't matter, it was what he was doing to her mind and heart with his snide tone. She raked the edge of her foot down his shin and then stomped hard on his foot, wishing she was wearing steel-toed boots. She'd found the perfect reason to own a pair.

"You are not going to endanger yourself one more minute. Not one. We're going back to the house and you're going to listen to everything I say. Out here, we're all in danger. What your female did, attacking me, put both of you in danger from every leopard here. And kicking my leopard? What if I didn't shift fast enough? What if I couldn't control him and he'd ripped your heart out? She's throwing a tantrum and you're letting her."

Her breath was trapped in her throat, closing off her airway. She could barely hear anything he said, but a tantrum? He'd ripped out her heart and he thought leaving was some kind of childish fit? Before she could find her voice and tell him to go to hell, he thrust her away from him.

"Fucking shift now, Sonia. Do it fast and head straight back for the house. You don't have a stitch on."

"Neither do you," she hissed, suddenly aware of how naked she was.

"Do you think I want you putting on a show for everyone? Shift. *Now.* You pull anything like this again, or draw attention to us, I swear you'll regret it."

"Just shoot me and get it over with, don't threaten me."

He was back on her in half a second, looming over top of her, his hands gripping her biceps, fingers biting deep as he gave her a little shake. "You're talking suicide, Sonia. *Fucking suicide.*" His voice was low but so intense it felt as if he'd roared it. If it was possible, his skin had gone pale under his permanent tan. "You're not going there. Not in your mind. Not in reality. That's unacceptable. You need to get past the emotion just enough to hear what I'm saying. I didn't know Bogomolov had anything to do with you. Already, I know I'm going to take him out. You *will* be safe from him. Just come back to the house and listen to me."

He had the upper hand. He'd brought six men with him, all leopards and all ready to take her down if she so much as made a move toward him. She nodded, because what else could she do? But believe him? Not so much.

Gatita took over, ignoring her mate, and started back toward the huge plantation house. Evan led the way, and Gatita followed with the others surrounding her. Sonia lost sight of Joshua, although she could smell his wild scent. He was bringing up the rear, following closely in her footsteps. She thought Gatita was magnificent. Totally magnificent. She looked like a queen as she padded through the swamp, refusing to be hurried. She set the pace and made it clear she was the one doing it.

The males surrounded her, but they couldn't force her to speed up. They didn't dare shoulder her; her mate would never have permitted it. Joshua was careful, now that she was in motion, to keep her moving. Sonia was certain he knew that if his leopard tried to reprimand her female, she would shift again and attack him.

It took a very long time to retrace their steps to his plantation. Twice, two of the leopards, one she knew was called Carter and the other Fergus, broke off from the group and backtracked, as if they suspected they were being followed. That made Sonia uneasy. She hadn't kept her voice down, not even when Joshua admonished her to. If the hunter had heard them and let loose his dogs, he might be able to track them. He had a gun. He could shoot any of the leopards, or it was possible they would have to kill him. That would be on her. An innocent man, probably one just trying to find food for his family, didn't deserve to be torn apart by leopards he stumbled across.

For the first time, she forced her mind to think beyond her own misery. Right at that moment, she thought she didn't care if Joshua died. She even thought she wanted him dead—that was until she realized a hunter could be trailing them. She didn't want anyone to die, least of all Joshua. Conflicted, so confused by her own vacillation, she urged Gatita to pick up the pace.

Fog had begun to creep through the trees, turning the dark night to a gray veil. There was little breeze and the insects were abnormally quiet, choosing to stay hidden when the pack of leopards invaded their territory. Sonia began to feel a kind of dread, her stomach knotting with every step they took. She didn't like the way the leopards were acting, taking turns to drop back and go along their back trail. She didn't like the fact that they were close to Joshua's home and she might not get another opportunity to escape.

*Why are the males so uneasy?*

*They caught the scent of an outsider.*

*Did you catch it?* Ordinarily, when Gatita smelled something, she shared it with Sonia.

*I thought, for a moment, I did,* Gatita admitted, *but it is elusive and it was gone within seconds. Still, the others have checked repeatedly.*

Sonia tried to think of a question that would gain her information. Talking with a leopard through images and heightened emotion was difficult sometimes. *Do you believe we are being followed?*

*Yes.*

Sonia's heart lurched. Joshua had been right to believe the hunter might hear her. He was stealthy as well. Any hunter capable of throwing seven male leopards and Gatita off his track and scent had skills.

*Get moving faster. I don't want the hunter shooting at us.*

*I do not believe he will shoot.*

Sonia blew her breath out in exasperation. Gatita was thoroughly angry with her mate. She didn't want to cooperate in any way.

*I kicked him for you,* Sonia reminded.

*They betrayed us. There is no forgiveness.* Gatita made that very clear. *By not warning me that your man was like Sasha, Shadow is equally to blame.*

*I agree,* Sonia said a little reluctantly. She didn't want Gatita doing anything that would get the male to turn on her. When they killed her, Sonia was determined they would kill the human, not the leopard, so Gatita wouldn't feel it as much.

The back of the plantation house loomed up through the gray fog. Sonia wanted to hide in Gatita's form, fear crawling down her spine. She would have to face Joshua again. It was the last thing she wanted to do, but it was inevitable.

*Do you remember what I did with my cell?*

*It was in the "go" bag.*

*That was a different one for emergencies.* She knew Gray had the bag around his neck. It wouldn't do her much good now. *What did I do with my everyday cell, the one I use for work?*

There was silence as Gatita navigated the branch leading to the upper deck. The other males fell back, making a show of circling the house so she would know she was a prisoner and if she got away a second time, she would be hunted down.

*Your phone was in the master bedroom, on the little table between the chairs.* There was the image in Gatita's mind.

Joshua shifted and opened the French doors to allow Gatita through, into the master bedroom. He stepped back to let them inside and then closed the double doors and locked them.

*Get close to the table.*

Gatita obeyed, her tail swishing dangerously as she padded

across the room to the table. Sonia shifted, her hand closing over the phone as she turned to face Joshua. His face was a mask, all traces of the man who had been seemingly loving and gentle gone. In his place was a cold, hard stranger. Dangerous as hell. Scary dangerous. His eyes were that crystalline blue, but now arctic cold, so cold she shivered. One moment he was across the room from her, the next he was on her, his hand closing around her wrist like a vise. He tore the phone from her hand and flung it across the room.

"What the fuck is wrong with you? Were you planning on calling Molly? Or Bastien? Do you want to get them killed? Do you think I'd let them take you from me?"

She detested being weaker than he was. He could so easily use his physical strength against her.

Joshua threw his hands into the air, then pressed his fingers to his temples as if he had a headache. "I've had just about all I can take from you tonight," he said quietly. "Do you need to use the bathroom, because we're going to talk. We have to talk."

He sighed again and ran his hand along the bloody rake mark across his chest. He looked vulnerable. Sad. He just stood there facing her, standing ramrod straight, blood dripping from his chest. His cheek. His thigh. Her heart contracted. She was terrified of him, believed he'd betrayed her, but her heart still clenched seeing him like that.

He pointed to the bathroom. "Damn it, baby, I know you're scared and you have every reason to be, but please. I'm asking you. I'm *begging* you. Hear me out."

She desperately needed to get away from him. Anything would be a respite. She nodded, trying to ignore the fact that her treacherous body knew he was close. It recognized him as the one who owned it, who ruled it. She wouldn't have minded so much if it was just her body, but he owned her heart. Her soul. He'd shattered both. She thought she wouldn't feel for him, but that look on his face, as if he was devastated. That moved her. That made her want to go over every word he'd said to her. To hear his voice, every nuance. She wanted to believe him. She turned and all but rushed toward the master bath.

"Leave the door open."

"I'm not leaving the door open," she protested.

He was on her again, catching her from behind, his hands on her upper arms, pulling her back to his front. Her close proximity was affecting his body the same way his was her. She felt his cock, thick and hard, pressed tightly against her. His hands were gentle on her, not hard and biting. His breath was warm against her skin.

"You all but told me you were willing to commit suicide, Sonia. *I* drove you to that. That man who loves you more than his own life. More than anyone's life. I'm not taking chances with you. You have to hear me out. If you still can't be with me after the threat to you is gone, I'll try to let you go. I won't lie to you. You walk out on us, my leopard will lose his mind. So will I, but I won't have you so unhappy that you contemplate taking your own life."

She closed her eyes. She couldn't take his gentle. His sweet. She didn't hear a single lie in his voice, but how could she trust herself? She didn't even trust Gatita to ferret out truth from lies. "I don't want that hunter's death on me, Joshua. Please tell the others not to kill him if he comes looking around."

"No one is going to harm him," he said. "Just get into the shower. I've gotten blood all over you."

He nuzzled her neck, pushing her hair from her nape. Each time she moved, even a little, his cock slid deliciously over her skin. She was ashamed for even thinking any kind of sexual thought, but it was far worse with her body reacting to his. She ached and burned, but more, her heart was bleeding.

"I'll take a shower with the door open," she conceded.

His hands dropped away, and he turned his back on her, pacing across the room. She noticed he didn't turn on the lights. She didn't either. She all but ran into the bathroom, straight to the shower. The hot water poured over her, and with it came tears. She didn't understand what was happening.

She loved him. *Loved* him. How did she see the truth through that? How did she see betrayal through that? She'd been in exactly the same situation, maybe a different kind of love, but love all the same, and the man she'd believed since her childhood had tried to kill her. Was it really a coincidence that Joshua had a meeting with Nikita? Was that even possible? She wanted it to be but . . . She didn't know what to do, what to believe.

She had a healthy sense of self-preservation. Maybe her body didn't and it still wanted Joshua the second he was close to her, but her brain screamed out to run. She didn't have that luxury so, standing under the spray of hot water, she forced calm back into the chaos. She had to think. She knew her brain was her greatest weapon. If she could think straight, she had a chance of divining the truth.

She turned away from the open door, where she kept glimpsing Joshua as he paced up and down the long, wide room. She hated seeing the blood seeping out of those rake marks, especially knowing Gatita had put them there in her defense. She hated that he kept pressing his fingers to his eyes, to his temples. She didn't like that tone of sorrow. The look of desolation on his face. Was he really that good of an actor? Sasha had been. Putting one hand on the wall of the shower, she ducked her head and closed her eyes, allowing the water to soothe her. She needed her mind to stop the chaos and let her think.

She wasn't aware of him until she felt him pressed up against her back. She started to turn, her heart beating hard, her sex clenching. His hand slammed hard into the wall beside her head, palm flat. His arm snaked around her waist and he laid his head between her shoulder blades, breathing her in.

"I told you I loved you, Sonia. I gave you more than I've ever given another human being, things about me I wouldn't want anyone else to know. I couldn't set you up for a fall. What would be the point? Baby, please. Please. Please. Just listen to me. Hear what I'm saying. Let me in past the hurt and hear me. I need you to do that."

His lips moved against her bare skin with every word. The water poured down over them. His arm was a band around her chest, right under her breasts, holding her under the spray, but it was the ache in his voice that threatened to drown her.

Tremors took hold, a thousand goose bumps, a million butterflies. She was *so* susceptible to him because she wanted to believe him. She wanted to hear the honesty in his voice—the hurt. And there was hurt.

"Sasha told me he loved me."

She felt the sweep of his lashes against her back. His breath was warm. "Did he? Did it feel the same? When I hold you, when I kiss you, when my cock is inside you and I'm moving in you, looking into your eyes, does that feel the same?"

She shook her head before she could stop herself. Tears were close. For him. For her. For her really fucked-up life. "I don't understand, Joshua. If you love me, why are you holding me prisoner? Why come after me when you knew I wanted to leave?"

"Nikita Bogomolov knows you're alive. He knows because I hung your painting over my fireplace. God, I love that fucking picture. I stand in front of it and just stare some days when I first get back home. I hate that he found you that way—because I wanted something of you in my home. I hate that he laid eyes on it."

His palm lifted from the wall and then slammed back down again. "You can't run from a man like that. I've done research on him. Our teams did research on him. I know far more than you're ever going to know about him because the man is a monster. He won't stop coming after you unless he's dead."

He sighed and pressed his forehead right between her shoulder blades. "I know you're hurt and confused right now, Sonia. I know it must feel like history repeating itself to you. I should have just sat you down right away and told you. Better yet, I should have blown his fuckin' head off right there in the great room. I can only tell you that I love you with every breath I take. I want you to feel that. Feel *me,* not them. Sort us out in your head so you know I'm real."

The arm around her waist moved so that his hand slid under her left breast, cupping the soft weight, his thumb sliding over her nipple. She told herself to stop him. She couldn't be with him, not until she knew exactly what he was, what his relationship with Nikita was, but she couldn't force her body away from him. It felt intimate. It felt comforting. It was Joshua, and she loved him with every beat of her heart. She pressed her forehead against the wall and let tears leak out, hoping the water washed them away before he could see them.

"What does that mean?" She whispered the question. Tired. Tired of being afraid. Of fighting. Of not knowing the truth.

"It means I have no choice but to kill him."

"Then Sasha would come after you. Who knows how many others? That's the way it works with them and if you researched, you would know that." She told herself to step aside, to turn and push him away, but she couldn't. She closed her eyes and savored the way his thumb strumming over her nipple sent little waves of heat shimmering through her bloodstream.

"I'm more than aware of that. I've got people watching them." He turned her very, very gently and then pulled her into his arms, so that her head was resting against his chest. "They're prepping for war."

Her heart thudded hard and panic welled up, cutting off her air supply. "I can't breathe." She felt faint. She didn't understand any of it. Why her father had chosen to rob a man as powerful and vindictive as Nikita Bogomolov. Why they had spared her mother and her. Why he'd forced her mother to sleep with him. Why her mother had let her believe the Bogomolovs were good people. Why had Sasha pretended to marry her? Or maybe actually married her. How could she be getting others killed when she hadn't done anything at all other than be her father's daughter?

Joshua reached past her to turn off the shower. He wrapped her in a towel and dried her off. "Nothing is going to happen to you. I swear to you, I'll protect you."

She had to know. She *had* to know who to believe. "I need the truth from you, even if it means you're going to have to kill me because I know. Did you take over Rafe Cordeau's territory?" She needed him to say it again. To lay it out for her in black and white. "Are you in the mob? Did I somehow get mixed up with the things you told me?"

She sank down onto the edge of the bed, looking up at him as he dried off his body. Her gaze didn't stray down to look at all that muscle, at the hard length of him she loved. Her eyes stayed fixed to his.

"I took over Cordeau's territory, and yes, I am technically part of the mob."

She swallowed hard. He hadn't even blinked. He'd looked right into her eyes. There was no feel of a threat, or regret. Just honesty. She took a breath, gulping in air when her throat closed.

"There's more to it than that, and you didn't give me the chance to tell you. It's complicated, but it's a life I no longer can get out of. I tried to explain it, but you . . ." He rubbed the towel through his hair. "Understandably, you couldn't hear what I was saying."

"So, say it again." She couldn't leave. She didn't want to listen, but she didn't want to think he would sell her out to the Bogomolovs. This was Joshua, the man she'd spent night after night with, lying on the bed, talking about everything and nothing. Laughing. She'd never done that with Sasha. Sasha had treated her gently, carefully, but he'd rarely spent time with her, not even in the bedroom.

"Get dressed, baby. You're distracting sitting there with all that beautiful skin. I can barely control myself when you're covered up. It's impossible when you're sitting on a bed with your body tempting mine."

That was Joshua. He sounded sincere, as if he really couldn't look at her without needing to touch her. He made her feel beautiful and wanted. She'd loved Sasha, and she knew now, it was a love that had nothing to do with an adult woman loving an adult man. She still loved Sasha. He'd been her best friend and confidant. He'd smoothed out every rocky road. He'd never made her feel as if he couldn't wait to touch her. She'd been the one to ask him why he didn't want her in the bedroom. He'd always insisted he did, and he'd make love to her, but then he'd go away—for weeks at a time. Joshua made her feel alive and vibrant. Wanted. Needed even.

"Baby"—he cupped her face with his hand, his thumb sliding over her skin—"don't look so sad. I swear to you, I would never harm you or allow anyone else to. You're mine. You gave yourself to me. You told me you loved me. I gave myself to you. All of me. Please have an open mind. Please."

She stared into his eyes and wanted desperately to believe him. That face. That voice. Those eyes. If his eyes were windows to his soul, right now his soul was shattered.

"The Bogomolovs know where you are through an accident. An *accident*. I didn't tell them. I wouldn't have wanted them to know, because I intend to kill them. Knowing you're alive gives them a slight advantage because they'll find out fast enough I have something to lose."

She slipped away from him because the temptation to let

herself get lost in sex was fairly high. She had to make sense of everything. Pulling a T-shirt over her head, she shimmied into a pair of jeans while he did the same. He held out his hand to her. She hesitated a heartbeat. Two. It was impossible to not take his hand, not when his blue-green eyes were so compelling. He closed his fingers around hers and led her out of the room, downstairs to the great room.

"Do you want a fire?"

She shook her head and sank into the wide-armed leather chair facing the seat he preferred. He took it and leaned forward. "You know that no matter how many times the head of the snake is chopped off, another crime lord rises and takes his place. There is no way to stop that. There will always be criminals, people who want to take from others. There will always be gunrunning and illegal activity of some kind."

She nodded, pressing her hand to her churning stomach. She detested this. Detested that he was going to make excuses for what he'd become.

His gaze dropped to her hand and then came back up to her face. "There are bosses like Bogomolov who are extremely violent. They are always greedy, hungry for more power and more territory. The Bogomolov family are Amur leopards from Russia. The man known as Alonzo Massi is actually from Russia and was a part of the *bratya* there. He is also leopard. There are a few leopard lairs in the *bratya*. They are the cruelest of crime lords."

She knew Nikita was cruel. She had seen his orders carried out when men had come to kill her father.

"In their lairs, they refuse to find their true mate. They take a woman capable of giving them a leopard and when she does, they kill her as a sign of loyalty to the *bratya*."

"Nikita's wife?"

He nodded. "He murdered her. He's looking for Alonzo. He's looking for you. He doesn't get either of you."

She touched the tip of her tongue to her lips, trying to moisten them. "What about you, Joshua, do you think because you aren't killing me that it makes you better than him? You're still committing crimes."

He nodded. "I know I am. I'm not denying that. It's necessary to keep up the illusion of being in this business. I can only shut down the worst of the criminals. I do it quietly and slowly from the inside, so it isn't really noticed. I have an explanation ready if any of the other bosses question me. What we're really doing is looking to take down the worst of the bosses. Men like Nikita. If the crimes are kept to the underbelly and the killing stays there, we let it go. If it leaks out and a man like Nikita goes on a killing spree, we take him down and replace him with one of our own. Just telling you this can get a lot of good men killed."

She frowned, trying to process what he was saying. "An undercover agent?" She wasn't certain she could believe that, although Drake Donovan's agency had sent him in more than once undercover if his stories could be believed.

He shook his head. "No, taking down a crime lord that way leaves the territory open for an even worse boss. We prefer to make the rules as best we can and keep the worst out."

"I still don't understand. Are you saying that you and some others are taking over territories mafia have and trying to weed out the 'bad' ones?"

He smiled at her and leaned back in his chair, resting his head against the leather, his eyes on her face. "Put like that, it sounds silly, but the reality works. We have someone taking apart the companies for laundering. He does it legitimately, although we find the companies in a not-so-legitimate way; usually we hack them. We disrupt the pipelines for drugs and gunrunning. We shut down human trafficking wherever we find it, and that is a moneymaker, so everyone wants in. We create pipelines through other territories and that makes it easier to monitor them."

"Essentially, you're working both sides of the fence."

He nodded. "Exactly. We have to appear, at all times, as if we are the head of a territory to the other bosses. We work with them, get to know them, and learn what we can safely take apart by disrupting shipments and hitting them in their businesses and books. We can weaken territories. The most difficult thing we do, and the most dangerous, is take down men like Nikita."

"The cops think you're dirty."

"We are dirty."

"But if the other members of the syndicate realized what you were doing, they'd kill you."

He nodded slowly. "Without a doubt. I won't lie about that." He kept his gaze glued to hers.

She felt the intensity of that stare right to her core. Every word sounded like the absolute truth, but who would be that crazy? Both sides, criminal and law, would hunt Joshua.

"It's a risk, baby, but something has to be done. Human trafficking has gone through the roof. The violence is escalating. Someone has to find a way to stop it. In any case, there will always be those rising to power. Power corrupts. Greed, violence, drugs, alcohol, all of it feeds into a pool of criminals. We fill any void and control the borders, so to speak, keeping the criminals as much in their own world and away from civilians as we can."

"You have a white knight syndrome so far to the right it's scary. Don't you see how truly insane what you're trying to do really is? You can't control what others choose to do. You just can't."

"The answer is to ignore it? Do you have any idea what is done to those women and children? We've stopped them, over and over. We haven't saved them all, maybe we haven't even slowed it down, but we've stopped some of them. That counts. It counts for the ones we got back. We've kept guns from going to terrorist cells over and over. That counts as well. We've weakened territories, we've messed with books.

We've turned over evidence to the FBI and found dirty cops and turned over evidence on them."

"They'll kill you if they find out it's you."

He shrugged. "I had no idea you existed, Sonia. I searched for you and couldn't find you. My family is truly fucked up and I wanted little to do with them, other than my cousin Evangeline. Ironically, she wanted little to do with me."

"Does she know the truth about you?"

"She knows the truth about her husband, and that means she knows the truth about me. Before all this, neither of us wanted anything to do with the Tregres. You talk about vile, ugly people, that would be my family. Other than my mother. She was the best."

She sent him a tentative smile. "I'm glad. I wish I'd had the chance to meet her."

"I do too, although she would never have approved of what I'm doing, and she'd most likely have told you to run for the hills."

"I tried that. It didn't work."

"You have a nasty little temper. You kicked Shadow. He's still sulking."

She shrugged. "He deserved it. And more. He can just not touch Gatita like that ever again."

"Leopards are rough, baby," he said softly.

"Maybe, but he was angry with her."

"She didn't believe him. You didn't believe me. God, Sonia, it hurt like hell seeing you so afraid of me. I couldn't take it. I never want you to look at me like that again." He leaned toward her. "Do you believe what I'm saying to you? Because if you don't, if you want evidence, I'll get it for you. I'll do whatever it takes so you know, with me, you'll always be safe. Tell me what to do to give you that. I don't want you to have one small doubt in your mind. Tell me how to do that."

She stared at him. The things he'd said to her were scary dangerous and so like him. The white knight. Atonement for his perceived sins. There was no saving him from himself. He was many things, but he wasn't a liar. He wasn't a betrayer. Joshua's loyalty ran deep. His sense of duty. He wasn't lying to her. He loved her. She chose to believe him because every cell in her body, every instinct she had, said he was telling her the truth and he loved her.

She had to believe. She had to push aside the hurt and fears from her past and look at the man sitting across from her. She could read him, that face, so familiar to her now. She had no idea if she was strong enough to stay with him and face what he had to do every single day. She had no idea if she would have the strength to walk away when she knew he was doing things that were very wrong.

"I believe you. I don't know exactly what to do with it, but I believe you."

He went still, as if he couldn't believe what he was hearing. For a moment, she thought she caught the shimmer of tears in his eyes, and that completely undid her. He lifted his head and his eyes suddenly glittered at her, going a deep crystalline blue that always took her breath.

He wasn't going to give in to the emotion because it was too overwhelming. She waited, holding her breath, ready to follow his lead to get them out of this moment neither could handle. She knew it would be sex, because sex was his go-to when he needed to be close to her. Right now, she needed to be very close to him, without talking. She didn't know what she would do or say if he asked her the wrong question before she processed everything completely.

"Since we're covering everything, I'm not down with you shifting in front of my men. At. All. You were stark naked. I promised myself I would put you over my knee for that."

A little shiver went down her spine, but she lifted her chin and narrowed her eyes at him.

"In today's society, adults have evolved, and they don't hit their children or their women." She said it in her snippiest tone and gave him her haughtiest look.

"I'm leopard and our society hasn't evolved that far, so you're in very real danger."

"Well, don't even think about doing something like that. I'd retaliate."

His eyes went pure crystalline. That sea of blue made her breath catch in her throat. A slow smile spread across his face, softening the harsh lines. "How would you retaliate, baby?" His voice had dropped low. Intimate. Insinuating all sorts of carnal things.

Her body went liquid, her breasts instantly ached, nipples peaking beneath the thin material of her tee. "Something you won't like," she threatened, having no idea what that would be, but she loved their game.

"Tell me, baby. I can't wait to learn what my punishment would be."

She lifted her chin. "No sex. At. All."

His smile turned into a smirk. "But I would be free to try to seduce you."

Sonia hastily shook her head. "No, you wouldn't. Absolutely not."

"That's the rule, and I'm up for the challenge. I'm going to strip you naked, right here, right now, and spank your beautiful ass until my handprints are all over it. Then you deny me sex, and I'll do my best to persuade you otherwise."

She squirmed, rubbing her thighs together as heat spread through her veins. Her sex spasmed. Clenched. Her clit pounded with hot blood and anticipation. "Don't you dare." That came out breathless. An invitation more than a demand.

He smiled like the predator he was. Just as he stood, his cell phone buzzed. He glanced down and frowned.

"Your friend Molly just got out of an SUV with tinted windows and is running up to the front door. Evan says she's crying."

# 15

SONIA jumped to her feet and started for the door. Joshua caught her arm. "Before you get caught up in the drama with your friend, I need to know we're good. You and me. You're with me."

"Is that a question?"

"Yes, and it requires an answer."

She nodded. She had to believe in someone. She had to trust at least one person. If he'd lied to her and ended up turning her over to Nikita, at least she could die knowing she tried.

"You'll stay with me?"

That was much more complicated. Would she stay with him? The girlfriend of a mobster? She didn't know that answer. "I have to think about that."

Every bit of softness faded from his face, leaving his features scary stony, ice-cold and more than a little danger-ous. She was looking at a mixture of the leopard and the mobster, not her Joshua. "Think fast, Sonia. You're fuckin' mine and you know it. You need me every bit as much as I need you."

"Thanks, Joshua," she said sarcastically, pulling out of his grip. Molly was already knocking on the door. "I love how very romantic you are."

"I don't know the first thing about romance, baby," he said, his voice like steel. His eyes like a glacier. "But I know when my woman is full of bullshit. You're fuckin' mine. Say it."

She glared at him and yanked open the door. Molly fell into her arms sobbing. He reached around the two women to catch the door and peer out. The gray fog obscured the view of the drive and the waiting SUV. They hadn't turned on any lights, not outside and not inside. He closed the door as Sonia took Molly to the chairs by the fireplace.

"Molly, do you need me for anything, or is this a girl talk?" he asked.

Molly glanced up, her eyes bright with tears, her lashes wet. She tried a watery smile, shook her head and waved him away.

"I'll be in the other room if you need me," he said, giving them privacy. If Bastien had broken up with her or upset her in any way, Sonia would want to have words with him. The less attention they received from law enforcement, the better.

Sonia waited until he was out of the room. "Tell me what happened. Did you get into a fight with Bastien?"

Molly shook her head. "It's worse," she whispered. "So much worse. I don't know how to tell you this. I love you. You're my first real friend, and you've been so good to me."

"Just say it, Molly. We'll work it out."

"A man came to the house. Several men, actually. They have Bastien held somewhere. They hit him, and I saw him go down. He told me to run."

She leapt up. Molly caught her arm, shaking her head. "Don't get Joshua. They said if I told anyone but you, they'd kill him." She waited until Sonia reluctantly subsided. "I did run, but they caught up with me."

"Did they hurt you?"

Molly shook her head. "No, but they scared me. They said if you didn't go out and get into the SUV alone, they would kill Bastien and throw his body in the swamp."

"Describe them," she said, but she knew. Her heart sank and she felt sweat trickle between her breasts.

"They had accents. Russian, I think. Is it your husband?"

Sonia nodded. "I think so. I think he found me. I can talk to him, try to get Bastien back." Nikita had probably already killed him, but she wasn't going to tell Molly that. "I'm going, but you have to tell Joshua. You *have* to. Give me a five-minute start. I may be able to tell you where to find Bastien if I get it out of the driver. If I do, I'll text you the location." She knew the first thing they'd do was take her phone.

Molly threw her arms around her and nearly crushed her. "I don't want you to go. I thought maybe we could think of some other way," she whispered in her ear.

"You know there isn't, not with these men. Honey, you have to tell Joshua. He's going to be angry, but you have to tell him no matter how scared you are. Promise me. He's my only chance to live. If Nikita doesn't shoot me the second I'm in the SUV, and that's always a possibility, then Joshua will have time to rescue me." Because if he didn't shoot her, that meant he was going to torture her.

"You're taller than I am, so we'll have to do this fast. We'll go outside on the front porch, but leave the door open, so Joshua and his guards think I'm going back inside. We'll talk for a few minutes, which will settle the guards down, both of us sitting in the chairs. Then I'll get up and walk to the SUV. You remain seated so it won't call attention to the disparity in our heights. I'll get in, we'll drive off. You stay seated as long as possible and then go into the house and straight to Joshua. You understand?"

Molly nodded. Hiccupped. Nodded some more. "I don't like this. Shouldn't we tell him now? They can follow the SUV right away."

"He'd never allow me to get into the vehicle, and then there would be no chance of getting Bastien back." They would kill Molly, Joshua and everyone else. Sonia wanted them away from the house.

"If I wait five minutes, how will they be able to track the car?"

She knew Joshua's men were out there, probably in leopard form. Leopards could smell the SUV and track it anywhere. That was her one chance, and she knew Joshua would come for her. She knew, no matter what, he would come for her.

She took a deep breath and put her arm around Molly. Raising her voice, she shouted to Joshua, "We're going to sit on the front porch for a few minutes."

He stood in the archway between the great room and the dining room. "Everything okay?"

"Just girl stuff," she said. "You know how ridiculous men can get."

He frowned at her, opened his mouth to say something, but she gave a quick shake of her head, as if she didn't want him to protest what she said in front of a weeping Molly. He nodded and stepped back into the other room. She breathed a sigh of relief and walked Molly out onto the porch, making certain not to turn on lights. She pointed to a chair and then sat beside her.

"It's going to be all right, Molly. Tell me about you and Bastien. What's he like?"

"He's so good to me. He spoiled me rotten and was so careful with me. No sex yet, just kissing, but I could tell he wanted sex. I wanted it too. He says he wants me very comfortable. He's asked Jerry to get the holes in the house plugged and doesn't want me to go home until that's done."

She hiccupped often and twice muffled a sob by pressing her palm to her trembling mouth.

"It's going to be all right, Molly," she reiterated. "Just please sit here for five minutes and then go straight to Joshua and tell him what happened and to follow the SUV."

Molly shook her head, catching her arm. "Are you certain they won't hurt you?"

Molly wasn't leopard. She couldn't hear lies, and she wanted to believe whatever Sonia told her. Sonia forced a smile. "They aren't going to hurt me."

"You said they tried to kill you."

She nodded. "But now I have a bargaining chip. Let me do this. Bastien is an innocent man in all this. He doesn't deserve to die. I have a chance. He doesn't. I need your cell and passcode."

Molly handed the cell over and gave her the passcode. Sonia didn't wait for a reaction. She had worked up the nerve to enter the SUV, and she had to do it before she lost it. She stood up, brushed Molly's face with a kiss and ran down the steps to the vehicle. The door was thrust open before she got there. She dove in without even looking at the driver.

"Go. Hurry, before they realize we switched places."

"Boss says not to draw attention. I'll hit it when we get to the street. Give me your cell phone."

Sonia recognized the man as Dmitri, one of Sasha's best friends. They were together quite often. He worked for Nikita as well. Her heart thudded when she righted herself in the seat and realized the driver wasn't alone. Two more men occupied the backseat. Even if she managed to grab the driver's gun, she wouldn't get away. She thought about lying and saying she didn't have it, but she knew Joshua would come after her no matter what. Breathing a silent apology to Molly, she handed the cell phone to him and he tossed it to the others in the backseat. They opened the window once they were on the main road and sent it flying.

"Do you really have Bastien Foret, Dmitri?" She kept her voice low, unconcerned, as if she didn't expect them to take her to the nearest swamp and feed her to the alligators. Surely, they wouldn't do that without Nikita gloating at her first.

"Yes. He's safe." He glanced at her. "Put on your seat belt." The vehicle picked up speed.

She complied with the order. So far, he was treating her gently. No roughing her up, no slapping her. No dragging her into the backseat so the others could have their fun while Dmitri drove. She glanced in the back. "I'm sorry, I don't remember your names." They didn't look all that familiar, although she could have sworn they looked a little like Sasha around the eyes.

"Koldan," the one on the right said gruffly.

"Vasili," the other told her.

Both looked directly at her. Yep. They were definitely going to kill her or they wouldn't have been so free with their names, nor would they have wanted her to see them. She took a deep breath and let it out. Dmitri was driving very fast, but controlled. She remembered that about him. More than once he'd picked up both Sasha and Sonia and taken them to a small, intimate café. They'd been among the few times she'd ever been out in public with Sasha. She supposed that gave Sasha plausible deniability that he was with her if her dead body turned up.

"Where are you taking me?"

"We'll switch vehicles. Leopards can track a car."

She stiffened. She'd all but forgotten Joshua had told her the Bogomolovs were leopard. Of course they would know leopards tracked vehicles. They'd prepared for that. She hadn't thought out her plan very well. She had to hope she could leave her scent, or Joshua would just track the new vehicle.

"Please make the call to have Bastien let go. He isn't part of this. He doesn't know anything." She knew it was stupid to even ask. Nikita's answer for everything in his way seemed to be to kill someone.

"He'll get loose on his own. He saw no one. By the time he makes his way to a phone, we'll be long gone."

She nodded, trying to hear the truth in his voice. Honesty had a tone to it, a note easily recognized. She was too tense, her heart beating too hard and fast to be able to discern if Dmitri was being honest.

*Gatita? Do you think he means it?*

*He sounded truthful, but then Sasha always sounded truthful. Joshua and Shadow sounded truthful. I am confused.*

Sonia stared out the window at the scenery passing by. Mostly it was a blur. Dmitri turned down a road just off the main highway near the town. There was a theater there. Several vehicles were parked together in the lot. He drove right into the center of them.

"Stay put. Don't remove your seat belt."

She nodded and stayed put. She didn't want a bullet in her brain. Joshua would lose his mind and go on a rampage. If he was really going to sell her out to Nikita, they wouldn't have found it necessary to kidnap her. She'd been right in believing in him. She held on to that. He would come.

The men got out of the SUV, each using a different door. Dmitri came around to her side, opened the door and stepped back. First, Vasili came to the door and leaned in to remove her seat belt. He turned and hurried to enter one of the other cars. Koldan was second, and he leaned in and acted as if he might pull her out of the darkened vehicle, but then he turned and went to another car. Dmitri actually lifted her.

"I can walk," she protested.

He kept her in tight to his chest. "No, you can't. Your scent would be on the ground. This way, they have to track multiple vehicles."

The door to the dark SUV opened in the back and Dmitri thrust her inside. The instant the door closed, she drew in his scent. Sasha. The man she loved. The one who had betrayed her. He reached for her, drew her into his arms and all but crushed her.

"You're alive. *Slava Bogu.* All this time, I thought he'd killed you. Why didn't you reach out to me? I would have come for you, protected you."

His arms were the same. She remembered them from her childhood. All the times he'd held her when she cried over her father. He'd known Nikita had ordered the man's torture and death. He'd known Nikita had been forcing her mother to sleep with him. Still, he'd been the one to pay for her mother's care. For the hospice expenses. For the memorial and cremation.

"Sasha." She whispered his name, tears welling up.

The vehicle sped down the road. She couldn't see through the blur of tears. If it had been Nikita coming for her, she could have been stoic, going to her death without drama or weeping, but even knowing Sasha had tried to kill her, she couldn't block out all those years, from her childhood on, of caring for him.

"You're safe," he whispered. "You're safe with me."

She knew better. She had believed him once. Just as she believed Joshua. What was wrong with her that this kept happening?

She pulled out of his arms. Immediately he dragged her seat belt around her. "We have a house. It will be well guarded. If my father or Joshua Tregre try to come for you, we have weapons that will give us the advantage in protecting you. It's all been planned out carefully."

She shook her head and stared out the window, afraid if she looked at him she'd start screaming. His betrayal cut deep. He'd been her everything after her mother had died. Not just after, before, after her father had been murdered. Then during her mother's illness.

"Look at me, *malen'kiy*, you have not even looked at me."

"I can't. I'm very confused by the things you're saying to me, Sasha. I don't understand why you're playing this game with me."

"Game?" He caught her chin and tugged until her head came up and her eyes met his. "What game? I thought you were dead or I would have looked until I found you."

"I *heard* you, Sasha. I came in early and I heard you and your father talking about me, my father and mother, and how you had to kill me."

He inhaled sharply. Dmitri shared a long look with him. The driver glanced back at her in the rearview mirror. She'd been an idiot to admit that, but she'd had it with the lies. She doubted if she was going to come out of this alive, so at least she'd get Sasha to look her in the eye and admit he wanted her dead.

"I have no reason to kill you, Sonia. I love you. You know that."

"Oh. My. God. I'm so done with the declarations of love and then finding out every man who says that to me is a criminal. Just pull out your gun and shoot me. Get it the hell over with." Her voice was swinging out of control, but she didn't care. She was ready to fling herself at him. All she had to do was unsnap the seat belt and lunge for him. Gatita would do the rest—except she couldn't quite make herself do it. Not yet. Not until she found out why.

The road they turned on was a narrow dirt track leading into the swamp and away from town. "Where did the other vehicles go?"

"Various houses we rented. The others will make their way back here. This property was the most defensible and has the better escape routes."

She took a deep breath as they parked in front of a large old plantation house. She recognized the architecture. It was very different from her home, but still quite stately and beautiful. Dmitri hopped out first. He and two others circled the house before going in. Dmitri motioned and someone opened Sasha's door. He slid out and then reached for Sonia.

She hesitated before sliding across the seat to him. Sasha

lifted her down and they walked together to the porch. *Gatita, look around. We have to be ready to move fast.* She took a slow, careful perusal of every aspect of the grounds she could see.

Sasha took her hand as they went up the stairs and entered the older, well-kept mansion. It was definitely a find. Trust Sasha to find it. Like Sonia, he'd always been interested in architecture. "This is beautiful," she ventured, trying to decide what to say, how to handle the situation. She needed to know what he wanted and he wasn't giving her much to go on.

"I found it online and then destroyed my entire laptop and hard drive so Nikita wouldn't know about it. He's on his way here with a large group of men. You know how he likes to make a show of force."

She hadn't known. She'd been kept in the dark until that day. She tugged her hand from his the moment they were inside and stepped away from him, her arms going around her middle for comfort. "Why did you lie about us being married?"

"You took what you heard out of context. You don't know the entire story."

"Then tell it to me," she invited. "And let Bastien go."

"He's safe enough. He'll get loose but it will take him a while before he can make his way to a phone to call for help. I imagine his girlfriend has already called for help, but they won't find him so easily. We've got time to prepare."

She threw herself into a chair, very conscious of the fact that she wasn't wearing underwear. She'd been with Joshua so many times, she felt him inside her. She felt his hands on her. She tasted him in her mouth. To look at Sasha, the man who was supposed to be her husband, made her feel guilt and shame, even though he'd tried to kill her by planting a bomb in her car.

"When did you know you were leopard?" he asked. He took a bottle of water from Dmitri and handed it to her. Light was streaking through the windows, the outside still gray with fog. "That was a shock."

"It was a shock when I smelled my husband's scent in the car just before it blew up," she countered.

He whirled around. "You think *I* planted that bomb?"

"Sasha, even my leopard smelled your scent. It wasn't just me." She tried—and failed—to keep the hurt out of her voice. To have time to regain her composure, she took a drink of water, allowing it to slip down her parched throat.

"I was there, in the car. I worried that he would try it. I was pulled from the car and taken physically into the house. There was a fight between me and the men my father had restraining me. He sat in a chair with a glass of bourbon in his hand and watched while they beat me. It was a lesson, he said, I had to learn to be strong. He didn't want a weak son, and you made me weak."

It was impossible to miss the ring of truth in his voice, and more, the behavior was so Nikita. He always acted a little detached and superior to everyone else. A surge of hope swept through her. Sasha, *her* Sasha, hadn't been the one to try to kill her.

"Tell me the entire story, Sasha. I'm a little lost."

He set his water bottle on the mantel and turned completely toward her so she could see his face. "My father's world is one of violence and revenge. There can be no loyalty to a woman, especially not one's wife."

Her heart jumped and then accelerated. He was telling her essentially what Joshua had revealed about Nikita Bogomolov.

"He killed my mother when I was ten. He made me watch as he beat her to death. He said no member of our family would ever put a woman first. Those kinds of women were to be fucked and then killed. He liked to say that."

She knew. She'd heard him. "What did he mean by 'those kinds'? I heard him say that about me and I thought . . ."

"He meant every woman. *Every* woman, Sonia. He didn't single you out because of where you came from. He singled you out because you were too important to me. Your father betrayed him, and that isn't tolerated. The penalty for stealing or really any infraction is death for the entire family. Nikita enjoyed making a statement. Your mother had been keeping our house since you were a baby. You were a beautiful child, a ray of sunshine in a world of madness. So was your mother."

She had always believed he thought that of her mother. He had spent a great deal of time talking to Valeria. She remembered him as a teenager, tall and handsome, his dark eyes flashing with smiles at her while she followed her mother from room to room.

He paced across the room. "Of course she would catch Nikita's eye. He wanted her. When your father made such a terrible mistake, he ordered him tortured and killed. He went to Valeria and offered a proposition. She could live in our home permanently and sleep with him whenever and wherever he wanted to pay off Roberto's debt, or he would kill both of you and be done with it. He made certain I was there. He wanted me to see how a woman would 'whore' herself out for her child or her own life. That was supposed to be another lesson, but I knew he did it so he could have Valeria."

"How could you stand him? Stand being in the same room with him?"

"I went to your mother and told her I would always watch out for you, that I'd do anything it took. I told her to make the deal with my father, but add that you weren't to know, that your childhood would be happy. Your mother took care of me after my father's many, many lessons. Broken bones, cigarette burns. He liked watching his men beat me. She was always there for me." He looked down at his hands. "Making sure you had a good childhood and remained alive was the only thing I could do for her. It was better than what I did for my own mother."

"Sasha." She breathed his name, her heart breaking for him.

"I couldn't save her. I tried, but I couldn't save my mother, Sonia. I was too young, not strong enough, but I vowed one day I'd take him down. He's just so good at what he does. Had he known you were leopard, you would have been a prisoner until you gave me a child. As it was, I was careful that couldn't happen. He might have killed you both, especially if the baby was female."

"I'm so sorry. I never realized how terrible he was, not until I overheard that conversation and I did a little research. I'd been so sheltered, I'd never even heard gossip. I was picking up the language, though, and things weren't adding up."

"I asked you to marry me in order to keep you close. Had I sent you away to school, which I considered first, he had already indicated he would have had you killed as an example. Your father's debt, he said, would never be fully paid. I couldn't actually marry you because then he would demand your death, but when I told him I made the same deal with you that he had with your mother, he left you alone—for a while."

He sighed and pushed a hand through his hair. "I was in a difficult position. You're so young. You were innocent. I had no right touching you. It didn't feel right, Sonia, and I tried to keep my distance. I stayed away as much as possible, while still keeping you safe. I went clubbing with Dmitri. I was seen around town. I threw myself into the business. I kept you home and away from him. When you wanted to have sex, as any normal wife would, I obliged, but I knew it was wrong for you."

"I love you, Sasha. I always have," she admitted quietly, "but I didn't love you the way a woman should love her man. It's different." She had to tell him the truth. She knew the difference now.

He nodded his head. "I'm well aware of that. I love you

too, but not the way a man loves a woman. You were like a little sister to me and touching you that way felt wrong. Still, you deserved to be happy, and without your knowledge you were almost kept a prisoner in that house."

"Thank you for trying to keep me safe."

"I did my best to grow strong, to recruit my own men, men loyal to me. I had to be extremely careful because if even one of them betrayed us, if there was a whisper of conspiracy against Nikita, he would have tortured everyone until someone talked. If he thought, for a moment, I was behind it, you would have been tortured in front of me. I apparently gave myself away by being too protective of you."

"You were always protective of me, even when I was very little."

He nodded. "But just before he talked to me, do you remember the accident you had? The one where a car nearly hit you? You were coming out of your yoga class and crossing the street to get to the car where your driver waited."

She nodded. It had been close. Very, very close. It had been Dmitri who had saved her that day, throwing her out of the path of the speeding car. They both rolled on the asphalt, scraping skin, but other than a few bruises, they were both fine.

She'd been surprised that Dmitri had been in the vicinity, but hadn't questioned it because she'd been so shaken by the near miss. Dmitri had acted angry. Her driver had scowled at him and they'd had a very heated exchange. That hadn't been anything compared to what Sasha had said to the driver. He'd pulled out a gun and put it to her driver's head and ordered her out of the room. She didn't know what had happened after that.

"He worked for your father, and he set me up by parking across the street," she guessed.

Sasha nodded, his eyes burning with anger. "Yes. Then he texted the hit man and he was supposed to make it look like an accident."

"Why? If you father had decided to kill me, why didn't he just do it?"

"He wanted me to do it, and when I made it clear I wasn't done with you yet, he gave the job to two of his men. I made the mistake of killing them both and threatening him."

She opened her mouth to say something, but the reality of his life hit her. The reality of Joshua's life was the same. They *killed* people. It was part of their world. Deliberately, she took another sip of water, taking her time to try to process everything he said. It fit. The way he'd treated her from the beginning of their marriage. She'd been so shocked by her mother's death and his marriage proposal that she'd gone numb and just let Sasha take over. She hadn't really woken up for months after. He hadn't touched her, saying she wasn't ready yet.

She'd been the one to go to him. She'd been hurt, afraid he didn't want her. He'd been patient and gentle with her, always loving, but after, she'd wake to find him sitting on the edge of the bed, his face in his hands. She'd even gone so far as to wonder if he was gay. He'd rarely come to her and only at her insistence. It made sense that he wasn't in love with her. He thought of her as a child. She'd grown up in his household and he felt protective of her, but he didn't love her the way a man loved a woman. He was right, they were more like little sister and big brother.

She pressed the cold bottle of water to her temple. How had she gotten here? How had Sasha, or Joshua? "Life sucks sometimes," she murmured.

"Nikita insisted I kill you, to prove that I didn't love you and my loyalty was solely to the *bratya*. He wanted to make certain I didn't love you more than our family." There was a sneer to his voice when he used the word *family*. "He wanted me to be like him. I knew I had no choice, if you were going to survive, but to break with him, and that meant killing him."

She gasped, one hand flying out to catch his wrist. "He's still your father."

"The father who murdered my mother," he said bitterly. "Do you think I can ever get that image out of my mind? *Ever?* He doesn't get you. You're going to live."

"Does he know you've broken with him?"

Sasha nodded. "It's going to be an all-out war." He rubbed the bridge of his nose, studying her. "I saw you in the bedroom with him—with Tregre. Then in the swamp it looked completely different, as if you were a prisoner, rather than being with him by choice."

Before she could speak, he shook his head and held up his hand to stop her. "It doesn't matter, you're safe with me. Tregre is just as dirty as my father. He may not have killed his woman, but he's ruthless in this business. In a very short time he's proven he doesn't shy away from violence. Nikita thought he could walk all over him, but that wasn't the case. He's a little afraid of Tregre, and that's something I've never seen. Tregre is in solid with Elijah Lospostos."

Sonia had heard that name come up several times in conversation, although it had always been in Russian, when they'd been sitting around a dinner table. Nikita had by turns cursed the man and then admired him.

"He's going to come for me," she said softly. "Joshua will, and I don't want the two of you fighting. He's my choice, Sasha."

He shook his head. "I spent years protecting you. I don't want you anywhere near this business. You get away and what do you do? You find the one man worse than Nikita."

"How is he worse?" Her heart thudded in her chest so hard she pressed her hand over it. "What do you mean, worse? Did he sell me out to Nikita? Is that what he did? Did Nikita pay him for the information?"

He turned away from her, pacing across the room, his strides angry, the set of his shoulders stiff.

"Don't lie to me, I need the truth."

"No, he didn't sell you out, Sonia. He doesn't need the money or to have my father owe him a favor. That should tell you something right there. He came up fast—too fast. As far as anyone can tell, he was never connected before. He just walked in and took over. No one knows who killed Rafe Cordeau, but we all know he's dead. His territory was wide open until suddenly Tregre comes out of nowhere and assumes the crown."

She let her breath out slowly in relief. He didn't know anything about Joshua, not really. "He isn't any worse than you. If you manage to kill your father, are you taking over the family business?" She couldn't keep the challenge out of her voice.

"Yes. I was born into this world. I don't know any different. I'm good at it. Yes, sweetheart, I'll always be what I was born. When my father is dead, the others will expect me to ascend the throne, and I intend to."

"Sasha, I love you. I really do. With all my heart, I love you. You'll always be my family, but he's my choice. I want you to get to know him. To take that time, for me. I'm asking as someone who loves you and needs you in my life, take the time to get to know him before you judge him."

"Damn it, Sonia, *no*. He's not for you. This life isn't for you. I forbid it."

She stared up at his furious face. "He'll fight for me. He will come after me and he'll never stop until he finds me. He'll fight for me. That's the kind of man he is."

"You don't know that. You can't possibly know him that well. I saw you in the swamp, a little female running from that pack of males. Imagine my surprise when that beautiful cat turned out to be you. I saw his leopard knock yours off her feet. I saw you shift and kick the crap out of the male. You were fearless. Beautiful. I was so proud of you."

She liked his praise. She'd loved Sasha since she was a little girl. She remembered going to his beautiful, amazing home, thrilled that they'd gone every day. She'd been four when she'd met him. He'd been a lot older, but he liked having a little sister to protect and look after. The connection between them was strengthened through his love for her mother.

"I love him."

"He manhandled you."

"He would never hurt me. *Never.*"

"I see bruises on your skin. Smudge marks where his fingers dug in deep."

She blushed. The marks were more than smudges and both knew it. He was being discreet. "It's not like that. We both get a little crazy. He doesn't hit me. He wouldn't."

"How would you know, Sonia?"

"I know you wouldn't hit me. No matter how angry you get at me, I know you would never hit me. I know the same about him. Whatever he's doing in his life, whatever led him there, that's his, not mine. He has to decide what's important in his life. You believe you were born to take over your father's business and you intend to do that. You just admitted to me you killed the men conspiring to harm me."

He nodded slowly. "I know I'm not a good man. I know what I am. I know I'll never have it all, the woman I can love completely and who can love me and look at me as if I'm everything to her. That's not going to happen for me because I know I'm not a good man."

"He'll come for me, Sasha. I love him, and I love you. I would never be able to forgive you if you hurt him."

"Do you think that matters to me? I *chose* you. You're all I have left. You are my family. *You*, Sonia. Do you think for one minute I'm going to turn you over to a man who is a fucking criminal? Once you're his, in our world, I can't interfere."

"That's just it, Sasha. I am his," she said quietly. "I'm his mate. Our leopards chose each other. She's had her heat and she chose him. I chose Joshua. I would every time."

He turned away from her, swearing in Russian. She closed her eyes and pressed the water bottle harder against her temple. She knew Joshua would find her. He would puzzle out the tangle of a trail and he'd show up—in force. Sasha was waiting for him, ready to ambush him. His men were hidden all around the outside of the house as well as the inside. She didn't want either man killed, but Sasha refused to listen.

"Let me call him. Talk to him. I can convince him to stay away. You can meet with him at a neutral location," she ventured.

He turned back to her, studying her face. "You can tell him the two of you are done and I'm sending you somewhere safe."

"I'll just find my way back to him." She said it quietly, not defiantly, just matter-of-factly, stating the truth. "I love him. I could be carrying his child. Did you think of that?"

He groaned, turned and flung the bottle of water at the fireplace. It hit, spraying water everywhere, bounced off and hit the floor, the rest of the water leaking out. They both stared at it as if that widening pool could give them the answers.

"Please, Sasha, at least get to know him. Give me this chance with someone I love. My leopard can hear lies. She knows he's telling the truth when he says he loves me. I feel it every time I'm in the room with him. Please just give us this chance. All of us. You, me and Joshua."

"I think that would be a very good idea," a male voice said.

Both spun around, Sonia's breath catching in her throat as she recognized Joshua's voice.

# 16

JOSHUA wanted to kill the bastard. Absolutely fucking kill him. Sasha. The man who had married his woman. He'd had her in his bed. In his home. He'd tried to kill her. A bomb in her car. Sonia was so young, and she should have had protection, but instead, the Bogomolovs, father and son, had tried to kill her.

They fanned out, following each trail, one leopard per vehicle, the others waiting, all armed, ready and willing to go to war. Sasha had taken her from him. She belonged to Joshua. She was his woman. No one was going to hurt her, let alone kill her. Every minute that went by felt like an hour, a day.

He loved her. It was that simple. He didn't know how it had happened or even when. He just knew he couldn't sleep without her next to him. He wanted to go to sleep listening to her laughter or the sound of her voice murmuring to him. He loved the scent of her in his bathroom. In his bedroom.

In every room of his house. She belonged with him because without her, he didn't have one single fucking thing.

The moment Kai told him where she was, he gathered his crew around him and they came up with a plan. He sent four scouts to map out every possible escape route, to count every guard. He didn't care if they were outnumbered or outgunned, he was going to get her back and kill the son of a bitch who took her.

His men gathered the information needed and brought it back to him. He was brilliant at strategy, he always had been. Drake had recognized that in him early and encouraged him to have confidence in his choices. He surrounded himself with good men, men he knew he could count on. All were experienced in battle and they were used to stealth work. They'd worked in the rain forests or small villages, going into terrorist camps and extracting prisoners. It was what they did best. This was no different. Sonia was a prisoner. She'd been taken, and they would get her back.

None of them liked that he chose to go in with just two leopards at his back. The rest were to surround Sasha's men and wait for the signal to take them out. He needed to get the lay of the land, and God help them all if the Russian had harmed one hair on her head.

*I'm coming for you, baby. Hold on for me.* He sent the message into the universe, hoping she got it. He detested that she might be afraid and feeling alone.

He slipped through their ranks easily. They were leopards, but they were used to dealing with humans, not other leopards. They had chosen to stay in human form, cradling their guns as they paced their routes. He studied them as he slipped past them. They moved well, the guns extensions of them, very familiar, as if made for them; they stayed alert. It made sense to use their human form in the city, even around the house. Still, had he been directing security, he would have had a few leopards prowling just to ensure nothing—or no one—got through their ranks.

He made it into the house through an upper-story window. That was careless as well. They should have had an alarm on every window. It was time-consuming to put them on houses like these, but it prevented mistakes. Letting them in was a huge mistake. Evan went first. He insisted and there was little, short of shooting him, Joshua could do to stop him. Evan and Kai were insistent they were there to protect him. He was insistent they were getting his woman back.

He heard her voice, talking softly. He heard the stress because he was so tuned to her every mood. She didn't sound afraid, only stressed, and that brought him up short. He nearly pulled the trigger to end the bastard, but at the last minute, he decided to listen. It wasn't easy to stop himself. He *wanted* to kill Sasha Bogomolov more than anything else in the world. If Sonia was married to him, he would make her a widow and clear the way for her to be his wife. He didn't care if that made him a monster.

The man had taken her from him, kidnapped her right out from under him. More, he'd broken a cardinal rule in doing so—he'd involved the police in the form of Bastien Foret. Joshua knew he'd grown more violent over the years. His mother's influence had faded as necessity and self-preservation had taken over in the circumstances he'd found himself in, but he'd never felt like this. Never. He was barely able to control himself.

He moved into position, knowing Evan had his back and Kai was rounding up the other occupants of the house. The moment he laid eyes on her, that he could see for himself Sonia was alive and no one had touched her, some of the killing fury, that demand for blood, eased in his churning gut. Still, like his leopard, he felt like snarling and raging. He wanted to beat Sasha into a bloody pulp and then butcher him.

"Sasha, I love you. I really do. With all my heart, I love you." Her voice, so low, was filled with affection and he nearly blew Sasha's head off right there and then.

"You'll always be my family, but he's my choice. I want

you to get to know him. To take that time, for me. I'm asking as someone who loves you and needs you in my life,
take the time to get to know him before you judge him."

Her family? The Bogomolovs? The ones trying to kill
her? What was she doing? Stalling for time?

"Damn it, Sonia, *no*. He's not for you. This life isn't for
you. I forbid it."

Sonia stared up at the fury on Sasha's hard features.
"He'll fight for me. He will come after me and he'll never
stop until he finds me. He'll fight for me. That's the kind of
man he is."

Joshua's heart clenched hard. Pounded. His blood thundered in his ears. She believed in him. There was absolute
confidence in her voice.

"You don't know that. You can't possibly know him that
well. I saw you in the swamp, a little female running from
that pack of males. Imagine my surprise when that beautiful
cat turned out to be you. I saw his leopard knock yours off
her feet. I saw you shift and kick the crap out of the male.
You were fearless. Beautiful. I was so proud of you."

Joshua was proud of her now. He'd been so then as well,
although at the time he'd been so fucking pissed at her and
terrified out of his mind when he'd realized she was willing
to commit suicide. He'd also been so upset that she'd shifted
and showed her beautiful body off to all his men—and apparently Bogomolov as well—he hadn't thought much beyond that. He knew, from what Shadow indicated, that
Gatita hadn't forgiven the male and refused to come out and
resolve the problem. He should have done a better job of
apologizing to her.

"I love him."

Joshua nearly groaned aloud. His entire body reacted to
those three words. The way she said them. A fact quietly stated.
Her gaze was steady on Sasha's and she didn't flinch when the
Russian glared at her. Joshua loved her even more in that moment. *Loved* her. With his heart. All the way to his lost soul.

"He manhandled you."

He had, but she'd been kicking the hell out of his leopard and he hadn't wanted the bad-tempered beast to think about teaching her a lesson. Still . . .

"He would never hurt me. *Never.*" She said it with absolute conviction and Joshua felt like his woman was bringing him to his knees.

"I see bruises on your skin. Smudge marks where his fingers dug in deep."

His woman blushed. His body hardened at the thought of the other marks on her, on her breasts, the inside of her thighs, her buttocks. He hadn't left much of her unmarked.

"It's not like that. We both get a little crazy." That wasn't the word for it. He was so addicted to her, to her mouth, her body, every part of her, that he didn't think a full second went by that he wasn't thinking about his cock and how it felt in her, surrounded by her. She got him into such a frenzy, he was out of control—and that never happened with any other woman.

"He doesn't hit me. He wouldn't."

"How would you know, Sonia?"

Joshua wanted to smash Sasha for that question. He would never hit her. He couldn't. He sure as hell wouldn't allow another man to abuse her either. Like putting a fucking bomb in her car.

"I know you wouldn't hit me. No matter how angry you get at me, I know you would never hit me. I know the same about him. Whatever he's doing in his life, whatever led him there, that's his, not mine. He has to decide what's important in his life. You believe you were born to take over your father's business and you intend to do that. You just admitted to me you killed the men conspiring to harm me."

He nodded slowly. "I know I'm not a good man. I know what I am. I know I'll never have it all, the woman I can love completely and who can love me and look at me as if

I'm everything to her. That's not going to happen for me because I know I'm not a good man."

"He'll come for me, Sasha. I love him, and I love you. I would never be able to forgive you if you hurt him."

There was no way to love her any more than he already did. Every time he thought that, she said something that melted his heart. That took him closer to her.

"Do you think that matters to me? I *chose* you. You're all I have left. You are my family. *You*, Sonia. Do you think for one minute I'm going to turn you over to a man who is a fucking criminal? Once you're his, in our world, I can't interfere."

Fuck Sasha. He wasn't keeping Joshua's woman, although from the conversation, as much as he didn't like it, or want to admit it, things sounded as if Sasha really cared about Sonia and was trying to protect her.

"That's just it, Sasha. I am his," she said quietly. "I'm his mate. Our leopards chose each other. She's had her heat and she chose him. I chose Joshua. I would every time."

Sasha turned away from Sonia, swearing in Russian, and she closed her eyes and pressed the water bottle to her temple as if she might be getting a headache. Joshua's heart contracted. He despised seeing her upset or in pain.

"Let me call him. Talk to him. I can convince him to stay away. You can meet with him at a neutral location." Joshua heard the hope in Sonia's voice, and it gutted him. She definitely didn't want the two men fighting.

Sasha turned back to her. "You can tell him the two of you are done and I'm sending you somewhere safe."

"I'll just find my way back to him." She said it quietly, not defiantly, just matter-of-factly, stating the truth. "I love him. I could be carrying his child. Did you think of that?"

Joshua's mouth went dry. His entire body froze. He hadn't thought of that. Not for a minute. What the fuck was wrong with him? When he'd first met her, he'd known she was in a heat and he didn't care one way or the other if she got pregnant because he knew she belonged to him and he'd claimed her. He hadn't thought about it since. He should have locked her somewhere safe, somewhere she and his child wouldn't be taken by the Bogomolov family.

Sasha let out a groan, turned and flung the bottle of water at the fireplace. It hit, spraying water everywhere, bounced off and hit the floor, the rest of the water leaking out.

"Please, Sasha, at least get to know him. Give me this chance with someone I love. My leopard can hear lies. She knows he's telling the truth when he says he loves me. I feel it every time I'm in the room with him. Please just give us this chance. All of us. You, me and Joshua."

Joshua felt it was a very good time to announce his presence. He couldn't take much more of her quiet declarations of her love and belief in him. Or her pleas. They sure as fuck didn't need the Russian's permission to be together and he intended to make that perfectly clear.

"I think that would be a very good idea." He spoke quietly, his gaze on the Russian, waiting to see if the man was going to live or die.

Both spun around, Sonia's breath catching in her throat as she stared at him. Sasha went for the gun in the holster beneath his shoulder.

Joshua shook his head. "You'd be dead before you got it out."

Sasha slowly dropped his hand to his side and regarded the intruder with a sour look on his face. "Joshua Tregre, I presume."

"I came for my woman." Joshua was making that perfectly clear from the get-go. "Sonia, come here to me. Give him a wide berth."

"He wouldn't hurt me," she protested.

"Sonia, don't you dare move from that chair," Sasha commanded.

Rage burst through Joshua's normal calm, reminding

him Zen went out the window when he dealt with anything having to do with his woman. "You have no fuckin' right to tell her to do anything. I should blow your head off for planting a bomb in her car."

"He didn't," Sonia said, jumping to her feet and flinging her body in front of Sasha's. Her arms were spread wide to cover as much of the man as possible.

"Just so you know, baby," Joshua hissed through clenched teeth, "I can take the wings of a fly. No problem finding a body part on him you can't cover. Get your ass over here before I take him out so I know you're safe."

He held out his hand to her, and if she didn't get over to him in the next thirty seconds, he was blowing the Russian's head off. That was the one target she couldn't cover.

"Sonia, you are not to shield me," Sasha hissed.

"Don't need you tellin' my woman what to do. I'm capable of handling her on my own."

She stomped over to Joshua, glaring with every step. He caught her wrist and thrust her behind him. "What do you mean, he didn't plant the bomb?"

"It's a long story, but he was trying to save me from Nikita. I'll tell you the entire thing at home, but right now, you two have to be friends."

"That isn't likely, baby." He dismissed her decree out of hand. He didn't take his eyes from the Russian. From the moment he'd suspected Sasha Bogomolov had been Sonia's husband, legal or otherwise, and there was nothing to prove the marriage legal, he had collected as much information as possible on him.

Sasha was a shrewd businessman, much more so than his father, who tended to rely on brute force. He didn't shrink from violence if it was called for, but viciousness wasn't Sasha's first choice.

"She needs to be safe," Sasha said. "Nikita is wholly focused on killing her, then me and finally, you. He's bringing a shitload of men with him."

"They'll all die here."

"You didn't look like you had an army built up," Sasha said. "Do you have even ten men you know are loyal to you? Ten that will stick when it gets ugly, because it will."

"I have a few friends I've reached out to," Joshua said. "They're on the way." He backed up a couple of steps and indicated the front door. "You go out there and call off your men. Sonia and I are going to walk out of your house and get into the truck one of my men is bringing around. There had better not be any mistakes. You'll be the first to die if you make one wrong move. Your friend Dmitri is next."

"Joshua, no," she protested. "Sasha is family to me."

"The man fucked you, Sonia," he snarled before he could stop the words from roaring out of his mouth. "Just for that alone I want him dead."

"Are you going to give me a list of every woman you've ever fucked so I can kill all of them? I'm betting there's a long list."

She was magnificent. Beautiful. Her hair looked wild. Her eyes held a fury only a female leopard could manage. Her chin was up defiantly. Those lips of hers, plump and soft and perfect to stretch around his cock, were pressed together in a line that made him want to push his tongue right through to all that moist heat. She'd stepped around him and both hands were fisted on her hips.

"Not certain I remember names, Sonia."

"Too long a list?"

"That and didn't spend more than a couple of hours with them. They weren't memorable. You, on the other hand . . . Evan." He raised his voice slightly.

"Got him in my sights, boss," Evan replied.

Joshua stepped right into her. Crowding her body. Letting the tips of her breasts nuzzle his chest right through the thin tee she wore. He caught the back of her neck in his palm and brought her to him, taking her upturned mouth. The moment his lips touched hers, need exploded through him.

He took his time kissing her, licking at her lips, using his teeth on her bottom lip until she parted for him.

His tongue swept in, claiming her. Part of him knew it was a dick move. He wanted there to be no question in the other man's mind just who she belonged to. The biggest part of him couldn't resist her, was totally lost the moment she'd gone all wild woman on him. He poured everything into that kiss—from love to ownership—and hoped she got each separate message.

She kissed him back. There was never holding back with Sonia, she just gave him everything she was. No one kissed like her. She wiped out everything that had ever come before her, good or bad. His arm snaked around her waist and pulled her closer.

"I know you don't want me to kill him, babe, but he's bound to come after you."

She pressed her forehead to his chest, looking down at her feet rather than into his eyes. "Then we take him with us. It isn't safe for him here, not with his father looking for him."

He frowned, catching her chin. The pad of his thumb slid over her soft skin as he forced her head up so he could look into her eyes. "Sonia. What is it? Talk to me."

"He's family. I'm sorry you're upset that we had . . . sex." She whispered the last word. "He is too. He didn't want that for me, but I insisted. I was afraid I wasn't a very good wife to him and I . . ."

"Stop, baby. That was me being a jackass. I love you. Whatever happened between you isn't my business. It never will be. You say he's a good man and isn't trying to kill you. That's good, but it isn't good enough for me. I have to know for myself. We'll talk it out, man to man, but not here. Sooner or later his men are going to get restless and then we'll have to start killing. Both sides lose. We're leaving. Now. You're going out the door with me and until we're safe at home, you're going to do everything I say the moment I say it. If you don't, there will be consequences. That's if we make it out of this alive."

Sasha had been standing to the side of the couch, watching them intently. "I'll take into consideration what you've said to me, Sonia." He looked at Joshua over her head. "You keep her safe or you're a dead man."

Joshua might have admired the man under other circumstances. He wrapped his arm around Sonia. "Walk right behind me, baby. Evan and Kai will be behind you."

She nodded. "I'm going to say good-bye to him," she announced, stepping away from Joshua toward Sasha.

He caught her by the pocket of her jeans, yanking her back to him. "No, you're not. You'll do all that after I talk to him and make my own assessment about what kind of danger he poses to you."

Sasha turned his back on them and went to the front door, calling out to his men with a soft two-way note indicative of the black-bellied whistling duck. His men came out of the shadows, looking a little perplexed.

"Let them through," he ordered.

The men looked shocked as first Joshua emerged, Sonia behind him, and then the two bodyguards, Evan and Kai, walking backward in perfect synchronization. Their leopards allowed them to know when the ground changed and to feel for any objects close. They moved in silence to the road and as they did, one by one the others joined them. All but Gray.

Sonia looked around for him. "Is Gray all right, Joshua?"

He glanced down at her. In the morning light she was gorgeous, her skin flawless. Eyes dark. Lashes long. He could see her nipples pushing against the fabric of her tee, the outline of the generous curve of her breast. "Gray's just fine. He's hanging back to make sure a sniper isn't up on the roof or in the trees looking to kill you or me. You're the one who needs to start worrying whether you're all right or not."

She frowned at him. An adorable little frown. It wouldn't

get her out of trouble, but it made his cock ache and he wanted to smile. He didn't.

"Why would I not be all right? Sasha didn't hurt me."

"No, Sasha took you from me. Wait, no, Sasha didn't take you, you went right out my fuckin' front door and got into his car. Then you drove away and told your girl posse to wait five minutes to give the bastard Russian a head start."

He saw the comprehension on her face, the quick glance darted his way. "Everything turned out all right. I'm alive. Did Bastien get back?"

"The point is that you might have been dead. There was a fifty-fifty chance he'd kill you. You were the one who thought he put a bomb in your car, yet you go straight to him when he tells you to. Do you ask your man for help? Hell, no. You just run off with your murderous ex-husband."

"We were never married."

Joshua caught her hand and trotted the rest of the way to their vehicle. He yanked open the door and as she climbed into the passenger seat, he slapped her ass hard. She yelped and glared at him. He indicated her seat belt and she snapped it in place. He shut the door with controlled violence. Every time he thought of that moment when Molly came running into the kitchen to tell him that his woman had delivered herself into the hands of her ex-husband, the man who had tried to kill her, it made him sick all over again.

Everything in him had gone still. Frozen solid. Ice had run in his veins then because it had to. He had to find her and then get to her. The rage would come after, but he had to be fully functioning while he hunted for her. He yanked open the driver-side door and set the car in motion.

"Is Bastien back yet?" she asked in a small voice.

"How the hell should I know?" He knew he sounded irritated with her and he needed to take a breath, but it was there again, that feeling that he'd lost her. That the one decent thing he had was gone. He'd let her down, let those maniacs get to her. "All that mattered to me, Sonia, was finding you. For all I knew they were taking a blowtorch to you."

She winced. "I'm sorry. I knew you'd come."

"It doesn't take long for someone to hurt you. Less even to kill you. Five minutes is too long. He had you a hell of a lot longer than that."

"I know. I'm sorry, Joshua. I didn't think beyond saving Bastien, and I knew you'd come." She repeated it a second time.

He glanced at her. "I'm not beating the hell out of you, babe, if that's what's putting that scared look on your face. Spanking maybe."

"Your spankings tend to turn me on, not make me cry," she pointed out. "I'm not afraid you'll beat me or spank me. I'm afraid for Bastien. I should have insisted Sasha tell me where he is. What if he can't get free on his own?"

"We'll find him. Let me get you home. Security is already beefed up. We've got a few surprises if we're attacked. And this time, Sonia, don't you move without telling me first."

She nodded. He could feel her gaze on him. "I really am sorry I worried you, Joshua. I was so scared for Bastien. If Nikita had him . . ."

"You fuckin' knew he was already dead if Nikita had him." He glanced sideways at her, letting her know he wasn't about to listen to bullshit.

They drove in silence, and then he suddenly pounded on the steering wheel with his fist in an explosion of violence. She jumped, her heart accelerating. She glanced at his stony features and then out the window. He knew he was scaring her and he had to stop, but he'd never experienced such fear. Terror.

His world had nearly ended. Every dream he'd ever had—given up—and then felt he got back when she came to him, was gone. He'd been sick. Since that moment in Borneo, when he'd gone berserk and annihilated the five men who had taken those three young girls from the villagers, he had managed to convince himself that monster was gone. Subdued. He was one hundred percent in control. He would never repeat that shameful act. When Molly told him his woman was gone, the monster was back instantly and roaring for blood. A leopard's killing blood.

What was the point of allowing her to try to explain anything to him right at that moment? He wasn't willing to listen. Or he couldn't. Either way, she had zero chance of making him understand why she drew Sasha's crew away from his home. Maybe she didn't know why she'd done it.

Silence filled the car and he glanced over at her. She stared out the window, but he saw the tears tracking down her face. She was quiet about it, crying in silence, not trying to use tears to get her way. The sight twisted his heart. He wanted to pound the steering wheel again, because the monster was loose and it was still afraid it had lost her. Lost her to the man who had claimed her.

*He had no right,* Shadow snarled. *None. She wasn't his. She was never his. She belongs to us.*

She did. Sonia belonged to them, but she wasn't property. *You heard her. She told him she chose us.* She had. He'd heard every word she'd said. He glanced over again, and she had turned her face even more from him and had pressed her fingers tightly against her lips. He couldn't take it. She was his, and he wasn't doing a very good job of taking care of her. She had to have been terrified to walk out to the SUV and put herself into the hands of someone she was certain had tried to kill her. She'd been incredibly brave—not thinking straight, but brave.

"Baby, don't cry." Joshua couldn't help the soft, velvet tone. She broke his heart crying like that. He reached out and brushed a tear from her cheek. "I'm angry that I nearly lost you. When she told me . . ." He broke off, the darkness in him roaring for blood.

Now that the monster in him was loose, he wasn't certain he could stay in control. It had taken those years at Jake

Bannaconni's ranch to bring him back his calm center. "Just know I'm happy I've got you back for more reasons than you know." He caught her hand, brought her fingertips to his mouth to kiss them and then pressed her palm tight to his thigh.

"I'm sorry," she whispered again. "I really am. I realize now, it wasn't the smartest plan. I just didn't want them . . ." She broke off and pressed her fingers harder into her lips.

They were home and he turned off the motor, but he didn't move. He hadn't thought he could hear her explanation and really listen, but he had the feeling her motivation hadn't been entirely about Bastien.

"Sonia. Were you protecting me?" Taking into consideration the way she was with Jerry and Molly, and if what she'd told Sasha had been true and she loved him, it would be fiercely, and yes, protectively. He wanted to swear all over again and this time pound his fist into the wall, but he forced back the monster threatening to swallow him and stayed silent and still. Looking at her.

She was beautiful in her disheveled state. He loved when she was put together, because she was gorgeous, but this was best. Her hair was falling out of the braid she'd used to tame it. Her tee was stretched tight across her breasts, so he could see the outline of the curves and the way her nipples were tight little temptations. Her jeans clung to her hips and rounded ass, cupping her bottom, putting all sorts of wonderful but dirty ideas into his head. She was barefoot, and she had small, delicate feet.

"Sonia, I'm not going to go crazy and hurt you, I am just asking for the truth."

She turned her face fully toward him and his breath caught in his throat. His body stirred. He loved her so fucking much he didn't know what to do with it.

"Can we just say I did something stupid and not get into the why of it? I acted impulsively, and I won't do it again."

He shook his head. "No, we can't." He pressed her hand

tighter against his thigh. His body felt burning hot and he knew she had to recognize the rise in his heat, know the way the fire rushed through his veins. "You were brave, Sonia, be brave now. We need to make certain this will never happen again. Tell me the real reason. Were you protecting me?"

She bit down on her bottom lip, nodding as she did so. "I didn't want him to get near you. I thought if he really wanted me dead, he'd have no reason to kill you. He might Bastien, but I couldn't prevent that one way or the other."

He took a breath and then another one, forcing his lungs to work again. Forcing himself to remain still, sitting in the seat beside her. He wasn't a hearts-and-flowers kind of man. He wanted to be that for her, but it was so alien to his nature he knew those moments for her would be rare. He was more hands-on, clothes off, anything goes any time of the day or night, no matter where they were. That was him showing her he loved her. That was his way to let her know she was beautiful and so amazing he had to show her what she did to him.

He couldn't imagine waking up without her now. Not being able to turn to her in the middle of the night when nightmares sometimes took him. She had eased the migraines he often got, so that they were fewer and far between. She was . . . his everything. "You can't ever place yourself in danger to save me. I'm able to take care of myself, Sonia. It's what I do and you have to trust that I'm good at it."

"I do know that you are," she agreed. She hesitated.

Here came the *but*. He forced himself to remain controlled, but he needed movement. He kissed the center of her palm and then slid out of the car, indicating for her to do the same. As he walked around the vehicle to her, he took his time, determined he wouldn't yell at her. She didn't need that, but he still wanted to shake her for putting herself in danger. She stopped moving once they got to the verandah and turned to face him.

"I love you, Joshua. I know the difference between real love for my man and affection and gratitude for the only person who was good to me during a terrible time. I don't want to lose you any more than you want to lose me."

"If that means you think it's okay to do what you did, stop right there. It's not. Not. Ever. *Never.*" He all but snarled the last word. Where the hell was his cool and calm? He knew what she was going to say, but he still reacted. "Give me your word you'll never do anything this idiotic again and you won't try to save me."

She made a little moue with her lips, sending fire streaking like an arrow straight to his cock, or maybe it was her defiance and his need to conquer. Or just her. Just Sonia.

"Joshua, I want to give you my word, I want to give you anything you ask for, but I'd be lying to you and I think you know that."

He yanked open the front door and all but thrust her inside. They were going to talk his way and she was going to understand she was going to give him her word and by God, she would keep it too. He'd forgotten Molly. The woman flung herself at Sonia, nearly knocking her down.

Swearing under his breath, he stood back and watched the two women. What were they going to say to Molly and hopefully Bastien? Sasha was capable of killing the man. If Joshua was being strictly honest with himself, he knew he could as well, given the right circumstances. The monster lurking in him was always out for blood, and if Sonia was threatened in any way, he knew he would kill to protect her.

"I'm safe," she reassured. "Sasha thought I'd been kidnapped and he wanted to save me. He wasn't the one who'd planted the bomb. It was his father. Sasha all along worked to keep me alive when his father wanted me dead."

"Oh, no," Molly said. "Bastien is pissed. He's after whoever kidnapped him and took me out of his house. He's really, really angry. If he finds out Sasha did it, he'll try to arrest him."

Sonia frowned. "That wouldn't be good." She glanced over her shoulder at Joshua.

He waited, wondering what she would say. Sasha had taken a cop prisoner. He'd sent that cop's girlfriend on an errand. Bastien would have been alone, wondering what they were doing to his woman. If that had been Joshua, and he found out who had done it, he would have killed them all. Nothing, no one, would have been safe until he got Sonia back. Even then, he would have exacted vengeance.

"You really didn't know who took him," Sonia pointed out. "They were Russian, but they could have been hired by Blake's family. You have no real idea who they were or what they wanted. The last thing you want is for the Russian mob to come after you and Bastien, Molly. Believe me, they never stop. If they want Bastien dead because he arrests one of their own, sooner or later it will happen."

Molly gasped and put a hand to her throat. "I didn't think about that."

"What did you tell him?"

"He was completely in the dark. He didn't know what they wanted and I just said they wanted you, Sonia. He's going to come here and demand to know what happened. I should call him and let him know you're safe. He's out looking for you, along with the entire police, sheriff and highway force."

"I'm sorry, your phone was thrown out onto the road," Sonia admitted. "And mine is smashed to smithereens."

Joshua took out his and handed it to Molly. "Call him, but if you don't want him to be looking over his shoulder for the rest of his life, you need to come up with a story."

He didn't like that they were protecting Sasha, but the man could be an ally now, when his father was sure to attack, and also after when he ran the Bogomolov empire. His mind began to come up with plausible stories for Bastien; after all, it was what he did best.

# 17

SONIA gasped with every smack on her bright red bottom. He gently rubbed the heat into her decorated cheeks, all the while strumming her clit with his other hand. He'd been at this for some time. His cock felt as if it might shatter, so full and hard it was brutal waiting. Angry sex would have been a great release, but he couldn't sustain anger at her. He gave her another smack, watching her face, seeing the flush spread, the way she bit her lower lip, hearing her small, panting cry of pure need.

*"Joshua."* His name came out in a breathless keen. *"Please."*

"Please what?"

"I need you in me." Each word was punctuated with her breath.

He fucking loved that. He loved holding her right on the edge, denying her release, taking her up over and over. She was so beautiful like this. Bent over the bed, hands fisting in the sheets, her legs spread out, his thighs between them while he played with her body. While he worshiped every inch of her.

She totally trusted him or she would never have allowed his kind of play. Why hadn't her brain remembered that trust when she'd needed it most? He gave her another smack, because just thinking about her leaving him, her talking suicide, her trading her life for his or Bastien's nearly broke him.

It had taken hours for the cops to leave. He knew Bastien was still suspicious, but he'd dropped his interrogation, allowing the others to do the job because he was part of the investigation. During those hours, with the police invading his home, he'd watched Sonia protect her ex-husband. She'd been brilliant at it. She'd been careful never to word her story the same way twice and she'd cautioned Molly to be careful of that as well. Molly, thankfully, hadn't known much. Sonia had handled the cops like a pro. She'd be an asset to him. She'd been cool under the bombardment of questions, known when to have a small breakdown and remained adamant that she never saw those who'd taken her.

She'd been beautiful sitting there, looking vulnerable. He'd seen more than one cop staring at her breasts, the way they jutted out under that tight tee. He'd been able to make out both nipples. When she'd moved, her breasts swayed, drawing attention to her lush curves. He'd sat with his cock a fucking rock, a steel spike with no relief. He hadn't been the only man in the room with his body out of control.

Once he'd thought about getting a sweater or something to cover her up, but that vulnerable, fragile, sexy-as-hell look had had every man believing her bullshit—with the exception of Bastien. Joshua's admiration and respect for her grew, but he detested the fact that it was Sasha she'd been defending. By the time the cops left, his need to stake his claim on her had grown to unhealthy lengths. He'd known it, but hadn't cared. Then he'd had to wait until Bastien took Molly home.

The moment the door was closed, he'd turned without a word, picked her up and tossed her over his shoulder. He'd taken the stairs two at a time, tossed her on the bed and ripped her tee right down the front. He'd been wanting to do that for hours. *Hours.* He had plans. She was going to suffer. Not the way he had, but still . . .

He'd spent an hour kissing Sonia after carrying her up to the bedroom. Kissing every inch of her. He'd needed that. Needed to feel her skin under his mouth and hands. He'd needed to know she was alive and with him. She'd cried out when he kissed her inner thighs and left strings of bright red strawberries and teeth marks, but he'd only nuzzled her clit and left her empty and needy to turn her over, a fast, abrupt move that had left her breathless.

He'd taken the opportunity to yank her down to the edge of the bed, kick her feet apart and wedge his body between her thighs. She'd thought she was going to get him, take his cock, have him bury it deep in her slick, hot sheath. She'd been very, very wrong. He'd caught the nape of her neck and held her down.

"Keep your arms out. Don't you dare lift them. You deserve everything you're going to get." It had been her only warning. The first smack had been hard. Hard enough to have her yelp. When he'd seen she was going to stay where he wanted, he'd plunged two fingers into her. Her keening cry was music to him. He'd known she loved this as much as he did—she liked rough. She liked the way the heat spread across all her nerve endings and sent fire straight to her core. He'd wanted to hear her say it. He needed it.

He smacked her over and over, rubbing in the heat between each whack and strumming her clit or curling fingers to caress that sweet little spot that drove her insane. "You really love this, don't you?" he asked.

"Yes," she whispered. "It isn't a punishment, if that's what you're thinking."

He knew that. He was careful to control how much force he used, just enough to warm her bottom and bring every nerve ending to life. Her breath came in sobbing gasps. Wet glistened on her thighs, an invitation to his parched mouth, and he took it, leaving a series of strawberries and bite marks up her quivering thighs while he indulged his need for her addictive taste.

He knew her. Every shudder of her body. The way her muscles rippled, the way her breath hitched right before she toppled. Each time she got close, he stopped, taking away his hands, his mouth.

"Joshua." His name was a long, drawn-out wail.

She tried to lift her head and he pushed her back to the bed, holding her still. "*This* is your punishment for nearly killing me. For letting those bastards take you. And, baby, I can keep this shit up all night. I'm *enjoying* myself. Are you?"

"No. I said I was sorry." Her voice came out a sob of need. Of pure hunger.

His woman, needy for him. He loved that. "You make music when you're so needy, did you know that? I fuckin' love the way you sound when you're beggin' me for my cock." His tongue swiped through all that heat. She was scorching hot. "Poor deprived, very bad girl. You love my cock, don't you?"

"*Yes.*" She bared her teeth at him and wiped the dots of sweat on her forehead along the sheet, trying to get some relief. "You? Not so much right now."

Sonia's eyes blazed with fire. With passion. Those beautiful lips of hers nearly sent him over the edge. He was dripping with a need of his own. He stood up, put one knee on the bed, so he was right next to her head. So his cock was inches from that mouth—the one he craved. He kept one hand on the nape of her neck, pinning her down, the

other sliding over his cock. A tight fist. It felt damn good.
Watching her stare with wide, desperate eyes felt even better.

"I could barely think. Barely function. You did that to
me. What if our child was inside of you? You put not only
yourself but our baby in danger." Anger flared through him,
bright and hot all over again, anger mixed with sheer terror.
The thought of losing her, a woman who could accept him
just as he was, walk by his side on a dangerous path, take
whatever he wanted to give in the bedroom or anywhere
else he wanted, had left a dark hole in him. The monster
had crawled out. She was all brightness. Despite her past,
she was still bright and happy and so sweet she took his
breath. He'd almost lost that.

He pressed the broad head of his cock against her lips.
Her gasp of air was warm. It carried the hint of desperation
and need. She parted her lips, her tongue touched him and
he nearly blew apart. He'd never been so hard in his life.
The hand at the nape of her neck bunched her hair, half
lifted her head and he thrust between her parted lips, filling
her mouth. So hot. So tight. Paradise.

He moved in her, trying to force his body to be as gentle
as he knew how—which wasn't much, but he watched her
face. When she closed her eyes, he tightened his hold on her
hair, pulling on her scalp until those impossibly long lashes
lifted and he was staring directly into her eyes. They were
so dark with lust he couldn't help the next thrust, his cock
swelling until he knew he was going to explode.

"Keep looking at me," he bit out.

Fire. It was pure fire. Pure paradise. He wanted to keep
feeling her mouth, her tongue, the way she sucked. The
squeeze of her muscles. There was no holding back. Jet
after jet rocketed down her throat. She tried to keep up, but
the angle on the bed was difficult. He didn't care. He refused
to let her up.

He loved the way she looked, her eyes bright, a little
dazed, that desperation still there, her hips squirming, still

marked by him. There were marks all over her body—his marks proclaiming she belonged to him. He loved that she wore them under her clothes, and he knew when they faded, there would be more, new ones.

He grinned at her, watched her lick her lips as he pulled his cock free and fisted it. "Look at that, baby, I'm still hard. That's because you're so sexy. Do you still want this?"

She nodded. "Please."

He stepped off the bed to stand behind her, admiring his handiwork. He loved looking at her red, round ass. She was gorgeous. He still couldn't believe he'd found her and she was so perfect for him. "You are still in trouble."

"What are you going to do?"

"I have plans for tonight, Sonia. Hell is coming and I'm going to need to be able to keep my mind on work, not on worrying about whether or not you put yourself in danger." He couldn't help rubbing his hand over her left cheek. It was still hot. His handprint was fading.

"I won't."

"You will. You're so stubborn." He bent to kiss the two indentations above her ass. "You need 'property of Joshua' tattooed right here, so every time I take you like this, every time I have to punish you like this—and I know damn well that will be plenty of times—I can look at it with satisfaction."

He bent his head to her because all that hot nectar belonging to him was escaping. She screamed when his mouth moved on her, devouring her, suckling, tongue alternately fluttering and stabbing. He pinched her clit and she went wild, bucking against his mouth. He lifted his head. "Don't. Don't you dare come."

"I can't stop."

"Find a way. If you want this, control yourself." He grinned, knowing there was no control. His own cock was out of control, once again harder than a rock. He loved her. He loved her body. He loved that she let him play like this.

Nothing restrained her. She could stop him anytime. One word. Getting off the bed. Anything at all to indicate the play was too rough for her and she knew he would stop instantly, but she stayed, arms stretched out, fists bunching the sheet, head thrashing, breasts pushed deep into the mattress.

He couldn't help himself when she struggled to control her breathing, taking in deep breaths to quiet her body. He turned his head, sucking her delicate skin as high as possible on her inner thigh, not stopping until his brand was there. He did the same thing to the other side. All the while his fingers moved in and out of her, curling and then uncurling, rubbing that sweet spot and then scissoring deep. She was panting, making little mewling noises.

He stood behind her, close, his feet spread, forcing her legs apart so she was open to him. He pushed the broad head into all that heat. She squeezed down on him, and he threw his head back. Ecstasy. Pure ecstasy. He drove deep and she screamed so loud he was afraid every one of his men would come running. It wouldn't matter if they did. Nothing could stop him. Her body surrounded him, hot scorching silk, slick with honeyed liquid, bathing him in her, gripping so tight he felt like he was in a living, silken vise, all those muscles massaging and milking.

"I can't . . . I can't . . ." Her head thrashed, her body bucking back against his wildly.

"Fly, baby, now. Go high." He drove deeper, lifting her hips into him, taking the lower half of her body right off the bed so he had more of an angle.

She screamed again, a long wail of joy as her body clamped down hard, convulsing around his. Over and over, the ripples kept coming and he kept driving right through them, feeling that burning pleasure that rocked him from his toes to the top of his head. He didn't know if she had one long continuous orgasm or if the hard pistoning of his body brought her up over and over fast, but those muscles worked his cock until he had no way to stop his release.

He'd never felt anything like it, that fire spreading through him like a storm, flames licking over his skin, through his groin, consuming him. His roar of satisfaction was nearly as loud as her screams. She milked him for every last drop, wringing him dry. He collapsed over top of her, his arms stretching out along hers to find her hands. He threaded his fingers through hers and tried not to let his body come down from that place she always took him.

They lay there, Joshua fighting for breath, fighting to keep it together. She'd taken him over. Taken his heart. His soul. She fucking *owned* him. He might say it was the other way around, but he knew every inch of him belonged to her. It was terrifying.

"Are you all right?" He pressed kisses into the nape of her neck and down her spine.

"Yes. But I can't walk. I'm not certain I can sit either."

He smiled and just the fact that she could make him smile when his heart beat out of control and deep inside he was panicking that he would lose her was a miracle. He rubbed her left cheek and then her right, his thumb sliding along those marks with reverence and pleasure.

"You don't deserve to sit. You took years off my life, Sonia." He rolled off her and pressed his fingers to his eyes. "*God*, baby. I never want to feel like that again."

She rolled to her side and put her arm around his waist. "I'm sorry, Joshua. I couldn't think beyond getting them away from you."

"I told you what happened in Borneo. What I became. What I did. That's what got out tonight. I could have hurt a lot of people. I would have. I would have walked through a river of blood to get you back. Understand that. Understand what I'm saying to you. You don't put yourself in danger. You or our children. Not ever. You can't ever let that monster loose on the world. I'm not certain you could live with the things he's capable of doing, and I wouldn't let you go."

There was a small silence. He opened his eyes, turned his head and looked at her. She had tears tracking down her face. "I won't, Joshua. I won't do that to you. I know it was bad in Borneo, but whatever you did, they deserved it."

"No one deserves the things I did. A bullet in the head, yes. What I did, no. There's always going to be that darkness in me, Sonia." He hesitated, his hand reaching for hers. He waited until their fingers were threaded together. "I'm always going to need what we have now, in the bedroom. You know that, don't you?" He wanted so much more for her and he vowed he'd learn gentle. He'd learn how to touch her with the reverence he felt for her, at least sometimes.

She nodded and leaned close to brush a kiss along his bicep. "I need it too. I wouldn't let you touch me that way if I didn't want it. I've learned a lot about myself in this last year. I've had to grow up and rely solely on myself. That was good for me. I know if you ever did something I didn't like, I'd tell you."

He had no idea he'd been knotted up inside. Waiting for her to tell him she couldn't handle the things he needed. He should have known better. She was—everything. He brought her hand to his mouth and brushed kisses along her knuckles. "I would stop immediately. I want to give you pleasure, Sonia. I love to hear you scream my name. Making you wait heightens what you feel."

She nuzzled his shoulder. "I'm aware of that. It's just that when you've got your hands or mouth on me, sometimes it's so intense I think I might lose my mind."

Only Sonia would admit so matter-of-factly that she was into their play as much as he was. "When you give me everything like that, your complete trust, it turns me inside out." He smiled at the her. "God, you're beautiful. Not just outside, baby; deep down where it counts. When I'm with you, I forget every damn thing I've ever seen or done. You take it all away."

"I'm glad."

Her lashes fluttered, and his heart dropped. He wasn't out of danger yet. She still had concerns. He couldn't blame her. He'd laid it all out for her and their future wasn't pretty. She was intelligent enough to know that his reputation as a crime boss would grow and the people she cared about were going to shun her.

"I love what I do, Joshua. I mean, I *really* love it. I want to work for Jerry and renovate old historical houses. I know I can modernize them and yet keep the original beauty. I'm good at it. I take online classes all the time, but more, I just have a feel for it."

She didn't have to tell him that—he saw her work. It was beautiful and brought the homes into the present century, making them safe and functional without compromising the beauty of the original architecture. She was so hopeful and he wanted to give her the world, but . . .

"I know you love working. I know you love what you do. I'll do my best to compromise, but you'll have to as well. You know, with what I'm doing, there's always going to be some danger. That means bodyguards. I have to have them on you at all times to protect you. At home, at work. Wherever you go."

He couldn't stop the acceleration of his heart. Sonia had learned independence and she wanted to keep that. He couldn't blame her. He detested having bodyguards. He'd been the bodyguard for several years and having to switch roles still wasn't easy for him, but he knew the necessity.

"I wouldn't be able to do my work with bodyguards, Joshua. I go into people's homes. That would be upsetting to them."

"They don't have to look like your bodyguards."

"Right." There was an ache in her voice.

He hoped that ache was because she feared giving up

work she loved, not him. "You were here every day for a month. Longer. You didn't suspect."

Hope flared in her eyes. "That's true. And I'd heard the rumors." Her face shut down again. Lashes veiled her eyes. "What about Molly and Bastien?"

His heart clenched hard. It felt as if a giant hand squeezed the organ and kept it up. He had to tell her the truth. "Once Bastien connects the dots and realizes those rumors are true, they aren't going to associate with us."

She turned her face away from him, her breath audibly catching in her throat. She turned onto her side, her back to him. "I don't have any other friends. Molly. Jerry. Do you think Jerry will do the same thing?"

He rolled to his side and slipped his arm around her waist, forming a protective shell with his body. First, he'd ripped her heart out when he'd revealed the truth about what he was, and now he was doing it all over again. He wanted to lie to her, but he'd promised himself he'd tell her as much truth as possible. He'd shield her from the things he had to do—the details of the dirty side of being a criminal, the boss, the one making the decisions on who lived or died, but he'd try to give her the truth in all other areas.

He didn't want to think too much about what he'd do or say if she asked him about the things Rafe Cordeau was into that allowed Joshua to live in that world. He buried his face in her hair. The thick mass was like silk and smelled like heaven. He tightened his hold on her.

"You don't know for certain that Jerry and Molly would turn on me." Her voice was shaky.

He swore to himself. He wanted to protect her from the firestorm that was coming. He knew they were probably going to war with the Russians. She'd believe it was solely about her, but Nikita would learn soon enough that Alonzo Massi was really Fyodor Amurov, and he'd share that information with Fyodor's uncles. They wanted the man dead. Joshua was never going to let that happen.

"No, baby, I don't. You're right. The odds are that they will, or they'll treat you different and you'll hate it, but there's a chance they'll be loyal to you." It was so small he knew he shouldn't give her hope. The hurt would be so much worse.

"She really likes Bastien. He wouldn't risk his career to be friends with us, would he?"

Her voice was muffled against her pillow, but he heard the ache in it. The pain. He detested being the cause of hurt to her. He tightened his hold on her as if his arms, his body, could shelter her from any unhappiness. "If Bastien remained friends with us, once the rumors start flying, others, including his department, could brand him as a 'dirty' cop. He's a good man, Sonia. I looked into him. Rafe had a few cops in his pocket. Bastien wasn't one of them."

There was a long silence. He stroked his hand down her hair, needing to comfort her and not knowing how.

"I don't have friends. I didn't growing up. My mother was my friend. And then Sasha."

He winced. He couldn't help it. Like him, Sasha was a good deal older than she was. And a mobster.

"What about school?"

She pulled in on herself even more, making herself even smaller. Her knees were drawn up tight against her chest. He curved his body around hers, his legs drawing up just as tightly so she was in a little cocoon of safety.

"I went to school until my high school years. Then I was homeschooled with tutors. I had to go to take tests, but there was no interaction anymore between me and other girls or boys. The few I knew in grade school drifted away. It was my mother and Sasha."

That name again. He was going to have a talk with the bastard, and if for one second he thought Sasha was playing her and would harm her in any way—*any* way—Sasha Bogomolov was going to die. He'd sent word to the others and they were gathering their armies to back him from the threat against his woman. He didn't need them for what he had to do.

Joshua pressed kisses along the nape of her neck. "I know you want Molly to always be your friend, and I hope she proves to you that she will be, but I also know you'll meet other women. Saria, Drake's wife. She's as sweet as they come. Emma, Jake's wife, is an amazing woman. She just gave birth to their third child. Alonzo is married to my cousin, Evangeline. She owns a bakery. They're all good women. There's more. Eli Perez's wife, Caterina. You'll like her. She was held here, raised with Rafe, and had to escape. He was a DEA agent for several years, now he works security for Drake. Elijah's wife, Siena, is pregnant with triplets. I'll take you to meet her."

He nuzzled the nape of her neck again, and then scattered kisses across her shoulders. "You won't be lonely, Sonia. I swear you won't. I'll make certain you meet women, good women, who will understand the situation you're in. They'll accept you."

"I don't even know how to make friends. Molly is just so easy."

She was tearing him up inside. He wanted to blame Sasha for keeping her in that mansion that was really a prison, but what would he do to keep her safe? Hell, he'd lock her up and throw the fucking key away if that's what it took. The business they were in was hard on wives and family.

"Molly's wonderful. I hope she doesn't listen to the rumors, or if she does, she doesn't care, other than to want you safe." He pressed his forehead against the back of her head. "Stay with me, Sonia. No matter how difficult it is, stay with me. I'll make you happy. I swear it. I'll try to learn to do all those things a man should do for his woman."

She turned then, still in his arms because he didn't let go. "I'm not going anywhere, Joshua. I'm scared. I don't want to lose Molly, but I know I love you. I know you're that man for me." Her eyes searched his. "You're certain there's no way out?"

He nodded slowly. "I'd be hunted until they found me. You can only run so long, and then you're dead. I took this job knowing that. I had no idea I'd find you or I wouldn't have done it. I would have remained as part of Drake's security force."

"Why doesn't Drake fall under suspicion?"

He dipped his head to press a kiss to each eye. She had beautiful eyes. Exotic. He loved her long lashes. He especially loved how her eyes darkened with passion, with so much desire for him when he was making love to her. Playing. He loved that she let him play and understood that the more he did, the more he was showing her what she meant to him. That trust. That connection between them.

"Drake is known internationally as the head of a security company. Everyone in the criminal world knows he's relentless and dangerous. Most have a standing rule to back off if he's involved. He doesn't take bribes and he's been offered insane amounts of money. His men are every bit as relentless and dangerous as he is."

"Leopards?" she guessed.

"A mixture, but he employs a good many scattered throughout the world."

"So how does he explain being friends with mobsters?"

"He doesn't. People assume he needs contacts to do the things he does. His best friend is Jake Bannaconni."

"That doesn't seem possible. He's a billionaire or something equally as off-limits to the average man."

"Jake has bank, baby, but the two of them go way back. He saved Drake's life in Borneo and then his leg here. They're tight. Jake can be . . . volatile. Drake rarely gets angry. He's always steady." He dipped his head to find her mouth.

He'd kissed a lot of women. He couldn't remember their

names or faces. He couldn't remember their taste. Sonia had found a way inside him. He craved kissing her. He found himself thinking about her kisses at the most awkward times. He traced the shape of her lips with his tongue, memorizing the shape and feel of them. Taking his time. She let him. Right in the middle of an important discussion, she let him.

His heart stuttered. Her mouth was his haven. Her body was paradise, his escape from his reality. She became his reality when he touched her. He straightened his legs, tangling them with hers while he poured his love down her throat, stroking her tongue with his, dancing, mating, commanding. He got back love, and he took it deep.

He lifted his head. "You always give yourself to me. Wholly. All of you. That first time with you, your body melted into mine. You were so fuckin' hot. All for me. All mine. Every time I touch you, it's the same way." He heard the reverence in his voice, the awe, but he didn't care. She deserved to know how much she meant to him, and there was no way to explain to her. She was giving up everything for him.

"If this was his idea, why isn't he looking dirty to the world?"

He didn't see that coming. There was a little bit of bite to her tone indicating to him she might not want to get along with Drake.

"He's a good man, Sonia. Give him a chance."

She made a face at him and kissed his throat. "He put you in danger, Joshua. You're the one looking dirty to the world. Not him. He may have cost me a good friend. My only friend. I don't know if I can do that."

"I didn't have to take this job. No one put a gun to my head. That was all me." He pushed his fingers through his hair in a sudden moment of contemplation. "I don't even know why."

"Atonement."

His heart jumped. "What the fuck, baby? What am I

atoning for?" But he knew. He knew exactly what. That monster inside him. The one he'd unleashed in Borneo. There were things one regretted in a lifetime. Things one couldn't take back or ever make right. "Don't answer that, just let it go."

She tangled her fingers in his hair and pressed her lips to his throat. The action had her breasts rubbing along his chest, something he loved. He cupped the soft weight in his hands and dipped his head to lick at a nipple with his tongue. His mouth closed around the tempting mound. Her skin even tasted like paradise.

Her arms cradled his head and she laughed softly. "How can I possibly have a serious conversation with you when you're distracting me? I'm not certain I can go another round, Joshua, my body's a little sore."

He lifted his head immediately, narrowing his eyes. "You didn't say a word. You have to tell me when I'm being too rough with you."

"You weren't too rough, silly." She kissed his throat and scattered more along his jaw to the corner of his mouth.

He knew damn well she was trying to distract him, and he wasn't having it. "That's unacceptable to me. You *always* tell me. *Always*."

"I enjoyed every single second of what we did together. I have no problem opening my mouth and saying if I think you're being too rough. We've had a lot of sex lately. I'm just saying I'm a little sore. I like the way I feel. I do. It reminds me, with every step I take, that you were inside me. I love that feeling."

"I'm not small, baby. Maybe we should consult a doctor . . ." He tried to fight down panic. He didn't have a lot to offer her and sex was a big thing for both of them. It wasn't one-sided. She loved it as much as he did. He couldn't . . .

"Stop, crazy man." She pushed her forehead against his heart and burst out laughing. "I'm not going anywhere. You don't have to change yourself for me. I love the way you touch me. The way you like to mark me. I love the way you play. You're being paranoid. We don't have to go to a doctor, although one might be needed for your head if you keep acting like a nut. A hot bath with salts will take care of it. I'm just too sleepy to go there."

"Well, I'm not," he snapped and rolled off the bed. It was difficult to leave the warmth and softness of her body, but damn it all to hell, she wasn't going to be sore. "You should have told me *immediately*." He snapped the command, warning her that if it happened again, his brand of retaliation would be worse than he'd given her tonight. Or better. Depending on what the outcome would be. He let himself fantasize while he started the taps running and looked through cupboards until he found some girly-looking lavender salts the maid had purchased when he'd asked her to get a few things along with the blow-dryer.

He tossed the salts into the tub and stalked back to tower over her. "You totally exasperate me, woman." She maddened him with need. With a deep hunger he hadn't known existed, or he could feel, until he'd laid eyes on her. Mostly she infuriated him because she was totally his woman in all things, but she insisted on that being true only in the bedroom. He wasn't having that, but the takeover wasn't going his way and he suspected it never would.

She had tucked the covers around her, creating a cocoon, so he could only see her eyes and the top of her head. "Go away, Joshua. I'm sleepy, and you're bothering me. If we're going to be truthful, *exasperate* is a mild word for what you do to me. You're so bossy."

*"Bossy?"* His eyebrows shot up. "I am the boss around here, or hadn't you noticed?"

"I try not to. You're already arrogant and demanding. God only knows what would happen if I ever made the mistake of acknowledging you as my boss."

He caught ahold of the blanket and yanked. Nothing happened. She had secured it tightly, rolling into it like a little burrito. She gave him a look, her brows drawn together, but her eyes were laughing a little.

"Go away. I'm tired."

"You should have told me you were sore, you little wretch." He reached up under the blanket and caught her bare feet.

"Don't you dare."

Deliberately he stroked her calves, over and over, watching her face. She narrowed her eyes suspiciously, although he could see them darkening, and that told him just the touch of his fingers got to her.

"What are you going to do to me if I do?" he taunted. "I'm bigger, baby. And stronger."

"Brains over brawn every time."

He knew she was trying to sound as snippy as she could, but excitement and laughter were getting in her way.

He circled her ankles with his hands, clamping down suddenly and yanking her toward him. She let out a little scream and grabbed for the mattress in an attempt to stop herself from sliding right off the bed onto the floor. He pulled her out of the blanket burrito so she landed on her bare bottom. The floor was cold and she let out a little wail, glaring up at him.

"You are so mean."

Joshua reached down and lifted her easily, cradling her close to him. Sonia put her arms around his neck and leaned into him. She was sleepy, he could tell by the way her lashes drooped. She looked drowsy. Sexy. His. He stopped just beside the almost full bathtub and just stared down into her face, drinking her in.

"What?" she asked softly, her hand cupping his jaw.

"I love you. So much. You talk to me, Sonia. Promise, you will always talk to me before you decide to run. Losing you twice in one day nearly killed me."

She didn't take her eyes from his. "I promise. Giving you my word means something to me. I won't break it."

"My word means something too. We're together. The two of us. We can work anything out if we talk right away. Don't wait. Come to me first and I'll listen to you."

"I hope you hear me when you're listening. I want us to be good together, but not at the cost of who I am."

He brushed a kiss across her lips and then gently lowered her into the water. She gasped a little when she put her feet down, but she sank all the way into it, allowing the hot water to close over her.

"I would never take that from you. I don't want you working away from home because I don't think it's always going to be safe, but it's important to you, so you'll do it. If you want to go back to school to further your education on the subject, I'm for that as well, but only if you agree to the bodyguards. They'll blend. They can look like workmen. Your assistants. Your driver. Whatever it is you need them to look like. Just no sneaking off, and we're good."

"You do know I've lived a fairly solitary existence. I've had a lot of alone time."

"Kiss that good-bye, baby," he said, trying to sound up-beat. He didn't feel much like laughing as he climbed into the tub, settling behind her, pulling her between his out-stretched legs.

She put her fingers to her lips, smacked noisily and blew the kiss into the air. She laid her head back against him. "Thanks for this. It really feels good." She closed her eyes. "I might fall asleep right here."

He put his arms around her. "Go right ahead. I'll put you to bed. I want you in here at least fifteen minutes or until the water starts to cool." He didn't look at his watch. The others would be waiting, but he wasn't impatient. He wanted to make certain his woman wasn't hurting at all. He didn't like the idea that he'd caused her any discomfort and made a small vow to be more careful—at least for a few days.

He nuzzled the top of her head with his chin, just holding

her, savoring the feel of her in his arms. He knew she was falling asleep, her body relaxing little by little.

"I love you, Joshua," she murmured.

That voice. Drowsy. So sexy it turned his heart over and made his cock as hard as a rock. He willed that portion of his anatomy to behave. At least for a few more hours. He had things to do. A woman to protect. Above all else, he would ensure Sonia was safe.

# 18

FYODOR Amurov was a big man. He could be intimidating if one didn't know him. He *was* intimidating when you did know him. He rarely smiled. Mostly when he was around his wife, but if he did smile, it almost never reached his arctic-cold eyes. He was like ice, inside and out. He was guarded by Gorya Amurov, a cousin who had been raised with him, and Timur, his brother. All three were fierce leopards, experienced, lethal fighters. They looked what they were—men shaped into killers.

Mitya Amurov was another cousin. He was extremely remote, very removed from the others. Quiet, he kept to himself, but there was no question when he walked into a room, he commanded it. Sevastyan Amurov shadowed Mitya, occasionally flashing a smile that could break hearts, but there was nothing behind it. Like the other Amurov men, Sevastyan was a big man, but more elegantly formed, the roped muscles that defined the shifters hidden beneath a smoother physique, but there all the same. Matvei, another leopard from the Amurov lair, was never far from Mitya either. He was a big man, even among the Amurovs, much like Fyodor.

Joshua had come to know and trust these men, but they were dangerous as hell and a force to be reckoned with. Each of them had a leopard that had been trained from the time the men were born to kill. To need blood. To hate. Those cats lived for the kill. Only Fyodor had found a woman capable of taming his leopard, and even she was a thin leash on the beast.

Both Fyodor and Mitya had brought several of their men with them, all leopards, all proven to keep silent in the face of whatever had to be done. These were all men Joshua could trust—all men willing to stand with him. It didn't hurt that they had a stake in finding Nikita and Sasha Bogomolov.

Sasha had chosen a vacation estate, one isolated and easily defensible. The swamp surrounded the house, edging in on it, trying to take back the property. No one lived there permanently and it showed in the way the bushes crept back persistently. Great cypress and gum trees rose up, branches stretching out like arms. Long fringes of moss waved macabrely in the night breeze, adding to the illusion that the house was surrounded by giant stick figures.

Joshua and the others moved silently through the swamp. They'd left vehicles a few miles down the road, not wanting lights or sounds to give them away. To prevent the leopards from scenting them, they used the spray Drake had given them. They were used to traveling with small packs around their necks, carrying jeans, shoes and weapons. The packs were small, so they didn't have much in the way of firepower.

They kept downwind of the other leopards just in case, circling around to get behind each sentry. They had to take them out silently, but not permanently. That would come later, if need be. Joshua shifted just behind the man, not bothering with clothes. He struck the guard hard, a short, ugly blow to the temple. He packed a lot of power and sent up a silent prayer that he hadn't killed the man.

He caught the guard and lowered him to the ground, did a quick tie and gag and then pulled on his jeans and shoes. Slipping over the railing onto the verandah, he knew the others moved into position, surrounding the house. He heard his heartbeat as he waited for the signal to go. It came in the form of an owl hooting. Each team was in place. He gave the signal to move on the house.

Before he could breach the door, Evan was there before him, giving him a look that told him to back off. Joshua had always been the one to go first, to take the biggest risk in any operation they ran. He was still getting used to the idea that his men protected him. It didn't sit well with him, and he was certain it never would. Not ever.

It took only a few minutes to subdue Sasha's crew. They were spitting mad, especially his personal bodyguards, their eyes promising retaliation. He didn't care. Sasha was dragged into the great room, where Joshua indicated he sit in a chair facing the fireplace. Sasha stared at him stoically. Joshua had been in countless situations with criminals, ruthless men ready to fight their way out of any situation, even a suicide mission. He could read men easily. Sasha Bogomolov wouldn't crack under torture. His body would give out long before his brain would. That didn't fit with a man afraid of his father—afraid his father would kill his woman.

"I don't believe we were formally introduced. I'm Joshua Tregre."

Sasha inclined his head. "I'm well aware of who you are."

The tone was neutral. Quiet. Joshua had trouble getting a handle on him. His leopard had gone insane, raking at him the moment he recognized the Russian as his number-one rival for Sonia. He'd watched this man with her, and even then, he couldn't tell for certain whether Sasha had his own agenda or he really cared for her and wanted her safe.

"Sonia told me the story, why you took her and why you

supposedly protected her from your father. I'm trying to understand why you didn't put a bullet into that bastard's head. If my father was threatening to murder the woman I loved, I'd kill him—if I thought he'd really do it."

"Oh, he'd do it. I was ten years old when he beat my mother to death in front of me. I will always have the scars he gave me that day when I tried to defend her." Again, Sasha stated the facts without emotion, looking at him with dead eyes.

Joshua paced across the room and back. He wasn't certain yet how to get his prisoner to tell him what he wanted to know. He either had an ally or an enemy. He had to know which. "You want me to believe your father beat your mother to death in front of you and you still haven't retaliated? That he put a bomb in your woman's car and you still let him live? You aren't afraid."

Sasha sent him a faint smile. "When you grow up with a father like mine, you lose the ability to fear."

"Like yours?"

Sasha shrugged. "He beat me at every opportunity. He shoved a gun into my mouth countless times. Mostly, he tortured and killed other men as examples of what he would do to anyone disloyal. He killed their families—including their children. He set his leopard on me more than once. Suffice to say, my father enjoyed hurting others, me included."

He turned his back on Sasha, pacing away. No one used their leopard like that. Certainly, they didn't turn them on their own child. Still, he knew it was the truth. Fyodor and Mitya both had fathers that did the same thing. Their lairs were run by cruel shifters.

"You're related to Fyodor Amurov." Joshua made it a statement.

"If you expect me to help you find him and turn him over to my father as a bribe to keep him from killing Sonia, think again. Fyodor is a good man. He did what he had to do.

Wherever he is, I wish him the best. Secondly, and more important, Nikita would go back on his word to you and he'd kill Sonia anyway. You can't trust him. No one can. He likes killing. I've seen him take out his weapon and shoot a man across from him at a nightclub because the man looked at him too long. He got away with it too."

"Why the hell haven't you killed him?"

"Sonia, of course."

Joshua's heart accelerated and adrenaline hit his system. He spun around and faced Sasha fully. "What the fuck does that mean? Sonia would be safe if Nikita was dead. At least according to you."

"If I missed, she would have been his first target, and I wasn't strong enough. I had to wait. To get my men in position for a takeover. Nikita always expects it. He has me watched. When he came back with the photographs of Sonia's painting, he thought I'd helped her escape. He thought I knew. He almost killed me."

"He didn't." Joshua made that very clear. He also made it clear he thought Sasha was giving him a line of bullshit.

Sasha shrugged again. "You are leopard, you can hear truth. Nikita didn't kill me because he realized I had no idea she was alive. I've worked my entire life to keep him from seeing any emotion, but I gave myself away. I was so relieved. So happy. The world needs Sonia. She's remarkable."

Joshua inwardly winced. He wanted the man gone. He wanted him to be the enemy. It wasn't shaping up that way.

"Why didn't you kill him? You're obviously strong enough now."

"Fyodor has been in hiding for several years. I wasn't willing to go that route. There are more of them."

"More?" Joshua raised an eyebrow.

Sasha nodded slowly. "Men who run their lairs cruelly. They murder their women and daughters. Or they sell the daughters to other lairs knowing the husbands will eventually kill them. I refuse to allow it to continue. Someone has to do something about it."

Joshua stilled. "So your plan was to remain with your father . . ."

Sasha shook his head. "My plan *is* to take over. The other *vors* will accept me. Takeovers occur often, and if Nikita is dead, it will be a natural ascension." He shrugged again. "Perhaps we will work together one day."

"You still think you're going to survive this."

"You will not kill me." It was a statement.

"You're pretty damned sure of yourself." Joshua flicked his coldest gaze over the man. "I could kill you myself for making Sonia believe you married her when you didn't."

"I will not apologize to you for saving her life. I couldn't marry her, but I could make her my mistress. She wouldn't have gone for that."

Joshua studied the man's face. "You really think I'm going to believe that after all this time you really plan to get rid of Nikita?"

"I have everything in place. I came here for Sonia. He knows that. He knows I will do anything to keep her alive, so that means I've declared war. If you're thinking of aligning yourself with him, know that killing me might buy you a favor, but it won't be keeping Sonia alive, if that's what you really intended all along."

He knew. Nothing gave Sasha away. Not his quiet tone. Not his stony features, not those dead eyes. Nothing. But Joshua knew the man intended to kill him, and Sasha fully expected Joshua's bodyguards to kill him. He moved fast, using his leopard's speed to leap toward the Russian, hitting him hard, driving him over backward, one claw of his big leopard raking down Sasha's arm to strip the gun from his hand.

"Don't shift," Joshua hissed. "You shift and you're dead. There's nothing I can do to save your life." More than anything, that act, trying to kill Joshua, told him that Sasha loved Sonia and wanted her free. Wanted her out of the business. "You didn't think this through. I love her. No one's going to take her away from me. You love her too."

He held the Russian down, pinned beneath his body, feeling the other's struggle for control as his leopard rose to try to save him. "If we're both dead, no one will save her. No one will be left alive to fight Nikita."

"Dmitri will see to her safety."

"He doesn't love her. We do. Together we're stronger. Don't you see that?"

"I see that you're in this business. Ruthless. Ready to kill at a moment's notice. It is not the life for her."

"Don't," Joshua hissed again when the body beneath him began to expand and contract as the leopard pushed against the human form in an attempt to emerge. "You're dead if you do. Your leopard's dead. Don't be a fool, Sasha. She loves you. She counts you as family. Don't you think she's had enough losses? You don't have to like me, but you should know, I can keep her safe. No one is going to love her more than I do. My leopard staked his claim on hers and she accepted. They're mates. There could already be a child. Think, man, before you throw your life away."

He'd frantically signaled to both Evan and Kai to keep them from shooting Sasha. Both bodyguards had their weapons out. Evan had his pressed against the side of the Russian's head.

*"Prekratit' bor'bu,"* a voice rang out. *"Ne bud oslom. Oni ub'yut tebya."*

Joshua held Sasha down, the words ringing in his head. *Stop struggling. Don't be an ass. They will kill you.* He recognized Fyodor's voice. He didn't turn his head, but continued to stare down into Sasha's face, watching for signs of surrender.

"These men are my friends, Sasha," Fyodor said, moving

into view. Flanking him, but with guns ready, were Timur and Gorya. "No one wants you dead, least of all me. Relax and live to fight another day, hopefully with us."

It took a few seconds for the adrenaline to fade before the coiling tension had eased in the Russian. Joshua let him up immediately. It was Fyodor who extended a hand to his distant relative and pulled him to his feet. Joshua noticed that Evan had stepped back, but his weapon was still out. He held it against his thigh in readiness.

"I didn't expect to see you alive," Sasha greeted. He hesitated and then stepped close to Fyodor to wrap him in a bear hug, patting him on the back. "You look good. Healthy."

Fyodor returned the hug and patting without hesitation. Joshua stepped back to allow the two Russians space. Timur and Gorya stayed close, both watching Sasha carefully. Even when the Russian turned his attention to them, they were much more wary than Fyodor appeared to be. Joshua wasn't buying the act. He knew Fyodor. The man had been an enforcer for years. He could kill Sasha in seconds if the Russian made one wrong move.

The men exchanged rapid greetings in their native language. Joshua could follow along fairly easily. Like most of the leopards employed with Drake's security company, he had learned multiple languages. Most shifters had an ear for languages.

"Don't have time," Joshua said. "Catch up later."

Fyodor nodded. "You're right, Joshua. I haven't seen Sasha in years. I hadn't heard his family came to the States. That's how long it's been. Nikita and my father had a break a few years back over who had jurisdiction over a cocaine pipeline. There was nearly a war. The situation was resolved, but the two men never were friendly after that. That of course meant we couldn't speak unless it was about business."

Sasha's gaze flicked to Joshua and the others, clearly

shocked that Fyodor was so open around them. "Why are you with them?"

"We're allies. Over here, as you know, we need allies, just as we did in Russia. Elijah Lospostos is with us." Elijah was a huge name in their business, and one you didn't drop casually. "I took over Antonio Arnotto's territory."

"Massi. You're Alonzo Massi."

Fyodor nodded. "Joshua is closely aligned with us. We came here to ensure you weren't leading him into a trap. Nikita has to go just as my father had to go."

"Lazar will hunt you to the ends of the Earth. He knows you killed his brother and he has serious money offered for any information on you. He won't stop, Fyodor, but even more than you, he's after Mitya. His own son. He wants him dead."

"That's no surprise," Fyodor said. "My uncle likes to kill. He lives for that pleasure."

"He wants to do it himself," Sasha cautioned. "He'll come for you, and if you know where Mitya is, he'll come for him as well."

"Mitya is here," Fyodor said. "In the next room. We didn't want to harm any of your men, but they'll mostly be waking up soon or they already have. We had to use ties just to be safe, but even with that, we've surrounded the place with our guards."

"Where is Nikita now?" Joshua asked. As far as he was concerned, they could do their happy salutations another time. "Focus on the problem. My woman is not going to die because you want to catch up on old times."

He knew he would come across as rude, but he didn't give a rat's ass. He needed to know where Sasha stood, if he could be trusted—which he wouldn't be for a long time—and where Nikita was.

"I don't know. I had a man shadowing him, but I haven't heard from him. That means Nikita killed him or he's being tortured right now. There's no other explanation. If he suddenly contacts me, I'll know he has a gun to his head. He was to check in every hour. He'd never been late until two hours ago. Nikita knows I left and he knows Dmitri is with me. He's never liked Dmitri. Before we could disappear, we had to get his parents and sibling to safety. Nikita would have had them killed."

"Bottom line," Joshua said. "He's on his way here."

"His best revenge against me is to get his hands on her. He would try to get both Dmitri and I to turn ourselves over to him in an empty promise to leave her alive. If we didn't agree, he'd torture her, record it and play it endlessly for us so that we saw every cut, the blowtorch and whatever other device he chose to use. He'd want us to hear every scream."

"That won't happen," Joshua said. "He isn't going to get his hands on her."

"You can't know that. Don't underestimate him. This might be your territory, but Nikita doesn't enter into a game without advantages. He would never come here himself unless he believed he would live through it, even for a big prize like Sonia. Now, more than ever, he's going to want to find her. I betrayed him. He knows she means something to me. Women, in our families, aren't worth anything. They can't matter to us. They'll shoot a dog if their sons like the dog too much. A woman gets treated far worse."

Joshua swore under his breath. He suddenly needed to get back to her. He had others watching over her, but that didn't mean she wasn't in danger.

SONIA woke from a sound sleep. One moment she was in dreamland, the next she was wide awake. Completely alert. Automatically she reached out toward her leopard. *Gatita?*

*It's smoke. There's a fire close. Too close.*

She leapt out of bed and ran to the pack she kept at Joshua's. Her loose-fitting drawstring sweats were there and she yanked them on. A tee was next and then her shoes. She ran

to the French doors. Just below her, the men were attempt-
ing to put out a fire on the verandah. It had spread across
the wooden deck.

"Gray? What's happening?"

"Fire started around the side of the house and spread. I
don't like it, Sonia. Too convenient. We were forced to call
the fire department, and that lets in strangers," Gray called
back. "We're going to have to get you out of here."

She put one hand on the rail and leapt, jumping to the
tree limb just off the lower deck. "Can I help?"

The fire was hot and spreading fast. It licked at the wood
hungrily. She backed away from the heat.

"No, stay back. I'll take you to your house as soon as
possible. Just stay out of the way."

The men worked frantically. In the distance was the
sound of sirens. She didn't like it any more than Gray did.
Nikita could sneak his men in, acting as firemen. She had
the sudden urge to call Joshua. She didn't even know where
he was. She looked around.

"Is Joshua still in the house?" she asked Gray.

"Sorry, sweetheart, he left earlier. Had an errand."

She stiffened. "What kind of errand?"

"I'm a little busy here, Sonia," he said.

"Was his errand Sasha?" Now her heart was pounding.
Joshua wouldn't kill Sasha, would he? He had believed her,
that Sasha was only trying to save her life, hadn't he? She
tried to recall his face when she'd told him.

He'd been still. Frozen almost. He hadn't looked away
once, watching her with the focused stare only a leopard
could give. She shivered in spite of the heat, wrapping her
arms around her middle. She thought she knew Joshua, but
there was a side of him she didn't know at all. He'd warned
her. He'd been fair. He'd said he had a monster inside him,
but she still thought he'd be fair.

She started back up the tree, deciding to call him, before
she remembered she didn't have a cell phone. He'd smashed

hers. She couldn't call him. She had a second one in her "go" bag, but she didn't know where it had been stashed. Someone, probably Kai, had taken it from her in the swamp. Flames burst into the sky on the far side of the house and the men went running in hopes of saving the hundreds-year-old structure.

She jumped to the ground and backed away, trying to get a better look without getting close. She ran into someone and started to step aside. Hot breath hit her neck and Gatita reacted, clawing toward the surface. Something exploded against the side of her face and she felt her knees give out. She'd been looking straight ahead, right toward Gray. He turned as her knees buckled. She tried to say something to him. Call out. There was no voice. No way to say a word because the world was going fuzzy. Dark. Grimly she hung on.

*Gatita, don't let me pass out. Stay hidden. He can't see you yet.*

Her head felt like a bomb had gone off, her insides mushy. Liquid. She was boneless and slumped to the ground. A shot rang out. Someone grabbed her shirt and yanked. Her body slid forward an inch or two. Deliberately she dropped her heels into the rotting vegetation and dug deep, hoping in the darkness no one could see.

There was more gunfire. Bullets spat into the leaves close to her and *thunked* into tree trunks. The man trying to drag her was forced to return fire. He tried to lift her one-armed, to use her as a shield. She sagged, keeping her weight as heavy as possible, pretending she was completely uncon-scious. The smoke drifted through the trees, heavy in the air, so that she had to fight to keep from coughing. If she did, her attacker would know she wasn't out.

Gray and three others abandoned the fire and came run-ning at them, utilizing their abilities as leopards, each leap covering twenty feet or more. They stayed in their human forms but called up their leopards for assistance. Her vision was a little fuzzy, but she saw them coming, and just as her attacker took aim, she dug her heels deep and shoved back, spoiling his aim.

Cursing, the man threw her to the ground and aimed at her head. A bullet took him backward away from her, and then Gray was crouching over her, looking around him, steady as ever. "You do live an exciting life, Sonia," he said. "Can you get up?"

She nodded. The action made her head want to explode. Clenching her teeth, she made it into a sitting position and then stopped for a moment. "He hit me pretty hard with something."

"I think he wore brass knuckles. You must have a pretty hard head to still be awake."

There was a trace of amusement in his voice and she couldn't help but respond. She sent him a small smile. "Are they going to be able to put the fire out?"

"We need to worry about you. Let's get you out of here. I'll take you to your house and send word to Joshua that you're there. Too many strangers showing up on the pretense of fighting the fire. Let's go. Can you make it through the swamp or should we take a car?"

She wanted to be all badass and go through the swamp, but she was still dizzy and a little nauseated. "I'm sorry, Gray, but I think I'll need the car."

He nodded. "I'm going to bring it around to the side yard. I'm stashing you close to the road, and you're not to move. You understand me? Once you're there, you wait only for me. No one else. Joshua is trusting me with your life and I'm not losing you."

"I can't go anywhere on my own," she assured. All she wanted to do was lie down and cover her eyes. The flames from the fire seemed to dance behind her eyes, burning her from the inside out. Her throat ached from the smoke. Every step she took around the house to the path leading to the road from the cabins in the back jarred her head. Even the old cabins looked good to her. Surely one of them had a bed she could lie in. After a few minutes of walking, the ground looked good enough to sleep on.

"All right. This is far enough. You sit down in this brush and wait for me. I'll be three minutes, five max. You understand me? Three minutes."

"That's all I've got," she admitted. "Much more than that and I'm on the ground asleep. My head hurts so bad and I want to vomit."

"That sounds like a concussion. Damn it. You need medical now." For the first time, he looked indecisive.

"I'll be fine," she lied, knowing Gray knew it was a lie.

He turned and jogged off. Sonia held her head with both hands and rocked, closing her eyes and praying she wouldn't throw up. Fire trucks and volunteers surrounded the mansion. She hoped they'd save it. She loved Joshua's house.

A hand gripped her hair and yanked her roughly backward, so that she fell hard. She stared into Nikita's face. His eyes burned into hers. "Get up. Men are so predictable. Always the heroes. Of course when you are injured he would gallantly go back for the car, leaving you alone. The little whore. Hopefully we'll have time to find out why my son is willing to betray me for you. Why a man like Joshua Tregre would give up valuable favors for you."

With every word, he gave a vicious yank on her hair until she got her feet under her. Tears blurred her vision from the assault on her scalp. He thrust her between two of his men. They grabbed her arms and dragged her toward the vehicle hidden just a few feet away and across the road. Nikita brought up the rear, flanked by two more guards. She was shoved in the SUV and then they were flying down the road, putting distance between them and the burning house.

"Are you going to tell me why my son would trade his life for yours?" Nikita was to one side of her on the seat, and he pulled her head back and licked up her throat. "We might have time for a little entertainment, boys," he added.

His men snickered. The one on the other side of her grabbed his crotch and lewdly laughed at her.

Nikita leaned close. "I know you think they'll find you fast. A little process of elimination. Find the houses in the area, somewhere remote for rent, and cross them off one by one. Simple, right? But we're not going to one of the several houses I rented. We're going to the last place they will think of looking. We're going to *your* house."

Sonia concentrated on her breathing. She had once thought of this man as family. He'd been the head of the household, and she'd always believed he cared about her. Now she knew he didn't even care about Sasha. Sasha hadn't told her what it had been like, controlling his leopard when his father had hurt him—and she knew he had. She knew Sasha's life had to have been a nightmare.

Nikita didn't like that she refused to talk and he caught her jaw hard and squeezed. "Pay attention, slut."

Gatita clawed at her. For a moment, her skin itched uncomfortably. *Don't. He can't know. We can't escape. There's no way to get them all. Someone will shoot us. We have to wait, and if he knows about you, he'll cage us.*

Sonia didn't respond to Nikita. He squeezed her jaw so hard she feared her bones would break. When she still refused to talk, he licked up her face, from her chin to her mouth. His men laughed. The Russian mobster caught the front of her T-shirt and ripped it down the front. She hadn't worn a bra, thinking she might have to shift, and her breasts jutted out, exposed to him and his horrible men.

One of them whistled. "Look at the marks all over her. Someone roughed her up."

"It couldn't have been my son," Nikita snickered. "He's no man. I may have to rethink Tregre. He might have decided to align himself with me by turning her over to me."

She stared straight ahead, refusing to bow her head or act embarrassed. Joshua thought she was beautiful. They were his marks all over her, claiming her.

"It took a real man to show a woman what she's made for. A man's pleasure," Nikita declared. He clawed at her breast, caught her nipple and twisted viciously.

A low cry escaped, but she clamped down, cutting the sound off. He let go, laughing. "Has Sasha been located? He has to be in the area. I want him found." Now all trace of humor had gone from his tone, leaving him looking nearly mad, an insane, perverted, very evil man.

"Not yet, Mr. Bogomolov." It was the driver who answered, his tone a little wary. He glanced uneasily at the other men surrounding Nikita. He made the turn into Sonia's driveway. "We're searching the last of the properties we had marked off now."

"What's taking so damn long?"

"Distance between the properties, sir." Again, it was the driver. He parked and shut off the SUV.

Nikita's men leapt out and raced around her house to secure it. Only when they nodded to him did he get out. Using her hair, he dragged her across the seat and out of the vehicle. She fell to the ground hard, bruising both knees. He leaned down, wrapping her hair around his fist, yanking it toward him. Abruptly he stopped, his breath hitching in his throat. He stared down at her, as if transfixed.

"You want help with her, boss?" one ventured, close.

Nikita whirled on him. "Don't put a hand on her, David." To her, he snapped a command, hissing it between his teeth. "Get up. Get up now." He pulled her hair, but not with the same savage intensity he had before.

Sonia managed to make it unsteadily to her feet. She swayed, afraid her knees would give out. Her head exploded with pain each time she moved too fast, and the way Nikita pulled her hair added to the teeth-gritting agony.

"Give her your jacket, David!" the Russian shouted. "Now!"

David didn't hesitate. He peeled off his leather jacket and put it in his boss's outstretched hand. Nikita put it on her.

"Cover up," he ordered, as if she hadn't been the one to rip her top off.

She pulled the edges of the jacket together, feeling for the zipper. It was huge on her, but she didn't care. She hated the way the men gawked at her. She didn't want them looking at the marks Joshua had put on her body. She knew, in a strange way, those marks made them think he was a man to be reckoned with. They even thought he might be an ally, a man who would use her and then turn her over to Nikita.

"Your key?"

There was no sense in having them break down her door or shatter a window. She took the spare key out from under the flowerpot sitting to the left of the door.

Nikita smirked at her. "Very inventive, my dear."

She handed the key to him and let him unlock the door. She'd seen her mother handle him, year after year. Little things. Her mother had given him deference, rarely opposed him and then only when it came to decisions made for Sonia's schooling or care. He took the key as if it was his due and opened the door. She went into the house without any urging, wondering what had changed him.

He was different. She didn't know exactly how, but he was. She went quickly to the middle of the room, staying away from any furniture, anywhere he might think she had hidden a weapon. She faced him, swaying, her head throbbing.

"Sit down, Sonia. You're going to fall on your face." He sounded irritated.

She complied immediately, grateful she hadn't fallen in front of him. Her fingers gripped the arm of her chair. "What are you going to do?" She whispered it, letting fear make her voice tremble. Let him think she was completely cowed. She had Gatita, her ace in the hole.

The dark, deep pits Nikita had for eyes stared at her until she shivered. He looked evil. She'd never noticed that before.

"I was going to torture you in front of my son. My plan

was to keep you alive for several days and let him suffer, watching your agony. Now I am not certain. Who made these marks on your body?"

She pressed her lips together tightly and then, as if she couldn't hold his gaze, she looked away from him. "A man by the name of Joshua Tregre."

"Did that man put those marks on your shoulder?"

She stiffened. She hadn't thought about those marks for a long time or the way they'd gotten there. She touched her tongue to her suddenly dry lips. She nodded slowly, her eyes jumping to his. Did he know? Was he aware those marks meant she was leopard? That she'd been claimed by another male? Did he think Sasha had put them there?

He exploded into anger, slamming his fist on the nearest table, picking it up and throwing it. When one of his men rushed to see what was wrong, Nikita slapped him twice, hard, calling him names and taunting him over and over. She realized he was goading the man to pull his weapon. When the man refused, Nikita took out his own gun and pistol-whipped him, then put it to his head and pulled the trigger.

She screamed. Loudly. A woman screamed when gangsters shot their own men and brains, blood and bone scattered all over her floor. She made certain her shock and horror were extra loud. She'd left her bedroom windows open, covered only by the insect screens. Surely the swamp would carry her voice to Gray. He would be looking for her by now.

Nikita stormed over to her and slapped her hard. "Shut the fuck up and let me think."

He hit her so hard her neck snapped back. She had to press her hand to her throbbing temple. The blow from the Russian made the one on her temple hurt more. She watched him pace across the room. He suddenly turned back to her.

"Did my son know?"

"Know what?" She frowned at him, trying to puzzle out what he meant.

He spat on the floor in disgust. "You don't want to fuck with me. Your sweet little pussy may have been able to lead my son around by his dick, but I can assure you, I'm not that man. If I keep you, you'll do whatever I say, when I say it."

"What are you talking about? You were with my mother. I'm not about to be kept by you." She was genuinely horrified. She'd expected to be tortured. She'd expected to be killed. She hadn't ever once entertained the idea that he might want to keep her. Rape her, yes. Give her to his men, even that. But never permanently keep her.

"I'm killing Sasha. He's worthless, the sniveling coward. He always has been. I'll need another son and I'm considering that your life was spared for a reason."

"What would that be?" she asked.

"To give me sons. As many as I want. I'll keep you alive for that reason, you little slut. I don't know how you escaped that bomb or kept your leopard secret from me, but Tregre wouldn't have put those marks on your shoulder if you weren't leopard."

Her breath caught in her throat. She closed her eyes and shook her head in silent denial. If she opened her mouth, he would hear her lie.

Nikita paced across the room. "Maybe a better plan is to send the others to kill Sasha, take you back to Miami and renegotiate with Tregre. If he had planned to turn you over to me, we can come to a solution. If not . . ." He shrugged. "Killing him shouldn't be too difficult."

Her heart accelerated at the thought that he might take her to Miami. He would definitely have the home-field advantage there.

# 19

JOSHUA stared out the window, his back to the others. Gray had brought the news to him in person. His trackers were out, not an easy thing to do on the highway, but they would find her. "Have Drake's people find out every vacation home in this area that has been rented." He glanced over his shoulder at Kai. He waited for the man to nod and hurry away, cell to his ear, before he turned back to stare into the night.

A madman had her. God only knew what was happening to her. Everything he had learned about Nikita boded ill for any woman he took, let alone Sonia. He felt sick. The hole inside him widened and the monster crept out until it was staring back at him in the window. He put his head down to breathe away the murderous rage, the need to pound his fists into human flesh, let his leopard loose to claw apart his enemies.

*Hold on, baby. I won't stop until I find you.* He wouldn't. That was his greatest flaw and his greatest strength. He didn't know how to stop, and for Sonia, he never would. He would find her and do whatever it took, for however long, to make certain she was safe and happy.

"That's too obvious," Sasha said. "He'd know you have resources, and he wants time with her."

There was a break in the Russian's voice. The first crack Joshua had heard, and he spun around to face him. Sasha's color was off, a thin scar running along the side of his face showing whiter against his skin. He was scared for Sonia too. No, it was more like terror. He knew what his father was capable of, more than any other. He'd witnessed it. This was his nightmare, just as it was Joshua's.

"Where would he take her?"

Sasha frowned. "I don't know the area, but it would be somewhere you wouldn't expect. The last place you'd think to look. I had that old hunting cabin on the island, maybe there's something like that."

There were a million old camps the locals had used or abandoned, scattered throughout the swamp. Joshua paced across the room. The others were silent, watching him. Waiting. He was the most familiar with the swamp . . . He had to clear his brain. Think. Images of Sonia raped, beaten. Tortured. His stomach lurched. He had to stop. He had to force his mind under control so he could think. Where could a man who didn't know the swamp take a woman to be alone with her? A place no one could hear her screams?

He needed to punch something—or someone. The devil inside him was riding him hard. He paced to get the adrenaline out, to force his brain to think. A house in the swamp, then. Not a vacation home. He'd need a local to direct him to the camps. Other locals would talk, especially if someone went missing, and it would be like Nikita to kill whoever aided him, buying his silence permanently.

"He'd want her alive as long as possible. He'd want me to see her suffer," Sasha said.

"So, he's coming after you," Fyodor said. "You're certain?"

Sasha nodded. "I had guards spread out. They didn't make a good showing against Joshua's men, but they're good in a firefight. We're a little out of our element here. The good news is, Nikita's men will be as well."

*Not good in the swamp.* Joshua repeated it over and over like a mantra. He'd want Sasha there to witness the torture he had in store for Sonia. Sonia. Images of her invaded despite his best efforts to stop them. Sonia in the swamp, that first night, her skin practically glowing. Her eyes when she looked at him, lying on her bed in her house. Her house . . .

He stopped in his tracks. Her home was just down the road from his. Gray said she couldn't have been gone more than a few minutes, five at most. He'd seen the taillights of the vehicle but when he'd given chase, it was gone. That fast. The trackers reported that it had gone straight to the highway. But had it? If it had stopped and dropped most of its occupants off first, and then sped away, the trail would continue to the highway.

His gut told him he was right. "Her house. They're at her house. That son of a bitch took her to her own home." The psychological repercussions would suit Nikita. He not only took Sonia from Joshua's house, but violated the sanctuary of her own home. That would stay with her for a long time. Nikita wanted her to know that he was all-powerful. He could reach out and get her anywhere. There was no safe place for her, no sanctuary.

He turned and started toward the door.

*"They're coming at us. Two carloads. At least fourteen men."* The warning came in his ear, the little radio that told him they were under attack any moment.

*"This direction as well. Coming from the north. Carload. Seven."*

*"And from the east. Have another carload. Seven here."*

He glanced at Fyodor with a raised eyebrow. Fyodor and
Mitya brought crews. Sasha had one as well.

"Tell Sasha's guards what's happening and release them.
If they try anything, kill them. No second chances." He
looked at Sasha when he said it. "You turn on Fyodor or
Mitya, I'll hunt you down, and the things I do to you will
make what your father did seem like a picnic," he warned.

"Dmitri." Sasha raised his voice. "Tell the men to fight
with Fyodor's crew. That's an order. I'm going with Joshua."

Joshua shook his head. "You're a powder keg for him.
I'm an unknown. I have a chance to get her out of there
without you. None, with you. Stay here and kill these fuck-
ers. They're his men, not yours. They came here for you,
shove it right back down their throats."

He didn't wait to see if Sasha argued. He slipped out the
front door, whistling for his men. He had no doubt that
Fyodor and Mitya could handle the men coming at them.
Most weren't leopard and that put them at a distinct disadvantage. The fact that none had come from the surrounding
swamp meant either they'd sent in leopards and the guards
hadn't caught them yet, or they had no expertise and were
too worried about the dangers to try it.

He signaled to Evan to slip through enemy lines and get
their car. His crew would know to divide and take the two
trucks they'd brought. Both were a distance up the road.
Most of them slipped through as leopards. He stripped,
rolled his jeans and put them in the small pack. They carried
their bigger firepower in the trucks, in special compartments. He snapped the pack around his neck and shifted,
rushing off into the night to find his woman.

SONIA made herself as small as possible. She wasn't certain
how best to act, but she didn't want to chance rousing Nikita's ugly temper. There were brains and blood just feet
from her. Twice, Nikita had stepped over the body of the

dead man. She couldn't look at it without feeling sick. She kept her hands pressed to her eyes, desperate for a plan.

He'd sent his men to kill Sasha. There was nothing she could do to warn him. She had no idea where Joshua was, but she hoped he was far away. Secretly, she wanted him to come rescue her, but now that the blinders were off, Nikita felt too powerful. Too invincible. Too evil. How did one defeat someone like him? Was there anything sacred to him?

How much time had passed since he'd sent out the crew to go after Sasha? Every minute was an eternity. She had to stall. He'd made up his mind to take her to Miami. She'd heard him telling his crew to get everything ready to leave within the hour.

"Why do you hate me so much, Nikita?" she asked softly. "I loved you. I looked up to you. I thought you were to be admired and respected. I had no idea you hated me so much you wanted me dead. Or tortured. I know I was very young when my parents started working for you. Did I annoy you that much?"

She wanted him to think about those days. She'd followed him around sometimes, singing him songs, dancing for him. Sitting in his lap and holding him when she thought he was sad. Wasn't he capable of loving someone? What of his own son? She remembered times Sasha had gone to her mother, the stain of tears on his face, and they'd disappeared into a bathroom. He'd been holding his side, or there were blood-stains on his shirt. Now she knew Nikita had done that to him.

"Little girls grow up and become sluts for men to use. That's their purpose." He waved his hands in the air. "All that women's rights crap is foolish. Women need to know their place. You serve a man. That's what you're made for." His voice rang with sincerity. He believed the garbage he was spouting.

"Why do you want to hurt me?"

He turned fully to face her, a half smile on his face. "I

enjoy it. I like hurting women. Or men. It . . . arouses me. Not the way Tregre put those marks on you; they're all superficial. They couldn't have hurt much. What I will do to you, you won't find pleasure in, but I will."

She couldn't go to Miami with him. Whatever happened had to happen here. If she was to escape, her only chance was the swamp.

"I'll enjoy watching other men use you, but later, after I get what I want from you."

She tried not to look the way she felt—terrified. He knew about Gatita. His leopard would tear her apart if she attacked him.

"Are you pregnant now?"

Her heart stuttered and then began to drum wildly. She shook her head. "I don't know. He . . ." She didn't know if he thought Joshua had forced her. If he thought that, Joshua might be safe from him. "I don't know. My leopard was in heat."

He smirked. Leered a little. Looked at her with contempt. "So were you. In heat. You probably seduced him. It got a little rough and you probably sniveled and begged him to stop. But he didn't, did he?"

She shook her head, looking at his face. Just the thought of Joshua raping her aroused him. She could see it in his flushed face, his darkened eyes and the bulge in his trousers. She forced herself to look away and push down fear. He would get off on her fear. That was part of his enjoyment of hurting others. How did men get like that? Were they born? Were they made? What difference did it make? He was there, a monster standing in front of her.

Joshua thought himself a monster because he went after men like this and sometimes, his rage blinded his ability to end their lives fast. He didn't truly understand what a monster was. She couldn't imagine Sasha's life, a young boy exposed to the cruelty of a vile, depraved man who enjoyed hurting others.

"What does your leopard do when you hurt others? When you hurt women?" she asked curiously. What would a leopard exposed to such violence do?

Nikita walked right up to her, caught her hair in his hand and jerked her head back. "He craves blood. The kill. Sometimes I let him come out and play. It's exhilarating to see that look on their faces, so much fear when they're hunted by a predator. He hates every woman I touch. He wants his mate. He wants sex. I don't let him have either and he's savage. Every time I come close to you, he rages for your blood." He laughed and let her hair go, stepping back as one of his men hurried into the room.

*Gatita, is there any talking to his leopard?*

*It is evil. It wants to kill you and me. It is like Sasha's leopard when he touched you.*

She pressed her hand to her mouth to cover the gasp of shock. Sasha had to fight his leopard every time he made love to her? She hadn't been his mate. Did that mean leopards couldn't be with anyone else? No, Joshua had. So that meant the continual exposure to violence changed the leopard as well as the man.

"We're not going to wait for them," Nikita declared. "If they can't handle that sniveling idiot of a son, they'd better not come home, Filat."

"Mr. Bogomolov," the man he'd referred to as Filat said. There was respect in his voice, but also steel. She remembered him from her childhood. He'd picked her up occasionally and given her cookies. She knew he was Nikita's closest and most trusted advisor. "If we don't get Sasha, there's a chance he can undermine us with the other *vors*."

"We're no longer in Russia."

"No, but we have to work with those here. Also the Italians. And this man Tregre. He's in tight with Lospostos. Lospostos runs a huge territory. He's powerful and right now, untouchable. If Sasha remains alive, he will always be a threat to you, your biggest threat. He cannot make allies

of these people. Shore up this alliance with Tregre. Get him
to kill Sasha if our men miss him."

"He knew where the bitch was and didn't tell me," Nikita
snapped.

Sonia could see he was thinking over what Filat had said.
He didn't necessarily like it, but first and foremost, Nikita
was a businessman. He didn't get to where he was without
doing what was best for his business.

"Be ready to move. Reach out to Tony. Tell him the
second it's done to call in. We'll leave then. You're right.
This is our best shot at getting Sasha and the rats that followed him. I want them all dead. And their families, Filat.
Every last one of them wiped from the earth."

"They've gone into hiding," Filat said, "but they'll have
to come out sometime. If we get Sasha, we'll get the others
and their families."

"While I'm waiting," Nikita said, his voice a smirk as he
turned and looked at her, rubbing his crotch lewdly, "I'll be
occupied with my newest little slut. You like her?"

Filat nodded. "You willing to share her?"

"If I do, it has to be soon. Tregre may have put a baby in
her. We'll get rid of it. Until then, we can have fun the way
we like. There's always her mouth. She'll learn to be a good
little cocksucker, won't you, Sonia?"

*Gatita. I'm not doing this. I'm not. If he comes near me,
I'm going to hurt him. He'll probably kill us. If not, he'll
beat the holy hell out of us.*

*I won't let him touch you.*

*His leopard is a killer. It wants to kill us both.*

Nikita started toward her as Filat laughed and put a cell
phone to his ear. He leaned against the counter as if he was
about to watch a show. Heart beating hard, she watched him
coming, feeling Gatita coiling and ready to strike. Her stare
was focused, the predator watching prey.

Nikita stopped abruptly and laughed. "Her leopard is
close, watching me. I can see her. I've never had a woman

who was leopard other than Sasha's mother. She was a timid, stupid woman, always so eager to please, completely unlike this one, Filat. This one's a fighter."

Filat straightened, his eyes on her, darkening with pure lust. "Tony isn't answering. They must be at the house. Just a minute, boss. This is going to be fun." His hands went to his shirt.

There was a slight sound and everyone turned their heads to see Joshua standing at the foot of the stairs, regarding them all with amusement. "You were going to start the fun without me? I found her, by the way. She fights like a wildcat."

Silence followed his statement. Sonia's mouth went dry. He sounded so sincere, but then every statement he made was true. The leopards listening for their human counter-parts would have to say he was telling the truth. She didn't dare look at him, even though she wanted to drink him in. How had he gotten in? Just waltzed past Nikita's guards and gotten in through her bedroom balcony? And where were Evan and Kai? They wouldn't let him just come alone.

"What are you doing here?" Filat asked carefully.

Joshua's face changed. He looked cold. Arctic cold. Like a glacier. "Came home to find my house on fire and the woman I've been fucking gone. I decided to go look for her. If she started it, I was going to beat her within an inch of her life. If she didn't, whoever had her clearly tried to burn me out."

"This woman is my son's wife," Nikita said.

"That's not exactly the truth," Joshua said. "Like you, I don't like being lied to. I don't do business with people prone to screwing me over. I didn't know who she was to you when you asked about the painting. I was already fucking her and I wasn't about to give her up until I knew if she was carry-ing my kid."

"Your leopard marked her." Nikita made it a statement. The way he said it, the ritual disgusted him.

"My leopard got off on that shit and so did I. Made her think she was special to me." Joshua's voice held a convincing sneer.

Sonia's breath caught in her throat. He sounded so frank. So real. Even Gatita had to acknowledge that what he said was the absolute truth. She had a choice. She could curl up inside and die, believing Joshua had truly played her, or she could fight back, whether he'd done that or not. She had choices. She might be in a room with predators, but she wasn't without her own weapons. She chose to believe that Joshua Tregre was her man and that he'd just walked alone into the lion's den for her.

*His bodyguards have to be close.* Gatita was positive. *They wouldn't let him come alone. Kai and Gray watch him all the time and Evan rarely leaves his side.*

That was true, and it made her feel better, although if he'd come with just those three men, they would have their hands full subduing Nikita's guards outside.

"You touch her?" Joshua's voice was casual. For the first time he glanced at her.

His gaze hurt. It burned. She felt it all the way through her skin, straight to her soul. Cold as ice. Not one trace of the warmth, or the heat or desire his eyes usually held when he looked at her.

She looked down at her fingers, twisting them together, trying to figure out his plan, forcing her mind away from betrayal. It was so easy to go there. Her father's actions had been the first betrayal, putting his wife and daughter in jeopardy. Nikita pretending she mattered in his household. Even Filat had been nice to her. And Sasha. She had believed Sasha had tried to kill her. It was a long list of men who had misled her into believing she mattered to them. Joshua was playing right into her worst fears.

"I decorated her, added to the marks on her," Nikita sneered.

Joshua's ice-cold gaze flicked over him. "That body belongs to me, not you, Nikita," he said softly. "The only marks on her should be mine. It's called ownership."

"I like your way of thinking, but I have to dispute your claim. My family had her first."

"And you lost her. For a fuckin' year. I'd say that was the end of your claim. She's got my kid in her belly and she isn't goin' anywhere." His accent deepened, but he looked the exact same. Tough as nails. No give.

Nikita held up his hand, his oily smile plastered on his face. "Bitches are rarely worth fighting over. This particular one led my son around by his dick until he was useless to me. Her family owes me a large debt. Her fucking father stole from me." His voice hardened, snapped like a whip when he mentioned her father. "I treated him like a brother, and he *stole* from me. So, I took his wife, and now I'll take his daughter as payment."

Joshua slowly shook his head. "That's not happening, Nikita. I can see why you would think you had a claim, but I can't let her go until I know if she's having my kid. I need a son."

"You're young. You can find others like her."

Joshua sent him a faint grin. "Because there's so many."

The mild sarcasm should have sent Nikita into a fury. Sonia remembered how he would get angry over the smallest perceived slight. She knew he had never forgiven her father. He wouldn't even say his name. He wouldn't allow them to say it. When she was young and didn't know the truth, she thought it was because he grieved for him. Now she knew it was because he despised him—and because of her father, her as well.

"I understand," Nikita said. "I wouldn't want to give her up if I thought she carried my child in her belly. Perhaps we should negotiate. The pipeline could be very lucrative. I would consider giving up my claim for a larger percentage."

Joshua shook his head. "With regret, I can't change that deal. It isn't just my deal. Elijah is a big part of that, and you

don't want to fuck with him—not when it comes to money
or product."

*Drugs?* Her stomach lurched. She pressed a hand to it
and breathed deeply to keep from vomiting. She was in so
far over her head. She had to trust Joshua. She *had* to. She
had no other real choice. He played both sides to get rid of
people like Nikita. It was just that he played the game so
well. Even Nikita, who barked orders at everyone, respected
him enough to bargain rather than pull out a weapon and
shoot him.

She glanced at the dead man on the floor. Joshua hadn't
even commented. The sight of all that blood leaking all over
her beautiful wood floor, now completely ruined, made her
stomach heave again. She wanted this to end. What was he
doing, just standing there, smirking a little, ignoring her as
if she was so much garbage?

"I would lose face in my community if I allowed this
bitch to live without compensation."

"You had your compensation, you son of a bitch, when
you took a blowtorch to my father and you made my mother
sleep in your filthy bed," Sonia snapped, loathing and contempt dripping from her voice. She couldn't stand listening
to him one more minute.

Nikita's face darkened with fury. He couldn't turn anger
on Joshua, but he could her. He always got his way. No one
thwarted him in anything. He had to listen to Joshua because
he needed an ally, but to him, Sonia was nothing but a play-
thing, a toy to be used and discarded.

He strode across the room, clearly prepared to hit her,
his fist clenched. Joshua was there first, his hand in her hair,
yanking her head up so that she had to look into his eyes.
All that crystalline blue blazed with anger.

"Shut. The. Fuck. Up." He enunciated each word. "I
thought I taught you to keep your fuckin' mouth closed. Do
you want another lesson?"

Instinctively she cowered away from him, pulling into

herself, trying to be smaller. She shook her head. The action hurt, not just because of his hand holding so tightly to her hair, pulling on her scalp, but because it made her temple throb. His thumb, as he slid his hand out of her hair, slid over the swollen, darkened bruise with exquisite gentleness.

"When men talk, Sonia, what do good little girls do?" His voice was a sneer.

"They stay quiet," she whispered.

He patted her cheek. "That's right." He turned back to Nikita. "She's learning. She's a fighter. Makes her a wildcat in bed, and I enjoy the lessons I give her far more than she does, because she doesn't want to remember."

*Why doesn't he give us a sign? Something. Anything.* She needed something to hold on to. That one little pass with his thumb could have been a mistake. She might have imagined it. *Gatita, what is he planning?*

*You did not imagine it. I felt his touch too.*

Okay. Okay, she could do this. If Joshua could walk right between Nikita and Filat without flinching, she could wait for his signal.

"We were speaking of compensation," Nikita said.

She risked a glance at him, and then at Filat. Filat was watching her carefully. Didn't he believe her cowed act? It wasn't an act, it was the real thing. Why wouldn't he believe it? She had to think, because she could see it on his face, that dawning comprehension that Joshua wasn't the ally they wanted.

Joshua had half turned away from her and she lashed out with her feet, kicking him hard enough to make him stagger. "Bastard," she hissed, leaping for the door. He caught her ankle as she ran past him, and she went down hard.

Joshua calmly put his foot on her throat. "We did this once before, Sonia. Don't you remember? You ran from me. Your female ran from my male. You seem to be a slow learner."

Nikita's laughter rang through the room. "I don't know,

Joshua, I could have such fun with her. Are you certain you
want the trouble? I'll accept compensation as a show of good
faith, but if she isn't pregnant, I ask that you turn her over
to me so I can try."

Joshua reached down and hauled her to her feet, walking
her backward without looking at her, to shove her back into
the chair. "I might consider that. I don't keep a bitch long,
although she's different. Once you're in her, you'll understand my reluctance to part with her."

An owl hooted outside the house in the direction of the
swamp. A second owl answered just outside the window. A
third bird sounded off, using a two-note call. Joshua caught
her face in his hands, leaned down and fastened his mouth
to hers. She expected rough. She got gentle. He ended the
kiss abruptly and whispered one word against her lips.
"Run." It was barely there, a stroke over her mouth, but she
heard it as if he'd yelled.

Abruptly, he let go, and as he straightened, he whipped
off his shirt and kicked off his shoes. He tore at his jeans,
already shifting. Nikita tried for his gun, but the leopard
was on him, stripping it from his hand. Sonia leapt toward
Filat. He already had his gun out. She managed to knock it
away from him. He caught her by the throat and squeezed
hard, looking straight into her eyes. She was already losing
air. One hand went to the zipper of the jacket, dragging it
down while she concentrated on shifting the arm so she
could rake down his stomach, trying to eviscerate him.

He screamed, leaping away from her. She ran, taking
the stairs several at a time. Glancing over her shoulder, she
saw Shadow and Nikita's leopard in a terrible battle. Filat
tore his clothes from his body and shifted, his cat racing
to Nikita's leopard's aid. She ran for her bedroom. Earlier,
when she'd been trying to escape from Joshua, she had
dropped a shotgun on her bed. She had extra ammunition
for it as well.

The sounds in her great room were terrible to hear. She had to hurry. Joshua had deliberately forced both leopards into attacking him to give her the time to run. There was no leaving him behind. She shoved shells into her pocket and ran back to the top of the stairs. The two males fighting Shadow were using a tag team method, going in fast, slashing and biting and jumping out so the other could get in.

They clearly had used the method before. Shadow was fast. Both other cats were bloody, sides heaving, but so was Joshua's leopard. She aimed at the leopard she knew to be Nikita. More than anything, for her mother, for Sasha, and even for her father, she wanted to kill him. She pulled the trigger just as he whirled in the air to renew his attack on Joshua.

The sound was loud, reverberating through the room. Behind Nikita, the cabinet disintegrated, wood flying in all directions. The leopards looked up at her, grimacing. Showing teeth. Calmly, she took aim again as Nikita's leopard reared into the air, claws extended. Shadow met him in the air, raking at the older leopard with his stiletto-claws, going for his exposed genitals. Nikita's leopard screamed and rolled away as they both hit the ground.

Filat turned to face her, his leopard's expression menacing, his eyes wholly focused on his prey. She held her ground as he began a slow, freeze-frame stalk. Nikita was her first target. She squeezed the trigger as his leopard rolled. He screamed. Howled. Blood sprayed the air. Filat didn't even turn to see the damage to his boss. He charged. She tried to slam bullets into the shotgun fast, knowing she wouldn't make it. She transferred the gun to her other hand to use it like a bat just as Shadow landed hard on the leopard's back.

Shadow was heavy with muscle and incredibly strong. He dug his claws in and sank his teeth deep into the neck. They rolled almost at her feet, but she ignored them, her eyes on Nikita's leopard as he dragged himself to his feet. His hind end was bloody, but from the distance she'd been, she didn't know how much damage the older shotgun would create.

The two leopards rolled down the stairs, Shadow never letting up on his hold of Filat's raging cat. She walked down the stairs, watching Nikita's leopard the entire time. He snarled at her. Growled a warning. He lowered his head, eyes focused in preparation of a charge. She lifted the shotgun, taking careful aim.

Nikita whirled around and raced toward the door just as she pulled the trigger. He screamed and wood disintegrated into splinters as he jerked open the door and ran through it. She raced after him. In the swamp, she'd give the advantage to the leopard. Gatita was too small and too inexperienced to fight him. She needed the shotgun.

The leopard had disappeared from view, but she saw a splash of blood in the grass just to the right of the verandah. She stepped back to get a better look and that saved her life. The cat sprang at her from above, trying to twist toward her when she moved back. He landed just feet from her. She pulled the trigger. It seemed impossible to miss at that close range, but she thought she had because Nikita's leopard rolled at the last second.

He screamed again, indicating he might be hit, but the wounds had to be superficial. Blood specked his side and coated his right shoulder. He rushed her. Once again she thought to use the weapon as a bat, but she knew it was a flimsy defense against the big cat. He was almost on her, so close she felt the blast of hot air in her face. She swung the gun as hard as she could, using Gatita's strength.

Shadow leapt out of the night, his front claws attaching to Nikita's cat's hind end. The leopard shrieked, the sound reverberating through the swamp. She hit. A solid strike that shook up her arm until she was numb. The two cats rolled away from her. She found herself on the ground, too close to the teeth and claws. Resolutely she stood and calmly inspected the weapon. She waited until Shadow had the cat on the ground again and she stepped closer to the raging leopards.

They broke apart and then both dove simultaneously into the air, crashing into each other, raking and biting at each other's head and neck. They crashed to the ground, teeth bared, legs locked together. The death lock was difficult to witness, claws raking, teeth biting, blood streaming from both cats.

Sonia stepped even closer. This was for all of them. Every single person Nikita Bogomolov had murdered to show how cruel he was. Everyone he'd murdered or had tortured for his amusement. His enjoyment. Every woman he'd raped and killed.

*Gatita, warn Shadow.*

*He says to leave it.*

*Tell him I'm killing this murderous demon and sending him back to hell. Now.* She poured determination into her voice so even Shadow had to hear it.

In one move, she pressed the muzzle to Nikita's skull and pulled the trigger. Shadow was already rolling away, distancing himself from the blast. Nikita's cat stared up at her, his eyes crazed. Slowly, they turned from amber to a dark color and she saw Nikita looking back at her.

She leaned close. "This bitch killed you. This slut. I'm going to live with my man and you're going to die right here. We'll burn you and bury you, and Sasha will have your empire."

A large hand yanked her back just as Nikita's leopard gave one last effort, his giant paw swiping at her thigh to try to open her artery. Joshua towered over her, swaying. Bloody. He wrapped her in his arms.

"Are you all right? Did they hurt you?"

He was a mess. A terrible mess. "You're bleeding everywhere. Where are the others? Evan and Kai and Gray? At least they should be here." She got her arm around his waist and started walking him back to the house. All the open wounds as close as they were to the swamp were a recipe for infection.

"Nikita had a crew with him. We have to get them all. We can't afford any of them left alive, although Sasha said he'd mop up."

"Sasha said it?" She looked up at his face. It was drawn. A little on the gray side. He was giving her more of his weight than she liked. "When did you talk to Sasha?"

"I had a little chat with him while you were getting your-self kidnapped."

She didn't want to go into the house where there were dead bodies and blood everywhere, but she needed to sit Joshua down and get a first aid kit. "We need Evan."

"You can handle it," he told her.

She glared up at him. "You have no idea what I can or can't handle."

He flashed a grin at her. "Baby, you put that fuckin' shot-gun to his head and pulled the trigger. You can handle patch-ing me up."

"I could handle shooting you," she said. "Patching you up is something I didn't study."

She got him past the dead body of the man Nikita had shot. Lying beside her stairs was the dead leopard. Filat. She glanced away quickly and continued toward the bath-room where the first aid kit was. "You wanted to have a chat with Sasha? Why?"

"If he was playing you, I was going to blow his head off." He said it matter-of-factly.

"God, you're so bloodthirsty. Sasha saved me."

"I'm not wholly convinced, but signs point that way so I'm taking a wait-and-see policy. You stay away from him." He lowered himself onto the bench she had at the end of the bathtub.

"Bossy much?"

"That jacket offends me. Take it off."

"Sheesh, Joshua, stop bossing me around and let me take care of these wounds. Some of them are deep. You need antibiotics and stitches."

"Butterfly bandages will work. I get ripped up all the time. Take off the jacket, babe. You must have another top around here somewhere."

She hesitated and pulled the first aid kit from under the sink.

He caught her arm. "Just show me. I'm going to see sooner or later and he's already dead. What do you think I'm going to do?"

She shrugged. "You're a bit of a maniac. I don't know. Go out and shoot him all over again?"

He grinned at her. "That's a possibility."

The jacket was already unzipped so she shrugged out of it, trying to keep from looking in the mirror. She knew there was a dark bruise over her nipple where Nikita had grabbed her so viciously. It still hurt. Not a single thing Joshua ever did to her hurt after, and yet Nikita had managed to do so without trying.

"I mostly hate that he touched me," she confessed. "He makes my skin crawl."

"He's dead now, but you're right, I want to put that gun to his head all over again." He leaned forward to brush a kiss over the bruise. "I'm sorry I couldn't get here faster."

"You got here," she said briskly, feeling the burn of tears behind her eyes. To distract herself, she began cleaning him up when she really wanted to throw herself in his arms, have a complete meltdown and be comforted. "Thank you for saving my life."

"You're more than welcome, although I might have done it for selfish reasons."

She smiled despite the lump in her throat. He was pretty torn up. She felt torn up. Their homes. She wasn't positive she could ever live in her house again, not after having Nikita and Filat there—and the dead man. "We don't have any homes left."

"Baby," he said softly. "Look at me."

She was kneeling on the floor, washing a particularly deep gash in his side, prepared to close it with butterfly bandages and cover it in antibiotic cream. She looked up at him. At his face. That stubborn jaw. Those eyes she loved.

"We've got us. You. Me. We're fine."

She took a deep breath and nodded. They'd sort it out.

# 20

SONIA had no idea of the extent of the operation against them. Joshua was fine with that. They'd handled it. Fyodor and Mitya had helped Sasha in defeating Nikita's men. They'd all gotten busy immediately, working through the night to erase all evidence. He'd called for help. Help came. They burned the bodies and buried the ashes deep at each location where a battle had taken place.

Sasha had gone back to Miami. Joshua kept Sonia occupied with cleanup and rebuilding on his house, so she never got a chance to see Sasha before he left. He didn't want them near each other until Sasha proved he was no threat to her. Or never. Never would do.

The lower verandah took most of the damage on three of the four sides. One wall had minor fire damage to it. Because the inside of his home was livable, he had every excuse to keep her with him. She woke several nights with nightmares and he held her close, careful of any damage to her body. He was gentle with her, learning how to like gentle as well as his rough play with her. He figured that was a good thing, because even if she wasn't pregnant now, she would be someday and he couldn't be rough then.

The first thing he'd done, even before work had started to clean up the fire damage, was to prepare a room upstairs, on the far side of the master bedroom, overlooking the swamp, for her studio. He brought her paintings there. All her brushes and paints in all the different mediums she liked to use. He had surprised her with it one morning and was rewarded most of the night. He hadn't been looking for a reward, but welcomed it all the same. That was his woman, turning the tables on him all the time.

Upstairs in his office, he heard the sound of hammers and found them comforting. Rebuilding. Together. At night, she rolled out her plans and they pored over them together. He heard her laugh and he closed his eyes, honing in on that melodic sound, feeling it move through him. They had a long way to go. He knew that. It wasn't going to be easy. He was in a dark, ugly world. She would always need protection. But she would be that sunlight for him.

He stayed where he was, letting her get her work done, even though he needed to see her. Molly and Bastien had been over a couple of times for a barbecue, and twice they'd gone to dinner in town together. He liked Bastien, but then, he knew he would. Tonight was going to be special because they had business to take care of before Molly's man began to believe the rumors flying around about Joshua.

Several hours later, he put the phone down. Arrangements were made. Sasha had agreed to the same terms for the pipeline as his father had, although he made it clear he was having to clean house and set things right on his end. He stared out the window. Sometime in the last few hours, night had crept in. The sound of hammers was long gone and voices had faded away.

He stood up and stretched and then paced through the

house looking for her. Usually, she was in the kitchen. She liked to cook. He could smell spices. She was bent over, pulling the pork roast from the oven. The night before she'd soaked it in a citrusy mojo marinade. He'd watched her make it, pretending to help. He loved when she looked serious, like she was now.

He'd contributed by handing her orange juice, lime juice and olive oil. He'd watched as she'd mixed it into a bowl with the garlic cloves and salt she'd crushed together. She'd added more spices, cumin and dried oregano, and then cut up fresh oregano. She'd made a puree out of it, and then, after scoring a diamond-shaped pattern into the roast, she'd rubbed her marinade all over it.

He found it fascinating to watch her. It was her face he loved to look at when she cooked. There was joy there. It was undeniable. Just watching as she'd poured the rest of the marinade over the roast, wrapped it and set it in the refrigerator to chill, had turned him on.

"That smells wonderful." He stated the obvious. "Tell me how you cooked it." That was the other thing he loved. Hearing the enthusiasm in her voice when she talked about doing what she loved. He would never be able to repeat what she said, but he listened to every word, every nuance of her tone.

"It's nothing special, honey," she said. She put the roast on the center island.

He crowded her, leaning in to kiss her neck. "Tell me." He couldn't very well say he craved the sound of her voice when she talked about cooking almost as much as he loved eating what she'd made for them.

"Silly." She scoffed, but she did as he asked. She nearly always did—in the end. Sometimes it took a little persuasion. Those were the times he knew he had a green light to be wholly himself. "It's just a pork roast. Oven is 325 degrees. Roast, pork skin side up covered in parchment. I add a couple of cups of water and then foil over the parchment.

When it's done, I remove the covering and then broil it for five to ten minutes until crispy." She showed him the roast. "It looks like that. I'm about to make the sauce by pouring the drippings into marinade that I saved from this morning and boiling it until it thickens. We have dinner!"

"What are you serving with it?"

"Fried sweet plantains, rice, green beans and pumpkin flan."

"Baby, you are amazing." He kissed her neck again and then left her to make her sauce.

Setting and clearing the table was his self-appointed job. After, they often washed and dried the dishes together rather than use the dishwasher.

"Actually, Joshua, I think you are. Thanks for making my life really wonderful. I had no idea anyone could ever be so happy." It came out in a little rush. She touched her temple and then ran her finger down the front of her tight tee, right over her nipple. The bruise had long since healed, but it still bothered her that Nikita had put his hands on her. "You came for me. I knew you would. I was able to stay calm and think, because I knew you'd come for me."

He cleared his throat as he put the dishes on the table, his heart accelerating. She did that to him, when staring down a madman hadn't. She hadn't talked about her time with Nikita, only telling him the minimum, and he hadn't pushed her. She'd dealt with far too much that day. The revelations about him. About Sasha. The fear of being kidnapped twice in the same day. He had been so afraid she would believe his bullshit story when he'd walked so brazenly in on Nikita and Filat. He'd known both men were extremely violent. He'd also known no woman was safe around them.

"I'll always come for you, Sonia," he assured. "I have to admit, knowing you were in their hands scared the hell out of me. I haven't gotten over it. I don't like you out of my sight. When you're working, I listen all the time for the sound of your voice."

She sent him a smile over her shoulder and it warmed him. Stirred his body. Every look on her face, from sweet and happy to sexy to angry, wreaked havoc with his body, but it wasn't a bad problem to have.

"I haven't wanted you too far from me either," she admitted. "I send the guys into town for supplies because I'm a little afraid to go by myself."

It was the first time she'd ever acknowledged that. He'd guessed it, but she'd never told him. "Next time you want to go into town, tell me and I'll go with you."

"You have your own work. I am not going to disturb you."

He set glasses out. She liked sparkling water. It wasn't his favorite, but it was hers and he made certain the house was always stocked with it. "I like going into town with you, babe. No big deal. Ask me next time."

She sent him a look, her nose wrinkling. "You always sound bossy."

"Because I'm the boss."

She made another face, but there was laughter in her eyes that faded quickly. "I couldn't believe when you walked into that room. I was terrified for you. I didn't understand what you were doing. After I heard the owls, I knew you were waiting for a signal to let you know the outside guards had been taken care of."

He nodded. She needed to talk. She still hadn't gotten to what had happened to her when she was alone with Nikita and Filat.

"Why didn't Evan come to back you up?"

"He had to chase down some of the leopards running away. Which reminds me, I've been biding my time, but tonight is the night."

"For what?" She poured the sauce into a gravy boat.

"I told you to run. I made it very clear that you were to get out of there." He carried over the bowl of plantains.

She set the rice and green beans on the table. "It was a good thing I didn't, you would most likely be dead."

"I doubt it, but you helped. Still, that's beside the point. You made me a promise." He began carving the roast. It smelled delicious. "I owe you a punishment and I'm collecting tonight."

Her eyebrows shot up. Her face flushed a soft rose. "I don't think so. Not when I saved you. If anyone is getting punished around here, it's you. You walked into that house without backup. You deserve it way more than me, and I think tonight's the night."

He laughed as he put the meal on the table. "I have news for you, baby. You're quite a bit smaller than I am. In some things, such as this, brawn wins every single time." He sank into the chair opposite her, his body hard.

She loved this game between them as much as he did. He'd always thought, even if he found the right woman, the one his leopard claimed, she wouldn't want his kind of play. He doubted that many women would even try, but Sonia was as hot as he was just talking about it.

Her eyes had darkened with desire. Her breathing had changed. Her nipples were hard beneath the T-shirt. His woman. So beautiful. He reached into his pocket and found the box. That small velvet box. He slid it across the table to her.

Her lips parted. "You aren't even going to wait until after dinner?"

"I have more surprises for after dinner. This is more suited to now." He watched her face carefully. She was unsuspecting.

Very slowly she opened the lid. Her eyes went wide with shock. Very slowly her lashes lifted until she was looking up at him. "Joshua?"

"Askin' you to marry me, baby. I want you with me here, every night. I can't sleep without you. Can't think without you. I'm so in love with you it's crazy. I hope you feel the same way about me."

She bit her lip, staring down at the ring.

"There's a little gold chain, Sonia. You'll have to wear it around your neck rather than on your finger, just to be safe. If you shift, your leopard will wear it. I measured her neck to make certain it would fit."

"Aren't you supposed to get on your knee?"

He put down his fork and leaned toward her, staring her straight in the eyes. "I plan to get on my knees tonight up in our room. You're going to be screamin' yes and my name over and over for hours. Right now, I'm not makin' you do that. You just have to say it once for me right now and I'll be happy."

She took the ring from the box and held it in front of her. The gold chain slithered onto the table. She put it around her neck. "Yes, then. The answer, right here, this once, is yes. I can't promise I'll be saying that again tonight. You might be, though. Begging, I mean."

He grinned at her. He couldn't help it. She looked beautiful with his ring settling between her breasts. "Take the tee off, so I can see it against your skin."

She raised an eyebrow. "You just want to see my breasts."

"That too. Take it off for me."

She did it slowly, pulling it up inch by inch until the undersides of her breasts peeked at him. As she pulled it up farther, he could see the ring nestled between the two soft mounds. She tossed it onto the chair beside her and continued eating, looking every inch a queen without her shirt on.

"You know, Joshua, it doesn't make sense that you think I'm going to say yes over and over tonight when I already said it now."

His woman. Smart. He fuckin' loved that about her. "You'll be saying no first and giving me all kinds of grief when I tell you the rest of your surprise. Not the little gifts I've got waiting for you—well, technically, they're for both of us; those are engagement gifts—but the rest of your surprise."

Now she had her fork down. "What rest of the surprise?"

Clearly she knew him now; her voice was wary and the look on her face full of suspicion.

"We're getting married right away. We fly out tomorrow, and we'll get married in Vegas. Molly's going to stand up for you. Bastien is coming along so they can have time away together."

"I'm not marrying you right away, Joshua. Are you nuts?"

He was calm. He had expected her objections. He continued eating, watching her. Thinking she was the most beautiful woman in the world and he loved her so much he could barely breathe with it.

"I haven't gotten over the fact that I was never married to Sasha, for one thing. And there's my house. I have to decide what to do with it. I don't like the idea of giving it up."

"You can't even walk into it. It isn't good for a house to stand empty. Especially here."

"You're not going to railroad me, Joshua."

He could see it on her face. That love. That softness. Sweetness. All for him. She was going to marry him. They both knew it, but first, they were going to have one hell of a night with her trying to hold out and him convincing her. Putting his mark on her. Claiming her his way. He couldn't wait.

Keep reading for an excerpt from

# JUDGMENT ROAD

The first book in the new Torpedo Ink
series by Christine Feehan
Available January 2018 from Jove

THE wind blew off the sea as the three Harleys made their way through the last series of snaking turns and hit the straight stretch on Highway 1 running parallel to the ocean. The night was well under way, a fact that Savva "Reaper" Pajari was well aware of. He had to report to the president of his club, Czar, the moment they arrived back in Caspar, but time didn't matter for that. Even if Czar was at his home in Sea Haven, tucked in close to his wife, Reaper would just hit the roof and climb in through the bedroom window. He'd done it more than once.

He lived for two things: riding free and fighting. He needed to feel solid muscle under his knuckles. He needed to feel fists hitting his body, tapping into that well of ice that covered every emotion. That swift explosion of violence and sweet pain as fists connected was his life, and had been his life since he was five. Now he needed to stay sharp somehow, in this new bullshit direction the club had taken.

He rode along the highway, aware of the others on either side of him. Brothers, some for over thirty years. Men he counted on. Men he called family. Still, he was apart from them and he knew it, even if they didn't. He turned his head toward the ocean. Waves sprayed up into the air, rushing over rocks and battering at the cliffs. Sometimes he felt like he was those battered rocks, time wearing him away, little by little.

His soul had gone so long ago that he couldn't remember having one. Now his heart was slowly disappearing. There wasn't a place on his body without a scar. He had another to add from this last trip. He also would have to have Ink tat his back, three more skulls to add to the collection of those resting in the roots of the tree on his back.

Viktor Prakenskii, the man known as Czar, was the best man he knew. Reaper's job was to stand in front of Czar, his self-appointed task from the time he was a little boy. He'd been doing it for so long now, he didn't know any other way of life. He stood in front of all his brothers and sisters—in Torpedo Ink, his club. He was proud to wear the club colors. He'd die for those colors and still detested any mission he ran if he had to take them off.

They turned off the main highway onto Caspar Road leading to the town of Caspar, where they'd set up home. They'd designed their compound around the old paymaster's building for the Caspar logging company. They had spent the first few months working on the building, turning it into their clubhouse. It housed multiple bedrooms, a bar, their meeting room—known as the chapel—and a kitchen. They shared bathrooms, whichever was closest to their assigned sleeping room. Czar had insisted each of them purchase a home nearby. He wanted those roots put down deep.

Reaper didn't give a damn where they all slept. As long as he could defend his club and their president, he was fine. The compound had a bed, and right now, he needed one. He was going on forty-eight hours without sleep. He'd stitched up the wound in his side himself, making a piss-poor job of it too, but all he'd had was a little whiskey to disinfect it, and that had burned like hell. It still did.

They rode up to the compound and Storm and Keys parked their bikes while he scanned the lot. Either Czar was home or at the bar. Reaper was fairly certain he'd be at the bar waiting for a report. He didn't like to disturb his wife, Blythe, or their four adopted children. Reaper didn't shut his bike down as he waited for the others to turn to him.

"Goin' to find Czar," he said, unnecessarily, but they were looking at him like he should say something. He didn't like stupid shit, like the formalities that seemed so important to others. He didn't care if people liked him; in fact, he preferred they stay the hell away, except for his brothers, who understood him and made it clear they expected him to at least talk once in a while.

"I can report in," Keys offered. "You could use the downtime."

Reaper shook his head. "Won't be able to sleep right away. I have to check on him anyway. You know how I am."

"Want company?" Storm asked.

He shook his head. "Not necessary. Savage will be with him, probably a few others. Get some sleep. We all earned it." Savin "Savage" Pajari was his birth brother. Like Reaper, he acted as sergeant at arms, protecting Czar at all times. Between the two men, they had their president covered around the clock whether he liked it or not. "I already texted Czar we were comin' in when we were an hour out."

He was certain if he did that, Czar would go to the bar rather than have Reaper come to his home—exactly what Reaper wanted. It was the new bartender. Reaper didn't like anything out of the ordinary. He didn't trust it. The woman was definitely something out of the ordinary. Code could find dirt on anyone, but he hadn't found a single trace of her anywhere. She worked for cash, under the table. She wore designer jeans, but she drove a beat-up car on its last leg, rust breaking through the paint. The fucking thing smoked every time she turned the engine over.

Torpedo Ink had a garage up and running. Did she take her car there to get it fixed? Hell, no. She drove off every night thinking no one knew where she was going. That was the hell of it. She drove back toward Fort Bragg, took Highway 20 and turned off at the Egg Taking Station, a campground in the Jackson Demonstration Forest. Why the fuck would a classy woman bartend in a biker bar, drive a beat-up Honda Civic older than she was, and be camping? It made no sense. He didn't like puzzles, and Anya Rafferty was not only a puzzle, but one big headache.

Reaper had watched her for over a month. Five weeks and three days, to be precise. He'd learned she was a hard worker. She listened to people, remembered their names and what they liked to drink. She flirted just enough to get good tips, but not enough to cause fights. She was generous with the waitresses, sharing tips she didn't have to share. She was careful and guarded yet gave the illusion she was open. She was kind to those less fortunate.

He'd watched her give a homeless man a blanket she carried in her car, and twice she'd brought him coffee and a meal. Twice she'd spent money he was certain she didn't have to get food or shoes for someone living on the streets. She seemed to have an affinity for the homeless, and he was certain she knew all of them by name. She volunteered in the soup kitchen Saturday mornings even though she couldn't have had more than a couple of hours of sleep.

She didn't flinch around the bikers, but it was obvious she wasn't from their world and didn't have a clue how to fit in. She took her cues from Czar and sometimes asked him questions. She'd never asked Reaper a single question, but she sent him a few shy smiles, which he didn't return. He'd spent more time in the bar in the five weeks she'd been there than he'd ever spent in a bar in his life.

Reaper glanced away from the compound, up toward the

bar. He could see the lights shining through the dark from the banks of windows. His heart accelerated. His cock jerked hard in his jeans. That was unacceptable, and that was why the woman had to go.

Everyone in his club had been taught to be in complete control of their bodies at all times. They had been beaten, starved, tortured and had unspeakable things done to them in order to shape them into disciplined killing machines. He felt very little emotion and certainly not physical attractions. The bitches partying hard, getting it on with anyone and everyone, did nothing for him. Not one thing. He often walked through a room full of half-naked or naked women and his body didn't so much as stir.

But one look at Anya Rafferty . . . Listening to the sound of her voice. Her fucking laugh. The way all that hair fell around her face like a dark cloud. A waterfall. She had more hair than two women put together, and he found he thought a lot about that hair when he should be thinking about keeping his president alive. Or himself. He refused to allow his cock to drive him. That part of his anatomy would never drive him. He didn't trust anyone, especially not a woman who made his body ache until his teeth hurt.

He sighed and turned his Harley, heading for the bar. He'd told Czar that Anya had to go. She was a problem. Nothing about her added up. Nothing. Protecting Czar was his number-one priority, and if she wasn't forthcoming, she had to go. He told himself that shit, but he knew it wasn't the truth. He hated bullshit. *Detested* it. Especially when he was trying to bullshit himself. He could make all the excuses in the world, but the truth was the bartender upset him. She got under his skin without trying.

Once in the parking area, Reaper swung his leg over his motorcycle and forced himself to stand upright, his two feet planted on solid ground. He'd been on his bike so long he wasn't certain he had the legs for earth any longer. Placing his dome on the bike, he did a casual sweep of the parking lot. In that one moment, he took in every detail of the cars and lines of motorcycles parked there. He recognized several of the bikes. Two prospects were lounging close, keeping an eye out. He didn't acknowledge them, but he saw every detail. He removed the small leather bag from one of the compartments hidden in his bike and made his way across the parking area toward the bar, still looking around to every parking spot.

What he didn't see was the bartender's old rust bucket. He paused for a moment at the bottom of the stairs, breathing deeply, not knowing if that made him happy or if his mind went somewhere he refused to acknowledge. She was gone. Czar had done what he'd asked and her presence was removed. That should make him happy. Well. He was never happy. He didn't know how to be. He'd forgotten. Relief maybe—except now he had to go to the campground and make certain she was okay. Damn it. He swore under his breath and climbed the steps leading up to the bar. His gut burned like hell with every step, but it wasn't nearly as bad as the ache in his chest.

Music poured out of the building, a loud, drubbing beat. That only added to the pounding in his head. He ignored it and yanked open the door. Raised voices and laughter mixed with the clink of glasses. Funny, now that it was an established biker bar, the place was hopping almost every night.

He stepped to the side of the door and took a long look around, noting every jacket or vest with colors. Mostly small-time clubs or weekenders. A couple of legitimate road warriors. Three wannabe hardasses, drinking, looking for women and most likely a fight. Five badasses sitting in the corner wearing Demon patches. They noticed him the moment he walked in. All five were packing and they weren't drinking, at least not enough to say they were there for a good time. He did a quick inventory of his body. He could move fast if needed. He never minded a good fight, and most likely, any minute, he'd be welcoming one. He let the Demons see his gaze linger on them before he allowed himself to scan along the bar.

He had a gun tucked in his waistband at the small of his back. Another was down in his boot along with a knife. A third gun was inside his jacket, easy access, just a cross-body pull and he was in business. The truth was, he rarely used a gun or a knife when he killed. He preferred silence, but weapons came in handy occasionally and he was proficient in the use of all of them.

He knew he was looking for the bartender. Anya. He fucking loved that name. It suited her face. Her voice. It was possible her piece-of-junk car had broken down and she had hitched a ride with someone. He didn't see her anywhere and it pissed him off that he'd even looked. Worse, the pressure in his chest grew.

Tonight's bartender, Preacher, looked harassed. He glanced up from the sea of customers and shot Reaper a welcoming grin, his eyes scanning for wounds. His gaze dwelt for a moment on the blood on Reaper's shirt and then jumped back to his face. Reaper gave him a nod, indicating he was fine and Preacher nodded back. He jerked his chin toward the hall behind the bar. There was a doorway to the left of the bar, but Reaper stalked across the room and flipped up the jointed wooden slab that allowed him to walk through the opening to get behind the bar. He moved down the long hallway straight to the office.

The door to the back office was closed, signifying a meeting of some kind was taking place. If the door was closed, any waitress or non–club member stayed out. Unzipping his jacket, Reaper went right on in, hoping Savage didn't put a bullet in him as he waltzed through the door. Savage was unpredictable at times. His brother gave a quick scan of his body, much the way Preacher had. Czar stood up to face him, doing the same. He frowned when he saw the blood. Shit, he'd forgotten his shirt was a mess. It wasn't all his either. Savage's gaze jumped back to his face.

"I'm fine," he said, to stop the questions.

Code had been poring over books with Czar, which was laughable. Czar hated number crunching and only pretended to listen to Code half the time. With Czar and Code at the table were two other club members, Absinthe and Ice, Storm's twin brother. All had their eyes on him and the blood on his shirt. Something was up to have so many gathered this late at night.

"What happened?" Czar snapped before anyone else could say anything.

Reaper tossed the leather carrier bag onto the table. "Assholes called us in a little late. Who the fuck goes off to hide leaving their wife and kid to face certain death because they don't want to pay a gambling debt? He's supposed to be the big-ass president of a club and he's hiding in a dark hole surrounded by his brothers, leaving his woman and child exposed." He poured a wealth of disgust into his voice, because, really? Who did that? Who could live with themselves? How could his brothers look up to him? "I wanted to cut his throat." He glared at Czar. "Don't send me on a mission like that one again. Next time, I won't have such restraint."

Czar studied his face. Reaper kept his expression blank. Czar shook his head. "First, tell me how you got blood all over your shirt. Is that yours? Or someone else's? Please tell me it isn't the client's."

Reaper shrugged because, hell yeah, some of it was that douchebag client's. The club was called Mayhem. Laughable. Truly laughable. In Reaper's opinion, the bullshit president had deserved to die, so, yeah, he'd shown restraint. "Maybe I didn't make myself clear. The weasel ran up a gambling debt and then, rather than pay it, when the goons showed up to collect, had his boys get him to safety. He went across two states and only then remembered he had a wife and daughter."

"And he contacted us to get them to safety," Czar reminded, his tone mild.

"*After* he made sure his ass was in the clear. Two days later, Czar. Two fuckin' days. He didn't even warn her. By the time we got there, so had the idiots who'd been sent to collect. Bodies or money." He touched his side. The burn of that blade going in was still fresh. "They decided to have a little fun with the two of them before they cut them up. Girl is fourteen."

"You stepped between the girl and the knife," Czar said.

Reaper didn't answer. What was there to say? Was he really going to let a pathetic excuse of a human being kill a fourteen-year-old girl and her mother? Not happening.

"How many stitches?" Code asked.

"What the hell difference does it make?"

"Someone's in a bad mood," Code observed. "Five? More?"

"Six. I don't need the doc. I took care of it myself."

A small hoot of derisive laughter went up. Reaper flipped them off.

"I gotta see this," Ice said. "If it's anything like the last time you stitched yourself up, you'll be looking like Frankenstein in no time."

"Already does," Code said. "Just a little."

Reaper glanced at Savage. He hadn't cracked a smile and there was a slight hint of worry in his eyes, but he didn't say anything.

"You taking antibiotics?" Czar asked.

"I will. I'll get them from the doc."

"Tell me what really happened, because otherwise, I'm going to think you're slowing down. You could have killed these idiots in seconds, Reaper. What the hell were you doing to take a hit that cost you six stitches?"

"We're done talkin' about this," Reaper declared.

"We're done when I say we're done." Czar's voice dropped an octave, low enough that the room went silent. Low enough to caution Reaper that his president wasn't asking.

Reaper shook his head. When Czar talked like that, he

expected answers. "Didn't want the kid to see me kill him.
I directed the hit where I knew it wouldn't do much damage.
She had Down syndrome and she was terrified. Her father
left them hanging out there like that. Pissed me off. I didn't
want the kid to suffer any more than she already had."

Czar sighed. "Reaper, she's the daughter of the president
of a motorcycle club. The Mayhem Club may not be as big
as the Diamondbacks, but they're violent. She's bound to
have seen things."

"She was terrified," Reaper repeated. "It was my call. I
had her close her eyes, turn her head away and then I killed
the bastard. Before she could look, I covered her eyes and
took her the hell out of there."

"You don't get to take chances with your life," Czar
hissed, slamming his palm on the table.

Reaper leaned toward him. Looked him in the eye. "I've
been takin' chances with my life since I was five years old.
I've been killin' that long. I know how to take a blade when
I need to."

"The point is, you didn't need to," Czar snapped.

"My call. I'm there, I have to make the decision. You'll
be happy to know I didn't kill her father when we delivered
them safe to him, although it took restraint. He was willing
to pay us the fee we asked for, but not pay his gambling
debt? He put his wife and daughter in jeopardy, Czar. What
kind of man does that?"

"The club paid for the fee to have us retrieve them and
bring them safely to him. The gambling debt is personal."

"You know, if they catch up with him, he'll give us up in
a heartbeat. He was already plannin' to do that. I killed the
two hit men. Whoever sent them out will want revenge."

"All of you wore a mask and gloves," Czar said. "He
never saw your faces."

"No, but Mr. Mayhem President put a tracker in with the
money," Reaper said. "He was plannin' on selling us out to
get out from under his debt. He'll give up the link online,

that's all he's got." He smirked. "Killed the club member followin' us and put the tracker in his fuckin' mouth."

"Code said you texted him to shut down our online operation and he did. We'll set up again later."

"Just so you know, full disclosure and all, I beat the livin' hell out of that pissant president, Czar. Don't know if he lived or not, but if he did, he's not going to be the same man. He was going to give us up and that tracker was the last straw. Already wanted to shove a knife down his throat."

Czar shook his head and pushed the bag of money across the table to Code. "Add that to everything else. We're in good shape. We've got most of the businesses up and running. Still working on some of the houses. Reaper, are you going to actually move into yours?"

Reaper shrugged. He had no idea what the hell he'd do with a house. Czar had insisted all of them have an actual home. His was on the edge of the cliffs with a stairway leading down to the cove and two roads winding around Caspar so he had access to the old logging roads. He liked to know he could escape anything easily.

"Soon." He just required a bed. He had one at the compound. He didn't need a house to go to every night. Empty. Echoing every time he walked through it because he'd put the minimum amount of furniture in it. A bed. That was pretty much it. Maybe, if he was lucky, the entire structure would fall into the ocean and he'd be done with it.

He changed the subject. "Got a few badasses sitting at a table. Waiting, Czar. They request a meeting with you?"

Czar nodded slowly. "Waited until you got here. Code found out a few things about them. They're from up north. Demons, smaller club, but already have a reputation. They want to talk about extending their reach, using us to do it."

"Probably drugs," Ice spoke. "We don't do that shit anymore. We're rehabilitated."

The others laughed. "Yeah. We're don't spread drugs around but we kill people when it's needed," Absinthe said.

"A few hardasses out there as well, think they're real tough from the way they're actin'," Reaper continued. "Look like trouble and they're drinkin' heavy. Talkin' loud. Didn't even notice when I walked through the door, but the others did. The Demons. We aren't a well-known club. Barely established. We aren't even the big club in this area. Why come to us?"

Czar shrugged. "Don't know until they talk to us."

"Did they indicate they found us online through the website Code made?"

Czar shook his head. "Don't think so. Think they chose us because we're here, on the coast." He studied Reaper's face. "I wouldn't meet like this with someone wanting us to do a hit." He made it an assurance.

Reaper moved away from the door toward the back of the room where the overhead light didn't quite reach. He was tired. Exhausted. Even if he went to bed, he knew he wouldn't sleep, or if he did, he'd have a nightmare. He had them often now, something he was careful not to share with the others—not even Savage.

"You up for this?" Czar asked. "We could tell them to come back."

"Told you, Czar, someone else should handle inquiries, make certain they're legit. We all have a lot of enemies, but you most of all. Don't like you out in front like this," Reaper said. He put his back to the wall, making certain he had a clear shot to the door. Savage was on the other side of the room. They'd have the five Demons boxed in.

"If you could, you'd build a wall around me," Czar pointed out.

"You've got Blythe and the kids," Reaper said. "Aside from the fact that you're the brains for all of us, you've got them."

Czar's face softened. "I've got all of you. I don't worry because I have my brothers." Still looking at Reaper, he continued. "Ice, go get them and bring them back. They come through the door one by one. You stay behind them. Box them in. Absinthe, you search them. Tell them they want to give up their weapons."

Reaper was happy Czar wasn't taking any chances. Absinthe could influence with his voice. He was smooth and charming, and the moment he put the suggestion in the minds of the Demons, they'd hand over their weapons without hesitation. If there was going to be a firefight, it wasn't going to happen on Torpedo Ink's chosen home turf.

"Stay to the left of the room at all times," Reaper said, all business. "Savage and I will have them in a crossfire. None of you want to get caught in that. We'll mark the ones between us we'll take. The rest of you look comfortable and friendly." He was good at planning death. He'd done it hundreds of times. Czar was equally as skilled, probably his teacher, since Czar was older. He'd been the one to get them all out of that hellhole alive.

Czar nodded his head and Ice was gone, leaving the door open. Reaper leaned against the wall, relaxed. This was his world, one he knew intimately, and a woman like Anya Rafferty, with her long dark hair and her bleeding heart, didn't belong anywhere near it. He sighed, realizing she'd crept right back into his thoughts.

He should have followed her all the way into the campgrounds. They were a good distance from the entry, if he remembered correctly. His club had had a shootout there. A massacre. It was a place where outlaws could hide, and that meant Anya wasn't as safe as he'd like her to be. He shut down that line of thinking. He wouldn't want *any* woman camping alone out there.

He straightened suddenly. What if she wasn't camping alone? There could be a man out there. She could be supporting some shiftless loser who didn't want to work or take care of his woman. He should have gone all the way in. Damn it. Now his head wanted to explode and wasn't in the game where it should be, just as he knew would happen.

The woman was wreaking havoc, and it was a damn good thing Czar had sent her on her way. Still, he had to check on her, just to be certain she was safe—just the way he would with any woman.

His bullshit meter was screaming at him but he ignored it as the first man stepped through the door. This would be their top enforcer. Sergeant at arms. The badass of the five. He studied the man's face as Absinthe took his weapons. Yeah, he was the real deal. What was he doing in a small-time club? There had to be more to the Demons than they had ferreted out. The enforcer passed over his weapons without a murmur, his eyes sweeping the room, taking in the setup, realizing he couldn't see either Reaper or Savage clearly.

Both men had a way of blurring their image. It was useful when hunting others. They'd developed the skill over the years, starting when they were toddlers and Czar had them practicing. Most of it was learning to choose the right place to stand. The shadows covering them. The stillness one needed so the human eye wasn't drawn in that direction.

The Demons came in one by one, just as Czar directed. Ice tailed them, closing the door behind them. Reaper made certain to watch each of them as they came through, noting which one would be the likeliest to start trouble—that would be Tether, the youngest, the one eager to prove himself. The first one, the one they called Razor, was the one Reaper determined was the most lethal. He marked him as the one to take down first.

"I'm Hammer," one said. "President of the Demons." His patch confirmed that.

"Czar." Their president extended his hand and shook. He indicated the chairs surrounding the oval table.

Only Razor hesitated. He realized sitting put them in a vulnerable position, especially without weapons. Absinthe had conducted a search of each man even after they'd obeyed his soft, whispered command to hand over their guns and knives. He was thorough about his search, knowing Czar was in the room. They all protected their president. Czar didn't always like it, but it didn't matter. He was their number-one priority at all times. In this instance, if things went to hell, it would be Code's job to take Czar down and protect him with his own body, while Reaper, Savage, Ice and Absinthe killed every one of the Demons.

Soft feminine laughter drifted down the hall and Reaper almost stiffened. Almost. He cursed under his breath but managed somehow to stay disciplined enough not to move. That sounded a lot like the bartender. He had to keep his head in the game, not worry about some woman that was probably sent to kill Czar. Well, okay, he didn't believe that for a moment. He'd think about her later, and the fact that those three hardasses were looking for women. Right now, the only thing in his world was replaying step-by-step in his mind how he would kill the Demons and protect his president.

Razor had to go first. Reaper would draw and shoot him in the head. Two bullets to make certain, although he didn't miss. The president would go second, even though Code and Absinthe would go for him as well. Savage would take the two sitting to either side of their president, the ones assigned to protect him, just as Code was assigned to Czar. The two were named Weed and Shaft. Their cuts had their road names as well as their offices. It was unusual for a president, enforcer, secretary and road captain to all come to a meet at once. Something big was up.

"How can I help you?" Czar asked.

There was a small silence while Hammer sized him up. Razor was clearly uncomfortable with the setup, but he kept his mouth shut. His gaze moved restlessly around the room, always looking for anything that might threaten his boss.

"I'll get right to the point," Hammer said. "Heard good things about your club. You're small, but you get things done. We've got a situation. We're small too. Three chapters. Good territory. We keep it as clean as possible. Don't have trouble with the locals. Hear you're in pretty good here as well."

Czar shrugged but didn't respond, his eyes steady on the Demons president's face.

Reaper had seen him give that look a thousand times. He'd learned it in the school where hardened criminals ruled, and if you wanted to stay alive, you didn't make mistakes, like flinching at the wrong time.

"We have a route that goes from our territory to here. Stops dead and then picks up on this side of Santa Barbara."

Czar shook his head. "This is Diamondback territory. You want something to go through their territory, you contact them, pay the fee and they'll take it through."

Hammer hastily shook his head. "They swallow any pipeline, use it for their own purposes and use a club like ours as pawns. They'd want a cut of what we're doing and that cut would be more than we could afford right now."

"You get caught, they'll declare war and wipe you out. They have more chapters than just about any other club in the world. They're loyal to their brothers and out of respect we're careful not to do anything that would step on their toes, like creating a pipeline without giving them a cut."

Hammer and his secretary, Shaft, exchanged looks. To Reaper they seemed a little desperate.

"What exactly is the product?" Czar asked.

"Counterfeit money."

Just the fact that Hammer told them straight up was another indication that they were desperate.

Czar leaned toward him. "I don't like bullshit. I'm two seconds from putting a gun to your head and pulling the fucking trigger. What are you doing here? My old lady is waiting for me and I don't like keeping her waiting. Not. Ever. So don't waste my time."

Instead of looking worried or even scared at Czar's words, Hammer looked as if he was relieved. He took a deep breath and told the truth. "This is going to make my club look weak, and we're not. We got in bed with a club that runs a gambling operation. We help launder the money. Recently they found out about the counterfeit operation we've been running. We keep it slow. Nothing big, feeding a few bills here and there along an eastern route we've got. They want to take it big-time."

"How'd they find out about your operation?" Czar asked, always going for the most pertinent fact immediately.

"One of our prospects decided to try his hand at gambling and got in over his head. Instead of coming to the club, he traded his debt for information." Hammer's tone was strictly neutral.

"Where is he now?" Czar's voice dropped an octave.

Just that tone put the room on edge. Reaper had seen him do it so many times, but each time it happened, he was always impressed.

"He didn't survive," Hammer said.

"Anyone else talkative in your club?" Czar asked.

"The men in this room are men I trust implicitly. The ones in my chapter, same thing. The other chapters wear our colors and I'll fight for them and with them, but I don't know them as well as I do my own brothers."

That was an honest answer. No one could know every man in every chapter of a club.

"They all in on the counterfeiting?"

He nodded. "Distribution. We have the plates. They're good plates. I've got a good man who knows what he's doing. We play it safe and don't get greedy, we can make it work, make it untraceable back to us. This other club wants to get greedy."

"How big are they?" Czar asked.

"That's the thing. They're Ghosts. They call themselves Ghosts."

Reaper stirred then, something he never did. That called attention to him and the Demon's enforcer nearly came out of his seat. Reaper ignored him. "A word, Czar."

That was never done either, especially by one of Czar's men. They always allowed Czar to make his play. They talked it over after.

Czar didn't give anything away as he rose and jerked his chin toward the only other door in the room. Reaper let him come across the room and then stepped so his body was between his president's and the Demons.

Czar closed the door and turned to him, his eyebrow raised but concern on his face.

"The bastards going after the Mayhem president's wife and child, the one we saved, it was the Ghosts after them. They weren't wearing colors, but they referred to themselves as 'Ghosts,' as in, I'd never see it coming because his friends are Ghosts. Last words out of his fuckin' mouth."

"You think the Demons are setting us up?" Czar asked.

Reaper loved his brother. Czar believed in him, in his ability to protect not only him, but his family and the others. He believed in Reaper's instincts, his gut. Right now his gut was telling him the Demons were in trouble with this new "Ghost" club.

Reaper shook his head. "Got a bad feelin' in there. They don't want to be, but they're scared. Somethin' more is going on than they're tellin' us."

Czar clapped him on the shoulder. "Never think for one minute that I don't need you, Reaper. It's always been you and me. We lived in hell. Now we're not, we're calling our own shots. Don't let the newness, the difference, fuck with your head."

Reaper knew he'd been taking chances with his life. Czar knew it too. Now, with his brother looking him in the eye, he nodded curtly, not wanting to talk about it. It was the damn woman. The bartender. That hair. That laughter. Her fuckin' skin. It looked so soft he'd been tempted to actually touch her. He didn't touch anyone unless he planned to kill them—then they were dead. No one touched him unless they planned to get dead—then they were. Not unless they were one of his brothers—he'd had to learn to tolerate that.

"Let me go in first, Czar," he cautioned. "Stay behind me. I'll get you to your seat and then slide back into position. Question him after I'm where I need to be."

Czar didn't argue as he often was prone to do when it came to matters of his safety. He detested the others putting their lives on the line for him, but as far as Reaper was concerned, it was the one thing Czar had no say in.

Reaper led him back in and over to the table without seeming to. He was casual about approaching the table, leaning in to snag some peanuts that were sitting in a can toward the middle. If they'd been at Czar's home, his old lady, Blythe, would have put those peanuts in a bowl. He sauntered back to the wall.

Czar waited until Reaper was nothing more than a blur, just as he'd asked him to. "This club you call the 'Ghosts,' are they an actual club? They ride? They have colors?"

The Demons president nodded. "They came to us with respect. We have no idea of their numbers. They're up by the Oregon border. We don't have much intel on them." He rubbed his jaw. "My fault. I should have looked into them more, but at the time my old lady was . . ." He shook his head. "No excuses. We did what we did. I need to be able to run my product through this territory. I need you to do it."

"You haven't said why. How did they get you to come to us? Did they specify us?"

Hammer shook his head again. "No, don't know if you're even on their radar. I think they're looking to get their hooks into the Diamondback club. A club that big must have gamblers. You and I both know, if they start a war with them, the Diamondbacks will swallow us."

"Even so, why not tell them to go fuck themselves? You don't know their size. They have no reputation. Why not just kill them?" Czar's voice was mild.

"They have my wife." Hammer dropped the truth right into the middle of the room and the tension went up a thousand percent. Suddenly there was no air.

Czar looked up to meet Reaper's eyes. Who the hell made war on women and children? Who had the balls to kidnap the wife of the president of the Demons and hold her until the club did what they were told?

"How long have they had her?" Czar asked, suddenly all business. He went from mildly interested to total concentration.

Reaper loved the man, the way his brain kicked into high gear and he was aware of every detail, absorbing it, coming up with ideas and sorting through them for pros and cons until he knew exactly what to do.

"They took her two nights ago. Gave me a week to get it done. Came to you first. Her health . . ." He shook his head. "She had cancer. Just finished her last treatment. Immune system is down. She's only twenty-six. Young. Damn it, I don't know where she is, but she's a good old lady. She'll keep her shit together and she'll know I'm coming for her. I just need to buy some time to find her."

"These people don't play nice," Czar said. "This isn't the first time they've used a man's family against him. In that case, they were there to kill the wife and daughter. I don't think you have a whole hell of a lot of time."

"You willing to help?"